STORMY
THE BARREL HORSE

by RALPH GALEANO

Edited by
Ben V. Hess III
Hugh K. Lankford
Sandra J. Galeano

Published by

Horseman's Press
Silver Star, Montana

Published by
Horseman's Press
P.O. Box 687
Silver Star, Montana 59751

First Edition
First Printing • 1500 • September 1996

Library of Congress Card Catalog Number: 96-94769
ISBN 1-57502-308-3

Original Cover Artwork
by Don Greytak

For your convenience, additional copies of Stormy may
be ordered on the forms found at the back of the book.

Printed in the USA by

*M*ORRIS
PUBLISHING

3212 E. Hwy 30
Kearney, NE 68847
800-650-7888

CHAPTER 1

In late spring, high above timber line in the northern Rockies, mountain peaks still glistened with a cap of deep snow. Lower elevations had been free of snow for several weeks. New grass reached toward the warm spring sun in the wake of the receding snow. A band of horses grazing below the snowline were enjoying the tender new shoots of sweet grass. It was a welcome change after a long winter of dry hay. The horses were content to be back in the hills after wintering at their home ranch in the valley below. The corrals at the ranch had become sloppy when the lower country began thawing out as the days became longer and warmer. A crew from the ranch pushed the band of mares up into the fresh, clean land of the mountains several weeks ago to forage for themselves and escape the muddy conditions around the ranch.

On this day, late in the afternoon, the weather began to deteriorate. Light winds turned into bitter williwaws that screamed down from the high peaks carrying stinging rain. Heavy black clouds rolling in from the Pacific Northwest promised the approach of a foul storm. One mare stood facing into the advancing storm. She held her head high and tested the fierce winds. High gusts ruffled the remains of her shaggy winter coat. Her mane and tail danced and whipped in the wind as she studied the changing weather. The aged bay mare looked back at the other horses on the exposed slope they were grazing. She gave a loud snort to alert the band and then moved off at a fast trot down the slope. The other mares had been growing uneasy, so when the old bay issued her command, they willingly followed her off the open slope.

They traveled along the top of a brushy coulee following the bay mare. The old horse came to a trail leading down

1

to the floor of the coulee. With surprising agility, she broke into a gallop and raced down the familiar trail. The rest of the band jumped out after her and within seconds were all safely on the canyon floor. Hidden in the narrow coulee, the horses relaxed and began grazing on scattered clumps of bunchgrass. The canyon walls protected them from the wind driven rain the storm was sending ahead as a messenger, warning all creatures to take cover.

Born fifteen hundred miles to the northwest in the Gulf of Alaska, the storm was moving relentlessly toward the high mountain ranges of Montana. A late spring, low pressure area bred this monster and sent it on a journey across the North Pacific Ocean, gathering moisture and saturating the cumulus clouds it generated. Heavy rain and winds pelted the Northwest for two days and now it was the high mountain country of the northern Rockies that would feel the full fury and ultimate end of the dangerous storm.

The coulee the horses took shelter in was an old friend to this bunch. They often hid here from rain or snow storms that moved out of the high country. This time of year the leader knew they would be comfortable and find new shoots of bunchgrass emerging around the clumps of sage and gooseberry brush dotting this ancient, dry watercourse. As the band of horses settled down to wait out the storm, they could hear the screaming wind above them being deflected by the steep walls of the coulee.

A feeling of security surrounded the band of horses. A few of the mares wandered up the draw to where the coulee turned toward the west, and its origin near the crest of the mountains. As they neared a bend in the dry gully, the mares felt the wind funneling down the gully. They turned and eased back toward the rest of the band.

This coulee took on a different character where the horses turned and headed back to the main bunch. From this point on, the coulee climbed toward the Continental Divide, twisting and turning for nearly two miles. All along its course, smaller draws intersected it like branches on a tree. Large boulders lay scattered along its bed.

Known as Dry Boulder Coulee, this gulch provided a welcome haven to man and animals alike during bad weather. Formed an eon ago, and hiding a frightening history of terror and death, the coulee was now a safe sanctuary.

The mares entered Dry Boulder at a point where the steep sides offered an easy way in and out. A good trail angled down the west side. Formed by countless hooves and feet over the centuries, erosion and use had made the trail fairly wide and easy to negotiate. Near the bottom, the coulee widened and was a good place to stay, especially on a day like this.

Sagebrush, gooseberry bushes, and junipers made up most of the vegetation, and it was sparse at best. Snake weed and small clumps of bunchgrass finished off the growth. Going out the east side of the draw, the trail angled wide and to the south as it climbed out on top. A few gopher holes were the only obstacles, and they could be avoided with any daylight at all. A horse at a fair gallop could cover the ground from one side of the draw to the other, in less than a minute. During the fall gathering, riders from the Bent Bar Ranch negotiated the draw on horseback at speeds that seemed reckless, while moving and chasing cows out of the high country. The Bent Bar hands had exceptional stock to ride and were all competent horsemen. It wasn't surprising that most riders wouldn't slow their mounts when chasing through Dry Boulder on this trail.

As the coulee continued its journey out of the mountains the brush grew heavier and the boulders rested closer together making travelers pay more attention where they were headed. Deer and elk used this part of the gulch more than horses or cows cared to. Their spooky nature made them feel more at home and protected in this brushy tangle. The sides became steeper as the elevation continued to fall. Large outcroppings of granite protruded from the walls at every twist and turn. A few game trails snaked in and out, but were brushy, steep, and narrow. Most travelers usually avoided these trails and found something more accommodating when wanting to cross this area.

The tangled, steep section continued down for almost a mile before the coulee leveled off and widened. Here the steep sides began to give way to gentler slopes and Dry Boulder started to show a kinder nature. It became almost pleasant on the final leg of its journey to the valley floor.

Evening was approaching and the mares settled in to wait out the coming storm. Nibbling and picking at the new shoots of spring grass, the girls were content where they were. Only occasional squeals and nips occurred when somebody thought they might be getting crowded by an unthoughtful neighbor. These were reminders that kept the pecking order lined out right. Mother Nature had equipped these horses with a built in weather warning system and right now that system was telling them to stay in the coulee for the duration of the storm.

One of the younger horses was restless and seemed agitated. She broke into a sweat and started pacing the area. Occasionally she would lie down, then quickly get back up. Her nervousness was irritating the rest of the bunch. A feeling of satisfaction passed through the band when the young mare finally wandered down the coulee.

Picking her way down the draw, she moved around scattered clumps of brush and boulders with a grace and smooth fluid motion that few horses possess and all horsemen desire. Her rear quarters were broad, deep and heavily muscled. A wide solid chest and beautifully muscled foreleg blended into her shoulders with a symmetry that gave her the balance and agility of a true performance horse. Her head reflected beauty and intelligence. Deep brown eyes were wide set and radiated kindness with an underlying glint of stoic courage. A small spot of white centered on her forehead, coupled with a white sock on her left rear leg were the only markings on her sorrel coat. Her flaxen mane and tail formed a striking contrast to her bright copper color.

Scattered raindrops were finding their way into the draw. The noise of the gusty winds above the coulee sounded ominous as the sorrel continued to pick her way through the rough part of the coulee. Alert and ears forward, she effortlessly moved around tangled brush and rock out-crop-

4

pings. It was late evening and she seemed determined to reach an unknown destination before full darkness enveloped the small canyon. She increased the pace of her travel down the draw and sweat began to moisten the hair on her neck. She knew the approaching storm and heavy cloud cover that was developing would bring darkness earlier than usual.

This young mare had a good reason to leave the band and look for a secluded spot in the canyon. She was heavy with her first foal and her body was sending her signals she couldn't ignore. She wasn't due to foal for another week or so, but as sometimes happens, storms and low pressure systems can throw Mother Nature's clock off and early foaling occurs. Forces as old as nature drove the mare and she was determined to find a special place.

She came to a spot where mountain mahogany bushes and sagebrush formed an almost impenetrable wall from one side of the draw to the other. On the east side of the wall of brush she found a game trail through the obstruction. She had to lower her head almost to the ground to get through because of the heavy brush and low canopy it formed. This passage was only used by game animals and was fairly tight for a horse to negotiate. With her muzzle almost touching the ground, she snaked down the trail.

The trail came out of the heavy brush into a small meadow. The ground was covered in a dense layer of old grass. New sprouts were pushing their way through the old grass and promised some form of nourishment. The lower end of the clearing was blocked by a wall of high brush. There was a small game trail leading into the wall of brush. On the east side there was the trace of a trail leading to the top of the coulee. A large truck sized boulder rested against the side of the draw just below where the faint trail started and stretched halfway across the meadow. Erosion had formed a steep drop between the start of the trail and the canyon floor. To leave the coulee, a traveler would have to make an upward lunge to reach the trail. Sage and greasewood grew halfway up and around the huge granite boulder making travel impossible between the canyon wall and the huge rock, for all except the smallest of critters.

The west side of the meadow was bordered by sheer canyon walls. This sanctuary had the makeup of being a small fortress and was well protected from the elements. With the limited access, predators would have a hard time sneaking up on anything in this meadow without being detected. There was old grass for bedding, new grass for feed, and steep walls and brush for protection.

The young mare carefully investigated every nook and cranny of this secluded meadow and seemed satisfied with what she found. This was what she was looking for. She felt a movement deep within her body and knew a task was at hand that would take all of her strength and stamina. Content now, she nibbled on the green grass as darkness approached and heavier rain began falling. What she didn't know was that this night would bring a nightmare of terror and horror that would take every bit of strength and willpower her strong body was able to give if she was to survive to see daylight. With the dangerous storm rapidly approaching, Dry Boulder Coulee was going to show a deadly side of its frightening history.

CHAPTER 2

Four miles south of Dry Boulder Coulee, along a high wind swept ridge, a lone rider was coming down out of the hills at a quick trot. Both horse and rider were anxious to get to the valley floor. It was late evening and they knew the consequences of being caught in the high country at night with a bad storm approaching. The rider planned on holding a fast trot until they reached the lower end of this ridge and then slowing to a walk as they crossed through a steep and dangerous ravine. Once they cleared the other side of the ravine she planned on kicking the nervous horse into a lope for the last few miles to the rendezvous with the other riders.

They had covered a lot of country today. Her job had been to check the high country for new grass and see if there was any snow left in the mountain meadows. She found a few scattered patches in the lower meadows that didn't amount to much. There were still large masses of snow above timberline, but that wouldn't bother the cattle since they seldom ventured into the rocky areas that were still snowpacked. Overall, she found an abundance of new spring grass. The cattle that wintered in the valley could be pushed up into these mountains in the next few days and be able to scratch out a living earlier than normal this year.

Heavy, wind whipped, rain drops were beginning to hit and sting both the horse and rider. Things were starting to get uncomfortable. Holding her mount to a fast trot, the girl thought back on all they had seen and done today. She had spent more time than her original plans called for. She didn't intend to be so late returning to the valley and meeting the other riders. It was ranch policy for all riders to meet at the end of the day on Gunpowder Creek. Lone riders could sometimes run into trouble in the hills and it was a secure feeling to know everybody waited until the last rider was in before heading home.

Checking out the high meadows was always an enjoyable ride for the girl. Late Spring was a special time in the mountains. New life was popping up everywhere. Along with the grass, that was the lifeblood of any ranching operation, new buds on Quaking Aspen and Cottonwood trees were making their appearance as well. Rose bushes and other varieties of mountain growth were waking after a long winter. The smell of the country was so fresh and clean it made life seem like a great new adventure was about to begin. Deer and elk were following the snowline as it slowly receded toward the high peaks. They were picking up the new feed as it appeared from under the melting snow. Each new shoot they found was a treat after the long winter of scarce forage.

Riding along, she saw several large bunches of elk and several small groups of deer. None of the animals seemed spooky and she was able to pass fairly close without arousing concern. A few of the younger animals had shown more curiosity than fear and she spent far too much time watching the animals watch her. Now, at this late hour and with miserable weather, she wished she had moved along faster and finished sooner. She covered all the country assigned to her today and accomplished what had been asked.

It was now too late to make the ride out by way of Dry Boulder Coulee as she'd planned. She wanted to look in on the band of mares turned out several weeks ago that were in that area. Her favorite mare was due to foal in a few weeks and she wanted to check on her condition. She had plans for the future and wanted that mare's foal to play a big part.

Ann's daydreaming came to an abrupt end when a gust of wind whistled by carrying rain that stung with the force of the wind driving it. The rain worked its way through the collar of her jacket making a chilly trail down her neck. Her mount wasn't happy about the conditions either. He transmitted his nervousness, discomfort and weariness through hide and saddle to his rider. The rider picked up the signals with an inborn ability a true horseman comes equipped with naturally. They listened to loud clashes of thunder that were starting to reverberate around them.

As soon as they reached the lower end of the ridge, Ann intended to stop long enough to pull her rain slicker from behind the cantle of the saddle and put it on before they rode through the ravine. They would have to traverse the ravine at a walk and the way the rain was increasing, she knew she would be soaked and cold by the time they climbed out the other side of the canyon. It brought comfort to her knowing she would soon have her slicker on for the remainder of the ride home. Other thoughts entered her mind as they neared the end of the ridge. Hopefully, the other riders wouldn't be upset about waiting a little extra time for her to show up. Things were looking better and thoughts of home and a warm meal were reassuring. If only she could relay these comforting thoughts to her nervous horse, maybe he would settle down and not jump every time a thunderclap rattled across the mountains.

They reached the end of the ridge just as the last rays of light disappeared. Ann eased Buster down the dark trail a little way to get some protection from the wind and rain while she untied her slicker from behind the saddle.

Clouds had been piling up against the high elevation of the mountains and cascading over the top as the center of the storm drew closer. Millions of raindrops falling through saturated clouds and striking other drops had been creating minute electrical charges that were very small at first. Severe updrafts in the clouds kept lifting and releasing these drops so that they collided again and again. The electrical charges increased with each collision until the cloud became a gigantic battery. Within a few minutes the electric charge in the cloud had reached an awesome force of fifteen million volts. This huge battery was fast approaching the point where it would overcome the insulating effect of the air and would seek a spot with an opposite charge to discharge and equalize.

Johnson rode into the clearing on Gunpowder just at dark and saw two riders already there, sitting and waiting. "The girl not showed up yet?" he asked.

"Nope, not yet," answered one of the men.

Johnson reined in toward the two and stopped close enough to carry on an easy conversation while they waited for the other riders. Johnson wasn't worried about the girl and the other three riders. He knew they would show up and soon they would be on their way home. Seven riders left this morning to ride fence lines and check the general condition of the range before they turned the Bent Bar cattle out for the summer grazing season.

The noise of the wind and rain hid the approach of three slicker clad horsemen as they rode into the clearing and joined up with the others. "Well, gentlemen, fancy meeting you here in this wonderful weather," Johnson said as a greeting to the three as they reined in. "As soon as Annie gets here we'll take off for the ranch and call this a day," he said.

"And it won't be too soon by the looks of what this storm has in mind," answered one of the riders.

Rain was falling hard and a steady drip fell from the wide brim of Johnson's hat. Salt and pepper hair showed from under the dripping brim. Lines resembling crows feet started at the corners of his eyes and ran toward his sideburns. He called them laugh lines, even though he knew that years in the saddle staring into the wind and glare of the sun of these high mountain ranges had put the lines there. Johnson's tall, lean body sat straight in the saddle as they waited for Ann. Darkness hid concern for the girl on his weathered face.

Johnson was foreman of the Bent Bar Ranch. Ranching was his life. It was all he cared to do. He tried other occupations in his younger years, but nothing else gave him the fulfillment he found in ranching. He signed on at the Bent Bar as a rider when he returned after the war. The ranch was a tonic to his battered soul. It helped him forget the sights and sounds of grueling battles as his unit fought their way across Hitler's Europe. Working on the ranch convinced him that this life was what he wanted. He never left.

Tragically, he inherited the foreman's job when the owners were killed in an airplane crash while returning to the ranch. Heavy icing in bad weather forced their private plane down. Johnson led searchers to the crash site in rough mountain country. They found Jim Olsen barely clinging to life in the wreckage. His wife was killed on impact. Their baby daughter, Ann, was found unhurt, wrapped in blankets in the rear of the small cabin.

Johnson remained at Jim's bedside in the hospital as his friend's life slipped away. During the war, under heavy enemy fire, he rescued Jim Olsen from a burning tank. He was awarded the Bronze Star for bravery for saving his best friend's life. They were inseparable.

Johnson's thoughts drifted back over the years. He remembered Jim's last words and the pledge he promised in answer. Jim gripped his hand and looked deep into his eyes. Johnson saw deep sorrow and pain.

"Johnson...the baby, Ann. Will you take care of her? She needs someone strong and reliable. Please, watch over and protect her... hold the ranch together for her and make sure she receives a good education," Jim said in a barely audible voice.

Painfully, Johnson recalled his friend's request and his own emotional answer. "Jim, don't worry about the girl. I promise you I'll devote my life to her. I'll run the ranch for her. I'll watch over her and see that she receives a good education. You can depend on me." As Johnson recalled that painful time so long ago, his uneasiness for the girl's lateness increased.

The men respected Johnson and felt privileged to work under him. He proved over the years to be a man of the highest order, his knowledge of cows, horses and these high Rocky Mountains was respected throughout the county. He was an easy going, slow talking, pleasant man to be around. Johnson had a way about him that brought out the best in the people that worked with him.

His skill at breaking and training horses was legendary. When working with new colts or even rank older horses, Johnson radiated a feeling of trust and kindness. The horses quickly accepted him and gave him all he asked and then some.

Thunder rumbled and crashed nearby and all six men had the same thoughts. Deep down they were thinking that they would be mighty happy when Ann showed up and they could head home. Six horses stood with heads hanging down and rain dripping off every part of them, waiting for the cue that would send them down the trail to the barn. The men were making small talk, but their ears were fine tuned, listening for the sound of approaching hooves.

The crackle of a thunderbolt echoed off the ridge above them and ended in an explosion as the burst of lightning hit the ground. The noise was deafening, the horses jumped and the eyes of all six men spun to the source of the frightening sound in time to see a bolt of lightning stretched to the ground in a bright forked path.

CHAPTER 3

Ann stopped Buster a short way down the trail that crossed the ravine to untie her slicker. She dropped the reins on Buster's neck and reached back to pull the slip knots holding the raincoat. As she jerked the slicker free of its ties, the noise and commotion it made spooked the nervous horse. At almost the same instant, the overcharged cloud could no longer hold the tremendous amount of voltage that had built. In a violent, cracking explosion, its deadly cargo was sent streaking toward earth in a fiery, crooked path. The forked bolt of lightning hit the ground on the ridge just above the trail that Ann and Buster were on. At the very instant Buster spooked from the noise and movement of the slicker being jerked free, the lightning hit above them with a thunderous explosion. It was more than the frightened horse could handle.

At the sound of the explosion, Buster's tense muscles uncoiled like a giant spring and he bolted in a great leap down the trail. Wildly frightened, he lunged down the narrow trail. Heavily muscled hindquarters dug in and accelerated him to a full speed run before the sound of the lightning bolt had even reached its full crescendo.

Caught by the big gelding's reaction to the flapping slicker and explosion of the thunderbolt, Ann was nearly thrown by Buster's first leap. On his first lunge she was thrown back violently into an almost horizontal position and her head slammed into Buster's hindquarters near his tailhead. As the horse jumped out from under her, she lost her stirrups and seat. Buster's acceleration threw her back onto the cantle of the saddle. Before Buster uncoiled for his second great stride, Ann's reflexes took over and her legs clamped tight high up on his withers and just below the pommel of the saddle. By the third stride she had partially regained her seat. She brought her body back near vertical, still maintaining a grip, her legs went down and her boots started searching for and trying to trap the wildly flailing stirrups. When Buster reached his full runaway speed the girl was firmly in the saddle with her right boot in the stirrup, searching for the left and reaching down with both hands for the reins along the runaway's neck. A microsecond later she was deeply seated, had both boots in the stirrups and had found the reins. Leaning back in the saddle and putting great pressure on the stirrups through the balls of her feet, she pulled on the reins as hard as she could, trying to slow and stop the runaway.

With an almost uncanny ability and skill, Ann instinctively regained her seat, stirrups, and reins while the frightened horse lunged down the trail. It was a remarkable display of horsemanship, executed so smoothly, it seemed as if she were simply an extension of the horse's own body. She was born to ride. Her earliest memories were of being horseback. She could ride before she could walk. Johnson liked to tell the story of her father carrying her around in his saddlebags before her first birthday. A gifted ability had enabled her to stay on Buster, but now she faced the difficult task of gaining control and stopping the runaway before he reached the first switchback turn on the rain slick trail.

The narrow trail hugged the walls of the cliff as it angled down the side of the steep ravine to the first switchback where it wound around and then angled down again in the reverse direction to the second switchback. From there it descended at a more gradual rate until it reached the rocky bottom of the gorge. Rain made the narrow trail slippery and treacherous. In full darkness, Buster raced headlong toward the first switchback turn and the empty void of space waiting on its outside edge.

The ravine switchback trail commanded respect from riders crossing this gorge. Ann didn't like to look down the steep sides to the bottom far below. It was frightening for her to think about a horse slipping or spooking on this trail. It was a long drop to the bottom. The almost vertical walls were covered in brush and concealed rock outcroppings that could kill or cripple any horse or rider that was unlucky enough to miss the turns or slip off the side and plummet onto them. She always negotiated this trail at a safe walk. Now, in pitch blackness, she was hurtling down it on a runaway horse.

Straining back on the reins with every bit of strength she possessed, Ann tried desperately to gain control. The gelding was resisting the bit, and all of Ann's efforts did nothing to slow him. As they raced down the trail, she felt brush growing out of the upper side of the cliff, slapping her right leg while the left side felt nothing. It was a grim reminder of the sheer drop-off. At this speed on the rain slick trail, Ann knew Buster could not possibly negotiate the hard left turn of the switchback, coming up fast as the trail reversed direction.

Ann knew she would have only one chance of making the turn. It would require all of her strength and a heavy dose of luck to pull it off. As the trail neared the turn, the distance of the vertical drop between the upper trail before the switchback and the lower trial after the switchback would lessen. The trail at the switchback resembled a "V" laying on its side. Her only chance would be to try to turn Buster just before the trail turned and crash down through the rocks and brush to the lower trial going in the opposite direction. If she stayed on the trail and attempted the turn at this speed, she knew they would ride right off the steep edge.

Releasing her hard back pressure on the reins, she shifted her weight forward and desperately stared into the black night. She searched for the approach of the switchback in preparation to jerk Buster's head around and go off the edge of the cliff the short distance to the trail below. She had one chance and timing would be critical. She would have to start pulling his head to the left before they reached the spot where she wanted to leave the trail.

Driving hard, Buster charged ahead oblivious to the danger he placed himself and his rider in. His natural instincts were to run when faced with a threat. Barely able to see as he raced toward the first turn, a glimmer of sanity started to replace the blind panic that overpowered him since the lightning and slicker had started him on this wild ride.

Ann knew they were close to the turn and her concentration intensified. Almost too late, a subtle change in the trail ahead warned her of the abrupt turn to the left and the black void beyond. A warning signal flashed through Buster's senses at the same time. Still not in control, Buster did not comprehend the full danger ahead, but saw the seemingly end of the trail and the blackness beyond. Confusion was fast replacing panic in the runaway horse's mind.

Fifty feet from the narrow turn and the precipice beyond, Ann reacted savagely. She knew it was now or never! With every bit of lung power she could summon, she bellowed out, "whoooaa," as she stood in the stirrups and leaned back against the reins. In order to gain control, she must first try to penetrate Buster's sense of reasoning with a severe verbal warning followed by a brutal physical cue. It was a desperate act, executed with violence and authority that she prayed would overcome Buster's panic, and cause an immediate reaction to her commands.

Buster was ready. He was terrified and confused. He was running wide open on a narrow, slippery trail, vaguely familiar to him. He now realized there were dangerous turns ahead. The trail seemed to disappear and now he urgently wanted guidance. When he heard the thunderous "whoooaa" and felt hard back pressure on the bit, relief swept through him and he immediately reacted. Swiftly, he gathered his hind legs under him and threw his front legs out in front. He sat down on his hind quarters and with his front legs stretched out stiffly ahead, performed a classic sliding stop maneuver.

Relief surged through Ann when she felt Buster react to her harsh commands. She gained control and Buster was again obeying her. Time was running out and the edge of the cliff was coming up fast. Buster had all four legs planted and was sliding toward the edge. When Ann felt Buster react to her stop command, she knew she must wait a split second for him to get his body positioned correctly for a stop before giving the next command. If she tried to turn him over the edge and crash down the short distance to the lower trail before he was fully committed to a total stop, his body would still be in a position to abandon the stop and continue straight toward certain disaster.

Ann felt Buster's hind quarters drop all the way down. He was totally committed. They were less than twenty feet from the edge and sliding swiftly toward the black abyss. Putting all her weight in the left stirrup, she pulled hard on the left rein pulling Buster's head and neck around. Now, spurring hard on the right side of the sliding horse, she hoped he would push off in the new direction with his powerful hindquarters and take them over the edge that would save them. Trying to obey the new command, Buster used his front legs to help turn his sliding body and at the same time pushed off with his strong rear legs.

They almost made it. Ann felt Buster's rear legs driving hard, but going nowhere. Buster could not get a purchase on the slick trail. His driving hooves could get no traction and slipped out from under him. The momentum of their violent maneuvers caught up with them.

Buster was sliding sideways with his front hooves over the edge they had tried to propel off of. Losing his balance, he went down on his right side. His front hooves came back onto the trail as they slid sideways into the switchback they tried so desperately to avoid. Ann knew the desperate gamble had failed and that they were going to slide off the switchback and over the steep cliff to the rocks far below. As time ran out, Ann pulled hard on the right rein and spurred on Buster's left side. She managed to pull the horse around again. Her desperate maneuver put them in a position that would send them off the edge facing into the void rather than sliding off sideways.

Fear screamed through every part of the young girl's body. She lost her valiant fight to save both herself and the horse. Eerily they went off the edge. Time seemed to stand still and there was absolute silence as both horse and rider plummeted toward the rocks far below.

Six men heard Ann's far off cry. The gusting wind brought the unmistakable sound of her voice screaming "whoooaa" ominously down the ridge. As one, they spurred their horses in the direction of the scream. They hit Gunpowder Creek at a dead run and crashed up the bank to the ridge above. In the lead by a horse length, Johnson yelled back, "She sounded like she was somewhere near the trail through the ravine. Let's get there fast." It was a needless order. These men were devoted to Ann and would go to any lengths to protect or help her. They urged their horses to top speed. Their mounts seemed to feel the urgency of the moment and strained up the ridge. Tired from the hard day's ride, the horses summoned new strength and raced into the wind and rain toward that far off cry.

From the switchback the cliff dropped straight off and Buster looked out into blackness as they fell. Airborne for what seemed an eternity, Ann clung to Buster with her legs in a death grip and leaned back in the saddle. One arm forward with her hand grasping the reins and the other thrown back high and behind her, she attempted an impossible balancing act. She pulled on the reins as they started a slow cartwheel with Buster's hindquarters starting up and his front end falling off. She slowed the start of the midair cartwheel a millisecond and then gravity regained control. Slowly Buster's front end started falling off again and Ann threw herself as far back in the saddle as possible while again pulling on the reins. Delayed another millisecond the inevitable fatal rotation started again and Ann knew she would not be able to stop it this time.

Suddenly, Buster's hindquarters hit hard on loose slide rock, slamming him down on his forelegs. Instantly, he went down on all four legs as the momentum of the fall carried them through dense brush. They slammed down onto a narrow, sloping ledge that was covered in brush and huge protruding granite formations. The ledge was littered with loose rock and sand. If she had not pulled Buster around to face the direction of the fall as they went over the edge, they would have hit the ledge sideways with no chance of survival. The slight delay to the cartwheel Ann accomplished with her instinctive balancing act kept them from crashing head first onto the ledge. They had fallen more than halfway down the cliff and miraculously survived the impact because of Buster's body position when they hit the narrow, sloping ledge.

Down on all fours now, their speed slowed as they crashed through heavy brush. A huge granite outcropping loomed up on their right side and they slammed into it. They hit a glancing blow and were deflected to the left. They passed between large rocks and hit more brush which slowed them even more. Still in the saddle, a glimmer of hope began to replace the cold fear that consumed Ann during this wild ride. She felt Buster try to gain control with his legs and stop this deadly plunge. In the darkness, Ann did not realize they had not landed at the bottom of the ravine but only hit a glancing blow on the narrow ledge still high up on the cliff.

Still sliding down the incline of the ledge, Buster began to overcome the forces holding him to the ground. He began to gather his legs under him and rise. He rose to a hunched-up crouch, while still in a slow downward slide on the loose rock. Relief surged through Ann as she mistakenly presumed they had survived and were on the canyon floor.

The nightmare quickly returned as she felt the ground fall out from under them again as they slid off the ledge. Instantly, she realized they were still high on the cliff. They had only hit a small protrusion and were again free falling through space. Despair reeled through her body and she cried out an agonizing wail of defeat.

Below the ledge, the forces that created this ravine had carved the face of the cliff in a gentler manner. The walls now had more of a slope to them rather than a sheer drop. A rock falling off of the ledge would hit the side of the steep sloping cliff face several times before it landed in the bottom of the ravine.

Ann's cry of despair was cut short as Buster slammed into the ground again. She was knocked sideways in the saddle as they hit the steep slope. Before she could fully regain her seat, they were airborne again. Instantly they hit again. This time she felt Buster gather himself and thrust off the steep slope. She realized Buster was controlling this mad descent by crouching and pushing off every time they hit the sloping incline. Ann instinctively moved to position her body weight in the saddle trying to give Buster every advantage in his courageous effort. Leaning far back, her arm stretched out behind her, Ann released all pressure on the reins to give Buster full control of his head. While still loosely holding the reins in her left hand, she clamped that rein hand around the saddle horn in a death grip and rode for her life.

Buster's new efforts to survive brought Ann back from the despair that engulfed her when they slid off the ledge again. Now they were a team, fighting together in a wild ride to survive. Buster came full circle. He had been out of control, but now was valiantly trying to control this death plunge. Adrenalin surged through Ann. Buster felt Ann's new resolve and it inspired him to greater effort. A bond formed, and each felt there was a chance to make an impossible ride and survive.

Buster hit hard and uncoiled like a giant spring. He had more control of the way they would fall by springing off the incline rather than letting gravity and their great momentum carry them down. They were covering thirty or forty feet on each jump and the slope was tapering fast. They landed on a flat area and their momentum almost took them all the way to the ground. Buster was fighting hard now and they pushed off again on another long jump.

Ann realized as they went into the air again that the flat, clear area they just hit was the lower trail on its last leg to the bottom of the ravine. She knew this lower part of the cliff had a gentler slope and the worst part of this plunge was over. When Buster contacted the slope again, they didn't hit as hard or travel as far. They hit again and Buster managed to stay upright and not hit and slide on his rear quarters as he had been doing. Now his leaps turned into more of a downhill crow hop. Ann let go of the horn and shifted her weight slightly forward to help Buster's new stride. Euphoria enveloped her as Buster came down into a stiff legged trot as the slope tapered into a shallow grade.

Together they rode down the steep face of the ravine and survived. Buster's gait changed from the jolting, stiff legged trot into a staggering walk as the ground leveled out. Buster staggered down the draw in a stupor as the adrenalin drained out of both horse and rider. Blowing hard, the gelding came to a stop. He stood wide legged with his head hanging near the ground as he sucked in huge amounts of air.

Ann sat slumped in the saddle as the rush of that great ride slowly ebbed. Heavy rain poured down on the horse and rider. Gusty winds found their way to the ravine floor. Ann slowly slid out of the saddle to the ground. She reached up and wrapped both arms around the horse's great neck.

Slight tremors started moving through Buster's body as strained muscles began to relax. Ann released her hold on Buster's neck and moved apprehensively toward his rear quarters. She knew the crashing and sliding they did had to have taken a toll on his rear legs and quarters. Buster stood still as Ann began a slow inspection. Ann peered close in the blackness of the night. She saw that both legs from his fetlocks just above his hooves all the way to his hocks were red and raw where the hair had been burned off from Buster's brutal contact with the ground. Both sides of his hind quarters were sticky with blood. She gently felt along his legs but found only skin damage and minor cuts and bruises. They were fortunate. Miraculously, Buster received only minor injuries.

Ann moved around Buster and loosened the cinch. As she worked on the wet latigo, she saw branches and pieces of sagebrush sticking out from around the saddle. They were reminders of the brush they slid through on the high ledge. "Buster, you and I are lucky to be here in one piece," she said. "We better get moving before we start thinking about what we just went through," she added as she picked the pieces of brush out of the rigging. She worked the latigo knot loose and slacked the cinch strap enough to give Buster more comfort. He was sore in his rear quarters and she didn't intend to ride him anymore.

Buster was breathing easier now and Ann took the reins from around his neck and started leading him toward the trail that led up the other side of the ravine. She had a feeling that if she delayed too long, the fright of the fall would take over and fear of the ravine trail would prevent her from using it again. Johnson had a saying about fear, "When you get bucked off, you better get back on just as quick as you can, before you lose your courage." It was good advice and she intended to put it into play right now.

Ann watched Buster as she led him toward the trail. He was sore and moved stiffly but she believed he could make it home. They travelled a short distance when Buster's ears perked up and Ann heard the unmistakable sound of a steel shoe hitting rock. It would be the other riders coming to look for her since she had not returned to the meeting spot by dark.

They came down the trail at a trot. In the dark they didn't see her leading the horse and she yelped out a "Hello", more as a warning that she was on the narrow trail than as a greeting. They all answered her call at once. Relief swept through them as they swiftly closed the distance to where Ann had stopped to wait.

As they came upon her standing in the trail holding Buster's reins, the lead rider knew they had encountered some sort of misfortune. Johnson was the first there. In one smooth motion he stepped out of the saddle as his horse came to a stop a few feet in front of Ann. He grabbed her in his arms and asked, "Are you okay, girl?" Before she could answer he asked, "What happened?"

The other riders crowded around on the narrow trail. Ann couldn't contain her emotions any longer. Her harrowing experience had pushed her to the limit. Now, with the arrival of the riders and the comfort of their presence, she let herself go. Tears flowed down her cheeks as she sobbed, "Lightning spooked Buster at the top of the trail on the other side. He jumped and ran. We couldn't make the turn at the first switchback and went off the edge!"

Incredulous horror swept through the men. They knew the trail and all, at one time or another, had misgivings about that drop off. There was utter silence as they imagined the horrifying experience she had gone through. Ann continued to sob. Johnson regained his wits and asked again (even though he was wondering how they could possibly have survived a fall like that) if she was hurt anywhere. She didn't think she suffered any injuries in the fall but wasn't quite sure. "I don't hurt anywhere, but Buster's hindquarters are scraped up, so I'm going to lead him home."

Gently, Johnson released his grip on Ann and followed one of the riders around Buster to check his injuries. They found the scrapes and slide burns. It wasn't pretty but they didn't find any life threatening injuries. The rider named Bill said, "He's beat up pretty bad, and he'll be hurtin', but I think he'll lead home okay." Everyone was trying to comprehend how they had survived. Quiet admiration and awe for Ann and Buster settled through the riders. They looked at her and the horse with respect and admiration that bordered on reverence. Skilled horsemen all, they wondered if they could have pulled off such a ride. It was the most hazardous ride they ever heard of, and their respect for the ability of both the horse and rider climbed as they learned each new detail.

Johnson brought everybody out of their contemplation by saying, "James, you lead Buster toward the ranch. Bill, you ride Annie double and we'll get this child home as quick as we can."

"Where's your slicker, Annie?" Bill asked.

"I lost it somewhere up the trail when Buster jumped from the lightning," she answered.

Six men started shucking their slickers for Ann but the rider named Casey beat them all. "Take mine, Annie, you look like a drowned rat," Casey said.

Ann had stopped crying. She looked at Casey and smiled. "I don't look as bad as you did when I told you I took a short cut off the high ridge, Casey," she said. Everyone laughed with delight. They were tickled that her spunk was returning, for they knew she was going to be fine. Ann put on the slicker and Johnson helped her up behind Bill. They started up the trail at a good trot.

High on the opposite side of the ravine, above a protruding ledge, a yellow rain slicker was caught in a knurled sage bush. The slicker waved and snapped in the gusting wind as if it were saluting the riders and horses climbing out on the far side of the ravine.

CHAPTER 4

Screaming wind and heavy rain greeted the riders as they rode out onto the ridge. Conversation came to an end and everybody retreated to their thoughts. Wind and rain carried words away and talk was hard. Hearing was even harder. The noise of the storm became a roar and high pitched shrieks of wind added to the unearthly sounds the riders heard as they hastened toward Gunpowder. Rain stung their faces and crept between slickers and skin. Heads down, they moved toward the lower country and the protection it would provide.

They crossed the Gunpowder and paused in the clearing where they waited earlier for Ann. James fell far behind. He was leading Buster at a slow walk to keep from aggravating his injuries. "I'm ridin' back and keeping James and Buster company," Casey yelled. Johnson lifted an arm in acknowledgment and motioned for the others to start toward the ranch. Casey was a good hand for volunteering to ride back and help the other two, Johnson thought. It was only a few more miles to the ranch and he knew things would be okay now that they were in the valley and on the last leg home.

Things weren't okay for a newborn colt far up the country in Dry Boulder Coulee. The young sorrel mare gave birth to a colt in the secluded meadow. The new colt was in trouble. The rain washed him off, it also cooled him down and now he was cold and shivering. He needed a bellyful of his mother's milk, and needed it bad. His instincts told him that if he got that first milk, it would warm and nourish him and give him the antibodies he needed to ward off any sickness that might threaten him.

The mare was doing her best to help the baby. She had been roughly licking and nuzzling him in an effort to clean and warm him. This was her first foal, but she knew what her colt needed to survive. She was exhausted from the effort involved in foaling, but knew this colt would be in trouble unless he nursed soon. She kept up a steady effort of nuzzling and licking. This seemed to encourage the colt to more shivering. The shivering was helping him warm up. The violent shaking was stimulating blood flow in his body and causing his temperature to rise after falling at birth, when he came into the world in the midst of a cold, wet storm.

He was just short of an hour old when he started making his first awkward attempts to stand. He knew where he wanted to go, he just wasn't sure how to get there. It was a difficult task, trying to control those four long legs. They didn't want to go where he wanted them to go. The sorrel mare stepped back for the first time and watched. She had a beautiful colt. He was a dark, blood red now, but when he dried he would be a beautiful sorrel like her. He had a small white spot on his forehead and a white sock on his left rear leg. Except for his sex, he was the spitting image of his mother. Deep feelings of love and protection enveloped her as she watched the colt struggle to stand. He was unusually heavy muscled for a newborn and those muscles strained and flexed in his vain attempts to rise. Rippling muscles on his forelegs expanded and bulged as he got his front legs out in front and strained to pull himself up. Shivering and shaking, he put pressure on those two long hind legs and started an unsteady ascent. Halfway up, he started swaying back and forth. The oscillations increased until he lost control and crashed back to the ground in a spray of water.

The mare moved back to the colt and started nuzzling him again. He felt the urgency of the moment and tried again. This time he got farther up on those shaky legs before losing control and falling back on his hindquarters. He sat on his hindquarters with his forelegs straight out in front, elevating the front half of his body. This felt comfortable, so he sat and rested for a moment. When his quivering body settled down, he made another effort. This time he really put some push into those two long back legs and suddenly he was standing on his own. You could call it standing, but it was more like a wobbly dance with his legs not exactly in step with each other. His dance slowed as he began to figure out what made those legs move and how to keep them all straight underneath him at the same time.

The new colt was up and gaining confidence with each passing moment. It didn't take him long to know what to do with those four long ungainly legs. He took a few wobbly, tentative steps and managed to not crash back to the wet ground. He stood a few feet from his mother and rested, all the while gaining confidence and coordination in this new realm of standing and walking. The mare let him struggle to get up and stand on his own. Now it was time to help him. She moved close against him and he felt the warmth of her wet body. He began nuzzling her, looking for the place that first important meal was hiding.

The colt was soon moving around the mare with good control and surprising coordination for a horse just over one hour old. His body temperature rose with the exercise of trying to stand. He was feeling better and started shaking his head back and forth as he moved around the mare. He found what he was looking for and started nursing like an old pro. The warm milk flowed into him, spreading a wondrous glow of new life and strength as it coursed through his body. He was gaining by leaps and bounds now. He stopped shivering and took a new, more relaxed stance on the legs that gave him so much trouble only a few minutes ago. He nursed with urgency and soon a comfortable feeling of fullness crept over him. He came out for a rest and his muzzle was covered with bubbles of milk. After a short while he went back in earnest and soon drained the mare of all she had to offer. He had a warm, full belly and began to feel drowsy. It was an eventful and tiring few minutes. His first sleep was just a blink away. He walked away from the sorrel mare.

In the rainy darkness she sensed him move off and followed a few steps behind. He walked over to the wall of brush on the upper side of the meadow and found a spot where heavy mahogany bushes formed a canopy over a layer of old grass. This spot would give him shelter from the weather and suited the colt just fine. He tried to lie down but found it difficult. His legs had to learn how to fold up just as they had to learn to unfold. The ground was a long way off and his legs didn't seem to want to get any shorter so he could lay on that pile of old wet grass. He made several attempts to get his head on the ground but with those long legs in the way it just wouldn't work. He had a big day. Exhaustion, a full belly and an urgent need for sleep solved the problem for him. He simply leaned in the direction he wanted to go and finally gravity took over. When his weight shifted far enough, he just fell over on his side. He became comfortable in a hurry and was soon sound asleep. Gratefully, the mare moved up and lay down close beside him. She wiggled in till their bodies were touching. Her body heat would transmit to the colt and keep him warm. She was running out of steam too, and felt totally exhausted. She was satisfied and knew she had done all she could to insure a good start for her baby. The colt picked a good spot. They were underneath the heavy layer of brush, lying on a bed of old grass. The mare would rest until the colt stirred and wanted to be fed again. Feeling safe and comfortable in their sanctuary, both horses were soon in a deep restful sleep.

High above timberline, heavy rains were falling on what was left of the snowpack. The deluge was melting the remainder of snow left in the high peaks. Rain pounded the top crust of snow and chiseled through to the soft mass below. The temperature of the underlying snowmass was dangerously close to the melting point before the storm arrived. Now, the rain started a high speed meltdown. As the top layer of snow transformed into running water, the meltdown accelerated, and the rate of thaw increased dramatically. The combination of heavy rain and melting snow was creating a significant amount of water in the higher elevations.

The ground had been absorbing the rain and snow melt for hours and was becoming saturated. As the volume increased and moved downhill, saturation steadily moved lower until the whole mountainside became saturated. Then, water flowed freely on the surface as it made its way to the valley floor. Hundreds of small gullies started gathering water and holding it until they overflowed and fed larger draws.

Dry Boulder Coulee was the main artery for the entire watershed on the east side of the Continental Divide in this area. It drained an area of over thirty square miles containing hundreds of small draws, coulees and dry stream beds. Every drop of water that fell on the mountains from Dry Boulder south, for about four miles, and north for over six miles, flowed to the valley, by way of Dry Boulder Coulee. The upper end of this big draw was steep and had many smaller tributaries snaking out toward the highest part of the mountains. Runoff water was gathering everywhere at an alarming rate.

The coulee was big enough to handle this unusual amount of runoff. In the century since it last carried floodwaters, the coulee had become overgrown with brush and debris. Huge boulders lay scattered along its length. Slowly, at first, it began collecting the runoff from all of its intersecting branches. The flow increased steadily as the night wore on. The band of mares hiding in the coulee watched the old stream bed slowly fill and start running water. They weren't alarmed.

The draw was big enough where they were, so they just moved toward the side of the canyon as the water rose. That would have kept them safe and out of the runoff, except for a staggering series of events that occurred in rapid succession. The saturated ground caused more water to flow on the surface, causing a small amount of erosion at first. The erosion gave the runoff a quicker path and increased its speed. The increased speed and volume caused more erosion and consequently a domino effect occurred. Just when the runoff from the snow melt and rain began accelerating, a cloudburst occurred above the high peaks.

The cloudburst was a phenomena that opened up the heavens and turned the heavy rain into a deluge with a fourfold increase in the volume of water falling to earth.

This torrent fell rapidly and joined forces with the water trying to run down the mountain. This unusual volume filled and jammed the stream beds and channels. Water began a rampant cascade down the mountain. Within seconds, every draw leading to Dry Boulder was running bank full of water and heading for the same big coulee. Tributaries began emptying into the main branch of Dry Boulder along a two mile section above the unsuspecting mares. The accumulation of water from all the intersecting draws hit the coulee within a matter of minutes. The result created a destructive flash flood. A four foot wall of raging water was now roaring down Dry Boulder Coulee toward the band of mares.

The charging wall of water smashed into brush and boulders. It uprooted large bushes and trees. It carried all but the largest of the huge boulders littering the draw. It was sweeping up a centuries worth of debris as it raced down the coulee. The leading edge of the flash flood was carrying brush, logs and trees. The eerie force of the onslaught was rolling car sized boulders along as if a giant bulldozer had gone berserk and was shoving them down the draw. Trees and logs were tossed in the air with wild abandon as that first terrifying wall of water smashed everything in its path. The concussion of the boulders and debris bumping and colliding sent tremors through the ground ahead of the deadly advance. The clamor and tumult created a pandemonium of roaring noise that broadcast a short warning of the approach of the flood.

Most of the mares in the path of the flood were lying down resting while they waited for the storm to pass. A few of the older girls stood around, backed against any brush they could find. Their old bones ached in this weather and standing was easier than lying in the wet grass. Suddenly, a small bunch of deer charged into the clearing and raced through their midst. They bounded up the trail on the east side of the draw and were gone over the top in a flash. This instantly alerted the old mares to an unknown danger. They knew the deer had spooked from something that might pose a threat to them as well.

Three of the older mares snorted, almost as one, when the deer came through. This alerted the girls stretched out on the ground. Before they could get up to check out the commotion, they felt a deep down quivering and rumbling in the ground as the first tremors of the flash flood radiated out in advance. The standing mares sounded nervous whinnies. The mares were all up in an instant looking up the draw toward an almost imperceptible rumbling sound. The noise grew louder and the ground trembled. A dark bay mare, the leader of the band, screamed a loud terrifying command. The whole band was frightened and when they heard the bay scream and leap out in a dead run, they were all right behind her. The bay mare raced across the canyon floor and jumped onto the trail the deer took a few seconds ago. She knew a mortal danger was close at hand. At full speed, the band raced up the wide trail after her, toward the top of the canyon.

One of the oldest mares was slower than the rest of the group and was the last one out of the coulee. She reached the trail four lengths behind the main band of fleeing horses. The trail was wet and slick before the horses and deer raced up it. Now, after being churned by the activity of the last few seconds, it turned into a muddy mess. She reached the edge of the draw and lunged up to get on the trail. She slipped and fell in the mud. Quickly, she scrambled to her feet. Out of breath, she paused and looked back over her shoulder toward a terrifying sound. Instantly, she was racing away up the trail after the rest of the horses. She had seen the frightening spectacle of the flash flood demolishing everything in its path as it roared across the meadow.

The old mare made it to the top in record speed. She hadn't run that fast in years. What she saw had made a race horse out of her. She took off after the band as they ran down the ridge, away from the terror in the coulee. They all made it safely out of the draw, seconds ahead of the flood. The torrent continued, gathering speed and volume. It was uprooting trees and brush as it swept down the canyon. Mother nature was redesigning Dry Boulder Coulee in a fearsome way and anything caught in the path was sure to fall victim to a dire end.

Deep sleep had claimed the sorrel mare and her new colt. They lay in the little meadow oblivious to the raging flood bearing down on them. Less than a mile away, the flood continued to grow and destroy everything in its path. Unconsciously the mare felt the approach of the flood through the trembling ground. As it neared, it became audible. By degrees, she awakened and slowly became conscious of something not quite right. Still not completely awake, she tried to comprehend what was bothering her. Like little needles sticking her at a faster and faster rate, her uneasiness quickly intensified. She became fully awake as an awesome noise enveloped her. The ground was rumbling and shaking. The colt awoke and jerked his head up as the sorrel mare tried to bolt to her feet.

They were too late. The raging monster reached them before they could escape. The mare was halfway to her feet when she sensed and then saw the incredible sight of the churning flash flood only yards and micro seconds away from them. Wildly, she swung her head down and clamped onto the rising colt's neck with her powerful jaws in a fierce grip that pierced his skin. She came fully upright with her legs spread in readiness and the heavy colt gripped firmly between her jaws. The wall of water and debris smashed into them with the force of an explosion. The mare was knocked down and carried away in the maelstrom of sucking, swirling water. They were slammed into the ground and then washed away with the leading wave, smashing into tree trunks and tangled brush borne along with the raging flood. Underwater, unable to breathe, she kept her grip on the colt as they were swept away.

Only seconds ago they were peacefully sleeping and now they were in a fight for their lives. The mare gave birth only a few hours ago and was still in a weakened state. However, she was a powerful young horse and gifted with physical talents few horses could match. Well developed young muscles reacted and held onto the colt as they were twisted and rolled in the turmoil and disorientation of this terrifying ordeal. Unaware of what caused this catastrophe, she knew she must save the colt. They were part of a mass of debris rolling and crashing along in the floodwaters. Branches and other debris came between she and the colt and tried tearing him out of her grip.

The leading edge roared across the clearing and smashed into the huge granite boulder that rested against the side of the coulee. Brush grew halfway up the sides of the boulder to just below where the faint game trail led out of the draw. They were thrown about like a grain of sand caught in an ocean wave as it pounded down on a coastal beach. They were churned up toward the back side of the catastrophic leading edge of the flood when it slammed into the huge boulder.

As the wave hit the boulder and washed over it, a small backwash occurred from the force of the water smashing into and then rising up and over the huge obstacle. She found herself in a swirling eddy between the side of the draw and the huge boulder. She was swiftly gyrated into the side of the bank and felt her back come up against the boulder as the forward edge of the eddy surged up and started over the rock. On her back, still tightly gripping the foal, she felt them rise even higher and knew they were going over the top. In desperation she kicked out with her hind legs against the water and used her powerful neck muscles to throw her head toward the bank. She felt the foal hit solid ground just as they crested the boulder. She let go of her precious colt as the force of the cataract carried her into the maelstrom below.

Miraculously, the colt had been slung onto the small game trail, just inches from the rising water. Sputtering and coughing out water, he clambered to stand. He was disoriented and totally confused. The rising water was rapidly climbing the trail toward him. Havoc and bedlam were just inches below and quickly moving up the small trail. He started away from the horrible scene below him. He was bruised and battered by the few seconds he had been carried in the forefront of the flash flood. His neck was stinging and burning where the flesh had been torn by his mother's ferocious grip. He moved jerkily up the trail farther from the danger below. Halfway up the steep trace he stopped and looked at the nightmare raging below. The boulder that provided the split second opportunity for the mare to make that tremendous effort of hurling the heavy colt onto the trail was completely obliterated by the rising floodwaters. The backwash that helped slow them, had dissipated with the hydrodynamic effect of the rising water over the granite monolith. The physical forces that came together at a critical time and enabled the mare to save the colt had lasted only a few seconds.

There was no sign of the sorrel mare. The coulee was totally consumed by water. Only blackness and the roar of the flood greeted the colt as he stared over his shoulder into the draw. Something important was missing. He knew he couldn't stay where he was, so he moved farther up the trail. At the top of the trail he was hit by a blast of wind and rain. He stopped and looked back again for his mother. There was still no sign of her. He didn't want to go very far without her. The colt felt she was close by and would come soon. He found a heavy line of small cedars and gooseberry bushes and moved into their protection. The bruises, and wound on his neck, were causing him pain. Chilled and sore he began looking for a comfortable hiding place in the brush to wait for his mother. In the darkness, he pushed aside low branches and walked into a small hollow formed by the brush and trees. It was matted with grass and had been used often by deer and elk to bed down, out of sight, during the day. It looked like a good spot to him. He would wait here for his mother to come. Curled up in the soft wet grass, the colt fell into a deep sleep.

The flood raged and roared down through the narrow part of the coulee. The mare was thrown about violently and collided with boulders and tree trunks. Barely hanging on to her last breath, she was thrust above the melee for an instant and managed to suck in a life saving breath before being drug down again. Still clinging to life, she tumbled and rolled with the wild flow. The surging water carried her down Dry Boulder Coulee faster than she could have made it in a dead run. She was carried through the narrowest part of the coulee where the floodwaters were squeezed into their most turbulent stretch on the way to the valley below.

The draw began leveling off as it left the narrow section of the canyon. It widened and was not as steep as it made its way out of the mountains. The mare was swept along as the headwaters of the flood entered the wider part of the canyon. The water spread out over a greater area and lost speed as the terrain became less steep. The rocks and boulders the torrent washed along, slowed and then stopped rolling altogether as the force of water lessened in the easier terrain. Logs and brush that swirled above and below the deluge now rode high atop the flood waters. The height of the water fell dramatically. In this lower canyon the flood took on the appearance of a swollen, fast moving river and lost the wild turbulence of the upper coulee.

The mare came to the surface and was able to keep her head above water for the first time since this disaster struck. Her legs occasionally bumped bottom as she flowed along with the torrent. Soon she was able to half swim and half lunge off the bottom with her hind legs. Her mind now turned to reaching the side of the draw and escaping the grip of the flood. She desperately needed to reach the safety of solid ground. She had expended tremendous energy trying to survive this holocaust. If she didn't reach safety soon, she would run out of energy and perish in the flood waters. Something was coming up darker than the darkness around her and she knew it must be a ridge or outcropping running into the coulee. With the last of her energy, she started lunging off the bottom and half swimming toward the dark shape. If she missed this chance to escape the flood she wouldn't have the energy to make another attempt.

She strained and lunged. Calling up reserves of energy that were hidden within, the mare swam for the low ridge coming into the coulee. She was close. Desperately, she tried to reach the bank. Ten feet short of reaching shore, the flood began sweeping her out and around the low bank. Defeat and loss engulfed her as the flood swept her away. She couldn't hold on much longer. She valiantly fought to save her colt and somehow managed to survive the violent trip down the Coulee on the face of the runaway wall of water. Now, it seemed as if she would surely perish in the calmer waters.

The ridge the sorrel tried so desperately to reach now offered one last chance. She didn't realize it, but the ridge extended into the water and continued to the bottom of the draw. As the current carried her onto the underwater ridge, she was jolted out of her despair. Suddenly, all four hooves hit bottom! She instantly scrambled against the current to stand.

Her hindquarters were into the current and water rushed around and over her back. The force on her was tremendous. The current was eating away her last reserves of strength as she tried to stand and brace against the force of water trying to carry her back into the mainstream of the flood. Summoning all the power she could muster, she made a tremendous lunge toward the dark bank. The first effort only carried her a few feet. She landed in shallower water and the force of the current was considerably less. Now it was easier and she lunged further. Each jump took her closer to the bank and was progressively easier. She was going to make it. With one last burst of energy, she left the clutches of the flood and lunged up the ridge onto solid ground. The courageous horse was out of the water!

Shaking with relief and exhaustion, she made her way up the gentle slope. Drained of all energy and barely able to walk, she pressed on up the hill. The mare was in a daze. She was numb and felt no pain from her injuries. The trail leveled out slightly and passed through a group of high rocks with brush growing around them. As she moved through the rocks, dizziness overcame her. Slowly, she started down onto her knees. Halfway down, she lost consciousness and collapsed onto the hard ground.

The storm had been pounding the area for hours. It moved east and slowly disintegrated across the high plains of the Dakotas. The band of mares nearly caught in its fury had run to the lower country and settled in near the swollen Gunpowder creek.

A big mule deer buck had been run out of the canyon by the flash flood. He hid above the draw since escaping. Dawn was just hours away, and he wanted to find a more comfortable place to bed down before daylight. The buck moved toward the edge of the draw to an isolated clump of cedars and brush he often used. He came up on the downwind side of the sheltered spot and stopped. His sensitive nose picked up horse odor and confused him. Horses never went into places as tight as that little hollow. They were too big. Ears forward he stared intently trying to figure out where the horse was. Startled, he heard a snoring sound and then light coughing. There definitely was a young horse in the brush. Disappointed, he trotted down the top of the draw to another spot he occasionally used.

The worst was over. The cloudburst emptied the heavens and their overloaded clouds of all the moisture they were carrying. In less than an hour, Dry Boulder Coulee funneled every bit of falling rain and snow melt to the valley floor. There it entered the wide plain and was absorbed by larger creeks and streams. The hungry soil of the valley would quickly soak up the excess. As the floodwaters slowly subsided, the debris carried by the flood was cast off and discarded along the full length of the big coulee. Like its predecessors centuries past, the flash flood had occurred instantaneously for a brief duration and then was gone as quickly as it occurred. When the last of the floodwaters had traveled down the big coulee, things would look a lot different. Dry Boulder Coulee would have a new look, come daylight.

CHAPTER 5

Casey pulled into the driveway beside Bill's house. He was early and figured he'd have to wait a while for his friend. He shut the engine off and started to get out. Before his feet hit the ground, Bill was coming out the door. "Crank'er back up, we need to hurry," he yelled to Casey. Bill jogged down to the pickup and jumped in before Casey even had the old truck started again.

"You sure give a lot of orders for somebody that's always bummin' rides to the ranch, my friend," Casey said jokingly. Deep down he was happy to see Bill ready.

"Quit the jabberin' and get this rattletrap rollin', or I'm gonna' get out and run to the ranch. I'll probably beat you there and you'd die of embarrassment," Bill said.

"I'd already be at work if I didn't come by here and pick you up, out of the kindness of my heart," Casey countered.

"I'm gonna' start wearing ear muffs so I don't have to listen to you," Bill said.

"You said that yesterday and the day before," Casey shot back. The engine coughed, and started running. Casey backed up and turned around. They headed up the valley toward the Bent Bar headquarters.

They had the same thing in mind. They were anxious to get to the ranch to see how Ann was and check Buster. Neither one could sleep last night, thinking about what happened to those two during last night's storm. "How do you think they made it off there?" Casey asked.

"Casey, I lay awake all night thinking and wondering about that myself. I just don't know," he answered.

"It must have been a miracle," Casey said.

"Somebody sure had to been looking after them," Bill said. "Buster is a stout horse and as quick and smart as they come. Annie sits a horse like glue. In fact, she seems to know what her horse is thinkin', way before the horse even thinks about doin' something. As handy as both of them are, they still had to have an awful big stroke of luck to come out of that one alive," Bill continued.

"I lay there and shook when I thought about them riding off the top of that ravine. I know that country good, and that trail puts a little shiver in me every time I ride it and that's in daylight and good weather," Casey said.

"Won't this bucket of bolts go any faster?" Bill asked without answering Casey's last comment.

The county roads were still muddy and slick after the rain they had the night before. They crossed the bridge over Gunpowder Creek where it cut across the road on its way out of the valley. They could see by the headlights that the creek was higher than normal. A faint hint of dawn was starting to show above the mountains when they pulled onto the lane leading to the ranch buildings. Casey drove straight to the barn and parked. Lights in the barn didn't surprise them. They knew Johnson would be there.

"How is he?" Bill asked as he walked in and saw Johnson in Buster's stall.

"Beat up, scraped up and hide gone off in a lot of places. I don't know why this horse is still alive," Johnson answered. "I'm glad to see you two here early, there's a lot we need to be checkin' on today," Johnson said.

"How's Annie?" Bill asked.

"Still sound asleep. She was limpin' by the time she got to bed last night, and I didn't wake her when I came out this morning. She needs a good rest," he answered.

"After that ride, she deserves it," said Casey. Bill and Casey helped Johnson finish doctoring Buster's cuts and scrapes. They discussed what it would have been like, going off the top of the cliff. They were still in awe of the ride Ann and Buster made.

"When the other boys get here, we'll feed the herd. You boys saddle up and ride up Dry Boulder and look for the mares. That was the worst storm I've ever seen in this country. I'm anxious about them girls, some of 'em are gettin' pretty close to foalin', you know," Johnson said.

"Right away," Bill said. Casey headed for the corral to get a couple of different horses than they rode yesterday. Those horses had a hard ride in the storm and a day of rest wouldn't hurt them.

"Who do you want to ride today?" he yelled back at Bill.

"Surprise me," Bill answered, "but just make sure he's broke," he added. Johnson chuckled when he heard Casey mumble something under his breath. He watched the young rider walk jauntily out of the barn.

Casey was twenty years old and had an admirable swagger about him that everyone enjoyed. He was a good hand and knew it. He was wiry, a little above average height and handsome. Sandy colored hair showed from under his wide brimmed hat. Light blue eyes combined with an easy grin made him popular, particularly with women. He wasn't bashful and enjoyed their company, too. Johnson was pleased to have him working on the Bent Bar.

Bill went to the grain bin and got a few pounds of oats to feed the horses before they left. He put grain in two different feed buckets and then put some in a couple of sacks that he slipped into his saddle bags. He went for their saddles while Casey was gathering the horses.

While the horses were finishing the last of their grain, Bill and Casey saddled them and tied on their slickers. They each put an extra halter and lead rope in their saddle bags. If any of the mares had trouble last night, they would be able to halter them and lead them home. They were ready and anxious to get started. Johnson was staring at them, but said nothing. The two riders mounted up and looked at Johnson to see if he had any last minute instructions. They waited for him to come back from wherever his thoughts had taken him. Finally, he blinked his eyes and as if talking to no one in particular, said, "That girl has to be the toughest and most skilled rider I ever met in my life." Embarrassed by their boss's rare show of emotion, they both nodded toward him and said nothing. They knew where he was. Then gruffly, Johnson said, "It's gettin' late, you better get started, if there's a problem up there and you need help, one of you ride back and let me know."

They rode out of the yard with the full dawn. It would be twenty minutes or so before the sun made its first peep over the mountains. They took turns opening gates through the pastures they crossed. The sun poked up above the mountains and promised to warm things up. The nights were still cool enough to leave a calling card of frost on the ground, so the promise of warmer temperatures was welcome to the two riders. They made their way along the east bank of Gunpowder for a few miles till they came to a decent place to cross near where Dry Boulder came out of the mountains. The trail wound through willows and cottonwoods as it followed along the creek. They came out of the woods in a clear spot and got their first good look at the creek in full daylight.

It was high and still carrying a lot of debris from the flash flood the night before. They were both shocked when they looked at the banks above the water line. They saw that the water had been a lot higher than it now was. The banks were covered in mud, sticks and branches, three feet higher than the water level now running down the creek. The old grass on the banks was laying down in the downstream direction as if it was groomed with a giant comb. Up and down the creek they could see the aftermath of the flood. A few tree trunks and the remains of trees, washed away by the flood, lay scattered along the creek where the receding water left them. This was the first clue that a flood had occurred last night. They were back at the ranch looking after their stock when the forces of nature came together and formed the flash flood.

"Something sure roared through here last night after we came past," Bill said.

"I'm glad it roared through after we crossed, or we probably would have gone with it, by the looks of it," Casey answered.

"It was late the last time we crossed Gunpowder above here and it sure wasn't that high then," Bill said. "We must have gotten one of them flash floods roaring out of the mountains caused by all that rain we had with the storm last night. It must have happened just after we got back to the ranch. They don't last long when they happen, but they can sure do a lot of damage. Johnson will be interested in knowing about this," Bill continued. "We better get across and on up Dry Boulder and look for that bunch of mares. I hope they didn't get caught in it somehow," Bill said.

"It looks a little shallower by the bend, just above the cutbank. We can angle across through that riffle and come out on the shallow gravel bar on the other side," Casey said.

"Whatever way we do it, I think we're gonna' end up with wet butts, cowboy," Bill said.

"How many times do I have to tell you, I ain't no cowboy, I'm a cowman and a darn good one," Casey answered.

"Countin' today, it makes four thousand times you've told me," Bill answered back. Bill wasn't looking forward to getting the seat of his pants wet crossing the swollen creek, it was still chilly this morning. He knew it would be a lot chillier if he had to ride up the coulee with wet pants. Casey gave him a cold stare after the last comment he made. Without saying another word, Casey spun his horse around and galloped straight at the creek where he pointed out they could cross the easiest. Bill watched him go, wondering what he was up to now.

Casey didn't slow down when he hit the shallows at the crossing. Water sprayed out and away from him as it got deeper. Then, light as a feather, Casey came up out of the saddle using his right hand on the horn. His boots landed on the seat of the saddle. Supporting himself with his right hand on the horn and holding the reins in his left, he rode across crouched above the saddle. The horse slowed as the water grew deeper and Casey jogged him the rest of the way across and up the far bank. He slipped back down in the saddle. He was dry as a bone. Bill watched with a grin on his face and shook his head at Casey's antics. Casey jogged back up the creek until he was opposite of where Bill sat grinning on the other side.

"Okay, Bill, it's your turn, there's nothin' to it," he yelled. "Do it like that and you won't get wet, and hurry up, it's gettin' late," he continued. Bill sat there and thought about the little feat Casey just pulled off. Casey knew Bill was not about to try it. He'd probably slip off in the deepest part of the creek and get drenched. "Either do it my way or get a helicopter to get you across, otherwise there's no way you'll make it across dry, cowboy," he yelled across with a lot of emphasis on the cowboy. Casey always scored in the high seventies or low eighties riding bareback broncs in rodeos. Bill had nothing but admiration for his friend's ability on horseback. Occasionally Casey would treat him to a display of his talents when he wanted to make a point of something. Still grinning, Bill headed downstream to where Casey had crossed.

Not wanting to give Casey something to talk about for the rest of the year if he fell off, Bill stayed in the saddle as he entered the water. When the water got just below his stirrups, he pulled his boots out and raised his legs as high as he could, still sitting firmly in the seat of the saddle. The water came up to the skirt of the saddle and splashed onto the seat as they jogged across. Bill felt the cold water penetrate through the seat of his pants and let out an involuntary grunt. He came out of the water and jogged up to where Casey was waiting with a smirk on his face.

"Can I ask you a question?" Casey asked when Bill rode up beside him.

"What?" Bill snapped.

"Is the water cold, cowboy?" Casey asked with a mischievous grin on his handsome face. Without answering, Bill urged his horse into a fast trot toward Dry Boulder. Knowing when to quit, Casey jogged after him and they both turned to the task of finding the band of mares.

They traveled up the west bank of Gunpowder for a short distance and then turned toward the big coulee. The mares were scattered along the top of the draw. The old bay had her head up and watched them approach. They were still almost a half mile away but she spotted them long before they spotted the mares. "That old bay sure don't miss much, does she, Casey?" Bill said.

"Not much, and the rest of them sure pay attention when she gives an order," Casey answered. They rode toward the scattered mares. As they rode closer to the horses, Casey and Bill split up. Bill rode around the band one way and Casey went around the other. The mares weren't bothered much by the riders circling them. They knew the men and the horses they were riding. At one time or another they'd all been handled by the two riders. Casey and Bill moved around the mares at a slow walk looking them over to see if there were any problems. After a close inspection they both met on the upper end of the band and stopped.

Neither said anything for a few minutes. They just sat and looked back at the grazing mares. "I'm gonna' count 'em one more time," Bill finally said.

"Okay," his partner answered. They both counted only fourteen. They brought fifteen mares up here earlier in the spring. In the last few minutes they both counted the horses at least a dozen times trying to make the missing mare show up.

"We're short one and I can't figure out who it is," Bill said. There was silence again.

"Flame!" Casey finally said.

They split up to look for the missing mare. Casey cut down into the coulee and crossed the bottom to angle back up the other side. While he slowly picked his way through the aftermath of the flood, he found it hard to believe what he saw. Mud and debris was everywhere. There was a new channel carved out in the ravine. In the bottom there was no vegetation left. It looked like a huge plow came through and tore up everything. He began to have misgivings about finding Flame alive. There must be a good reason why she wasn't with the rest of the mares. If she had been caught in this terrible flood, he didn't see how she could have survived. He angled up the easy slope to the top of the coulee. When he reached the top, he rode up the coulee toward the mountains. Bill was going to ride up the other side. They planned on meeting high up Dry Boulder where a good trail crossed. The mares were seen in that area a few days ago. Maybe they would find the young mare still up there.

Bill headed up the coulee on the right side as it climbed toward the mountains. He scanned all the areas he could see. He traveled close to the edge of the canyon so he could look down into the draw. He came to a hogback ridge and looked down that trail but saw nothing. A large pile of rocks and boulders hid his view of where the young mare was lying.

After her ordeal she had collapsed in utter exhaustion and slept through the night in a spasm racked trance. Unconsciously she dreamt of her colt and where she had thrown him to the bank. The scene kept replaying through her mind all through the night. The first rays of sun penetrated through the outcropping of rocks and felt good on her bruised hide. She heard the ringing sound of a steel shoe hitting rock somewhere above her and came awake.

Bill started moving again, traveling along the rim of the coulee. He looked at the devastation below and wondered what happened here last night. One thing he knew for sure was that any animal caught when the flood came through would have had a hard time surviving. Occasionally he caught sight of Casey pulled up on the other side, looking into the draw. If anything moved, one of them was sure to spot it. He rode to where a faint trail led down to the bottom of the draw. He looked into the draw and saw most of the brush that had been there was gone, but that big old boulder was still lying where it had been, probably for the last million years. It would take a lot to move that big rock, he thought. He felt his horse suddenly tense up and look toward a thicket.

The mare known as Flame struggled to get off the ground. Pain shot through her in a hundred places as the agony of movement tortured her bruised and torn body. She lay back on the damp ground. Consciousness was bringing back a nightmare of memories. Suddenly, she remembered the birth of her colt and then the nightmare of the flood. Flashbacks of being overwhelmed by a wall of water and slinging the colt toward the bank raced through her mind. She struggled up against the pain. She must return to the area where she gave birth and look for her colt. She remembered the big boulder and the narrow game trail leading out of the coulee, and the effort of throwing the colt above the water and feeling him hit solid ground. Blood started oozing out of a wound on her front shoulder. The flesh had been torn when she slammed into a boulder during the ride in the front wave of the flood. Her leg and neck muscles were stiff and painful. Excruciating pain enveloped her when she tried to walk.

A higher order than pain dominated her resolve. She must find her colt. Painstakingly, she made her way toward the top of the coulee. She only made it a few feet before she had to stop and rest. Pain and dizziness enshrouded her. She started again and went further. She kept moving and slowly her stiff muscles began to respond to her effort. She came out on top of the trail and paused. She looked toward the higher country and knew where she needed to go. Determined, she ignored the pain and started off.

Alerted by his mount, Bill stared into the thicket. Startled, he heard a low nicker come from the brush. Involuntarily, his horse moved closer toward the greeting. Highly curious, Bill started to dismount and make a closer inspection. Just as he reached the ground, a blood red colt stepped out of the bushes and stopped. Stunned and amazed, Bill and his horse just gaped at the bedraggled foal. The little colt broke the spell by nickering again. He received a return hello from Bill's horse and tentatively started toward them. Bill knew he had to be careful to not spook the colt. He started talking low and soft, but didn't make a move. If he spooked the little fellow and he ran off, he would never be able to gain the colt's confidence again. The colt's very first impression of him had to be good. He must have no fear of this strange thing that only had two legs, Bill thought.

It was hard to say who tried harder, Bill or his horse. Bill murmured soft words toward him and his horse encouraged the colt with low welcoming nickers. Slowly the colt approached the horse and rider. He didn't seem frightened. They had to keep it that way. A hundred questions raced through Bill's mind. Where was his mother? How am I gonna' get him home? These were just a few of the things that were flying through his mind as the colt continued toward them. He knew if they succeeded in getting the colt to follow them home it would be, in part, because of the friendly gelding he was riding. Would the colt think the gelding was his mother? The colt came close enough for the two horses to touch muzzles. The colt started a chewing motion with his jaw while holding his head up toward the gelding. It was his way of telling the big horse that he wanted to be friends.

Bill didn't move as the colt began exploring the gelding, nuzzling him as he went. They both knew what he was looking for. Bill knew the critical time was coming when the colt stopped and stared at him. He was going to have to use all the horse sense he could muster to win this orphan's confidence. Slowly, he rubbed his gelding to get the horse's scent on his hand. Then he gently extended his arm toward the colt. The colt watched him raise his arm to his muzzle level and hold it there. Bill stood stock still as the colt approached his outstretched hand. The colt sniffed his hand. Relief ebbed through Bill as the colt smelled horse scent and didn't become alarmed with his presence. Slowly Bill raised his arm and touched the colt on his forehead. The colt tolerated the touch and then moved back closer to the gelding. Bill took his first gamble and stepped toward the colt who was inspecting the undercarriage of the gelding to see if he could find breakfast. Bill reached up and laid his hand on the colt's back. He noticed clotted blood on both sides of the colt's neck and was careful to not touch the wound. He didn't want to cause the colt any pain and have him jump away at this critical time. Slowly, he began gently touching the colt on all parts of his body.

Casey rode out on the rim rock on the other side of the canyon. He could plainly see what was taking place on the opposite side. He let out a surprised shout when he saw the colt standing beside Bill and his horse. He immediately knew what happened and what Bill was attempting with the new found colt. Casey couldn't see a mare any where around them and a shiver of dread passed through him. He couldn't cross the canyon here so he turned and started back the way he came. That's when he looked across and saw a lone horse slowly moving along the top of the draw toward where Bill stood with the new colt. Instinctively he knew it was Flame and that the colt with Bill was hers.

But why was she so far away from the colt and why was she moving so slowly? Casey asked himself as he started down the canyon. He loped back toward the nearest spot where he could cross. When the canyon widened, he found a likely spot and started down. He slowed to a walk and figured he better take his time. It would be better to let Bill handle this himself until the new colt got used to him. Then again, Flame was making her way toward them and another rider coming in now might upset things. Casey decided to ride to the top of the coulee and watch from a distance. Bill would be able to see him and could signal if he wanted help.

He rode out of the canyon and stopped his horse on a high spot where Bill would be sure to see him. He had a good view of Bill and the horses. Bill had spotted the mare and was walking his horse down to meet her. The colt was following behind. When they were about a hundred yards apart, the mare spotted the colt and let out a high piercing whistle. She broke into a painful trot toward the colt. Both Bill and Casey saw she was dragging and favoring her right front leg.

When the colt heard the unmistakable call of his mother, he came to a stiff legged stop. With his ears ramrod stiff and pointing, he stared in the direction of her call. He soon spotted her and whinnying loudly, trotted to meet her. Bill stopped leading his horse and stood back and watched. It was a sweet reunion. They nickered to each other and the mare started nuzzling the colt from one end to the other. The colt began looking for a meal. He quickly found it and went to work nursing with an honest hunger. Bill grinned in pure pleasure as he watched the mare and her colt. He got a good look at Flame and could see a deep wound on her right front shoulder. Her hide was scraped clean of hair in a big area on her rump and again on her withers. There were other places where her hair had been scraped off and ugly bruises and welts were showing through her skin. She was a mess. He waved to Casey and saw him start leading his horse toward them. They would have to figure a way to get her off the mountain without adding to her injuries.

Casey eased his way up to Bill. Bill moved off from the mare and colt to give them time to get reacquainted. He was squatting holding the reins of his horse and just watching. When Casey reached Bill, he squatted beside him and neither said a word. They were both trying to piece together the puzzle of the mare and colt and why they were separated. Because of the beat up condition of the mare, she obviously had been caught in the flood and somehow survived. The colt had a neck wound but that was all. He evidently escaped the flood, but how?

"Something is strange," Bill said.

"Did she have the colt up here and then somehow get caught in the coulee alone when the flood came through?" Casey asked.

"Well, that would explain her beat up condition and why they were separated. She was coming from somewhere down below when I first saw her," Bill answered.

"That colt was born last night, I'd say he's not more than twelve hours old," Casey said. Bill murmured agreement and they both watched the colt finish nursing. The colt walked around the mare a couple of times and then lay down almost underneath her. The mares eyes were bright as she looked back at her colt resting beneath her. She felt better now that the colt had fed. Stiffly, she lay beside him and closed her eyes.

"They have both had a rough time, we may never figure out what happened to these two last night, but I think they're probably lucky to be alive," Bill said.

"That's for sure," Casey answered. "Well, just look at them. They're built better'n any horse on the ranch, or the whole county, for that matter. We know Flame is tough as nails, she's strong and quick on her feet. I think that mare accomplished some sort of exceptional feat to save her colt from the flood, not to say anything about saving herself," Casey said.

"They're definitely an outstanding pair of horses," Bill said as he handed his reins to Casey. He eased over to where the horses were lying. The mare opened her eyes but didn't get alarmed when Bill bent over in front of her and looked at her injury. Bill saw that her flesh was badly torn and would need stitches. Blood was still oozing out of the wound, but would probably stop soon. He walked over to Casey and took his reins. He motioned for Casey to follow him.

They led their horses to a small clump of cedar trees. Bill tied his horse to one of the trees and loosened his cinch. Casey knew he planned on staying here awhile. "When she wakes, I'll give her some grain from the sacks in the saddlebags," Bill said. Casey nodded and waited to hear the rest of Bill's plan. He knew both horses needed attention and they had to get them off the mountain to get help. "The wound is bad, it needs stitches. She'll have to walk out of here and it will probably start bleeding again. That'll help clean it, so I don't think that will cause a problem. They need to rest awhile and then we'll start down. I'll watch them close and rest them when they need it. You start for the ranch and get one of the stock trailers. I'll get them off the mountain and across Gunpowder Creek. I'll bring them to wherever you're waiting with the trailer and we'll haul them the rest of the way home," Bill said.

"That sounds like a good plan," Casey said. "Do you want me to wait with you till they wake?" he added.

"No, I'll be fine. Be sure and find Johnson to let him know what we've got here and what we plan on doing," Bill said.

"Okay," Casey replied. He mounted and said, "I'll see you down below in four or five hours, Bill." Bill waved at Casey and turned around to look for a comfortable place to sit and wait for the two horses to awaken.

Casey headed downhill at a walk for the first half mile, then he kicked his horse into a lope. He had a ways to go and a lot to do before Bill got to Gunpowder. He made good time and rode into the ranch just a few hours after leaving Bill.

He saw Ann come out of the barn as he rode up. She was limping but looked fine otherwise. Ann saw Casey riding in and waved to him. A warm glow passed through him when he saw her wave and head his way. She wore a long sleeve blouse tucked into her jeans. Light makeup accentuated her face and Casey wondered why he never noticed how pretty she was before this morning. He could see her blond hair was still damp from the shower. Casey admired her trim figure as Ann walked toward him.

"How's the famous ravine rider today?" he joked as he stepped out of the saddle.

"I'm just fine, thank you," she said

"You don't look so fine, the way you're limping," he answered.

"Well, I've got a bruise on my right thigh. A boulder got in our way last night. It's still sore," she said with a twinkle in her blue eyes. Casey was pleased, and laughed at her last comment as he unsaddled his horse.

"Buster is in a lot worse shape than I'm in. We just finished doctoring him again. I think he likes all the attention he's been getting, but he deserves it. He's a real hero in my book," she said.

"Buster will heal just fine. You'll just have to use another horse for a month or so," Casey said.

"I'll have to semi-retire from the barrel racing circuit for a while," Ann said.

"I don't think your competition will mind at all," Casey said.

"I'll fall behind in the overall point standings, but there are worse things in life," Ann said.

Casey picked up his saddle and headed for the tack room. "Annie, where's Johnson?" he asked as he walked into the barn.

"Right here," Johnson said from the other end of the barn. "Where's Bill and what did you find out about them mares?" Johnson asked.

Casey related the story of finding the evidence of the flood. He told about finding the mares and riding up the coulee looking for Flame. When he got to the part about the new colt, Ann asked so many questions, Johnson finally had to interrupt so they could get the rest of the story. Johnson and Ann were intrigued by the mare's condition and how she survived the flash flood. Ann interrupted again and asked him how the colt survived the flood unscathed if the mare was so beat up. "That's the real mystery of this whole deal. Bill and I haven't been able to figure that out yet, except to say that Flame is a strong, healthy filly and must have put out some kind of terrific effort to save that colt," Casey said. He told Johnson of their plan to walk them off the mountain to Gunpowder Creek and trailer them from there to the ranch.

"Annie, would you go in the house and call Doc Brown and ask him if he could meet us here in about three hours? Tell him about the mare's shoulder and the condition of the colt," Johnson said.

"Consider it done," Ann said as she took off for the house. When she was halfway there, Casey and Johnson saw her stop, turn and start back toward them as fast as her bruised thigh would let her.

"You know what's coming now, don't you, Casey?" Johnson asked.

"Yep," Casey said.

Ann came back and before she could even open her mouth, Johnson said, "Annie, would you like to go with us to pick up Bill and the two horses?"

"You bet!" she chirped and was gone again at a fast limp for the house. She could hear Johnson and Casey laughing when she reached the house.

Casey put his horse away, then he and Johnson hooked up one of the stock trailers to a pickup. Casey put some hay in the trailer and a few ropes that he thought they might need if they had trouble loading the horses. He was anxious to go but knew Bill wouldn't get there for quite a while. Johnson asked him more questions about what he saw and what the coulee looked like. There were flash floods before, but it sounded like this one was a real monster, Johnson thought. They talked about the storm and how it caused the flood. They knew how heavy the rains were. "I am just glad we were back home with Annie before that flood hit and weren't stuck on the wrong side of the crick' last night," Casey said.

"Amen," Johnson replied.

When they pulled into an open meadow alongside the creek, they saw Bill and the horses. He had haltered Flame and was leading her slowly down the ridge. "Look at the colt!" Ann said. They could see the little reddish horse following behind his mother.

"We should name him Survivor, after what he went through last night," Casey said.

"Oh no! There is only one name for him and it should be Stormy. He was born during that terrible storm and must have endured a frightening night, he should be named for the storm!" Ann said forcibly.

"Stormy, that's kinda' catchy and sounds like a good name for him," Johnson said. It was settled. The gangly colt coming out of the mountains behind his courageous mother would forever be known as Stormy.

Bill rode down to the creek and saw that the water had receded considerably, since he soaked his seat early this morning. The colt should be able to cross with no problem, he thought. He led the mare across and the colt splashed in right behind her. When Johnson saw the colt jump in without hesitating, he was relieved. Their ordeal last night had not left a lasting fear of water on the mare or her colt. They were both plucky critters', he thought. Johnson, Casey and Ann waited until Bill led the mare all the way to the trailer before they moved. They didn't want to spook the horses now that the worst was over.

Bill rode up and handed the lead rope to Casey. "Any problems?" Casey asked.

"None," Bill answered. "When they woke, I fed Flame some grain while the little guy nursed. When they were done we started down. She sensed I was there to help, so she let me halter her easy. We made our way down slow and at her pace. I think that colt is going to be a real winner. After all he'd been through, he was still full of energy. He kept running in front of us bucking and jumping. His neck needs some attention, but besides that, he's healthy. Flame's shoulder needs to be sewed up, but as you can see, she made it here without too much loss of blood," Bill related to them.

Casey had backed the trailer in alongside a heavy row of brush and opened the loading gate to make a kind of natural pen. Bill loaded his horse into the front half and closed the divider. Johnson led the mare into the rear and tied her off. The colt stood nervously at the rear. Casey and Ann came in behind the colt and coaxed him toward the trailer and his mother. With the brush on one side and the loading gate on the other, he had no where to go. Hesitating no longer, he gracefully jumped into the trailer. Casey closed the gate. All four Bent Bar hands climbed in the front of the pickup and headed for home.

When they arrived, Doc Brown was waiting for them. They unloaded the horses and led them into the barn. Flame and Stormy were put into one of the bigger stalls. Doc cleaned up the mare and inspected the wound on her shoulder. He gave her antibiotics and then cleanly sewed the torn flesh together. "It will take a while but this shoulder will heal good. The rest of her injuries are superficial and with good care will heal completely," he said.

"Now, somebody help me corner the colt so I can look at that wound on his neck," Doc said. Ann was in the stall before anyone else could move. They eased him into a corner and slipped a small halter on to hold him while Doc looked him over. Doc Brown cleaned the wound on both sides of the colt's neck. He straightened up and said to no one in particular, "Hand me the flashlight out of my bag." He carefully inspected the wound with his light while everyone wondered what he was looking for.

"These are teeth marks. I've never seen this before, but the mare must have grasped him here with a powerful grip for some reason," he finally said.

CHAPTER 6

Word spread fast through the valley about Ann and Buster's ride off the high cliff. When she limped off the school bus Monday morning, there were a dozen classmates waiting to see her and ask a thousand questions. They all knew Buster and many watched Ann ride him in junior events at the rodeos and horse shows along this part of the Rockies. The two did so well in performance events that they were celebrities around town. Everyone felt like Buster was an old friend and they were all concerned about his condition. She was terrified during the ride and all the questions were bringing back the memory of those wild few minutes. She knew shortly after getting off the bus, that she would be glad when this day was over.

When she entered the school house, there were a half dozen teachers waiting to ask the same questions over again. Mainly, everyone wanted to know if she was frightened during the ride or fall off the cliff and how Buster managed to stay upright during their free-fall. "I was so busy riding Buster and trying to figure out where we were going to land next, that I didn't have time to worry about being afraid until we somehow ended up on the bottom of the ravine. Buster is pretty scraped and bruised but he'll heal in a month or so. He should be in good shape and back in condition for the Fourth of July Rodeo at the High Valley fairgrounds, I hope," Ann replied.

The first day back in school was a blur and she couldn't keep her mind on her classes. She kept seeing a black void at the end of a slippery trail. She was anxious for the day to finish so she could get back to the ranch and tend to the horses. They were cleaning and treating the wounds on Flame, Buster and Stormy twice a day. When she told the story of Flame having her colt and then being washed away in the flood, her classmates and teachers listened in complete silence. Ann told about the wound on Stormy's neck and what they thought happened. They believed Flame evidently saved the new colt by somehow throwing him out of the flood's path.

The kids in her class wanted all the details of the events that happened on the Bent Bar ranch during the storm. She told the story as best she could. The day seemed to drag on forever and when the bell finally rang after her last class, she was more than ready to head for home. There were a lot of things she wanted to take care of on the ranch and she was anxious for the bus to leave and head up the valley toward the Bent Bar.

When the bus stopped to let her off, she saw Johnson's pickup waiting for her. She was glad to see him. It would save a quarter mile walk down the lane to the ranch. Her leg was still sore from the boulder they collided with on the way down the cliff. "Hi, Johnson. Thanks for picking me up. That's awful nice of you," she said as she climbed into the truck.

"No problem. Thought you'd rather ride than walk today," he answered.

Ann wondered if this might be a good time to approach him about Flame's new colt. She was nervous about bringing up the subject and decided to wait before asking about the colt.

"How's the leg feeling today?" Johnson asked.

"It's a lot better and the swelling has gone down," she answered.

"Good, how are you getting along walking on it?" he asked.

"Pretty good, it doesn't hurt at all now," she said.

"Well, I think after we doctor Buster, he should be led around to give him a little exercise. Those bruised muscles need to be stretched, he'll get mighty stiff if he just stands around in his stall all day. The exercise will help him heal faster too," Johnson told her.

"Great, I'll change clothes and then go to the barn and doctor him. Then I'll lead him around the arena a few times and see how he feels," she said.

"How about Flame and the colt?" she asked.

"Flame is one sore filly, she needs care and rest now, the colt is fine. He's quite a character, he's been trying to run and buck in the stall and just doesn't have enough room," Johnson said. "Maybe in a few days we'll turn them out in the arena and let them have more space in the daylight hours," he said.

Without thinking, Ann blurted out, "What are you gonna' do with the colt?"

Johnson turned his head and looked at her for what seemed a long time. Finally, he said, "Same thing we do with all of our colts. We'll halter break him and let his mother raise him for six months or so and then we'll separate them and wean him. We'll turn him out until he's two and then break him to saddle. If the ranch needs another horse when we break him, we'll keep him on here. If we don't need any extra horses, we'll take him to the sale ring with the other colts we'll sell that year. You know what we do with the extra colts, Annie. They bring in needed income for the ranch. How come you're asking anyway?"

"I dunno," she answered.

Johnson pulled into the yard and parked. Ann jumped out and shouted, "Thanks for the ride!" and took off for the house to change clothes. Johnson got out and watched her go. I wonder what she has on her mind now, he thought.

Ann went to her room and slammed the door. She was upset with herself for asking about Stormy. She had to approach this situation with more tact than she had shown in the pickup. After all, Johnson was the one who would make the decision on what to do with the colt. She wanted that colt for her very own. She knew he was exceptional and was afraid someone might offer to buy him before she had enough money to make the ranch a reasonable offer for him. Deep down, she felt that if Flame had a colt, it could very well turn out to be an outstanding rodeo performance horse. Flame was such a great mare that possibly she would pass her athletic abilities to her offspring who might have even more ability. Wouldn't that be something? she thought.

She wanted the colt badly. Buster was good. She won a lot of events on him. He was quick and fast. Ann knew that to compete in the arena and win, she had to have a horse with a superb ability and a rock solid disposition. Buster was fast but she didn't think he could carry her all the way to a State championship.

Besides, she needed a horse coming behind Buster. Buster wasn't a youngster anymore. A younger horse would be faster for that final run to the finish line after the last barrel. She believed she had the ability to train a colt to win. Flame's colt had the conformation and disposition to make a well disciplined arena horse if he had the right training. In fact, after what the colt went through and survived, made her feel that he was truly an exceptional horse. How many other horses could have lived through that ordeal? He is really special. He could be one of those champions that only come along once in a great while, she thought.

She had saved two hundred and thirty six dollars. She knew that wasn't enough to buy the colt. When the school year ended she would earn wages working full time on the ranch. By the end of the summer, she could probably have enough money put away to make a reasonable offer. That was four months away and somebody with cash might come along in the meantime and buy him. Maybe Casey or Bill would loan her the money or maybe Johnson would let her put a down payment on the colt until she could earn the balance. That way, she could be sure no one else bought the colt. The first thing she had to do was find out what Johnson thought the colt was worth. She put on her work clothes and in a state of anxiety headed for the barn. She entered the barn and walked down the alleyway. When she passed Johnson's office she stole a nervous glance through the open door. She saw him poring over paperwork, but he didn't notice her. She continued on to the horse stalls.

She first stopped and looked in on Flame and Stormy. Flame turned and looked at her. The colt curiously moved over to the gate and sniffed her outstretched hand. What a friendly colt, she thought. Then, all at once he whinnied, spun on his hind quarters and jumped back to his mother. Ann laughed and walked toward Buster's stall.

Buster came to the gate and met her with a friendly nicker. "How are you, Buster?" she asked as she entered his stall. Ann had pampered Buster. His dark brown coat gleamed. His black mane and tail were combed and trimmed. Except for the injuries to his hind quarters, he looked exceptionally well.

"I'm sorry about what happened, maybe I should have given you a little warning before I jerked my slicker free," she told him. "But then that lightning scared me too, so I don't know. I think you could have picked a little better spot to spook, though," she added.

"What's important is that you both used your head and made some right decisions," Johnson said as he walked up. He startled her. She hadn't seen him come out of his office.

Ann's mind went into overdrive when she saw Johnson standing there. She still didn't have a plan to approach him with about buying the colt. "Well, thank you sir, occasionally we do something right," she answered.

"I'll help you work on the horses, that's a lot more interesting than the paperwork I've been muddling through all day," he said.

"Thanks" was all Ann could think to say. Maybe an opportunity would arise to bring up the subject of the colt and how much Johnson thought he might be worth, she thought. Ann went to the room where the medical supplies were and got containers of antiseptic and wound dressing. She picked up some gauze pads for cleaning and went back to Buster's stall. Johnson was putting a halter on the gelding when she got back.

They cleaned Buster's scrapes with the antiseptic and then applied the wound dressing. Buster stood for the irritation and gave them very little trouble. They were finished in a few minutes and ready to move to Flame and Stormy. "Buster, I'll be back in a few minutes to take you out for some exercise," she said as they left his stall.

"You need to pick out another horse to use here on the ranch. We're gonna' move the cows out of the valley this coming Saturday and we'll need your help," Johnson said as they walked down the alleyway toward Flame and Stormy's stall.

"Okay, I want to stay off Buster for at least a month. He should be okay to ride then and that will leave a whole month to get him in shape for the Fourth of July rodeo. I want Buster to be in better condition and form than he's ever been in. We need to win the barrel event," she said.

They haltered both horses and Ann commented on how Stormy seemed to go along with whatever you wanted to do with him. "It's the breeding, Annie, our Bent Bar horses have been bred to get along with people. A good ranch horse needs to be dependable, we need them like they need us. I won't tolerate outlaw horses on the place. They're the ones that get you hurt. I'm a little upset with Buster running away like he did during the storm. He's been a good horse since the day he was born, I guess the lightning was too close for him. But--he redeemed himself by controlling that fall off the ravine trail. Not all horses could have handled something as demanding as that. Buster was wrong to spook, but he must have realized it and started obeying your commands before the first turn of the trail. His breeding and training had a lot to do with your survival. An average horse would not have been able to handle that situation. The outcome would have been different if you had been on just any old horse. Buster also happened to have the advantage of having one of the best riders in the country on his back that night. He couldn't have done it without you either. You were both a real team," Johnson said.

Ann flushed with pride at Johnson's last statement. The man wasn't known for passing out undeserving compliments.

They worked on Flame and she gave them her full cooperation as they cleaned and medicated her injuries. As they worked, Johnson related to Ann the breeding program the ranch pursued in their horse herd. She was interested to know more about that subject. "What important traits do you look for in a horse you want to keep to be part of our herd?" she asked.

"Well, Annie, there are a lot of things that make a good horse. It's hard to find any one individual that has everything you'd like to see in an animal. I like to develop horses that carry as many good traits as possible. Intelligence has to stand pretty high on the list. For instance, Buster realized what was happening was not good and made adjustments before it was too late. A horse short on brains would have run right off the cliff and neither one of you would have had a chance. You can tell a lot about a horse's mental make-up just by watching the way he carries himself. An intelligent horse always seems to have an alertness about him. He's aware of what's happening around him and he doesn't fly off the handle. He'll tolerate some situations his rider may put him in even though he believes there's an easier way to get the job done. That's real important. A good example is your barrel racing. You take off running toward the side of the arena then all of a sudden you ask your horse to make a three hundred and sixty degree turn. Well, that doesn't make a lot of sense to the horse. He just came from that direction, so why go back there again. Instead of fighting your commands, a good, smart horse will turn where you tell him and trust your judgment one hundred percent. In other words, a smart horse will obey every cue you give him, no matter what he thinks he should be doing," Johnson said.

"Well, then Buster scores high in that department, doesn't he?" she asked.

"He sure does, he's got what we like to see in a horse. A good, smart horse is usually the one that has a pleasing disposition toward most people. He's smart enough to know you're in control and he might as well get along with you rather than fight you and make it harder on himself. However, if a person abuses a horse consistently, then sometimes the smartest horses can also turn into the most ferocious outlaws that ever lived. They'll come at them with murder in their eyes."

"Some of the smartest horses I ever knew were rodeo bucking horses. They are treated as good or better than most pleasure or work horses. Their whole job is to pitch that rider as quickly as they can. They know that the quicker they unload him, the quicker they'll be returned to a nice clean corral, so they come out rip-snorting and acting like the devil is in them. Some of them look as mean and fierce as can be imagined. Once their ride is over, a smart one becomes very docile and easy to get along with. With different training a smart bucking horse could be one of the better performance horses, either a good roping or barrel horse, for example."

"Next, we want ability, and lots of it. We need horses that are quick on their feet and fast. With all the roping we do on the ranch, a fast horse is a must. We'd waste a lot of time if our cows could outrun most of our horses during a roundup or branding. They have to be able to follow a cow, no matter what kind of move the cow or calf makes. You know how quick a calf can be when he wants to get away. Our horses need the ability to turn on a dime at a dead run and be back at full speed in just a few leaps. They also have to be able to make a fast sliding stop, then gather themselves and be ready to go off in a whole new direction when the rider gives the orders. A horse has to first have the natural talent of an athlete. When you combine that ability with good training, you come up with a horse that's a pleasure to ride and work. If we can breed a horse with all of those traits and have a good tolerant disposition, then we've got a good ranch horse. That's what we've been developing on the Bent Bar for as long as I've been running the outfit," Johnson said.

"We sure seem to have first-rate horses. Or, am I just prejudiced?" Ann said.

"Generally we've got top quality stock, but don't forget that other outfits develop good breeding programs too. Occasionally we'll buy a mare or colt from another outfit if I feel that animal has traits that would be beneficial to our herd," Johnson said.

"Is that why you hauled Flame to Wyoming to breed her last year?" she asked.

"Yep, the stallion we bred her to has everything we look for. Plus, he has more natural ability than any horse I've seen in a long time. I think it was a good investment. Just look at that colt. He's exceptional, if we don't keep him, he'll be worth a lot of money to someone looking for a rodeo performance prospect," Johnson said.

Ann's heart sank with Johnson's last statement. How could she ever buy him now. In desperation, she said, "Well, he probably would have been worth something if it wasn't for those ugly scars he's gonna' have on his neck. I don't think anybody would pay much for him now. Those wounds on his neck will scar after they heal and look terrible."

"Annie, I don't think those scars are gonna' affect this young colt's performance," Johnson answered. Then he fixed her with one of those long piercing stares he used when he was trying to figure out something. Ann flushed with embarrassment. She felt guilty about using the wounds on the colt's neck to try and reduce his value. After all, she didn't know if the ranch would even consider selling the colt.

When they finished treating Flame, Ann eased over to the colt and extended her hand toward his nose. He took a few sniffs and decided it was okay to let her approach closer. She rubbed him along his shoulder a few times and then gently slipped a halter on his head and secured it. Johnson snapped a lead rope on the halter and they carefully started to clean and treat the area on the colt's neck. Ann was daydreaming about how to bring up the subject of buying the colt. She was pouring antiseptic on to a cotton ball, the ball became saturated but she kept pouring the liquid.

Quizzically, Johnson watched her continued pouring the fluid even though it was running off the cotton onto the floor of the stall. She was so immersed in her thoughts about the colt that she didn't realize what was happening. "Whoaa, girl, whoaa!" Johnson said loudly, when he saw she was not aware of what she was doing.

Startled back to consciousness, Ann blurted, "Johnson, we can't sell this colt to someone else, you have to give me a chance to buy him. I don't have enough money now, but by the end of summer I should have earned enough to pay for him."

Surprised, Johnson stared at the girl. He had no idea she was interested in the colt. It all started to make sense now. First, with her excitement about the colt, when they first saw Bill leading Flame down the ridge with the colt following. The day of the storm, she said that morning she wanted to finish early and ride over to Dry Boulder Coulee to look in on Flame. Now today, with her comments about the value of the colt and the scars he would probably have on his neck after his wounds healed.

Before he could answer her, she was off and running at the mouth again. "Buster is good but he's getting older and I just don't feel he has that extra special quality it takes to make a state champion. I want to win a state barrel championship and I want to train my own colt to do it. This colt is so special, I think he's the one that probably has what it takes to win big. I'll pay any price you think he's worth, if only you'll let me make payments," she quickly added.

Johnson was flabbergasted and didn't know what to say. He was holding Stormy, who had bolted away from the girl when she made the loud outburst. Flame had quizzically turned her head to look at Ann. She flushed even more when she realized Johnson was staring at her and that both Flame and Stormy were also giving her the eye. She realized she lost control of her emotions and the very hint of a tear started to show.

Johnson still hadn't spoken. He seemed to be gazing through her. She regained control and settled down. Without saying anything more she went back to work on Stormy. She finished and still Johnson said nothing. She took Stormy's lead rope from Johnson, looked him right in the eye and said, "Please give my request some serious thought. I would really like to own this colt, sir." With that, she slipped the halter off the young horse and started out of the stall.

"Hold on there, young lady," Johnson commanded. "I have been thinking about it ever since you brought it up. There are some other things I don't think you have considered about paying for this colt. Mainly, the fact that you were to be saving for your college tuition with your wages. You've only got two more years before entering college and we both know you really need to start saving now for that big expense. It takes a lot of money to go to school. If you buy this colt, that's going to put a big dent in your college funds and could jeopardize your education. I realize this is an exceptional stallion, however, I think that at your age education is more important. You'll have the rest of your life to ride and train horses. Other good horses will come along," Johnson said sternly.

"Mr. Johnson, (she hardly ever called Johnson Mister, unless there was something of tremendous importance she wanted to say.) I have considered that expense and this colt plays a big part in my plans for college. I know I can score high with Buster for the next few years in the barrel racing circuit. We're both good, you know that. You also know that the university awards scholarships for the College Rodeo Team. I believe Buster and I can ride our way into one of those scholarships. By the time we reach that arena, because of his age, Buster might have a hard time competing. With your help, I can have Stormy trained to ride and win against the best. If we can do that, I'll continue to receive tuition help through the rodeo scholarship. That will take away a big portion of the financial burden." Pointing back toward the colt, she continued, "So, if I owned this colt, he would actually help me through school. The investment now will pay bigger dividends in the future. So you see, sir, I have put some thought into it," she dramatically said as she finished her unrehearsed speech.

Johnson stared at her with his piercing, steely eyed glare. His silence was unnerving and Ann started to fidget under his glare. Was he trying to think of nice way to tell her that the colt was not for sale? Or, worse yet, had he already agreed to sell the colt to someone else?

The colt had every element he described in the perfect ranch horse. Had one of the other ranch hands already made an offer for the colt? Anyone who had seen the colt since they brought him home would have recognized the outstanding qualities the young stallion possessed and would certainly want him. The longer Johnson took to answer her the more she began to believe the colt had already been sold. A feeling of loss began to slowly creep over Ann. The terrible realization that the colt was not to be hers settled on her like a huge weight. It was as if all her dreams of the future had been snuffed out by Johnson's long silence. The colt was the center of those dreams and now it seemed that he must surely be lost. As hard as she tried, she could not hold back tears. Worried that they would soon turn into a flood down her face, she turned away from Johnson and stared down the alleyway toward the colt's stall. She did not want him to see her crying. It was dead quiet in the barn.

Johnson broke his long silence. His words sounded like an explosion in the silent barn. "Sounds to me like you have some grand plans for that colt. Some of what you say makes a lot of sense. But you're betting on something that hasn't happened yet. You can't go to the bank with the ones that haven't happened. Sure, I know you'll be able to pay for the colt, but I don't want your education to suffer in the process. He's an exceptional colt, we all can see that. I bred Flame to a total outcross from our stock on the chance she would have a colt such as Stormy. His dam and sire are both remarkable animals. Stormy will develop into an outstanding stallion. This ranch would welcome the offspring he can produce in the years to come."

"And I sure do believe you and Buster can do all you say you can do. That includes winning a state barrel racing championship. You're both top notch and I'll always be behind you one hundred percent. You would surely be a top contender for one of those scholarships they offer. So like you say, that would go a long way toward your tuition. I have to make sure you use your money prudently and don't get in the habit of spending it unwisely," Johnson said.

Ann turned and looked at Johnson. He could see the streaks on her face from the tears she had tried so hard to hide. She riveted her attention on Johnson. Gruffly, Johnson continued, "I suppose that we could work out the finances for college if we had to. The colt is a good stallion prospect for our broodmare program. If the ranch sells you Stormy, then it would only be fair that the ranch retains breeding rights for our band of mares. If you agree to that, I think we can make a deal," he hastily finished.

Ann screamed in happiness. She ran, jumped up, and threw her arms around Johnson in a bear hug. "Oh, Johnson, you'll never regret this, I promise," she cried.

"Okay, Okay," he said. "Now maybe you'll get busy and give Buster the exercise he needs," he added.

Ann released her hug. "You watch. Stormy, Buster and I are gonna' go a long way, and we're gonna' make you proud of us," she said. She took off toward Buster's stall. Halfway there she stopped and turned. "Hey, Johnson, there's one thing you didn't tell me," she said.

"What's that?" he answered, grinning.

"You never told me how much money the ranch wants for Stormy!"

Still smiling, he said, "Well, considering that he's gonna' grow up with those ugly scars on his neck, he's probably not worth much."

"He is too worth a lot!" Ann quickly answered in Stormy's defense.

Turning serious, Johnson said, "The ranch will sell Stormy for five hundred dollars provided you agree to the ranch retaining breeding rights. You can pay half now and the balance at the end of the summer. If you agree to that, then he is yours."

"I agree, but, will you loan me fourteen dollars, I only have two hundred and thirty six dollars saved," she said all in one breath.

"Okay," he said with a laugh.

Ann was now the proud owner of a beautiful sorrel colt named Stormy.

CHAPTER 7

Ann's social activities in school started to take a back seat compared with her interests in her new colt. She was anxious for school to let out everyday so she could head home and care for the horses convalescing in the barn. A naturally good student, her grades remained high even though she spent more time with the horses. She intended to keep her word to Johnson and earn a scholarship to the university. She knew scholarships were offered for outstanding grades as well as horsemanship. She studied harder and her grades showed improvement over their already high level.

Her ride down the cliff became just a memory. She didn't think about the horror of it very often. Still, she was reminded occasionally when someone asked her about the ride. It was talked about in town and soon the story spread across the mountain country. Sometimes visitors to town would ask about the story in the cafe. If Casey happened to be there at the time, he was always more than happy to relate the details of that stormy night. People listened in absolute silence as he went back over Ann's ride and the description of the steep walls of the ravine the girl and her horse had ridden down. He described the incredible ordeal the mare endured while saving her newborn colt from the flood. He related the story of how he and Bill found the mare and colt far apart and about the wounds on the colt's neck. He let listeners draw their own conclusions about what could have happened to the mare and colt during the flood.

It didn't take long for Ann and Buster to become more well known for that ride than they were for their success in barrel racing. An article appeared in the newspaper describing the frightening experience. Soon, when anyone mentioned they were from the Bent Bar Ranch, they were almost always asked about the girl and horse they heard about riding off a cliff. The Bent Bar hands were proud of Ann's feat and were always ready to recount that night. Ann wanted the whole thing forgotten and didn't like to talk about it. When asked about the ride, she briefly described what a great job Buster did getting them down. Then she talked about Flame and the shape she was in when she was found.

Buster's scrapes and bruises were healing well and Ann's constant attention showed in his recovery. She exercised him daily in the arena. He loosened up quite well and in no time was showing a bit of friskiness again. Almost a month passed since he was injured. He was looking better everyday. Ann decided she would give him a few more days of rest and then saddle him for the first time since the storm. Flame was taking longer to recover from her experience. Her wounds were healing well on her back and sides, the deep wound on her shoulder was coming along okay but Doc said that her shoulder would take quite a while to heal. They were turned out in the arena with Buster for a few hours everyday for exercise. Ann led the mare around the arena a few laps each day to keep her shoulder from stiffening. She gradually loosened up and was able to move easier as time went by.

Stormy showed no ill effects from his experience. He grew like a fertilized weed. His neck injuries healed well. He was left with matching black scars on each side of his neck. They were each just a few inches long now, but like a brand, they would grow larger in proportion with the colt as he grew in size. They would stay with him for life as a reminder of his birth during the worst storm to hit this region in over a century. He gained complete mastery of his long legs. He ran like the wind around the arena when he was turned loose for exercise. Anyone nearby when Stormy started running always stopped and watched the young horse race around the perimeter of the arena. He put on such a show that it would have been hard not to watch. Even Buster and Flame watched the colt closely when the urge struck him to run and buck.

He followed a pattern when he was getting ready to put on a show. Buster and Flame learned to pay attention when they saw the colt start his antics. They both were victims of his exuberance in running and kicking out with his long hind legs. An occasional misdirected hoof from the colt's play could sting. He would start out trotting around the two older horses shaking his head as if he was inviting them to join him. With his tail straight out, he would circle the other horses a few times and then in a tremendous burst of speed, race toward the far end of the arena. When he reached the other end, he would turn and follow the fence at full speed back toward the other horses. Buster and Flame would nervously watch him race back. He would put tremendous effort into reaching top speed quickly.

The racing colt would run straight toward the other horses. At the very last instant he would turn in a spray of flying dirt to avoid colliding into them. Anyone watching would think he couldn't possibly avoid running into them. After a few laps up and down the arena, he would settle into a high stepping, proud trot and jog around Flame and Buster a few times before settling down. He was a joy to watch. When Ann exercised either of the injured horses, Stormy was always right there walking and trotting along side and generally making a nuisance of himself. The exercise pace was too slow for him so he traveled along jogging around Ann and the horse she was leading. He was a pest and she had to continuously shoo him away.

She spent a lot of time watching the colt. His speed and quick turns always drew her attention. He would run straight toward the fence and just before crashing into it, gather himself and spin away in another direction. His young muscles were developing quickly with all the exercise he was getting. Everyone enjoyed the colt except Buster and Flame. They had to watch Stormy closely to keep out of his way in case he got too rambunctious. As Buster began feeling better, he started trotting after Stormy as if he wanted to watch over the colt and keep him out of trouble.

Flame was still sore and her efforts to keep up with the colt were painful so she kept a close eye on him from a distance. Buster adopted the colt and worried after him like a mother hen. Stormy treated Buster like he was a big brother and continuously nipped and aggravated the older horse who didn't seem to mind.

Things were going a lot better around the Bent Bar than they had a month ago. The cattle had been moved out of the valley and into the mountains where they would graze through the summer. The work load decreased considerably since the cattle were taking care of themselves and didn't have to be fed everyday. Buster and Flame were well on their way back to good health. The colt was obviously in good shape and healthy. The flood was history and Ann could look hopefully toward the future. In a few more days, school would be out for the year and she could concentrate on getting Buster back in shape. With just over a month to go before the Fourth of July rodeo, Ann knew they had a lot of work to do. She decided to set her barrels up in the arena to give the horse a chance to get used to them.

Ann rolled three fifty-five gallon steel drums into the arena. She used them to practice the cloverleaf pattern of barrel racing. Buster, Flame and Stormy watched as she measured the distances between the barrels. Stormy cautiously approached the first barrel Ann set up. Slowly he closed on the barrel with his neck stretched out and his head low to the ground. Ann stopped to watch him and was soon giggling at the importance Stormy was trying to give the barrel. He snorted, then backed up and sniffed the air trying to figure out what it was.

"You'd think that was a grizzly bear the way he's treating that barrel," Bill said from behind Ann. She hadn't seen him come into the arena. Ann laughed at his comment and walked over to where Bill was sitting on the top rail of the arena fence.

"How are the mares doing?" she asked.

"Great, no problems that I could see. We really have a good crop of colts this year. I could stay in them hills all day and just watch the new calves and colts running and playing, but I don't think the boss would like that too much," he said. Ann knew Bill had ridden into the mountains today to look in on their cattle and horses and check on the general condition of the range.

They sat on the top rail and watched Stormy close in on the barrel again. He got within stretching distance and slowly moved his head closer. Carefully he stretched out and touched the barrel with his muzzle. The instant his muzzle touched the barrel he let out a startled snort and bolted away in imagined terror. He tore around the arena at full speed and avoided the three barrels as he ran. Ann and Bill laughed in amusement. Casey heard the laughter and came out of the barn to see what was going on. He had been with Bill in the hills and was putting his saddle and tack away when he heard their racket. He walked over and climbed up beside them.

"What's that crazy colt doing now?" he asked when he got comfortable.

"Stormy thinks Ann just put a pack of wolves in the big corral with him," Bill answered. They all laughed and watched the colt slow down and start to approach the barrel again. Down at the other end of the arena Buster and Flame were watching too. Their reasons were different than the riders sitting on the rail laughing. Buster and Flame were watching to make sure they weren't run into when the colt charged in wild panic around the arena. They knew that he sometimes lost control.

Stormy neared the barrel. This time he had his courage up and approached more quickly. He got within five feet and circled it a couple of times with his head snaked out toward it. He stopped and snorted. It still didn't jump up and bite him, so he moved closer and touched it again. He jerked his head up and looked around. Everybody was watching quietly in anticipation of his next move. They didn't have to wait long. He let out a loud snort and started prancing around the barrel as if he had just conquered it and was now claiming the barrel as a trophy. With his head held high and his tail straight out in victory, Stormy broke into a choppy lope around the barrel and then accelerated to full speed down the arena. Halfway down he caught sight of another barrel and headed straight for it. He went into a dirt flying slide and stopped a few feet from the new barrel. He cautiously approached this new threat and circled it warily. It didn't take him long to defeat this barrel. He was soon sniffing and touching it. This one didn't pounce on him either, so he let out a victory snort and took off in a high speed run.

He went by the riders sitting on the rail at full speed and raced past Buster and Flame. He turned and headed for the last barrel that was intruding into his domain. He slowed and circled this barrel at a gallop. He closed the distance between himself and the barrel but maintained his speed as he circled. "It doesn't look like you're even gonna' have to train that colt, he's already training himself to be a barrel racer," Casey said as they watched Stormy circle the barrel.

"It sure looks that way. I'm just thrilled to death with that colt," Ann added.

"We all are," Bill said.

Stormy finished circling the barrel and stopped. He reached down and touched it with his muzzle. He sniffed around it and then casually walked off toward Flame and Buster. "I guess he just decided those barrels weren't gonna' hurt him and that he'd let them stay awhile," Bill said, as Stormy walked away from the last barrel.

"Well, I guess the fun's over, I'd better get back to work," Casey said as he started climbing down.

"I'm with ya'," Bill said and followed Casey.

Buster watched Stormy racing around the barrels and charging back and forth between them. He was a veteran barrel racer and recognized the barrels for what they were. He hadn't had a saddle and rider on his back in a month but somehow he knew his vacation was going to end and he would soon be back to work. Stormy came right up beside Buster and nuzzled him on the neck, then walked off and flopped down on the ground next to Flame. It was almost as if the young colt had asked the older, experienced horse for approval.

Delighted with the show, Ann climbed down. She finished measuring the distances between the barrels and set all three in place. She marked their positions. She knew the horses would probably push them over and get them out of alignment in the next few days and she wanted to be able to set them up quickly when Buster and she started practicing again. When Ann finished aligning the barrels, she went into the barn to get a lead rope for Buster. She came out and walked down the arena where Buster was standing, watching her approach. The clever old gelding knew what was coming.

Ann snapped the lead onto his halter, and led him to the far end of the arena. She planned to walk Buster through the pattern a few times before she saddled and rode him through. She had placed the three drums in a triangle pattern. The starting line was located sixty feet from the base of the triangle, which was formed by two of the barrels. Those two barrels were placed ninety feet apart. The third barrel was the apex of the triangle and located just over one hundred feet down the arena from the base. She stopped Buster thirty feet or so behind the starting line and studied the course. Ann formed a practice of running through the course in her mind before making her actual run. Even though she would only be leading Buster through the pattern on the ground, she still paused and imagined the route they would take through the barrels. They would begin behind the starting line and head slightly to the left of the first barrel positioned on their right. They would make a right turn completely around number one and come out of the turn heading slightly to the right of number two. They would make a left turn around number two and come out heading slightly to the right of barrel number three, at the apex of the triangle. They would make a left turn around number three and come out heading toward the starting line. Then they would sprint for the start-finish line to complete the cloverleaf pattern.

"Let's go, Buster," she said as she started leading Buster toward the first barrel. She stepped out and Buster followed just behind her right shoulder. They walked through the pattern and returned to their starting point. It didn't work very well. Flame watched from a distance but Stormy trotted along with them getting in the way. Ann shooed him away and they started out for their second circuit of the course. As they were going around the first barrel, Stormy came flying by them, circled the barrel and raced toward his mother at the other end of the arena. When he pulled up beside Flame he turned and watched Ann and Buster heading toward the second barrel. As Ann reached the second barrel, they had company again. Stormy raced down the arena and ran around the barrel in the opposite direction Ann and Buster were attempting. Ann yelled as he went past and Buster snorted in irritation as the colt raced by. He ran back to where Flame was watching. He was having a great time and Ann knew her training session wasn't going to be successful as long as the frisky colt was in the arena with them. Tomorrow she would have to put Stormy and Flame in their stall before beginning. When they reached the third barrel, Stormy was already there. He was impatiently prancing around the barrel waiting for them. "I hope you like these barrels in a few years as much as you do now, Stormy," Ann said to the colt while she and Buster tried to maneuver their way around the barrel while the excited colt pranced around them. "I think we'll call this a day, Buster, we're wasting our time as long as Stormy is here trying to help us," Ann said.

She walked Buster across the finish line and kept going straight for the barn. She put Buster in his stall and fed him. Then she went back to the arena and led Flame back to her stall. Like a shadow, Stormy followed right beside them. She put the mare and her colt away. It was a start anyway, she thought, as she finished up. After feeding, she paused at the gate to their stall and studied Stormy. Ann watched the colt nurse while Flame ate her grain. Stormy's muscles were developing and because of the running he had just done, were standing out impressively as he strained his body nursing. The muscular structure on his chest and forelegs was exceptional, Ann thought, as she admired the colt. His hind quarters were wide and muscular with a large crease running along the top of his rump. She felt he had a tremendous amount of potential. His actions today in the arena showed good athletic ability. Certainly he had shown intelligence when dealing with the ferocious barrels.

Stormy was working out better than Ann even hoped for. The next two years would be important. He would soon be turned out with Flame to graze and grow on the good grass of the high mountain meadows. Riders would look in on the livestock in the hills often, watching for illness or injuries. Stormy would be brought back to the ranch in the fall to winter with the rest of the horses. Then, after he had been weaned from his mother, Ann would start training him. She planned on establishing a very strong bond with the colt this winter while they worked on his ground training. He would spend his second spring and summer in the mountains again with the rest of the horses. When the spring of Stormy's second year rolled around, Ann would be graduating from high school. She would not turn him out to the mountains that summer.

That was when Stormy's training would begin under saddle and things would get serious. Ann knew she had almost two years to wait before riding her colt. It seemed like a long time. Those two years would be filled with important training to prepare him for the championship competition she wanted to pursue. More than ever, after watching him today, she knew she had an excellent prospect for winning. Doc Brown was due at the ranch in a few days to check Flame's shoulder. That meant Stormy would soon be gone for several months. She would miss the little guy, but she and Buster had a busy schedule planned for the summer. As she watched him in the stall, she realized how much she had grown to love the little colt. She knew she would be happy to see him return in the fall so she could start working him and be near him again.

"Have you decided to sell him back to the ranch yet?" Johnsons asked from behind as he walked to where Ann was admiring the colt.

"Not on your life," Ann replied. "You should have seen him running the barrels by himself today," she said.

"I heard the commotion and looked out to the arena and saw him cutting up. He surely has some speed, doesn't he?" Johnson said.

"He's fast and quick. Just what I need to make a first class contender. I know one thing. I sure am going to miss him when we send them into the mountains for the summer," she said.

"Well, that's going to be very soon. I imagine you could take them up the first of next week," Johnson said.

"Friday is my last day of school. Starting Saturday I'll be able to work full time, so that will work out good for me," Ann said.

"That will work good for the ranch, too. The spring horse sale is Saturday and I'm hauling our extra two year old colts to the stockyards to sell. I could use your help," Johnson said.

"Count on me. I'm anxious to get started full time and pay off my debt for Stormy," she said.

"We'll be gone most of the day. I want to get there early so we can get our horses through the livestock inspectors before they get too busy. We'll stay until the end to see what kind of prices green, two year olds are bringing and how our stock matches up with the rest," Johnson said.

"We always get top prices, why should it be any different this year?" Ann asked. "Hopefully it won't. I like to stay on top of the market and see what's being offered from year to year. You have to stay one step ahead of the competition, you know," he said.

"How many halters will we need?" Ann asked.

"We're selling the six horses Bill has been working with. I'll want you to ride them into the sale ring when their number comes up on the roster. A horse always seems to bring a better price with a pretty girl riding him around the ring," Johnson said.

"Oh, baloney. People know we breed and train good horses, that's why we always get a good price," she laughed at Johnson.

"Whatever you think, young lady, just be ready to start loading horses at daylight Saturday," Johnson said.

"I'll be there with bells on," she said.

The last day of school on Friday seemed as if it would never end. The students and faculty treated it like a party, rather than a regular school day. It was a formality and everyone was anxious for it to end. The kids discussed their plans for the summer with their classmates. The more studious consulted with their teachers to see what kind of studies they could pursue over the summer to be better prepared for next year. Ann needed a list of reference books on the subjects she would be taking her junior year. She wanted to be well prepared next fall. She discussed the subjects with her counselor and wrote down a list of books that would be helpful. Feeling satisfied, she gratefully joined her friends and classmates in the happy atmosphere prevalent on that last day.

She was up and ready well before daylight on Saturday. She dressed in work clothes and packed a small case with clean jeans and a new blouse that she would change into before riding the horses into the sale ring. She went out to the corrals where Bill worked the horses. No one was there, so she headed for the barn to get the tack ready. On the way to the barn she could see the lights of Casey's truck coming up the county road. She could hear it too. Casey's truck was not in the best of condition and you could hear it miles away.

She poured some grain into a sack to take along, then went to the tack room and pulled her saddle off the rack and carried it to the front of the barn. She went back and collected six halters, several lead ropes and a hackamore bridle that she would use on the horses ridden into the sale ring. Ann often watched Bill and Johnson work the two year old colts and helped out whenever she could. The horses they were taking today were well mannered and would respond to a hackamore. They were not finished horses, but would turn and stop on command. The new owners would be able to finish their training to suit their own needs. Buyers were always anxious to buy Bent Bar colts because they knew they would be getting a well started horse with good bloodlines that would be easy to finish training. Johnson had built a solid reputation for the Bent Bar through the quality of horses it produced.

Ann stacked all the equipment they would need in front of the barn and then carried the six halters and lead ropes over to the corrals. Casey parked his wreck in the ranch yard and he and Bill were walking toward the corral too. "It sounded like your truck was blowing up coming up the road, Casey. I could hear you coming miles away," Ann jokingly said as they walked up.

"She always makes a lot of noise in the morning. Nellie doesn't like to get up this early and then have to pack all of Bill's weight around to boot," Casey shot back.

"No comment," Bill said. Ann laughed and headed toward the corral gate with a halter. They heard Johnson's truck start on the other side of the yard. "I'll go help Johnson hook up the stock trailer while you two are catching the horses," Bill said.

"Okay," Ann and Casey said in unison.

Ann and Casey started methodically catching and halter-ing the six horses. They led them out of the corral and tied them to the rail fence. Ann headed back to the barn to get the brushes and curry combs. She stacked them alongside the gear she collected earlier. Johnson and Bill drove over to the front of the barn. They loaded the gear and feed in the trailer tack compartment along with Ann's saddle and overnight case containing her good clothes. Bill drove the rig over to the corrals to load the horses, as Ann and Johnson walked over to help. In a few minutes they had all six horses loaded and the tail gate closed and latched. Daylight was just starting to show above the mountains when they finished.

"Casey, you have James help you with the other horses in the corrals today when he gets back from checking the cattle. Bill's gonna' ride along to give us a hand with the colts at the stock yards," Johnson said.

"Yes sir," Casey answered.

"Watch for Doc. He's gonna' try and get out to look at Flame today," Johnson said.

"I'll keep my eyes peeled like a hawk," Casey said.

"And please watch Stormy for me," Ann added.

"Stormy? Who's Stormy?" Casey innocently asked Ann.

They all laughed and Ann said, "You know who Stormy is, Mr. Smart Guy."

Bill got in the driver's seat, Ann sat in the middle and Johnson jumped in the shotgun side and slammed the door. "Good luck," Casey shouted.

"Thanks," Bill answered as he pulled away and headed for the road to town.

"Looks like we're early enough to stop in town and have a cup of coffee," Johnson said as they pulled out.

"I can go for that," Bill said.

Bill drove down the lane and pulled out onto the county road. On the way to town Bill and Johnson discussed the colts they were taking to the sale. Bill worked with the colts since their training began. Johnson oversaw the training, but mostly left the actual training up to Bill. Bill would have Casey or Ann help occasionally when a particular animal warranted some extra attention, but Bill knew the horses better than anyone else. Johnson took Bill's advice on which animals he thought they should keep and which ones to sell. They discussed each individual colt's good points and where Bill felt a particular horse needed more work.

Ann paid particular attention to the discussion about the colts. She valued Bill's knowledge and wanted to know everything possible about each individual horse before riding them into the sale ring. She wanted to show all of the good qualities the horses possessed. If she rode the horse well, demonstrating all of its qualities, they would receive a higher price for each animal. Ann wanted to be prepared. She knew the horses fairly well from helping in their training. Occasionally she would ask Bill or Johnson a question about an individual horse she wanted to know more about.

The sun was showing itself when they pulled into town. "Which restaurant do you want to go to, Annie?" Bill asked.

They all laughed, it was an old joke. There was only one restaurant in town. "How about Molly's," Ann said.

"Molly's it is," Bill said. They drove through town to the restaurant. Bill pulled the truck off on a side street next to

Molly's. They could see other trucks and trailers parked in the area and knew the cafe would be crowded with people on their way to the sale.

Inside the busy restaurant, they found an empty table toward the rear. They sat down and waited for Molly to take their order. Everyone in the small cafe knew Johnson, and most knew Ann and Bill. There were a few strangers here this morning, but that wasn't unusual for a horse sale day. Ann felt self-conscious when she saw several people staring at her. She knew they were wondering about her and Buster and their perilous ride. She tried to make herself as inconspicuous as possible. It wasn't long before someone asked her about that ride. A respectable looking older gentleman walked up and said good morning. He was an old friend of the Bent Bar crew.

"Morning, young lady, Johnson, Bill," he said and nodded to each in turn as he said their name.

"Morning, Sam," they all said at once.

Sam's honest face and cheerful demeanor made him welcome wherever he went. His grandfatherly appearance belied his rugged character. He oversaw the operation of his ranch with a firm hand. Despite his years, Sam carried himself remarkably well. "What did you bring in today, Johnson?" Sam asked.

"We've got six of the nicest colts you've ever seen. Bill's got them coming along good. They'll make some mighty fine horses when they're finished," Johnson answered. Ann noticed that the chatter and noise in the cafe slowed when Sam walked up to their table and asked about their horses.

"I'll bet they will. I'll be interested in seeing them," Sam said. Almost all conversation stopped except for the talk at their table. It became quiet in the cafe. Everyone was trying to hear what Johnson had to say about the Bent Bar horses.

"Well, Annie, I hear that you and Buster had quite a ride a while back. Is it true, that you and your horse rode off the top of the trail that goes down into that steep gorge above the Bent Bar?" Sam asked. Ann felt her face begin to flush when Sam asked that question. She could see and feel the eyes of everyone in the restaurant on her. It became so quiet that she was sure you could hear a pin drop. Everyone wanted to hear that story and was anxious to hear what she had to say.

"Yes sir, that was me. Buster did a miraculous job and got us both down okay with no serious injuries," Ann answered.

"Well, I heard about that ride. I'm sure glad you and your horse weren't hurt," Sam said. Before Sam could ask any more questions, Molly came up to take their order. Ann was relieved to see her. Sam said, "Well, I guess I better go, I'll see you at the sale."

Johnson noticed a rough looking pair of men sitting at the table next to them. They had both been paying a lot of attention to the conversation between Sam and the Bent Bar crew. Their clothes were dirty and a distinct whisky odor came from their vicinity. Both wore dirty western hats and had a ragged appearance. Neither had used a razor for quite a while. As Sam turned and started to walk away, Johnson noticed one of the men stick a muddy boot into Sam's path. Sam didn't see the man's boot and innocently tripped over it. The grubby man jumped up and yelled, "Watch where you're going, old man, you stepped on my good boots!" The other greasy character laughed at his partner's attempt to humiliate the older man.

Johnson jumped up and grabbed Sam's arm to steady him. He stared hard at the man and said, "He wouldn't have tripped if you hadn't stuck your muddy boot in his way." The man looked at Johnson towering above him, icily glaring down at him. Hastily, he averted his eyes and sat down without a word. "Are you okay, Sam?" Johnson asked.

"Yeah, thanks, Johnson," Sam said and then walked away. Johnson returned to his table as the conversation and noise returned to normal.

"Do you want to order now?" Molly asked when Johnson sat down.

"Yes, Molly, I'll have coffee and one of your tasty donuts," Bill said, breaking the tension. Ann and Johnson both ordered the same and Molly left. Bill and Johnson watched the two men that caused the trouble with Sam. They were getting up to leave and they both wanted to make sure the undesirable pair left the restaurant without causing any more trouble. The two characters went to the register and paid their bill. The short one that caused the trouble turned and looked back toward Johnson. He saw Johnson staring at him and quickly turned and walked out.

Molly brought their order and their attention turned to coffee and donuts. They left the restaurant and headed for the stock yards. Bill drove to the far end of town and turned onto the road leading to the stock yards. He pulled into the parking area in front of the loading chutes, turned and backed up against one of the chutes next to the brand inspector's office. He backed all the way in but unfortunately didn't get the trailer lined up with the chute. "I never get this thing lined up right on my first try," he said. He shifted gears to pull ahead to try again. Just as he pulled forward, a muddy looking, old, beat up, blue pickup, pulling a two horse trailer pulled out in front of him. He had to slam on the brakes to keep from hitting it. Everyone in the pickup saw the two nasty characters from the cafe in the cab of the old truck. The short one who had tried to trip Sam was wickedly grinning at them as they pulled away. They could see he was missing a few teeth and his remaining teeth were yellowed with tobacco stains. They watched as the dirty pair parked at the far end of the yards.

"Boy, that's the worst looking outfit I've seen around here in a long time," Bill said.

"I sure agree with you," Johnson said.

Bill backed up to the loading chute again, and this time lined the trailer up perfect. "You got lucky that time," Ann said. Johnson and Bill both laughed.

They unloaded their horses into the small corral connected to the loading chute then went into the brand inspector's office to fill out the paperwork. "Good morning, Duke," Johnson said to the man at the counter, bent over filling out forms.

Duke looked up and recognized the Bent Bar crew. He was average height with the rugged looks of an outdoorsman. Duke wore a wide brimmed hat and the uniform of the State Brand Inspection Department. He had a no nonsense look, but when he saw Ann he smiled and said, "Heck of a ride, Annie."

"Thank you, sir," she said.

"What have you got for me today?" the inspector asked Johnson.

"We brought a half dozen two year olds, four colts and two fillies," Johnson answered.

"Any brands, scars or unusual markings?" Duke asked, as he reached for the ownership forms.

"No brands and nothing unusual," Johnson said and handed Duke a list describing the six horses.

"Did you breed and raise these horses on your ranch?" Duke asked as he began filling out the forms.

"Yes sir," Johnson said.

"Johnson, I know you don't like to brand your horses but it sure is good insurance against having one stolen," Duke said.

"I know you're right, Duke, and I should probably start considering it. We've never had any trouble before, but I guess there's always the first time," Johnson said.

"I was just going over the Stray List the state issues every month. It's a list of missing horses and cattle that have been reported throughout the state for the previous month. There's a good description of the missing animal and the circumstances surrounding the disappearance. There's been a slightly higher incidence of missing horses lately, mostly unbranded. You know the price of canner horses is pretty high. Packing houses are paying top dollar for horse meat. That could tempt a few no-goods to pick up an un-branded critter now and then to sell to the canneries. Generally it's the old or crippled horses that are sold to packing houses, but sometimes I see a perfectly good horse go on the auction block to be sold for meat. Without a brand, it's pretty hard to positively identify a horse. I just inspected a couple of unbranded horses that I can't positively identify and I don't know the two characters that brought them in. They had bills of sale for both horses so I have to recognize them as the rightful owner. I know those horses will be sold to buyers from the packing houses. They both have a mean eye, but I think they were probably good ranch horses at one time," Duke said.

"Was it two grubby looking characters driving a beat up old pickup that brought in those horses?" Bill asked.

"Yes, it was and they had an out-of-state license plate and address. They'll stick around till after the sale, collect their proceeds and be long gone before the sun goes down. Come on, let's go and inspect your horses. I've got to make a detailed description of each horse's markings as I find them," Duke said. They went out into the corral and Duke started methodically inspecting each horse even though he had known Johnson for years.

"I don't know how anybody could slip a rustled critter past you, Duke, the way you look them over," Johnson said.

"It can happen," Duke answered.

When he finished the inspection, Duke gave Johnson copies of the paperwork and assigned them a corral for the horses. He gave each horse a sale number and instructed Ann and Bill to have their horses ready to ride into the ring when their number was called. They moved the horses down the alleyway through the stockyards to the corral Duke had assigned. The sale started at 10:00 A.M. so they had time to groom the horses before it began. Bill would stay with Ann to help her saddle each horse. Johnson gave them both last minute instructions and then wandered off to chat with friends.

Ann and Bill tied each horse to the corral fence and started brushing and combing their manes and tails. Ann asked Bill more questions about each horse as she worked. "These are all well mannered horses, Annie, they won't give you or anybody else any trouble unless you give it to them first. Then you better look out, bad treatment just breeds trouble. Once a horse is mistreated, they naturally go on the defense and fight you every step of the way. Johnson's favorite saying about training a horse is that when you finish a training session, be sure you're both still on good terms and that you finish the day as friends. Then the horse will be glad to see you again and won't mind being caught the next time you want to work with him," Bill said.

"That sounds like sound advice," Ann said.

"It sure is. Well, Annie, we're done here. Why don't you go and change your clothes," Bill said.

The sale was held in a small indoor arena. Both cattle and horses were sold at the High Valley stock yards, but today was strictly a horse sale. The arena was sixty feet long and thirty feet wide. There were bleachers for the spectators and buyers on one side. The other side had large doors on each end for the stock to come in one way and go out to the holding pens another way. The auctioneer and his secretary were positioned above the sale ring on the side opposite the bleachers. They sat between the livestock entrance and exit doors, where they could view both the animals being shown and the bidders in the bleachers.

Johnson found Sam and they headed for the arena to find seats before the crowd showed up. They found seats in the center of the bleachers where they could see well, and settled in to wait for the sale to start. Several other local ranchers came in and when they saw Johnson and Sam, they moved in that direction to find a seat near the two old friends. Soon there was a comfortable group gathered to watch the sale. They passed good natured banter back and forth and generally enjoyed each other's company. "It takes a horse sale to bring people out," Sam said to no one in particular.

"Everyone's interested in horses," Johnson answered.

"I haven't seen some of these people in six months, but have a horse sale and they start crawling out of the hills," Sam said. The sale barn became crowded as time neared for the sale to start. Johnson noticed Sam staring down the bleachers toward one of the doors. He followed his gaze and saw Sam watching the two rough looking men that caused trouble in the cafe.

"Hopefully that smelly pair will stay on that end of the barn," Johnson said.

"Their rightful place is in the manure pile behind the corrals," Sam said. Everyone laughed and turned their gaze toward the ring. The auctioneer had just come out and was setting up for the sale.

At ten o'clock sharp the auctioneer rapped his gavel and said, "Ladies and Gentlemen, we have a few opening announcements to make and then we'll get right down to selling horses. We have a fine selection to offer today, they range from green colts all the way to finished roping and arena horses. As usual, we'll have canners too. All horses rode into the ring will be described by breeding and the amount of training they have. The riders will answer any questions a bidder may have. All horses are sold as is and the stock yard gives no guarantees as to soundness. All buyers will receive a bill of sale on horses they purchase. Any horses that are run through without a rider will first be offered to the high dollar bidder. If no one bids a suitable price for the animal then we'll offer the horse for sale at so much a pound for his total body weight. All bidders must have a registered number, if you didn't register, please do so now. Before any animals can be removed from the premises, they must be paid for in full and you must obtain a travel permit from the state brand inspector before transporting. If there are no questions, we'll start the sale."

The entrance door opened and a rider rode a big bay gelding into the ring. The auctioneer announced the owner of the horse, gave a brief description of the breeding, what the horse had been used for and whether it was a ranch horse or used for rodeos or pleasure riding. He then opened the bidding. The rider rode the horse at a trot to the end of the ring, spun him around and loped back to the other end. He made the horse stop and back up. He swung a rope around the horse's head to show that he wasn't spooky. He stopped the horse, jumped off and lifted one of his front legs. In just a few minutes he displayed the horses disposition and the extent of his training. It was a well trained horse and the bidding moved rapidly. He was sold quickly, and the rider rode him out of the ring. The auctioneer kept the pace of the sale moving swiftly. They had a lot of horses to sell and didn't spend too much time on any one horse.

Ann had her first horse saddled and ready to go. The Bent Bar horses would be shown in succession, so Bill and Ann would be busy. Ann was next up. She mounted and looked down at Bill. He could see she was nervous. He winked and said, "Show em' what kind of horses and riders come from the Bent Bar."

Before she could answer the big door opened and she sent the colt into the arena. She jogged the colt to the far end of the ring. At the end of the ring she gently turned him in the opposite direction. The crowd was surprised when she then jumped the horse into a full run toward the other end. There wasn't much room in the small arena. It was a daring move on Ann's part. She heard the crowd yell out in approval when she put the horse into a sliding stop just before reaching the opposite end. She then spun the horse around, loped to the center of the ring, and stopped him completely. Standing in place and making him use his hind quarters to pivot on, Ann spun him around to the left one full turn and stopped again. She then spun around one full turn to the right and stopped facing the crowd. The crowd was definitely pleased. The auctioneer interrupted the murmuring crowd. "Some of you may have heard about the horse and rider that slipped off the cliff during that bad storm a while back and survived an unbelievable fall to the bottom. Well, the girl showing this horse from the Bent Bar ranch is that very same rider. She somehow managed to control the horse during the fall and rode him all the way to the bottom," the auctioneer said. The crowd started clapping their hands and applauding. She flushed with embarrassment at the attention and started the horse off in a jog around the arena. "I can surely vouch for the quality of the horses that come from that ranch, now what am I bid on the first Bent Bar horse to be offered today?" he continued.

In the stands, Johnson puffed up with pride when he saw the audience's reaction to the auctioneer's statements about Ann and the Bent Bar. Sam poked Johnson in the ribs and said loudly, "I'll vouch for them too."

Bill was peeking through the door so he could see what was going on. He was mostly responsible for the horse's training, so the comments from the auctioneer made him feel good. The bidding started and Ann continued to put the colt through some very fast maneuvers. The price kept increasing until it reached a point that was higher than most bidders were prepared to pay. When Bill saw that the bidding slowed, he entered the arena and walked to the center of the ring. The auctioneer was asking for more bids in an attempt to get the price higher. Ann ran the horse straight at Bill and slid him to a stop. As the horse was stopping, Ann was bailing off. She stepped back and Bill pulled the saddle off and set it to the side of the ring. He gave Ann a boost up on the colt. She jogged the horse around the arena bareback while the auctioneer urged the crowd to bid higher for this fine horse. Bill took the saddle and headed out to get the next horse saddled and ready while the auctioneer was completing the sale. When no one would bid higher, the auctioneer banged the gavel and shouted into the microphone, "Sold," he then added, "Sir, you just bought a mighty fine horse." Ann rode the colt out into the alleyway. She jumped off and removed the bridle. A handler led the colt to the pens where the sold horses were held until their buyers claimed them.

Ann took the bridle and ran to where Bill had the next horse saddled and ready to go. She slipped the halter off and put the bridle on. She swung into the saddle and the ring man opened the big door to let her into the arena. The action continued with the auctioneer giving details of the horse, while Ann put the horse through some demanding maneuvers that showed the ability and training of the animal. Johnson was pleased with the prices. He knew that Ann had a lot to do with the high prices they were receiving. She was really putting effort into showing just how good these horses were. "Johnson, your crew really knows how to show the best that a horse can give. They're runnin' those horses through their paces as smooth as I've ever seen it done. You ought to be mighty proud of them," Sam said.

"They do a good job, and yes, I am very pleased. Thank you, Sam," Johnson said.

The sale continued at a fast pace. It seemed to Ann that she had just gotten started when Bill said, "You're doing a good job, Annie, this is our last one."

She was surprised that they moved so swiftly. She rode the last horse into the ring and put extra effort into the exhibition. "Come on, boys, this is your last chance to own one of these exceptional horses. This is their last one today, so let's see everyone get in on the bidding and try to buy this horse for your very own," the auctioneer urged the crowd.

The bidding took off quickly and the horse was sold for the highest price they had received for any of the horses. As Ann rode out of the arena, the auctioneer thanked her over the loudspeaker for doing a great job of showing the horses. She smiled and waved, and received a round of applause from the crowd. She was pleased with the sale. Bill came over and helped her unsaddle. He complimented her again on doing a good job. "You really did good, Annie. Now, if I had shown those horses, we probably would have only received half the price for them. Maybe Johnson will consider giving you a raise," he said.

"I would love that, then I would be able to pay off Stormy faster," she said. They carried Ann's saddle and the rest of their gear out to the pickup and put it away.

"Let's go into the barn and watch the rest of the sale from outside the arena for a change," Bill said.

"Okay," Ann said.

They worked their way back into the building. They couldn't find seats, so Bill led the way through the crowd to an area in the rear where they could watch. The horses they watched go through the arena were all good horses and the sale moved right along. None of the horses brought the high dollar their horses had and Annie and Bill were delighted to see that the bidders placed a higher value on their horses.

The auctioneer moved the sale along with hardly any delays. Soon all of the riding horses were sold. "Folks, that's the last of the broke horses. We'll move onto the canner horses now," he said. (These would be the horses that the canneries would bid on. They would be butchered and subsequently used for canned animal food.) When the crowd heard that there were to be no more riding horses sold, they started to leave. Bill and Ann stepped out of the way as the crowd filed out. They knew Johnson always stayed with his friends until the last horse had been sold. When most of the crowd had moved out of the building, Bill and Ann moved to where Johnson and Sam sat with the rest of their friends.

"Bill, you and Annie did a great job today. I think we got a fair price for our horses and I'm pleased with the way you two handled the whole affair," Johnson said.

"Thank you, sir, but Bill did most of the work," Ann said.

"Ha, Ha," laughed Bill. "We'd of only gotten half of what we did if I had shown them," said Bill. Johnson and Sam laughed.

Ann and Bill found seats near Johnson and sat down to watch the canners sell. Ann didn't like staying for this part, but she knew it was part of life and had to be endured. She had a high respect for horses and found it very hard to watch, knowing how they would end up.

"I see the stink bags from the cafe are still here," Bill said. Ann followed Bill's gaze and saw the two dirty men sitting at the far end of the ring.

"Duke said they brought in a couple of horses that he was sure they were trying to sell as canners," Ann said.

"That's right, he did, and that would sure fit them two. I'm glad we don't see their likes around here too often. They're probably waiting to see what their horses sell for so they can collect their check and disappear," Bill said.

"If they're really their horses," Sam added.

The auctioneer called for everyone's attention and said, "Okay, let's get started with the last of the horses." The entrance door opened and a very old horse was ushered in. He walked in and stopped, and stared at the few people left in the bleachers. The auctioneer started the bidding and a few buyers sitting in the front row started what seemed like a rehearsed bidding war. They knew what canners would sell for on today's market and none would bid over a few cents per pound of what their competitors were bidding. It was almost as if they were taking turns buying the horses as they came into the arena. The old horse sold fast and other horses were sent into the ring to be sold and sent on their final journey.

Ann's heart cried out in sympathy as the door to the ring opened and a dark chestnut mare limped into the arena. She took a few tentative steps into the ring and stopped. Ann could see she had been severely injured and would be lame for the rest of her life. Her owner was obviously trying to salvage what money he could, by offering her to the cannery buyers. The mare started moving again but bobbed her head up and down as she tried to walk on the injured leg. She was obviously in great pain. She made her way to the perimeter of the ring and stopped. The auctioneer started the bidding and his voice crackled around the small sale barn. In his shrill voice, amplified by the P.A. system, he prodded the buyers to bid higher.

The mare stopped directly in front of where Ann was sitting. She could see pain in the mare's eyes as the old horse slowly turned her head and scanned the almost empty bleachers. Deep hurt radiated from her dark, liquid eyes. The mare slowly turned her head in Ann's direction. She stopped her head as she saw the few people sitting in·Ann's section of the barn. The mare seemed to stare right at Ann. Ann saw sorrow and hopelessness reflecting from the suffering eyes. The mare seemed to know that she was in an inescapable situation and that her life would only be measured in hours now. Ann saw that the mare had once been a proud, beautiful animal. She imagined what the horse must have been like in her prime. The old girl still carried a trace of bygone beauty and grace. There was the hint in her overall appearance that she had spent a productive life as a ranch or working horse, and had probably raised her share of colts. Sadness enveloped Ann as she watched the once proud horse struggling to understand why she had been brought to this arena, and deeply frightened by the unusual events. She had been suddenly pulled from her home pasture and thrown in with strangers amid the hubbub of the stock yards. She wanted desperately to be back on her home ranch in familiar surroundings with the people and horses she had spent her life with. Ann was trying hard to hold back tears she could feel forming as she watched the pitiful scene unfolding in the arena.

Suddenly, a loud slurring voice sounded from the far end of the sale ring. Influenced by the whiskey he had been nipping on during the sale, the short dirty man with the stained and missing front teeth was yelling out derogatory comments toward the pathetic looking mare. "Whoever buys that old plug better bring the dogs and cats in here to eat her, cause she's so beat up she'll never make it to the slaughter house," he shouted out toward the bewildered mare. It became very quiet. Everyone stared at the filthy man that shouted the insensitive words.

"Mister, I'll tell you once to keep your comments to yourself, if you shout at these animals again, I'll have you removed from this sale ring. Do you understand me?" the auctioneer sternly said. He stared back at the auctioneer and mumbled something unintelligible under his breath.

"Let's finish this sale," the auctioneer said. Ann was furious with what the man said. She felt Bill tense up when the man shouted out. Bill had compassion for animals and became angered when anyone abused them. In his early thirties, Bill was tall and lanky. He was physically strong and tough. Hard ranch work kept him in good shape. Ann thought that man would regret his outburst if he found Bill's steel gray eyes staring down at him in close quarters. Bill might rearrange the man's looks because of all the trouble he's caused today.

The sorrowful mare was sold to the highest bidder. The ring man slowly moved her out through the exit door into the corrals to await her fate. The grubby man kept his mouth shut while she was moved out and the sale continued. Two horses were run in. They were neither lame nor hurt, that Ann could tell. They were terrified and raced around whinnying loudly. They were wild and the ring man had to jump behind the barrier that protected him from mean or crazed animals. These horses had been treated badly and they had revenge in their eyes. When they were sold, the exit door opened and they raced out to the alleyway beyond. They would be herded into a pen to await being picked up by their buyer.

When the two horses were gone and the exit door closed, Ann saw the two nasty characters get up and leave. "Good riddance," she heard Bill say.

"I'm glad to see them go, too, Bill. I hope we never run into them again," Ann said.

"That last pair of wild horses must have belonged to them, since they left after they were sold. I sure won't miss them," Bill said.

A few more horses were run into the ring and sold. The sale came to an end and the auctioneer thanked everyone for coming. Johnson stood up and motioned to Ann and Bill as he and Sam headed for the door. When they got outside, they saw Johnson waiting for them. "You two did such a good job today I think the ranch can spring for lunch at Molly's, if you're interested?" Johnson said.

"I'm all for that, how about you, Annie?" Bill said.

"Sounds good to me too, let's go," Ann said.

"Would you join us, Sam?" Johnson asked his friend.

"You betch'a," Sam said, and they headed for Molly's.

Over lunch they discussed the results of the sale. Johnson was pleased with Ann and Bill. He praised the way they handled the horses. On the way back to the ranch, Ann was very quiet. She became immersed in her thoughts about the pitiful old mare that had brought tears to her eyes and the callous men who were so insensitive to her plight. She vowed to herself that any horse she ever owned or controlled would be retired to the ranch when their useful life ended. They would never be subjected to the fate of the old mare. She thought about the nasty men that were at the sale and was glad they were not seen again.

CHAPTER 8

Ann stopped Buster and looked back to see if she could see Stormy. She saw the young colt investigating a tree stump about fifty yards behind. "This looks like a good spot to take a break," she said to Buster and Flame. She slid out of the saddle and led Flame over to a tree and tied her off to a low branch. She led Buster down to the creek to see if he wanted a drink of the cool mountain water. Buster sniffed the water and sloshed his muzzle around in it but didn't drink, so Ann led him back and tied him near Flame. Stormy came charging up the trail and slammed on the brakes just as he got to the other horses. "Take it easy, youngster, you're gonna' run into somebody someday, and I don't think they'll like it very much," she said.

Ann untied Flame and led her down to the creek. Stormy followed them to inspect the creek and see if it offered any entertainment. He checked out everything they came to, since leaving the ranch. The colt was curious. This was a big day. Stormy saw the running water and heard the noise the creek made as it tumbled over the rocks and boulders. Ann watched as he stopped and stretched his neck toward the fast flowing creek. He intended to give this interesting spot the respect it deserved, just in case it had some surprises in store for him. Ann led Flame to the water's edge and watched as she drank deeply. Stormy came alongside Flame and stepped into the creek. The cold water penetrated his skin and he jumped away from the water. Almost immediately he stepped back in and sloshed his muzzle, splashing water on the mare's face as she tried to drink. Flame stopped drinking and raised her head. She looked down at the frolicking colt and watched him play.

Ann wondered what thoughts were going through the mare's mind. Was she thinking about the last time she and Stormy crossed Gunpowder Creek? Could she be remembering the night this young colt was born? Were the terrible memories of that night returning to haunt Flame? Did Stormy have any recollections of the night he was brought into this world? Ann's memories of that stormy night were vivid. She could recall every terrifying second of her plunge to the bottom of the ravine. She wondered if they would ever know the circumstances surrounding Stormy's birth and how Flame received the terrible wound to her shoulder. She felt an overwhelming gratefulness to Flame for bringing the frisky sorrel colt into the world and keeping him alive during that awful night.

"Stormy, do you remember the last time you crossed Gunpowder?" Ann directed her question where the colt was standing in the creek and pawing the water. At the sound of Ann's voice, Stormy stopped pawing and quizzically looked at her with his ears alertly pointed. "I think you really do know your name, young man," she said to the colt. Stormy whinnied and then started ferociously pawing the water. Water splashed everywhere. It seemed that the colt was really enjoying seeing the water shooting out from his flailing hoof. Ann and Flame were getting wet from the colt's battle with the water. Ann hastily led Flame out of the creek away from Stormy. She took her up the bank to where Buster was tied.

Ann sat down on a log near the horses and watched the colt play in the creek. "I guess we'll just never know what happened that night. Thankfully things worked out okay," Ann said to the horses. When Stormy tired of fighting the creek, he came up the bank to the spot where Ann and the two horses were waiting. "If you're finished playing in the water, we better get going. We've got a long way to go and still have to find the band of mares," she said. She looped Flame's lead rope around the saddle horn, untied Buster and climbed in the saddle. "Okay, Stormy, let's cross the creek and head for the high country," she said. They moved across Gunpowder Creek and climbed the bank on the other side. She pointed Buster toward Dry Boulder Coulee. She kept their pace down to a slow walk and every twenty minutes or so would stop and let Flame rest.

On the day of the horse sale, Doc Brown came out to the ranch and examined Flame. He gave her a clean bill of health. A few days after Doc's visit, Johnson suggested Flame and her colt be moved from the barn to the grass in the high country. He felt they would be better off in the clean environment of the mountains. Green grass would be better for her and the colt than the rations of hay she was getting in the barn. Ann saddled Buster early and left the ranch at daylight to lead Flame and Stormy into the mountains. James told her the mares were staying in the area of the upper coulee with their new foals. Ann was anxious to find them and see the new colts.

She was looking forward to watching Stormy's reaction when he saw the other colts and mares. He would have plenty of playmates to run with. Poor old Buster tried his best to keep up with Stormy but Ann knew the young colt needed the companionship of other young foals. She was going to miss him, and hoped she would be able to ride up frequently throughout the summer to see him. They made their way along the edge of the coulee heading higher into the mountains. Flame was moving right along and seemed to be enjoying the trip. Ann watched closely, but Flame showed no indication of favoring the injured shoulder. Ann was pleased to see the gallant mare's recovery was going so well. She felt that by the time Flame and Stormy returned to the ranch in the fall, Flame would be completely healed.

Ann and the three horses made their way toward the upper end of the coulee. She knew Buster and Flame would spot the mares long before she would and alert her to their whereabouts. When they arrived at the spot where the trail angled down and crossed the coulee, they still had not seen the mares. Ann rested the horses at the top of the canyon for a few minutes. She had a good vantage point, but did not see the other horses. They angled down into the coulee toward the meadow in the bottom. When they reached the small meadow, Ann could see fresh horse droppings. She got off Buster and decided to let the horses graze a few minutes. She could see the area had been grazed recently, so she felt the band of mares would be close.

Buster was glad to be out in the mountains and moved along as if he had never been injured. He was completely healed and Ann knew that he needed exercise to get his muscles back in top shape. This was his first real ride since the night of the storm and he seemed to be doing fine. They had taken it easy so far and Buster didn't even blow hard on the long uphill trail. He moved along eagerly and she could feel his enthusiasm for the ride. He was glad to finally be out of the barn and in the open country again. The way Buster was acting today, Ann felt that with daily workouts, he would soon be in competitive shape.

Getting back in the saddle and leading Flame again, she headed up and out the west side of the coulee. Stormy was still excited about the trip and ran back and forth on the trail ahead. He left this country when he was hardly a day old. This was the first time he had been away from the home ranch since he arrived there as a newborn. They came out of the coulee onto the foothills below the high peaks of the Continental Divide. Ann stopped to look at the majestic beauty of this tremendous range of mountains. High peaks stretched to the south as far as she could see. This land was full of life. The fragrance of spring growth was invigorating. She could see a small band of elk high in a small park just below timberline. Below her, along the rolling hills falling off toward the valley far below, Bent Bar cattle and their calves grazed on the lush grasses that grew here. To the south, she could see a pair of eagles soaring on thermal currents rising from the valley floor. It was breathtaking country and she paused to enjoy the splendor of her surroundings.

Ann started again to find the band of mares. They were close now and Ann knew they would soon find them. They could see great distances from these high rolling hills. The mares were probably down in a shallow draw or just out of sight behind a ridge and hidden from view. Ann turned Buster toward a ridge angling down from the high peaks.

They climbed the ridge to get a better view of the surrounding country. Ann climbed Buster to the highest spot on the ridge and stopped again to look for the mares. She scanned miles of country but still could not see them. She started Buster down the ridge and decided they would continue riding south.

They reached the bottom of the ridge and rode through a timbered draw. They came out of the timber onto an open plain. Suddenly, Ann felt Buster tense under her and she followed the direction of his gaze. "Whoa, Buster, what have you found?" Ann asked as she stopped. Buster was staring down the hill toward a ridge top a half mile away. At first Ann didn't see a thing. Soon she picked out the dark bay mare, the leader of the band, standing on top of the far ridge, looking in their direction. "There's the old girl. She'll have the rest of the band close to her. Good job, Buster. I'd of never noticed her watching us from that far distance. It's all downhill now. Let's head over there and see what Stormy's gonna' think of his new family," Ann said.

Buster was anxious to get to where the mares were. Ann let him jog down the hill and over to where they had seen the leader watching them. When they arrived, the bay mare was gone. They travelled across the top of the ridge to the far side. They found the horses below, in a small, pleasant meadow. They were all staring up the hill at Ann. Buster and Flame whinnied down to their old friends. Stormy ran up and looked down into the meadow. Ann watched his body go rigid when he saw the strange horses. He stared hard and then looked back at Flame to see if she thought they may be a threat. Her friendly whinnies toward the other horses told him that they must be friends. From below he heard the unmistakable sounds of the band whinnying a welcome to Buster and Flame. Ann took time to look the band over before riding down. She could see well from her position and counted the mares and their colts. She counted fourteen mares and a dozen foals. There'll be a lot of sniffing and bickering going on when we get down there and everybody starts to become reacquainted, Ann thought. Buster was starting to fidget. He was anxious to head downhill and see what was going on in the meadow. Flame was trying to pull loose and head down too. "Okay, let's go," she said. They started down the ridge. Ann looked back and saw Stormy nervously bringing up the rear. "Don't worry, Stormy, you'll feel awkward for a few minutes, but you'll get to be friends very soon," she said. Horses are like people, she thought. Sometimes things are a bit awkward when meeting strangers for the first time.

When they rode into the meadow, the mares crowded around sniffing and nickering at the newcomers. Stormy plastered himself against Flame so close that Ann giggled at him. He wasn't sure about this situation and decided he'd let his mother handle it. Ann slipped off Buster and pulled Flame up close. She reached up and rubbed Flame along her neck. "Flame, you take good care of this kid of yours and try to keep him out of trouble," she said to the mare. She reached out and touched Stormy on his forehead, "I'll see you as often as I can, Mister Stormy, I hope you grow big and strong on the mountain grass this summer. Take good care of yourself." Ann reached up and released the buckle holding the halter on Flame, slid the halter off, and pushed her head away. She mounted Buster and moved a short distance away to watch the horses become familiar with Flame again and inspect her new colt.

Stormy wasn't sure what to make of all the new horses and the attention he was receiving. Ann watched him put his ears back and warn a few of the strangers that were getting too nosy. The old bay that dominated this bunch pushed her way right into where Stormy was trying to defend himself. She nickered and touched muzzles with Flame. Stormy laid his ears back, then reached out and nipped the bay to warn her to not get so close. The old girl let out an angry squeal and reached down and bit the young colt hard on his withers. Stormy was caught off guard by the bite. He had only known kindness since birth and this savage attack by the big stranger was a shock. He spun around in fright and ran. Flame turned and trotted after him. She understood that Stormy was learning the pecking order of this band. The bay mare wasn't wasting any time teaching the youngster who was boss.

Stormy bolted and ran to the edge of the meadow. He turned and was relieved to see Flame trotting toward him. The bay was a force to be respected and she had quickly put her painful imprint on the colt. Stormy would think long and hard before he ever nipped at her again. She frightened and humiliated him in front of these strangers. He decided he would stay a good distance away from her. Flame stopped beside him and gave an affectionate nuzzle. Stormy watched apprehensively as a few of the horses and foals that followed Flame, moved close to him again. He would think twice before he bit anybody again without a good reason. He let one of the foals get close enough to sniff and touch muzzles. Before long, he recovered from the bay mare's lesson and was showing an interest in the playful foals.

Ann watched Stormy's introduction to the other horses with amusement and a great deal of satisfaction. The exercise he would get running and playing with the other foals would develop his young muscles and stimulate growth. These mountains would be a good place for the colt to spend the summer. She watched as a few of the foals tried to encourage Stormy to run with them. He watched with great interest as they ran to where he was standing beside Flame and prance and half rear in the air near him. He took a few stiff legged steps toward them and looked back at Flame. She didn't act as if there was anything wrong with the other foals actions. Encouraged by Flame's lack of concern, Stormy broke into a trot toward the other foals. They in turn took off running and bucking around the meadow and Stormy excitedly ran after them. Before long Stormy lost all of his apprehension toward the other horses and was happily running and playing with his new friends.

Reluctantly, Ann touched Buster's sides with her heels and started across the meadow to head back to the ranch. She was well satisfied with the way things were working out. Flame made the trip easily and showed no ill effects from the exertion of climbing into the high country. Buster was going along fine and showed his old bounce as they made their way along the mountain side. Ann's thoughts turned to the rodeo coming up in a few weeks. After today's ride, she felt she could get Buster in shape to compete in barrel racing and hopefully win or place high in the final standings.

The High Valley rodeo was well known for the caliber of horses and riders who entered. It drew competitors from hundreds of miles around and occasionally produced champions who went on to compete in national events. In the last few years, Buster and Ann had done well in their event. They made it to the finals for two years in a row. If they could win this year, then maybe they would become recognized as strong competition. That would certainly help in Ann's quest for a slot on the college rodeo team and the tuition assistance the rodeo scholarship would provide. She would be able to feel Buster out in the next few days and see if he was ready for some hard arena work. This was a long ride today, and was the first strenuous exercise Buster received in a long time. Maybe I'll let him rest tomorrow and then start on some arena work on the next day, Ann thought.

They worked their way down the mountain and away from the small herd of horses. They crossed brush covered draws and passed through timbered side hills on their way to intersect Dry Boulder Coulee. They arrived at Dry Boulder in a bad area to cross. The sides were steep and the only trails down were made by jack rabbits and deer. Ann knew they would come to a good crossing farther down the canyon. They reached that crossing and made their way into the coulee. Ann got a good look at what the flood left behind in this lower, wider area of the canyon. Debris was scattered everywhere. It would be a long time before this area returned to normal, she thought.

They angled up the hogback on the trail leading out of the draw. Buster started puffing and Ann stopped him beside a group of rocks and brush they were passing. This would be a good place to rest, she thought, as she touched the reins and gave Buster the cue to stop. Ann slid out of the saddle and turned Buster so they could look into the canyon they just crossed. She stood beside him holding the reins and leaned her cheek against Buster's neck. She could feel dampness on his neck and he was breathing a little fast. Buster worked up a sweat on the way out of the coulee. "You might be sore tomorrow, Buster," she said to the horse. "You can rest for a day and then we're gonna' have to really get with the program to get you in shape for the Fourth."

After a few minutes, Buster's breathing slowed and they started again toward Gunpowder Creek. They crossed the creek and were back at the ranch well before dark. It was a good workout for Buster. Ann rode him into the open barn and tied him near the tack room. Ann noticed that he had a tired look while she was unsaddling him. "A day's rest will do you good, old boy," she said. She brushed him down and fed him in his stall. Things sure seem lonely in here without Stormy and Flame, she thought as she walked by their empty stall. A twinge of loneliness passed through her as she thought again of how she would miss Stormy. Things were going to get busy this summer and before she knew it, summer would be over and Stormy would be back running around the arena. She finished and left the barn to find Johnson and tell him about her day and the mares in the high meadow.

A few days later Ann was working Buster around the barrels in the arena. She started out walking him through the pattern. It was boring, just walking, but it was a good way to warm up Buster and get him used to the pattern again. He had a tendency to cut the barrels too close. Ann made him maintain the right distance. He had to form a correct turn in his mind, one that he would habitually follow as they rounded the barrels, whether walking or in a flat out run. He had to form a pocket around the barrel and not develop a tendency to cut the corner too close and knock over a barrel. Ann patiently worked Buster through the pattern, and after four circuits he started maintaining a distance that would enable them to make a snappy turn at a fast run.

When Ann was satisfied Buster was executing the turns properly, they took a break. Boredom was the worst enemy a trainer had. A horse that loses interest will never attain the high level of perfection needed to win. You must always keep it interesting, Ann thought. After a few minutes, Ann started Buster again. This time they trotted through the pattern and Ann worked at maintaining the proper pocket around the barrels. Repetitively, they trotted through the pattern a half dozen times before Ann stopped near the barn and dismounted. She loosened the cinch and tied Buster to the fence. She wanted to give him a twenty minute break before they practiced at a lope. Ann didn't want to overdo it. She wanted to start Buster at an easy pace. The worst thing she could do would be to rush and have him come up lame. Easy does it, she thought.

They had three weeks left to train before the High Valley rodeo. There were other barrel events throughout the summer and if they did well on the Fourth of July, Ann planned on entering a rodeo on Labor Day weekend in another town. The competition would be stiffer and there would be more entries than the High Valley rodeo. It would be a higher level of competition and she felt she needed to ride against the best to sharpen both her and Buster's abilities. She walked in to the barn to see if Johnson was still in his office.

"Can I interrupt you?" she asked when she saw him.

"Sure, I wanted to talk to you anyway," he said. She went in to his office and sat down near his desk. "How's Buster doin'?" he asked.

"Real good, he's a little bored with walking and trotting through the barrels, so I'm gonna' give him a little break and then go through at a lope a few times before we quit for the day," she said.

"Is he showing any signs of favoring his hindquarters?" Johnson asked.

"Not so far. I think he's gonna' be just fine. I want to work him slow and try to have him at his peak a few days before the rodeo. Then give him a few days off before we go for it," she said.

"Sounds like you're engineering a regular campaign for the Fourth," Johnson said.

"I am, I want to win. That's what I want to talk to you about," she said.

"Uh Oh," Johnson said. "What have you got up your sleeve now?" he jokingly asked.

"A driver's license. I need one," she said.

"Well, I guess you better get it before you get stopped by the sheriff," Johnson said. "You do a lot of driving around the ranch and I've sent you into town to get parts for our equipment when we were busy during haying season. I think it would be a good idea," he continued.

"When do you think you could take me to town to take the test?" she asked.

"Find out when they'll be giving the examinations again and make an appointment, and we'll go on that day," he said.

"Okay, that would be great," Ann said.

"By the way, what brought this on?" Johnson asked.

"Well, I know how busy you get around here. I think I could be more useful if I could run a lot of the errands that need to be done. I know you don't like to ask me because I don't have my license. I'm old enough now, so there's no reason why I shouldn't have one. Besides, I want to compete more in the rodeo circuit and I don't want to have to ask you to haul me and Buster all over the country," she said.

"Sounds reasonable, but I enjoy taking you and I'd probably go anyway, whether you had your license or not," he said.

"Thank you for being so kind. I'll find out and make the appointment," she said.

"See ya' later," Johnson said and bent back over the feed bills he had been studying.

Ann left and walked to Buster. She tightened the cinch, untied the reins, and got back in the saddle. "Are you ready to pick up the pace, Buster?" she asked as she walked him around before going back to the barrels. When he loosened up, Ann walked him to their starting line and turned to face in the direction of the first barrel. She studied the pattern for a second and then kicked him into a slow lope. Buster jumped right out, glad he didn't have to walk or trot around the pattern this time. He tried to slice the turn on the first barrel and almost ran into it. Ann expected him to do that on this first pass at the higher speed. She pulled him off the barrel slightly and he maintained a good position for the remainder of the turn.

They came out heading for the second barrel and Buster tried to increase his speed. Ann held him back and they went into the second barrel holding a steady lope. Buster executed the turn, easily holding the proper distance between himself and the barrel. He tried racing to the last barrel, but Ann again held him back. Buster had a bad habit of getting too excited going into the third barrel and chopping the turn. He tried to slice too close around the last barrel and Ann ended up hitting it with her left leg before she was able to rein him away. They came out of the turn with Buster fighting the bit and wanting to race for the finish line. Ann held him to a slow lope as they headed toward the finish.

At the end of the arena, Ann stopped and turned Buster around to look at the pattern. "That first time was a little rough, Buster, we're going to have to smooth our performance quite a bit before we start winning again," she said to the gelding. She held him still, behind the starting line for a few minutes until he settled down. The faster pace had gotten Buster excited and he was fidgety. When Buster realized he'd have to hold still and not dance around like he wanted, he settled down and waited for Ann's next command. Ann walked him off and made him perform a three hundred and sixty degree turn. As he came out of the turn facing the first barrel, Ann urged him into a lope. Eagerly, he pushed off. As Buster's front legs neared the barrel, Ann shifted her weight slightly to the right stirrup and touched him gently on his left side with her boot heel. His position going into the turn was good and Ann was giving him cues to start the turn. He made a smooth maneuver and came out lined up right for the second barrel. "Well done," Ann said as they headed for the next barrel.

When they reached the point where they should start to initiate the turn, Ann gave Buster the cue to turn and he over reacted. He turned into the barrel and Ann's leg knocked it over. She tried to make a correction too late and they ended up going away from the barrel toward the starting line and didn't complete the turn. She stopped him immediately. She got off and led him over to the fence. She tied him and walked back and set the barrel back in place. Buster executed the turn around the first barrel perfectly and Ann blamed herself for the poor turn on the second. She wondered if she had given the cue to turn too soon, causing Buster to turn into the barrel. She decided to wait a few minutes and try again.

When they began again, Ann concentrated on every move Buster made. She remained tuned to his every motion. The execution of their turns improved dramatically. The improvement made her realize that not only did Buster have to get back in shape, but she was rusty in giving the orders and riding the horse to the best of his ability. Buster was trying hard and obeying her cues. If she started him too early, or too late, their precision would suffer. They made a few more runs and they both improved. Ann still held Buster to a lope and soon they were loping around the barrels holding a good pocket going in and coming out of the turns. It was a good start. Ann was happy with what they accomplished and decided to stop before Buster lost interest.

They worked for over an hour and Buster was starting to show a slight amount of dampness on his neck and chest. It was time to quit. It had been a good workout, and they ironed out mistakes both horse and rider made. Ann felt satisfied as she led Buster toward the barn. She loosened the cinch and pulled off the saddle. She led him around the arena for a few laps to cool and settle him down before she put him away for the day. When Buster was relaxed and dry, Ann brushed him to loosen and groom his matted hair from the sweat he generated during the training session. She carefully brushed the area where the cinch tightened on Buster's girth. They were just weeks away from their first competition and Ann had no intention of overlooking any matted hair or other irritant that could rub a sore on Buster by the action of the cinch around his middle. A girth sore now could stop them from entering the rodeo. She finished and led Buster to his stall. "I'll see you tomorrow, Buster," she said as she latched the gate.

It was late in the day and when she walked by Johnson's office, she could see a conference was in session. Casey, Bill and James were seated in front of Johnson's desk. At least once a week, Johnson gathered his top hands together to discuss details concerning the operation of the ranch. Evidently, that was what was going on now, Ann thought as she stopped outside the office.

"Come in, Ann," Johnson said when he saw her. "We're going over some things that need to be done in the next week. James has been checking the cattle and horses in the high pastures at least twice a week. I'm going to need him here to help get our equipment in shape before we start our first cutting of hay. I'd like you to take over that ride when James is helping the haying crew. You would have to ride into the mountains and check the condition of the animals and watch for any that may need doctoring or attention," Johnson said.

"Wonderful, that's my favorite job. That's so much fun, I feel guilty taking it away from you, James," she said and drew laughter from Johnson and the rest of the crew.

"Ride up there the first of the week and check on things. James will be free the latter part of the week and can take it from there. Occasionally we'll want you to fill in for him, but we'll let you know in advance," Johnson said.

"How'd Buster do today?" Casey asked.

"Better," she smiled.

"You better get him in first class shape. We're gonna' need at least one winner on the Fourth," Bill said.

"What's that mean?" Ann asked.

"Casey's goin' to sign up for the bareback event and we hear the competition's gonna' be mighty stiff this year. Just in case he goes airborne early and doesn't score, we need a winner from the Bent Bar to uphold our reputation," Bill said.

"Don't worry, Casey will win," Ann said in his defense.

"Thanks, Annie, at least I've got one supporter around here," Casey laughed.

Buster continued to improve and Ann seemed to be getting back in her old groove. It became second nature for her to give Buster his cues to turn or move out at precisely the right time. They overcame Buster's tendency to slice the turn. The incidence of running into the barrel and knocking it over decreased encouragingly. Communications between the horse and rider became fine tuned and mistakes were less frequent. Ann gradually increased the speed of their runs. They were running a fast pattern. She still had not asked for 100% of his speed between barrels or on the race to the finish line.

Buster had quick acceleration and speed. His speed was wasted if they made a bad turn and knocked a barrel over. That would give them a five second penalty. It took a lot to make up a five second penalty. Ann knew the proper execution of the turns was more important at this stage than pushing Buster to top speed. They continually practiced their turns maintaining the same distance from the barrel. Ann worked Buster hard. It became automatic for him to line out so they would be in the same position every time they started to execute the turn.

They became more and more consistent. Ann wanted Buster to circle the barrel at high speed maintaining a constant arc between her knee and the barrel. If they circled too close, their speed slowed alarmingly and precious split seconds wastefully ticked off the clock. If they circled too far out, the distance they traveled to complete the turn increased and took longer to cover. They had to operate at the perfect distance from the barrel to complete the turn in the shortest possible time. The perfect distance was the distance Buster could drive hard with his rear legs around the barrel at his fastest possible speed.

When Ann felt comfortable with the consistency of their turns, she started asking Buster for more speed. He willingly gave all she asked for. They began riding like a team. Soon they were performing exceptionally well. Ann was starting to feel confident in their performance. Mistakes were ironed out as soon as they happened and became increasingly rare.

They trained and worked according to a well planned schedule.

During the week before the rodeo, Ann started pushing Buster faster. She felt extremely good riding him hard through the pattern. They rode as if they were one as they raced around the barrels. Ann cut down on the number of circuits they made during the last few practice sessions. During the last days of practice, Ann urged Buster to his fastest speed and pushed him hard for at least two circuits before quitting for the day. Ann felt they were ready and she was eager for the weekend to arrive. She asked Bill to time them with a stop watch on the last few days of training. He gladly agreed. Ann knew they were running fast but she wanted to know exactly how good they were doing and the stop watch would tell her. Ann tied Buster to the arena fence and went into the tack room to get the stop watch.

When she came out, she smiled. There sat Johnson and Casey on the top rail of the fence and she could see James trotting up on his horse on the outside of the arena. Where did they come from, she thought. Just a minute ago, Bill was the only one in sight. "Where in the world did you all come from?" she asked.

"Oh, we've been around. We've been waiting a month to see how you and your horse are going to do," Casey said. Johnson smiled down at her.

James rode up and slipped from the saddle right onto the top rail of the fence. "Did I miss anything yet?" he asked.

"Not yet, I think she's getting ready to time a run," Johnson answered.

"Oh good! I've been waiting for this," James said.

"Heck, we all have," Bill said from the arena.

"I don't know where all of you buzzards came from. This place was deserted a few minutes ago. But I'm glad to see we'll have an audience, cause it adds pressure to do good and maybe we'll break the world's record," Ann laughed.

"If you do, I want your autograph!" Casey hooted from his perch.

"I wound the watch and I'm ready when you are," Bill said.

"Okay Bill," Ann said. The group on the fence became quiet and watched Ann mount Buster and walk away. When she got to the far end of the arena, she jogged back toward the starting line. She was limbering him up before asking him to run at top speed. She could feel Buster's anticipation. She knew Buster was ready and that he knew she was going to let him go as hard as he could. It was a good communion between horse and rider.

She jogged past the starting line and turned back toward it. She positioned Buster to start. Ann studied the course and went through the run in her mind. She could feel Buster fidgeting and knew he was ready. She looked toward Bill and saw he was ready to start the clock when she passed the starting line. She nodded at Bill and kicked Buster hard with her heels. Buster jumped into a full run. When they passed the starting line he was almost at his top speed. They reached the first barrel and Ann sat back a little to slow him as they started into the turn. Buster cut the turn short in anticipation. He had to collect himself halfway around and then drive off toward the second barrel, costing them time. They went into the second barrel more in control and made a perfect turn. Buster was on the right lead and came out driving away hard with his powerful hind quarters. The turn around the last barrel was smooth and fast. They kept a perfect pocket between them and the barrel, and Buster came out running full speed toward the finish line, with Ann urging him faster. Except for losing a split second on the first barrel, Ann felt they made a good run as they raced past the finish line. She pulled Buster into a sliding stop. Ann turned and rode toward Bill, who was reading the time.

"Sixteen and nine-tenths of a second," Bill yelled out.

"Wow, we've got to shave a little off that time to win on Saturday," Ann said. She looked toward the fence where the men were sitting and asked, "Did you rail birds see any mistakes?"

"Well, I think you lost a few tenths by starting to pull the horse up a stride or two before crossing the finish line. You need to keep running clear past the line. Don't pull him up till you're a stride, or even two, past the point where you think you should start stopping. The clock doesn't stop till you go by, so go by flat out and you'll improve your time," Casey said.

Ann listened intently. She contemplated every word. She felt he was giving good advice.

"It appeared from my angle, that on your dash to the first barrel, you headed Buster too close, cutting the pocket down and causing him to slow unnecessarily going around in a tighter turn," Bill said. Ann slowly nodded her head as she visualized these mistakes. She felt fortunate to have such expert critics on hand to evaluate her rides.

"I see. Johnson, did you or James notice anything that would help improve our run?" she asked.

"Honey, I think Bill and Casey already mentioned the only rough spots I could see. You looked smooth as silk on the rest of the run," Johnson said. James nodded agreement.

"I can see where we need improvement on those two things. Let me walk Buster around a minute and we'll make another run and see if we can eliminate those bad points."

Ann walked Buster around the arena to give him a breather and herself time to concentrate on the moves she would make to polish the problems pointed out to her. She had an unconscious feeling that they were crowding the first barrel, and now that others had noticed it, she would concentrate on holding Buster off the barrel a little more. She could make slight adjustments to correct that problem. She would also keep Buster wide open until they were a stride past the finish line and then set him back into a faster stop to avoid the traffic at the end of the arena. Casey's right, I'd rather go by the clock at thirty miles an hour as opposed to the fifteen or twenty we'd be doing if we were already slowing down when we passed the line, Ann thought. "Okay, Buster, let's try another run and see if we can implement some changes and improve our time," she said.

She turned Buster around far enough behind the line so when they started their run, they would be running at top speed past the line and clock. Ann correctly reasoned that she could reduce her time by passing the clock at full speed going and coming. She gave Bill the nod and sent Buster racing toward the first barrel. She didn't have to encourage Buster to reach his top speed quickly. He was more than anxious to give Ann all the speed she asked for. Ann held him slightly more to the left of the first barrel as they approached. Buster drove hard around the barrel. Dirt flew as he pumped his powerful hind legs accelerating out of the turn. "Wonderful!" Ann shouted as they raced for the second barrel. That's the ticket, she thought. Improving their speed on the first barrel would snap up their run and give them a faster time.

They went into the second, flawlessly rounded it, and were away toward the third in a flash. They completed the third barrel and Ann urged Buster toward the finish line with all the speed he could muster. She held him wide open past the line and then sat him back in a sliding stop. "Yahoo!" she screamed. They made a perfect run and she knew the time was going to be good. The men sitting on the rail were clapping and hollering too. They knew she had an excellent run and were happy for her.

"Way to go, Annie," Bill yelled. He held up the stop watch and said loudly. "A good time. Sixteen and three-tenths seconds."

Ann held her arm up in the air and pumped it up and down in a gesture of happiness. "Good job, Buster, they better look out for us on Saturday," she said.

They worked out again on Thursday and had good times and flawless runs. They were coming together as a well functioning team. Ann was pleased with their performance. In two days they would have to perform in front of the crowd at the rodeo grounds and the stakes would be for keeps. This would be her start to seriously contend for championships to help her reach the goal of a college rodeo scholarship. After the Thursday workout, Ann put Buster away for a full day's rest. She planned on both of them taking a day off and resting before the big day on Saturday.

If they placed high enough on Saturday, they would qualify for the finals on Sunday and be able to compete for the

High Valley championship. A bad run on Saturday would eliminate them, so Ann wanted to be sure they were both in excellent shape. Ann knew they were at a keen edge of performance and were running very well. She didn't want to push it and practice right up to the last minute. Sometimes a horse that was at the peak of his ability could become stale with too much practice and perform poorly. If they took Friday off, she felt they would enter the arena on Saturday fresh and ready to run the barrels to the best of their ability.

She was ready for a break. They had trained hard for the past month. The training pace increased along with the pressure as the rodeo drew closer. Ann thought about the events coming up in just two days and felt a twinge of nervousness flutter through her body. Gee whiz, I'm getting butterflies already and I still have two days to wait. Hopefully I'll settle down by Saturday, she thought.

Friday came and seemed to speed by. She finished her ranch chores and then set about getting her tack and equipment ready. She oiled her saddle and bridle, and decided to replace the cinch as she worked. She groomed Buster and combed and trimmed his mane and tail. She wanted them to not only ride a good race, but to look good doing it.

Casey came by and asked if she was ready for tomorrow. "I think Buster and I are running good and I've got all of our equipment ready, but I have to admit, I'm a little nervous. I hope I settle down before tomorrow," she said.

Casey laughed and said, "I know just how you feel. You gotta' talk yourself out'a being nervous. If you weren't nervous then you aren't worrying enough. When you worry, you push yourself harder and you become better prepared to go the extra distance to win. Being nervous just shows that you want to win. Nothing wrong with that. I think it's good for a competitor. Makes you sharper."

"Well, you're riding bareback broncs tomorrow but you don't seem to be nervous. How do you talk yourself out of being nervous?" she asked.

"Oh, it's easy, Annie. When I get out there tomorrow and crawl on that bronc's back, I just settle right down and concentrate on the job," Casey said.

"Come on, Casey, quit beating around the bush, how do you do it?" Ann asked again.

Casey saw Johnson and Bill walking through the barn toward them and really tuned up to the subject. The bigger the audience the better he liked it. "Well, since you ask, I'll tell you. First off, I realize that I have a fan club out there watching me. All the pretty girls in town will be rooting for me to win. Now, you know I can't let them down since they consider me the hero of High Valley. So, I tell myself this, settle down, Casey, all the girls in town are watching and you gotta' do good. Don't let your fan club down. The time to be nervous is past. The time to ride like the champion you are has arrived. More importantly, I keep telling myself, the simple fact that if you ride this bronc and score high, you might win the event. If you win the event, your fan club will be crawling all over themselves trying to get a date with you and you'll be able to pick out the prettiest girl in town to take to the dance on Saturday night. Well, those thoughts settle me right down and I get rid of my butterflies in a hurry, that's how I do it," he finished up.

Bill heard Casey's speech and laughed, "Yep, I'm sure you're telling yourself all them fancy thoughts while you're crawling on the bronc's back. Where do you get all the time to do that? If I remember right, you spend all your time asking me how the rigging looks and a hundred other things, while I'm helping you climb on board. Just before the gate swings open, I see so much fear in your eyes that I don't think you can even remember your own name, no less your fan club," Bill said in a mocking voice.

"Now, Bill, you know that's not true, I'm as cool as an ice cube when the gate opens," Casey said indignantly. Johnson and Ann laughed at their friendly sparring.

"Annie, have you got everything ready to go tomorrow?" Johnson asked.

"I think I do, but I'll probably forget something," she said.

"Hopefully you won't. Why don't you take one of the ranch trucks and a stock trailer and haul Buster to town in the morning. I know you're anxious to try out your new driver's license," Johnson said.

"That would be great. I want to get to the fairgrounds early so I can register and get Buster familiar with all the noise and hoopla that will be going on," Ann said.

"How about you, Casey? How do you want to handle tomorrow?" Johnson asked.

"I would appreciate the weekend off. Hopefully, I'll place high on Saturday and will ride in the final go round on Sunday. If Bill could be there early enough both days to help with my rigging and get me mounted and away okay, that would be a big help," Casey said.

"No problem. You two take both days off. We'll cover for you here and still be able to get to town early enough to help you or Annie if you need us. You're both a big part of this outfit and we're looking forward to watching you perform. We'll be at the rodeo grounds by mid-morning at the latest. Casey, watch for Annie in the morning and give her any help she might need when she shows up," Johnson said.

"You can bank on that. Thanks for the time off," Casey said. Casey looked toward Ann and lightly said, "The Bent Bar rides again."

CHAPTER 9

It seemed to Ann that she lay awake, tossing and turning all night. She went through the barrels at least a hundred times in her sleep. She was glad to see the first light of dawn sneaking through her bedroom window. Ann jumped out of bed and into the shower, then dressed in the clothes she prepared the night before. When she got to the barn, Johnson was already there. "It's hard to beat you to work in the morning," she said to him.

"Bill and James are here, too. We want to get the ranch work done so we can get to town early. In case you haven't heard, we've got two Bent Bar hands riding in the High Valley rodeo today and we don't want to miss it," Johnson said. Ann giggled and headed for Buster's stall to grain him before they left for town.

While Buster was eating, Ann went back to find Johnson. "Which truck shall I take today?" she asked.

"James hooked the two horse trailer to the red truck. Take it. It's all gassed and ready to go," he said.

"Thanks, I'll get it and pull over to load my tack," she said. She found James with his head under the hood of the red truck when she walked up. "Is something wrong?" she asked.

"No-No, I'm just checking the oil. I want to make sure you don't have any trouble," he said.

"Thanks, James, and thanks for hooking up the trailer for me," she said.

"Well, it's all yours now and good luck in the ring today," he said. Ann smiled at James and crawled into the driver's seat. She drove over to the barn and started loading the tack and feed in the trailer.

Afterwards, she checked on Buster. He was cleaning up the last of the grain. "Buster, this is the day we've been working toward. I guess we'll find out if all our training and practice is going to pay off. Are you ready to go?" she asked. She slipped a halter on him and led him down the alleyway. At the back of the horse trailer, she stopped him and laid the lead rope across his withers. She tapped him on his hip and Buster stepped into the trailer. He moved all the way forward and Ann stepped in beside him and tied the lead onto one of the rings in front of the feed tray. She stepped out and closed and latched the gate.

Ann was ready to go. She felt nervous about heading for town with the truck and trailer on her own. Whenever she pulled a trailer before, one of the men had always been with her. Johnson knew she still had trouble backing the trailer and making it go where she wanted. So where did he disappear to this morning? she wondered. Ann wanted the comfort of his last minute instructions before she took off on her own for the first time. James or Bill were nowhere to be seen either. She really didn't want to leave without some sort of last minute words with one of the men. She walked into the barn to Johnson's office. No one was there. Ann looked at her watch and saw that it was getting late. I hate to leave without saying good-by to somebody, but I better get going, she said to herself. She got in and started the engine. She tooted the horn and pulled out of the yard heading for the county road that led to town.

When she pulled away, Johnson, Bill and James walked back into the barn. On Johnson's instructions they made themselves scarce about the time Ann was ready to leave. Johnson knew Ann would be nervous about going to town without one of them along. He figured the best way for her to build confidence in her ability, towing a trailer, was for her to just do it and make her own mistakes without them present and giving advice. He thought she'd do okay if they left her alone. "Well, boss, she's on her own now. I don't know who's more uneasy about her going off on her own. You or her," Bill said.

"You can bet it's me, Bill," Johnson laughed.

Casey had been nervously pacing the parking area behind the arena. He kept watching for the red truck to show up. Johnson asked him to watch for Ann this morning, and to help her get the rig parked only if she absolutely needed help. So far, there had been no sign of her and Casey was getting worried. She should have been here by now, Casey thought. He walked around and talked to friends and other competitors. The back lot was turning into a busy little city. It was filling up with trucks and trailers. Everyone was unloading horses and setting up the area they would occupy for the weekend. Competitors came from far distances and most camped right on the rodeo grounds. They set up portable corral panels for their stock. It wasn't long before horses were being groomed and saddled across the whole of the back lot. The parking area was taking on a carnival atmosphere and everyone was looking forward to the upcoming competition.

Casey finally spotted Ann pulling into the parking area. His first instinct was to run over and start directing her into a parking spot. Johnson told him to let her make her own mistakes, so he slipped over to the area she pulled into and stayed out of sight.

Ann had a bit of a fright when she pulled into the parking lot and saw all the trucks, trailers and people congesting the area. I should have gotten here earlier. I'll just take it nice and easy and try not to get myself in a jam, she thought. She slowly pulled into the lot and drove around the perimeter looking for a place to park. Ann was hoping to find a spot she could pull straight into without having to back up. She drove around the area twice, but couldn't find an easy spot. She drove around again and found a spot with lots of room to pull up and then back into. "Well, I guess it's time to grow up, here goes nothing," she said. "Hang on, Buster," she called out.

Casey was peering around the corner of a friend's trailer a safe distance away from where Ann had pulled in. He watched her stop and get out. She walked back into the area she wanted to park and looked it over. He could tell she was jumpy about backing the rig. There were trucks and horse trailers already parked on each side of the spot she had chosen. He watched her look around and kick at some unknown object on the ground. "Go ahead, girl, it ain't gonna' park itself," he said to himself. Ann looked at the rigs on each side of her spot and then headed for the pickup. "I hope you make it on the first try, Annie," he thought. Casey knew that if an inexperienced driver had trouble backing a trailer on the first try, it became more difficult each succeeding try. They seemed to get more and more confused with each aborted attempt. He hoped it wouldn't happen to Ann.

"Just remember what you were taught. Steer the opposite way I want the trailer to go," she said to herself. Very carefully she started turning the wheel and backing up. She watched her rear view mirrors on both sides and could clearly see both of the parked rigs and her progress as she backed into the spot. Casey was holding his breath. She slowly backed into the space without hitting either of the rigs on the sides of her spot. Casey watched as Ann backed all the way in without incident. She stopped and got out and walked back to inspect her job. He watched as Ann looked at both sides of the trailer. She parked much too close to the trailer on her right. There was barely enough room to walk between the two rigs. She decided to pull out and back in again to line her rig up more in the center of the parking spot. Casey was too keyed up to watch any longer, he headed in her direction.

Ann pulled the rig out and was just starting to back in again when Casey walked up. "Hey, Annie, want me to back it in for you?" he asked.

Ann started to say, "gladly," but caught herself in time. Instead, she said, "Thanks, Casey, but I think I've got it now." She said a silent prayer and eased the trailer back into perfect position.

"You backed er' up like an expert. You must have had a good teacher," Casey said.

Ann laughed and said, "I sure did, I had the best teachers the Bent Bar has to offer."

"Let's take care of Buster and then get over to the office and register," Casey said.

They backed Buster out and tied him alongside the trailer. Ann hung a net full of sweet smelling timothy hay near Buster. "That'll keep him busy while we're signing in," Ann said.

"Okay, let's get going. Can't keep the fan club waiting," Casey said. They started toward the office to register and pay their entry fee. Casey kept stopping and talking to people on the way. He seemed to know everyone in the fairgrounds. He paid particular attention to female competitors and introduced Ann to some of her competition. Normally she knew most of the girls riding in the barrel race, but there seemed to be a larger number of contestants from other areas today. She would have to run a good race in order to qualify for the finals against this caliber of competition, she thought, as Casey jabbered away with one of the girls from another county. Ann poked him in the ribs to try and hurry him along. He got the hint and said to the girl he was talking to, "Well, you watch for me, I'll wink at you when I bust out of the chute on that bucking horse."

"Okay, Casey, I'll be watching," the girl said. Casey waved at her and he and Ann took off for the office.

"Casey, you'd better quit stopping and talking to everyone or we'll never get registered before the rodeo starts," Ann said.

"Don't worry, girl, they'd never start this show without us," he said. They stopped to let a young woman riding a well built buckskin horse pass in front of them. Casey watched intently as she rode past. "Now that is a work of art," he said.

"You're right, that is a beautiful horse she's riding," Ann said.

Casey took his stare from the horseback woman and turned and looked at Ann. "I wasn't talking about the horse, Annie," he said.

Ann laughed and said, "Oh, I'm sorry, Casey."

"Do you know who that was?" Casey asked.

"No, I don't," Ann answered.

"Well, young lady, you will before the day's over. That was Marsha Miller. She's one of the top barrel racers in the state," Casey said.

Ann looked back toward the girl on the buckskin. Ann had heard of Marsha. She knew the girl was currently one of the top ten barrel racers in Montana. She knew Marsha always had the best of everything. Her family owned a large ranch and generously supported her in her efforts to become the state champion. She certainly is beautiful, Ann thought, as she watched Marsha ride away. She carried herself with elegance. The buckskin she was riding seemed to accentuate her beauty. Ann read about her and the buckskin barrel racer in the newspapers. They were good, and they would be hard to beat. Buster and I will have to really operate at the peak of our ability today, she thought.

"Wake up, Annie. We better get going," Casey said. Ann said nothing, she just walked briskly toward the office. Seeing the beautiful girl and her well trained horse had been disconcerting. Ann trained her horses herself. She certainly asked for advice when she needed it, but mostly did all of her own training. She didn't own expensive clothes like Marsha was wearing and now she was beginning to feel a little inadequate after seeing her competition.

Casey seemed to read Ann's mind. He took off after her and caught her by the arm. He made Ann turn and look at him. He could see the doubt in her eyes. "She looks pretty fancy and she surely is riding a good looking horse, isn't she?" Casey said. Ann looked up at him and nodded. "I'll bet anybody my best horse, that they would never be able to make a ride like you and Buster did. Why, I'd bet they would both just fall to pieces if they were ever faced with the challenge that you faced riding off that cliff on a black stormy night. That was the greatest feat of horsemanship I've ever heard of. I really feel privileged to work on the same ranch with a rider of your caliber. Fancy clothes don't make a rider or horse perform any better. You've made a lot harder rides than what you're facing today. So, relax and just concentrate on making the best possible ride you can. Besides that, I think that when you smile, you're more gorgeous than Marsha Miller ever thought about being," Casey said.

Ann stared into Casey's eyes. He had just made her feel like a million dollars. What Casey had said instilled a wealth of confidence in Ann. "Casey, can I sign up to be a member of your fan club?" she asked. They both laughed. Ann felt great now and she was more determined than ever to do well in today's event.

They registered and paid their entry fees. Outside the office they stopped and looked over the program for the day's events. Ann saw that barrel racing didn't start until about one o'clock. "What are you gonna' do till your event comes up?" she asked Casey.

"Things won't start happening for me till about three o'clock so if you need any help, I'm at your service," he said.

"No, I don't need any help, I'm gonna' work on Buster and start warming him up about noon. Why don't you go and see your friends or whatever you want to do. If you see Johnson or Bill, please tell them where I'm parked," she said.

"Okay, and I'll see you before you ride. Remember, you're the best rider here, so don't get too nervous," he said. Ann smiled, then turned and walked toward the competitor parking area.

She took Buster's hay net and put it inside the trailer. She didn't want him running on a full belly. She groomed him and combed out his mane and tail. He was looking good with all the attention she had been giving him lately. He knew what was up. With all the noise, people and other horses coming and going, he knew he would be ridden short and hard today. He had been to a lot of rodeos and had become accustomed to the commotion. He was relaxed now but deep down he knew things would change shortly.

When Ann was satisfied with Buster's condition, she saddled him, but left the cinch loose until she was ready to ride. She chatted with the couple parked next to her. They were part of the drill team that would perform during the Grand Entry parade. Ann planned on riding in the Grand Entry and was pleased to meet these people. As they were talking, Johnson walked up with Sam. Ann introduced them to her new friends. When Johnson said he was from the Bent Bar ranch, the people looked surprised and then looked at Ann. "Then we must be in the company of a real celebrity, you must be the girl who made that incredible ride," the man said.

"That's her," Sam said.

"We are really pleased to meet you and we'll be cheering for you today," the lady said.

"Thank you," Ann said.

"Are you ready, Annie?" Johnson asked.

"As ready as we'll ever be. We'll ride in the Grand Entry and then I'll keep Buster saddled and warmed up till our event starts," she said.

"Good, then if you don't need us, Sam and I will try to find seats in the grandstands," he said.

"Okay, and thanks for checking on me," she said.

Johnson and Sam walked away. Ann smiled when she heard Sam say to Johnson, "Johnson, it looks to me like she got that rig backed in there okay, what were you worried about?"

Johnson and Sam made their way toward the grandstands overlooking the arena. "How are your cows doin'?" Sam asked Johnson.

"They're comin' along good. We've had a good spring and there's plenty of grass in the high country. Both the cattle and horses look butter ball fat this year. The calves look great and are growthy for sure. How about your place, how are things going for you?" Johnson asked.

"Fine. Just fine. We've got about the same conditions on our range, lots of grass for a change and hopes for a decent amount of moisture through the summer to keep it coming," Sam said. They entered the grandstands and started looking for seats.

"Hey, Johnson. Hey, Sam, up here." They heard someone calling out. They looked in the direction of the voice and saw Duke, the brand inspector, waving at them.

They made their way toward Duke and could see there was room for them to sit. "Hey, Duke, thanks. We'll just crawl in here with you if you don't mind," Sam said.

"Not at all, I'd enjoy your company," Duke said as they sat down.

"This is a good spot with a good view of the whole arena. Annie's runnin' the barrels and one of our top hands, Casey, is riding bareback broncs today," Johnson said.

"Well good, that gives me somebody to root for," Duke said.

They stopped talking when the announcer started testing his microphone. Loud squealing noises came out over the speakers. The announcer tried to get the system working right and stop the irritating squeals. "Test 1, 2, 3," he said and then the squealing started again. "I guess it's just part of rodeo to have to put up with that noise until somebody figures out the right adjustments for the amplifier," Sam said.

"You're on the rodeo board of directors, Duke. Next year, why don't you pass a law that says the amplifier must be adjusted before Sam arrives, so he doesn't have to listen to it," Johnson said. The three men laughed at Johnson's remark and people sitting nearby laughed with them.

Ann heard the squealing noises. "The announcer is getting ready," the man parked next to her said.

"Sure sounds like it," Ann answered.

"I guess we better snug up our cinches and ride over to the staging area," he said. They rode over to the arena and met with the coordinator of the Grand Entry parade. He assigned Ann a position. She lined up with the other riders. Ann listened as the announcer welcomed everyone to the High Valley fairgrounds and continued on about the day's events. He briefly went through the program and reminded everyone that today's events would determine who would qualify for the final go rounds scheduled the next day. The recorded music of the Grand entry started. The riders loped into the arena following the flag bearers. They made two trips around the arena at a fast gallop and then pulled up and stopped with all the riders facing the stands.

The crowd applauded, and the announcer introduced the singer for the Star Spangled Banner. The National Anthem was sung and the crowd enthusiastically applauded. "Now sit tight, ladies and gentlemen, and get ready to enjoy one of the finest rodeos in the state of Montana," the announcer said to the crowd. Loud applause greeted him again and the riders raced out of the arena following the flag bearers.

Ann had time now to concentrate on preparing herself for her run. She walked Buster around the outside of the grounds while the preliminary events started. She stayed close enough to the arena to be able to hear the announcer's voice and be able to keep track of the progress of the different events. She saw Bill and Casey working on Casey's bareback rigging. She rode over to say "Hi" and wish Casey luck.

"Hello, Annie," Bill said when he saw Ann ride up.

"Hi, Bill, I'm glad to see you made it. Casey's gonna' need all the help he can get today," she said.

"I'm ready and rarin' to go, Annie," Casey said.

"Barrels will probably start in twenty minutes or so, I hope you'll be over there to watch my run," she said.

"Don't worry about that, we're just making a few last minute adjustments on Casey's riggin' and then we'll be in the chute area so we'll have a good view of the whole arena," Bill said.

"Okay, I'm going to head over so I won't miss watching the runs ahead of me. I'm scheduled as the sixth rider," she said. Ann waved and started Buster toward the arena.

"Hey, Annie, just remember that you're from the Bent Bar, that makes you a top hand," Casey yelled. Ann smiled and waved back. Good old Casey, she thought.

Ann took Buster out of the grounds and loped him for five minutes to warm him up. Then she rode over to the gate used by the contestants to come and go from the arena. She saw the other barrel racers all gathered in a group and rode over to them. She knew about half of the girls and was soon in conversation about how everyone was doing. She saw Marsha Miller impatiently walking her horse around the area. "I wonder how ole miss priss is gonna' do today?" one of the girls said.

"She's probably worried about getting her britches dirty during her run," another girl said. Several girls laughed at the remarks. Marsha wasn't known to be overly sociable with the girls she was competing against. Her wealthy family gave her privileges the other girls didn't enjoy. She had the advantage of being able to buy the best barrel horses that were available. She didn't train her horses. They were trained by hired professionals. The buckskin she was riding today had been under professional training for months, and was an outstanding animal.

"Well, we've all got to ride around the same set of barrels and anything can happen," Ann said to the small group. They heard the announcer reading off times and listing the winners of the event before the barrels. They listened as he cautioned all barrel riders to get ready and be in the alleyway ready to go when their name was called. "Good luck, everyone," Ann said.

They watched as the arena crew set up and measured the distances between the barrels. Things were going to start happening now, Ann thought. The barrels were run very fast and the contestants didn't have long to wait for their turn. Crews in the alleyway made sure all the riders were ready. They had the rider whose turn it was to run, move into the arena. The next rider was positioned "on deck," ready to move out, when the current run was finished. If the rider scheduled next did not move into position within thirty seconds of being called, she risked the possibility of forfeiting her run. There were many events and riders scheduled for the day's performance and the programs had to move right along in order for all the activities to take place on schedule. There was no time for delays caused by riders being late. The judges had the option of scratching riders who violated the thirty second rule.

"We're moving right into the girl's barrel racing, the judges have indicated they're ready to go," the announcer said. He called out the first rider's name and the name of the horse she was riding. She moved her horse into the arena and the judges gave her the go-ahead to start when she was ready. The rider began and raced for the first of the three barrels. In the alleyway, the riders moved up one notch. The girl that had been "on deck," moved up to the entrance of the arena and the "on deck" position was filled by the next girl on the list. Things moved quickly. The first girl raced through the pattern and came across the finish line in a full run. She performed well and the crowd cheered when the announcer called out her time. It was a good run of sixteen and seven-tenths seconds. Ann heard the time and thought the competitors were good and that she and Buster would have to put in a flawless performance to remain in the competition. In just a matter of minutes, Ann heard her name called to be "on deck." She moved Buster into position.

Buster listened to the noise and watched the other horses and people throughout the day. He had been here before and knew that he would soon be making a run in a noisy arena surrounded by hundreds of cheering people. Ann reached down and patted Buster's strong neck. She felt the slightest amount of moisture on his neck from the loping they did before riding to the arena. Good, you're still warmed up and in perfect shape to break into an all out run in a few seconds, she thought. She felt a tenseness in Buster and knew he was ready. The rider ahead of Ann came racing back across the finish line and slid to a stop in the alleyway. Ann moved into the arena before her name was even called.

The announcer called her name and introduced her and Buster to the crowd. Then he said, "This horse and rider are well known in this country. They're from the Bent Bar Ranch. While checking their summer range this spring, they were accidentally forced to ride straight off the top of a deep gorge. Miraculously they completed one of the most astonishing rides ever accomplished in these mountains. It happened during a ferocious storm. They survived and came back to compete for us today at the High Valley Rodeo. Let's hear a big welcome for Ann Olsen and her horse, Buster!" he said. The crowd applauded. Embarrassed, Ann waved and then looked at the judge to see if she was cleared to start her run.

He gave her an affirmative nod. Ann felt Buster under her. He transmitted readiness as she turned him to face the course. Quickly she went through the run in her mind preparing for each barrel. Buster was fidgeting. She must push off soon, she thought, or Buster's high level of readiness may suffer if she delayed. She had concentrated on bringing Buster through this day, gradually building him to a point where he would be eager to run. The time was now. They must run hard.

In one quick motion, Ann slacked the reins and moved her legs away from Buster's sides. Her body posture dropped down and slightly forward as she gave the gelding the unmistakable cues to break into a full run. He needed no further urging. Buster was away and reaching top speed as they passed the line and the timer started the clock. Ann concentrated on making gentle corrections to hold Buster slightly off the first barrel. She refrained from making any severe rein movements. She didn't want Buster to overreact and break his stride, causing unnecessary time losses. They wheeled perfectly around the first barrel and Ann felt elated as Buster sprinted for the second barrel. They entered the pocket and precisely circled the barrel in a high speed turn. Running for the third barrel, Ann encouraged Buster to higher speed. They were in the groove now with only one barrel left to negotiate. They approached at high speed and almost imperceptibly, Ann leaned back in the saddle to slightly check Buster's great speed. He responded and adjusted his speed to enter the turn. Buster went into the turn with dirt flying behind him. They came out heading for the finish line with Ann urging Buster to his utmost speed. Ann knew they were having a good run and pushed Buster past the finish line before pulling him into a stop.

As Buster was coming out of his sliding stop, the next rider was moving into the arena under thunderous applause for Ann and Buster.

Buster was excited and breathing hard. He started a prancing walk as they moved out of the alleyway past the riders still waiting their turn. Ann noticed Marsha staring at her with a cold glare as they rode past. "I guess she wasn't too happy with our ride, Buster. Well, she's got something to ride for now," Ann said. She stopped outside the alleyway and waited for the announcer to read their time.

Ann didn't have to wait long. She heard the announcer say, "The time for Ann Olsen, riding Buster, is sixteen and forty-two one-hundredths seconds. She takes the lead with the top time posted so far. A good ride for the young lady who hails from right here in our own High Valley area. Let's hear a good hand for her." He didn't have to urge the crowd very much to applaud the home town girl. Ann was delighted when she heard the crowd roar their approval. She rode over and wished the riders still waiting "good luck." The girls all complimented her on her good time. Everyone except Marsha Miller. Marsha just looked the other way while Ann was talking.

She rode Buster out of the area and tied him to a hitching post out of the way of the active contestants. Ann wanted to watch the remaining riders to see if her time held in first place. She wasn't disappointed. Their time held the lead. Ann and Buster finished with the highest time of the day and easily qualified for the finals on Sunday. Marsha Miller and her buckskin horse placed second, right behind Ann, with a time of sixteen and fifty-five one-hundredths of a second. Ann was pleased to be in first place. They beat the favorite, Marsha, by more than a tenth of a second. Their intelligent training had paid off today. Tomorrow, the pressure would really be on, Ann thought. Marsha was behind and would probably push herself and her horse right to their limits to try and capture the lead. The other riders were just a few tenths of a second behind Marsha, so anything could happen on Sunday. They would have to have another flawless run to capture first place. The rider with the lowest total time for the two days would win the High Valley Championship.

She rode Buster to their trailer. She was anxious to get back to the arena and find Johnson. Bareback bronc riding would be coming up shortly and she didn't want to miss Casey's ride. She unsaddled Buster and brushed him down. She gave him a hug around his neck and praised him for the good run. Buster knew what affection was and enjoyed every minute of it. Ann hung his hay net in easy reach and took off for the stands to watch the rest of the rodeo.

She entered the stands and walked along looking up into the crowd trying to locate Johnson and Sam. Halfway down the arena, toward the chutes, she heard her name called. Ann looked up to see them standing and waving at her. She made her way up through the bleachers to where they were sitting. "Annie, you sit that horse like you were part of him, that was a wonderful ride," Duke said as they made room for her to join them.

She smiled at Duke's compliment and looked at Johnson. He was grinning from ear to ear and shaking his head back and forth in approval. Ann was pleased. "Annie, you're leading the pack today and we're sure proud of you," Johnson finally said.

"Can I have your autograph?" Sam jokingly asked.

In the parking lot behind the bucking chutes, Bill was watching Casey rummage around in the front seat of his pickup as if he were looking for something. "What's the matter, Casey?" Bill asked.

"I can't find my other spur," he said.

"That sure don't surprise me with all that junk lying around in there. Why, I bet there's a fortune in empty pop cans lying on the floor boards. Don't you ever clean your truck out?" Bill asked.

"Come on, Bill, help me find my other spur, I'm runnin' out of time. They're gonna' start bronc riding soon and I only have one spur," Casey said.

"Well, Casey, I don't see where you have a problem. Just rake that bucking horse with that lone spur. That way you'll know which way he's gonna' jump and you can be ready for him," Bill said.

"Very funny," Casey said.

"Just think, Casey, if you win with only one spur today, your fan club can start calling you "One Spur Casey" and you'll be famous," Bill said.

"You're just a barrel of laughs, Bill," Casey grumbled.

"If you can't find it, then we better get moving before you miss the whole event. Maybe you can borrow a spur from one of the other riders," Bill said. Casey stopped rummaging around and mournfully looked at Bill. This was a catastrophe of major proportions. He would feel naked without his own spurs on. They were part of him. Wearing different spurs would be like a blind date. Neither one knew what to expect from the stranger.

Casey knew he was out of time and had to get over to the chutes. Reluctantly, he slammed the door on his old truck and picked up his bareback rigging. He looked at Bill and said, "Let's go." Bill thought he looked like somebody who just lost his best friend.

As they made their way toward the bucking chutes, Casey walked along dragging the boot that was missing the spur. The other spur seemed to jangle loudly. The noise from the lone spur seemed odd and strange to the two riders. They were both aware of the missing jangle of the lost spur. By the time they reached the chute area, Casey had developed a definite limp. Bill looked over at Casey and said, "By golly, I think you've gone lame on me, Casey, we might have to shoot you." Casey didn't answer. He just looked down at his boots.

Bill watched Casey look up from his boots and start casting his gaze around the bucking chutes. There was a lot of excitement. Cowboys were moving horses around and opening and closing gates in preparation for the bronc riding event. Casey was wondering what he was going to do. Should he borrow a pair of spurs or should he just borrow one spur? Would I ride better knowing that at least one of the spurs was mine? Casey wondered.

"Hey, Case, look what I found," Bill said loudly. Casey spun around and looked toward Bill. He saw Bill bent over and reaching behind a corral post. Bill looked in Casey's direction and saw that Casey's attention was riveted on him. Grinning, Bill slowly began to stand upright while removing his hand from behind the corral post. In his hand was Casey's missing spur.

Casey took two long strides and reached Bill. He snatched the spur from Bill and said, "You thieving booger, you had that spur all along!"

"No, No, Casey, you got it all wrong, I just found it sticking out from behind that post," Bill said, grinning.

"Why, I oughta' break one of your arms. I've really been flustered trying to figure out how I was gonna' ride and win with only one spur," Casey shouted.

"Some thanks you're giving me for saving your bacon. I wish I'd never found it now," Bill said, still grinning. Casey glared at him. Finally, he turned and stomped away toward chute number three, where he was due to ride in a short time. He heard Bill laughing as he walked off.

Casey would be the fifth rider out and the second rider out of chute number three. He had a few minutes to get himself ready. He drew a horse named "Moon Shot." He knew from talking to other bronc riders that Moon Shot was not a ferocious bucker. He would have preferred to have drawn a horse with a better reputation for being hard to ride. Casey crawled up on the fence near chute three and watched as the handlers loaded the four bucking chutes with the horses that would be ridden by the first riders. He thought about Moon Shot and his chances of marking high on a horse that wasn't exactly a great bucker. The harder the horse bucked, the better chance the rider had of getting a high score. Casey felt like he was starting out at a disadvantage. He needed a good ride today, to get to the finals tomorrow. He wasn't sure Moon Shot was going to give him a wild enough ride to earn a high score. Anybody can ride a horse that don't buck hard, Casey thought.

Casey watched as the first riders went about the job of getting their horses rigged up. The horses tried to fight and kick in the confines of the small chutes as the men worked to cinch up the bareback rigging. The air was alive with excitement. Horses squealed and whinnied and men yelled instructions to each other as they put their rigging on the horse they had drawn to ride. As Casey watched the excitement growing around him, he began to feel the first faint signals of nervousness. Here come the butterflies, he thought to himself.

"Things safe around here yet?" Bill said. Casey turned and looked down into the alleyway behind the chutes.

"That was the meanest trick ever pulled on me. You have one thing to look forward to, Bill, and that's trying to figure out how I'm gonna' get even with you. And you can bet your best pair of boots that I am going to get even," Casey said. Bill grinned and climbed up on the fence beside Casey. "This first bunch of horses are gonna' be ridden out of here in the next few minutes and then I'll be up. The only trouble is that I'm not too proud of the horse I drew. He's not enough of a hard bucking horse to score high," Casey said.

"I heard that about Moon Shot this morning, when I learned you drew him," Bill said.

"I have to ride him, so I'll just have to hope he'll give me a halfway decent ride," Casey said.

"Make him give you a decent ride!" Bill said.

Casey looked over at Bill and in a very serious voice asked, "How do I do that?"

"Give him something he's never had before," Bill said. Casey waited for Bill to continue, but Bill just sat there and said no more. Casey knew that when it came to understanding a horse's mind, Bill was as good as anybody in the country. Johnson taught Bill all he knew over the years and Johnson had no equal as far as Casey was concerned. Bill was one of the few people Johnson would trust to make all of his own decisions on breaking and training their ranch horses. Bill seemed to know what the horse was planning for his next move before the horse did.

"Bill, I'm running out of time. What do you mean about giving him something he's never had before?" Casey asked.

Bill grinned and said, "I'll tell you what's on my mind if you promise to forgive me for swiping your spur."

"Okay, Okay, you're forgiven. Now tell me what you're thinking," Casey urgently said.

"Alright, listen close, Case. Ride that horse different than he's ever been ridden. He's used to riders coming out and spurring him down both sides, from his neck to his flanks.

He's gotten into the habit of putting up with it. He knows it will only last eight seconds and then be over. Confuse him, aggravate him, make him mad. Do whatever you have to, to throw him off his normal routine and he might surprise you and everybody else and give you one heck of a wild ride," Bill said.

"Have you got any suggestions on how to do that?" Casey asked.

"Sure I do. Look how quick you got all out of kilter walking around with only one spur. Your whole mental state changed and you became aggravated with me. You were suddenly thrown a curve and you didn't like it. Do the same thing to Moon Shot. Rake him harder on one side than you do on the other, it'll confuse him and make him think something different is happening. After a few jumps, switch to the other side if you can and rake him hard on that side and easy on the other side. You might be able to irritate him enough, so he'll decide to try and get rid of you in a hurry and buck harder than he ever has before."

Casey stared at Bill for a few seconds. Slowly, a wicked grin started to appear around the corner of his mouth. "Bill, you are one slick Son Of A Gun. You planned that whole episode with the spur to get me in the right frame of mind, didn't you? I was so aggravated with you that I was ready to fly off the handle and do something crazy. It just might work. I'm gonna' ride Moon Shot so he won't know what side he's gonna' get tickled on next!" Casey excitedly said. Bill sat there grinning. He was proud of himself.

The arena judge gave the announcer the signal that the first bareback bronc rider was ready to go. The announcer called the crowd's attention toward the end of the arena where the chutes were. The gate on chute number one flew open and a hard bucking roan horse came flying out. The horse bucked hard straight ahead and then started a series of spinning, twisting jumps and threw the rider before the eight second horn sounded. The crowd gave the rider a good round of applause and he waved his hat to them as he picked himself up. He didn't ride the bronc for the required eight seconds, so he didn't score.

The next three horses out of the chutes put on a show and their riders stayed with them and scored high. As the riders left the chutes on the bucking horses, men started immediately loading the chutes again with the next horses to be ridden. Moon Shot was sorted into chute number three. Bill and Casey got busy cinching the bareback rigging and flank strap on the horse. Casey gently settled on Moon Shot's back and placed his hand in the grip on the rigging. He adjusted his grip until it felt just right. He sat on the horse lightly with his boots up out of the way resting on the sides of the chute. He pulled the brim of his hat down tight and looked out into the arena where the last rider was being picked off his horse after a successful ride. Moon Shot was nervously snorting and stomping his front legs in anticipation of what he knew was in store.

Just a few more seconds and the judge will look my way to see if I'm ready to go, Casey thought. He looked nervously toward Bill who was on the fence next to him. Bill was waiting to jerk the flank strap tight whenever Casey gave the signal to open the gate. He planned to jerk the strap hard to aggravate Moon Shot into a better performance. Bill caught Casey's glance and read the nervousness in his friend's eyes.

"Settle down, Casey, your whole fan club will be watching today," Bill said with a grin. He saw the faintest trace of a smile start to break on Casey's face. Casey pulled his hat brim down again and looked toward the judge. The judge pointed to Casey. Casey nodded back indicating he was ready to ride. The gate to chute number three swung open and Bill jerked the bucking strap tight.

Moon Shot didn't waste any time. He leaped out in a four legged jump and hit the ground stiff legged. He jarred Casey hard when he came down and Casey had the fleeting thought that maybe Moon Shot was going to buck harder than he had in the past. But then he lunged off in a half hearted crow hop and bucked lightly when his front legs hit the ground. Time to go to work, Casey thought. He had been spurring Moon Shot evenly on the first few jumps. Now Casey changed his tactics. He brought both his legs up high along Moon Shot's neck and raked down his neck on only one side. On the opposite side of the horse's neck, Casey barely touched him, and used that spur to maintain his balance as he brought his legs back under the rigging. Moon Shot jumped away from the side Casey raked him. Casey reached up and intermittently spurred on the same side as he used the horse's momentum and timed his spurring to bring his legs back under the horse in a way to help maintain his solid seat on the easy bucking horse. This time he felt hesitation in Moon Shot, just before he jumped away from the spurred side again. Casey thought that something better happen quickly before the eight seconds ran out. On his next jump, Casey spurred again, but when he felt Moon Shot jump away from the spurred side, he immediately spurred on the opposite side. The unexpected shock of being spurred on the other side surprised the horse and he desperately tried to change direction and escape away from that spur.

In mid air, he tried to turn his body away from the aggravating spur. When he hit the ground his legs tangled and he almost went down. Casey stayed with him. Moon Shot recovered and started to buck harder in the new direction. Moon Shot was losing control. The shock of almost smashing into the ground out of balance on his last jump, jolted him out of his normal routine. Now, Moon Shot became alarmed and lost his reasoning. When Casey felt him recover from the near fall and try to buck away from the irritating spur, he switched sides again, and really put pressure on the horse.

This time it was too confusing for the horse to react sensibly to the constantly changing side of the irritating spur. Moon Shot became enraged at this unusual rider and exploded in anger. His only desire now was to remove the irritant from his back as quickly as possible.

Bill watched from the chutes. When he saw Moon Shot come down out of control and almost fall, his excitement began to rise. He could see confusion in the horse and realized Casey was executing their strategy perfectly. Now Moon Shot began bucking as if his life depended on getting this rider off his back. He sunfished violently, twisting his body in mid air as he tried to throw Casey. The young rider buckled down and began to concentrate on staying with the enraged horse. Moon Shot spun and bucked. He twisted and turned in a wild rage, but still the rider remained on his back. Casey had to stop the unusual spurring pattern he used to infuriate Moon Shot and concentrate on staying with the frantic bronc.

Casey's hands were full now and he was in danger of being thrown. The crowd began shouting encouragement. Moon Shot was putting on a spectacular bucking show as he called on every bit of energy he possessed to dislodge the wily rider. Bill and the riders at the chutes began cheering for Casey as they watched the drama unfold. The crowd in the stands came to their feet and the noise from their cheering became deafening.

The odds turned, and now it was Moon Shot who seemed to be giving the orders as he ferociously dealt bruising, head snapping jolts with each pounding jump. Casey rode well, but now the extreme effort the horse was putting out was catching up with him. On each succeeding jump, Casey's timing began falling farther and farther behind Moon Shot's violent maneuvers. Casey prayed for the sound of the horn, ending the eight second ride. He could feel himself losing control and desperately tried to stay with Moon Shot. Casey seemed to separate from the horse's back more and more with each buck. Soon his timing was thrown so far off that when he was coming down on the horse's back, Moon Shot was coming up into his next buck. It was like a bat hitting a ball and the effect of the opposite forces colliding dealt harsh treatment to the flailing rider.

Casey knew he was about to be bucked off. Tenaciously, he tried to hang on for one more jump. Bill's theory about getting Moon Shot to buck harder worked better than they had figured. Now Casey knew he was just one jump away from being violently separated from the horse and he still hadn't heard the horn that would end this ride. Suddenly, Casey felt himself catapulted into the air and Moon Shot bucked out from under him.

Trying to maintain his dignity after being thrown, Casey managed to control his flight through the air and miraculously was able to land standing straight up. Moon Shot brutalized Casey during the last part of the ride. He was in a daze after taking the beating Moon Shot dished out after his unconventional spurring. Casey staggered around trying to keep his balance. He had never ridden a horse that bucked so hard or that was as hard to ride as Moon Shot, once he unleashed his hidden fury. Surprised by the explosive reaction to his spurring technique, Casey looked in awe at Moon Shot. He was still bucking furiously toward the end of the arena.

Slowly it began to dawn on Casey that there was a tremendous roar coming from the grandstands. The announcer was shouting into the microphone about Moon Shot and the show he just gave the crowd. Casey's eyes began to focus and he looked around and realized everyone was on their feet applauding and cheering. He looked over to the chutes and saw Bill yelling and waving his arms in an unmistakable victory gesture. A horse and rider abruptly appeared and Casey saw that it was the pick up rider.

"What a ride! Are you okay, Casey?" the rider shouted above the roar of the crowd.

Casey began to realize that the cheering was for him. He thought he was thrown before the eight second horn sounded. Could it be possible he was so busy trying to stay on Moon Shot that he just simply didn't hear the horn over the noise of the crowd? Casey wondered. He looked up at the pick up rider and asked, "Did I ride him to the horn?"

"You sure did, and even a few extra jumps after it sounded," the pick up rider said.

Casey composed himself and looked back at the stands where everyone was still cheering. He swept his hat off and waved it toward the crowd in a happy gesture. He was rewarded with more cheering. He puffed himself up and jauntily walked toward the chutes.

Bill was grinning from ear to ear when he got there and yelled out, "Way to ride, Casey!" Everyone was congratulating him at once. He took it all in as if he knew all along he had ridden the horse to the end. He savored the praise and wasn't about to let on that the horse gave him the ride of his life and that Moon Shot had been totally in control for the last few jumps.

Smiling crazily, he climbed up beside Bill and whispered in his ear, "Bill, you don't know what happened. That plan of yours worked too good. That crazy horse unleashed demons and threw me around like a rag doll, I was barely able to hang on. That was the longest eight seconds of my life."

"But you did ride him, Case, and what a ride it was. I wish you could have seen the moves that horse made. It was beautiful, and you really rode him. I don't know what you did to draw him out like that but it sure brought out his hidden talent. Moon Shot will never be regarded as a slouch again and you can bet he will command respect from bronc riders from now on," Bill happily said.

The announcer's voice captured their attention. They listened for Casey's official score. "Ladies and Gentlemen, that spectacular ride by the cowboy from High Valley's own Bent Bar Ranch takes today's lead with a high score of 84." The crowd cheered in approval.

Smiling happily, Casey said, "I wish he wouldn't call me a cowboy. I'm a cowman."

Bill slapped Casey on the back and said, "That's gonna' be hard to beat, partner. Your fan club will be proud of you."

At the mention of his fan club, Casey looked at Bill and said, "Come on, I'll buy you a cold drink over at the midway." They climbed down from the chutes and headed for the crowds in the spectator area. Casey wanted to indulge himself a bit and soak up praise from the crowd. Bill smiled as they made their way toward the stands. His plan had worked well enough for Casey to earn an impressive score on Moon Shot.

"Casey, hey, Casey!" Casey and Bill stopped when they heard Ann's voice calling. They turned and saw Ann, Johnson, Duke and Sam making their way through the crowd. They were all smiling. Casey was anxious to see them. He wanted to bask in the glory of his ride. "Casey, we're both in first place in our events," Ann excitedly said.

"We sure are, the Bent Bar crews are hard to beat," Casey said.

"I'll vouch for that. Son, that was one heck of a ride. That horse bucked with a vengeance. He sure wanted you off of his back," Duke said.

"He didn't like me too much after his first few jumps," Casey said.

"Whatever his reasons were, he sure put on a show and the crowd loved the way you stuck right with him after he exploded like he did," Johnson said.

"The thanks should go to Bill for getting Moon Shot to blow up like that," Casey said and grinned at Bill. Everyone quizzically looked at Bill, who just smiled, but said nothing.

A pretty, dark haired girl walked up and congratulated Casey on winning. Ann didn't recognize her. She must be from another county, Ann thought. Casey's attention shifted to the admiring girl and he turned away from the group he was talking with. He took her by the arm and began telling the story of his ride as they walked away. "I thought I was in trouble for a while, but then I figured out what shifty old Moon Shot was up to. I just changed my style to stay one jump ahead of him,"they heard Casey say.

"Hey, Case, where are you going? You promised to buy me a cold drink," Bill shouted.

Casey turned and yelled back, "I'll catch you later, Bill."

Bill grinned and said to no one in particular, "Shifty old Moon Shot, huh. It looked to me like shifty old Moon Shot launched him into outer space on that last jump."

Everyone laughed at Bill's sarcasm and Johnson said, "Come on, I'll buy everyone a cold drink."

Ann wanted to care for Buster so she excused herself. She said she wanted to get Buster back to the ranch early so he could rest up in familiar surroundings. Tomorrow would be a big day and they both needed their rest to be in top form for the finals. Johnson agreed. He said for her not to wait up for him tonight as he was going to stay in town with Sam and Duke and maybe take in the dance later in the evening. "Okay, if you're staying in town, then you could keep an eye on Casey and try to keep him from getting in any trouble tonight," she jokingly said.

Johnson laughed and said, "That would be impossible, he'll be so tied up with that pretty little filly he just walked off with, that he wouldn't pay any attention to me anyway." Ann winced at Johnson's remark about the strange girl Casey had taken up with, but managed to smile. She felt a slight twinge of irritation when the girl came along and took him away.

"Well, have fun tonight. I'll look after everything at the ranch," she said. She left and walked toward the parking area. Ann was happy with the outcome of the day's events. Now she was anxious to start preparing for the finals on Sunday. The competition was going to be tougher and she wanted both herself and Buster to be well rested and ready to meet it head on. She loaded Buster and headed for home.

When they arrived at the ranch, James was waiting by the barn to hear the results. Ann pulled in close to the barn and got out of the truck with a smile on her face. "Well, darn it. Tell me, Annie, how did you and Casey do?" he said.

Ann smiled proudly and said, "Two rides. Two winners."

"Hooray, the Bent Bar does it again," James excitedly said.

"I'll tell you all about it while I unload Buster and put him away," she said. James helped Ann with Buster. They put him in a clean stall and gave him a small amount of grain and a ration of good grass hay. Ann related the day's events while they worked. He listened closely and was delighted when Ann told about winning the barrels and Casey pulling off a winning ride on a horse that had a poor reputation for bucking. Ann told James about the crowd's reaction when Moon Shot unexpectedly blew up and started bucking as if his life depended on it.

James slowly shook his head back and forth in admiration of Casey's wild ride. "Ole' Case is really something," James said.

Ann was awake before daylight Sunday morning. This was the big day. She had to hold her lead and make a faster run than Marsha in order to win the finals. There were other riders that would be trying to overtake her and Marsha for a chance at first place. Buster and I will have to go in there really trying hard, she thought. When she got to the barn it seemed strangely deserted. She turned on the lights and saw Buster looking over the gate of his stall. He gave her a welcoming whinny. "Good morning to you, Mr. Buster. I hope you had a good night's rest, because we've got a lot to accomplish today," she said. She fed Buster and then went out to the trailer and pulled her saddle out of the tack compartment. While Buster was eating she carefully went over every bit of the rigging on her saddle. She looked for any frayed or broken straps or cinches. She wanted to be sure everything was still in first class condition and would not fail during their run. She reminded herself of the old saying, "Because the nail was lost the shoe was lost. Because the shoe was lost the horse was lost." A broken strap or cinch had cost more than one barrel racer a championship, she thought.

She finished checking her equipment and went back to Buster's stall. Using a large brush, she began grooming him. As usual, Buster stood stock still, enjoying the attention. She didn't hear Johnson come into the barn and was startled when he said, "Good morning." Surprised, she turned and looked in his direction.

"Good morning. Are you okay?" she asked. He was looking rough around the edges this morning.

"I'm fine. I got home late last night," he said.

"How about Casey?" Ann asked.

"I don't know, he was still going strong when I left the dance," Johnson said.

Ann decided to change the subject and said, "I'm almost ready to go. Can I help you with any chores before we leave?"

"No, you go ahead. I'll see you at the rodeo. Good luck, Annie. I know you can win," Johnson said.

Ann arrived at the rodeo grounds earlier than she had yesterday. She was rewarded with lots of open parking spots. She parked perfectly on her first attempt. Ann unloaded Buster and tied him at the rear of the trailer. She had lots of time before the start of the day's events and wisely used it grooming and rubbing Buster down. When she was satisfied with her preparations, she strolled around talking and chatting with other competitors. Occasionally someone would ask about her ride off the cliff. She wished that night would be forgotten. She saw the buckskin horse that belonged to Marsha Miller tied to a fancy horse trailer with living quarters built into the front. Curiously, she walked in that direction to get a better look at the impressive outfit.

As she neared the trailer, the door to the living quarters suddenly opened and Marsha stepped out and glared at Ann. Embarrassed, Ann said, "Hi, my name's Annie Olsen."

There was a long silence while Marsha stared at Ann. Finally Marsha said, "Aren't you the girl who got lucky yesterday and managed to finish with a good time?" It was like a slap in the face. Marsha's insinuation that luck was the only reason for her good time inflamed her. Ann's first reaction to the callous statement was to lash out with a verbal defense of her ride. She stared back at the older girl while she tried to compose herself and maintain her dignity. Furious inside, Ann told herself to let the rude comment pass as if it hadn't bothered her. She was surprised that Marsha showed such small character for a rider of her ability. She thought Marsha Miller, who was in the top ten of the state standings, would have shown more integrity than she had in her obvious attempt to degrade her ride.

Smiling sweetly, Ann said, "I get lucky once in a while." Then still smiling, Ann turned and walked away. Marsha succeeded in irritating her. Ann was furious about the rude comment. She and Buster worked hard training and preparing for that ride. Luck had nothing to do with it, she thought. She told herself that she had to forget that incident and not let it affect her ride today. She tried to put it out of her mind and raise her spirits to the happy level they had been before encountering Marsha.

Ann walked over to the bucking chutes to see if Casey had shown up. She saw him leaning against the fence talking to one of the other riders. As she approached, she heard him describing how he managed to get Moon Shot to put on that great performance. Casey saw her coming and waved as he continued to tell his story. Ann had to wait a few minutes for him to finish. He finished his story and looked down at Ann. She smiled back in amusement. She knew what really happened. She also knew Casey wasn't going to give away the secret of how he provoked Moon Shot into that outstanding performance. Bill taught Casey a useful trick and Casey was going to keep that technique to himself.

"Good morning, little lady, how are you today?" Casey said.

"By the looks of you, I think I'm probably in a lot better shape than you are. Did you get any sleep last night?" Ann asked.

Casey laughed and said, "Yep, I went to bed right after the dance." Then Casey said, "It's almost lunch time, how about if I buy you a hot dog?"

"That sounds good to me," Ann said.

They had lunch at one of the stands in the midway and discussed the coming events. Casey thought they were both in good shape to win the final go around. Ann listened as Casey talked about the good lead they both had and how he was really hoping they would put in good rides today and finish as overall winners in each of their events. "That would be great for me, you know how badly I want to win. The more wins I have to my credit over the next two years will certainly help me obtain a scholarship to the university," Ann said.

"That's true, and the more points I score, the better chance I'll have of making it to the World Championship Rodeo someday," Casey said.

"There's no doubt in my mind that you'll make it there, Casey. Johnson said he's never seen a more natural bronc rider than you," Ann said seriously. Casey looked down at Ann and gave her the biggest smile she thought she had ever seen.

"Did the boss really say that?" Casey asked in unrestrained delight at hearing of Johnson's praise of his riding ability.

"I wouldn't tell you if he hadn't said it," Ann said sternly.

"Well, then, I better not let him down. I drew a good horse today, so I should be able to turn in a high score on him. Maybe I can capture the win and one of those shiny belt buckles they're giving to the winners. Maybe we'll win two buckles for the Bent Bar, Annie," Casey said.

"I hope so," Ann answered.

Casey's ego rose a few notches when he learned of Johnson's opinion of him as a bronc rider. Ann noticed him turn serious for a change. He said, "Ann, I think I'll head over to the chutes, I want to check out my rigging and make sure everything is in good shape. If Johnson thinks I'm that good, I don't want to let him down."

Ann left Casey and went to her trailer to check Buster and make final preparations for her ride. The day was moving right along and the first events would be starting shortly. The Grand Entry was scheduled to begin soon. She saddled Buster and passed the time chatting with her neighbors.

She was in position at the arena entrance when the announcer called for the start of the final events of the High Valley Rodeo. They rode in the Grand Entry Parade and Ann was pleased to feel Buster's enthusiasm as they loped around the arena with the other riders. After the National Anthem, they raced out of the arena, and the rodeo began. Ann rode Buster to an area where she could lightly work the horse, and ready him for their final run. She thought about Marsha's jabs and felt irritated by her uncalled for comments. She wondered if Bill and Johnson would be in the stands to see her run.

Ann scored the fastest time on Saturday. That meant that she would be the first to ride today. She walked Buster back to the arena when she heard the announcer calling the winning times for the event preceding hers. She wanted to be ready to run when they called her name. As Ann was nearing the entrance to the staging area, she saw Marsha ride up on her buckskin. Marsha qualified with the second highest score behind Ann. She would be "on deck" while Ann made her run.

As Ann moved into position to enter the arena, she passed near Marsha. She heard Marsha sarcastically say as she rode past, "Good luck, little Miss Olsen." Ann knew it had been another deliberate attempt to infuriate her. She realized that Marsha was trying to make her lose concentration and cause her to perform poorly. Although Ann reasoned with herself to forget the comments and focus only on the ride, she was unable to keep Marsha Miller out of her mind.

The judge held up his arm and motioned for Ann to move into the arena. Ann moved Buster into the arena and tried to forget Marsha. She heard the announcer introduce her as the leader of the event and then talk briefly about the barrel racing event. Ann could feel Buster's eagerness. He seemed unsettled and Ann wondered if he was picking up her distress over Marsha's remarks. No time to worry about it now, Ann thought.

Ann received the nod from the judge. She nervously turned Buster in a three hundred and sixty degree turn and stopped him in position heading for the first barrel. She took a deep breath and tried to settle down. Buster was jumpy under her and she knew they better go before the anticipation built to a destructive level.

She jumped Buster out toward the first barrel and he raced away as if he were glad to be unleashed. As they neared the barrel, Ann realized they were going to crowd it. She gently tried to pull the horse to the left of the barrel. Buster obediently changed his direction slightly as they came into position to start the turn. Buster managed to complete the turn at a high rate of speed and sprinted away toward the second barrel. Ann was relieved that they executed the turn so well after having to make a correction.

They were running good, but as they approached the second barrel, Ann sensed indecision in Buster. Almost too late, Ann realized she had been unconsciously holding Buster wide of their normal pattern for the second barrel. She over corrected with heavy rein pressure to bring Buster back in line for a better approach. Surprised at the force of the rein pressure, Buster obeyed the command and changed leads to try and follow her cue. That put them on a collision course with the barrel and Ann violently pulled Buster back to the right to avoid hitting the barrel. It worked. Buster darted to the right and then almost immediately Ann reined him hard to the left to make the turn. Buster's speed fell off in the confusion of their approach. He accelerated away from the barrel and Ann knew they lost precious time.

Buster came out of the second barrel at a very slow speed and now it took him an extra stride to reach full speed again. Ann commanded herself to settle down and concentrate on nothing but the last barrel. Their time suffered and they had to attempt to recover it. They seemed to have lost the fine edge of proficiency they needed to win. They reached the third barrel and Ann felt indecision in Buster as he lowered his inside shoulder at the start of the turn. She immediately slacked the reins. She was trying to give the horse confidence again in her commands. By slacking the reins she was hoping to let Buster know she was not going to change his direction like she had on the second barrel. It was the right move. She felt Buster lean into the turn and accelerate away as hard as he could drive. They raced past the finish in a wide open sprint trying to recover lost time.

It was a good run, but Ann knew they might have jeopardized their chances for a first place finish. Ann rode Buster into the alleyway and turned to anxiously wait for her time. Marsha rode into the arena to prepare for her run.

Ann watched Marsha confidently move her horse into position. A growing feeling of uneasiness spread through Ann as she awaited her time. She felt terrible. She let Marsha's needling affect her ride. Live and learn, thought Ann, as she waited. After what seemed an eternity the announcer read her time. "Ann Olsen, riding Buster, scores a time of sixteen and eight-tenths of a second." Ann's heart fell. They ran the course almost a half of a second slower than yesterday. The other riders would have to perform very poorly in order for her and Buster to hold their lead now.

She watched from the back alleyway as Marsha made her run. Disappointment flooded through Ann as Marsha made a blistering run. The buckskin seemed to effortlessly race through the barrels executing the turns with a precision he had not shown Saturday. He had great speed and they flashed around the third barrel and raced for the finish line on a run Ann knew would be extremely fast. Her time was announced and Ann reluctantly admitted that Marsha and the big buckskin horse were indeed good. Now she could see why they were in the top ten in the barrel racing circuit. Marsha's time was a sizzling sixteen and twenty-five one-hundredths of a second.

The times were added together for both days runs. The rider with the lowest combined total would win, with succeeding low times placing second and third. Marsha's overall time was more than four-tenths of a second faster than Ann's total time. Well, I better hope I can hold on to second place at least, Ann thought as she prepared to watch the remaining riders make their runs. When all riders completed their runs and the times were tallied, Ann was pushed back and finished in third place.

Dejected, she rode toward her trailer. She thought about her ride and knew she had been wrong to let Marsha's jabs affect her. "That will not happen again," she said with firm conviction. Buster flicked an ear back toward her as if he was agreeing. Ann laughed and reached down and patted her old friend fondly on the neck and said, "It was my fault, Buster, but don't worry. I won't let her bother me again."

Ann unsaddled Buster and rubbed him down. She hung his hay net in easy reach and headed for the stands to find Johnson and Sam. The thought of relaxing in the stands and watching the rest of the rodeo as a spectator seemed appealing to her. She got to the stands and found them in the same area as yesterday.

Sam and Johnson tried to console Ann about her ride. She shrugged it off and said, "Well, at least I placed third. That will earn me a ribbon and some points in the overall standings. Now I know what it takes to beat a champion. I'll be more prepared next time I have to compete against her."

"The more you ride, the better you'll get," Johnson said.

Casey was getting ready to do just that. His draw for the finals was just being tucked away in chute number one. The horse was a big gray and he had fire in his eyes. Bill grinned at Casey as they watched the crew trying to load the bucking horse into the chute. The horse wasn't cooperating with his handlers and he kicked out at the sides of the chute when they finally got him inside and the gate closed. It sounded like he was trying to tear the chute apart and Bill and Casey moved out of his way. "I'm glad that chute's built as stout as it is," Bill said.

"He's sure trying to tear it apart," Casey said.

"What did you say his name is?" Bill asked.

"His name is Bootlegger, but I think they should have named him The Demolisher. Look what he's trying to do to that chute," Casey said as the big gray horse kept kicking and banging.

"He better settle down or we'll never get your rigging on him," Bill said.

"We'll get somebody to hold his head while we rig this character up," Casey said.

"I'm sure glad it's you riding him and not me. This horse is wild," Bill said.

Casey looked over at Bill and grinned. "Bill, this is just what I was hoping for. When I learned I drew this critter', I was absolutely overjoyed. Why, Bootlegger here is the answer to my prayers. He is a real champion when it comes to bucking. He's a pro. He makes the rest of the stock look like they belong on a "merry-go-round". He'll give me a ride without even having to ask for it. If I can ride him, I'll score high again and that silver buckle is going to belong to me when the day is done," Casey said.

They had someone hold Bootlegger's head against the side of the chute and he temporarily settled down. They got him rigged and Casey delicately lowered himself onto the gray's back. Bill could see fire in the horse's eyes. "Casey, you better make your best ride, cause this old boy means business," Bill said.

Casey turned serious as he glanced at Bill and then focused his attention on the hostile gray. Casey concentrated on the horse under him as he considered the best way to ride.

"If I'm gonna' ride you to the horn, I'm gonna' have to respect you, and pay attention to you, Bootlegger. Every move you make, I'll be there before you. I'll be easy on you. I know you're gonna' give me everything I need to win. I'll follow your moves so close you won't even know I'm on your back. I'll watch your head and you'll give me a clue to your next move. I'll feel your quarters as you gather yourself to throw me off and I'll know what direction you plan on sending me. I'll be ready for you. When you stretch out and try to twist yourself in two, I'll know how you have to land. I'll try to land going in the same direction. When you swap ends I'll probably be late following you, so I'll tuck down a little on the inside. When you hit the ground again you'll throw me right back where I need to be. Yes sir, Bootlegger, you've got my attention and I am going to give you all the respect you deserve."

"Casey! Casey! They're ready for you!" Bill shouted. Casey jerked his head up and came out of his deep concentration. He looked into the arena and saw the questioning look of the judge. They were waiting for his signal indicating that he was ready to ride. He pulled his hat brim down tight on his forehead and adjusted his grip in the rigging. Bill watched as a determined cast settled on Casey's face. Casey looked at the judge and nodded.

Casey never knew when the gate was pulled open. His whole living, breathing world was consumed with total concentration on the gray horse under him. Bootlegger erupted into the arena amidst a spray of flying dirt. He took off in three great leaps toward the grandstands to build up speed and momentum. He hit the ground with his front legs off center from his heavy hind quarters. The momentum from his speed carried his hind quarters past his front end and he reversed directions at breakneck speed. He let that great momentum carry him around for a full turn. Before he lost all the energy from those first great leaps, he kicked out hard with both hind legs and somehow twisted his powerful quarters in the air in an attempt to challenge the rider with two different directions of travel.

Casey was up to the task and he rode Bootlegger through the unusual maneuvers with a grace and skill that was delightful to watch. The gray used up his kinetic energy from his first burst and now he had to regain the forces that propelled him in his initial attempts to dislodge Casey. He raced away gathering speed and used precious time on the clock. Bootlegger was an intelligent horse. His first attempt failed to throw the rider and now he changed tactics. He went into a sequence of conventional bucking and spinning. Casey was still in control and when Bootlegger slacked off of the hard twisting maneuvers, he felt like he was going to win this one. The horse bucked straight away and became easier to stay with. Casey maintained his determined concentration. He didn't want to take any chances at this stage of the ride. He knew a horse of Bootlegger's caliber could still have a lot of buck left in him.

Casey heard the eight second horn and a feeling of accomplishment passed through him. He made a good ride. He saw the pick up rider pull in close. Casey deftly reached out and grasped the rider and at the same time shifted his body from the bucking horse to the back of the pick up rider's horse. When Bootlegger was safely out of the way Casey swung down to the ground and walked swiftly toward the chutes. The crowd gave him a standing ovation.

He scored a seventy-eight on Bootlegger. With his high score on Moon Shot, Casey easily won the High Valley Bareback Bronc riding event. He was all smiles when the final results of the event were read by the announcer. He won a silver buckle.

CHAPTER 10

From her vantage point high atop the ridge, Ann looked out across the mountains. She was studying the terrain trying to pick out the best trail to take down into a small meadow where she saw a group of cattle grazing. She wanted to check the stock in this remote pocket of the mountains. It was now her job to scout the high country since James was busy haying.

The crew was haying and Johnson needed all the help he could get until they had their winter supply baled and stored. The weather was clear and dry. Conditions were perfect for drying the long windrows of hay that were cut. There was always an air of uneasiness after the hay had been cut and they waited for it to dry so they could bale it. If it rained on the grass before it dried, the quality would suffer. The winter feed supply depended on harvesting the hay crop without it being damaged by rain or hail.

Ann looked forward to taking over for James and riding the range looking for any problems with either the cattle or horses. Occasionally, fences needed repair and the range rider had to carry a small arsenal of tools and equipment in the saddle bags. Before leaving the ranch headquarters, Ann loaded Buster's saddlebags with pliers, staples and other odds and ends she might need to repair any fence problems she might encounter. So far, there were no problems. All the cattle were in good shape and the fences she rode by were okay. She checked the remote water tanks that stored water brought by pipelines from springs in the higher country. When their stock grazed the dry areas of the mountains they needed a water source nearby or else they would return to areas that had water and over graze them. These remote tanks helped insure the animals would graze the whole range. All of the tanks were running water into the overflows, so Ann knew the pipelines were okay.

"Buster, if we get that little bunch of cattle checked and there are no problems, we can make a beeline for the Dry Boulder country and see if we can find the mares before darkness sets in," Ann said. Buster quizzically pointed his ears in Ann's direction. Buster was in great condition now. His coat was shiny and his muscular form stood out impressively. Ann continued to work Buster at least three times a week on the barrels since they competed in the High Valley rodeo. She wanted him to remain in top shape for other events coming up during the summer. The work on the ranch also helped strengthen Buster and he was running the barrels as well or better than he ever ran them before.

Ann picked her way down the side of the ridge and rode toward the meadow. The cows heard her coming. When she broke out of a small clump of timber and rode into the meadow, she was greeted with the sight of the white faced cattle watching her and Buster approach. She talked to the cattle as she circled them. They all seemed to be in good health. Their ears were up and their eyes were bright as they watched her slowly ride around them. They carried a fair amount of body fat and she could see the grass in the meadow was deep and lush.

"Girls, you and your calves all look good. I won't bother you very long. I'm just looking you over to make sure you're okay and then Buster and I will leave you alone to go about the business of raising your babies. You can look forward to us checking on you about once every week for the rest of the summer. James is needed on the ranch. I'll be taking his place until school starts in the fall," Ann said to the cows as Buster slowly circled them.

"Everything looks good here, Buster. What say we take off for Dry Boulder and look in on Stormy, Flame and the rest of the mares," Ann said as she turned Buster and headed out of the meadow. Buster stepped right out. He knew which way home was and he wasn't bashful about showing a lot more enthusiasm going, than he did coming. When they got back on top of the ridge, Ann slacked off on the reins and Buster took off across the side hills in the direction of Dry Boulder Coulee.

The mares were easy to find and Buster first saw the old bay mare when they were still almost a mile away. As usual, the mare spotted them first and was standing on a high spot watching their approach. The band was spread out behind her with their heads down grazing. A few of the colts were grouped off to the side of the main band. When the colts saw the horse and rider approaching, several of them started whinnying a warning and inquisitively trotted in the rider's direction. The colts placed great importance on the discovery of Ann and Buster. They whinnied loudly and looked back at the band to make sure everyone knew someone was coming.

Ann saw Stormy among the group of colts approaching. Buster whinnied loudly when they were within a quarter of a mile of the other horses. Buster was anxious to reach the band and Ann let him break into an easy lope across the open bench land they were crossing. When Buster whinnied, they heard an answer from the small group of colts trotting toward them. They watched as Stormy separated from his friends and broke into a run straight for them. He recognized Buster's voice and was anxious to see his older friend.

With head held high and his tail straight out, Stormy raced in their direction. Ann watched as the whole group of young foals broke into a run, following Stormy. She pulled Buster to a full stop so they could watch the approaching band of colts. It was a sight that was a joy to behold. The bright sorrel colt led the pack and moved toward them with a speed and grace that thrilled Ann. Stormy quickly outdistanced his friends and raced toward them whinnying his greeting to Buster. Buster started fidgeting as Stormy drew near. He knew how the young colt liked to race up to other horses and slam on the brakes at the very last second.

Stormy hadn't changed. When he was almost upon them, Ann pulled Buster off to the side to try to get out of the colt's way. It wasn't necessary. Stormy's control had improved since his days in the corrals with Flame and Buster as his playmates. Still going flat out, Stormy sat back on his haunches and transitioned from a full run into a sliding stop. He came to a full stop just a half stride from Buster and Ann. He proudly stood back up on all fours and moved right to Buster. They touched muzzles and nickered softly to one another. They both seemed happy to see each other again.

How Stormy had grown! His short time in the mountains had done wonders. His coat was bright and shiny and it seemed as if he had grown a foot. Ann looked him over closely as he and Buster exchanged greetings. His muscles were developing and his condition appeared excellent. The lush grasses that were so nutritious for Flame and the young horse were plentiful this time of year. The horses were showing the benefits of summering in the mountains. Ann stepped off Buster and Stormy moved up stretching his muzzle toward her. Pleased, Ann rubbed him lightly on his forehead.

The other colts arrived, but they held their distance a short way from Ann and Buster. One curious filly took a few steps in their direction and Stormy quickly laid his ears back and warned her off. These strangers belonged to Stormy and he had no intention of sharing them with any-one else. Ann laughed as she watched Stormy warning the other horses not to get too close. He seemed to have achieved a high rank among his peers and Ann noticed the other colts kept their distance and did not dispute his claim to the newcomers.

Ann mounted Buster and moved him in the direction of the mares. Stormy proudly trotted ahead of them, leading the way toward the band. The rest of the colts followed at a respectful distance. "Stormy, it sure didn't take you long to become the leader of the foals. How are you getting along with the old bay mare these days? Is she treating you any better than she did the first time you met her?" Ann asked. She remembered how the bay mare had lashed out at Stormy and chased him away when Ann had first brought him into the mountains earlier in the summer.

Ann and Buster circled the band looking for any injuries or problems with the horses. Stormy stayed with them as Ann inspected the mares. When Ann spotted Flame, she reined Buster in that direction. Stormy trotted in front, toward his mother. Flame moved toward them and when they met, Ann stepped out of the saddle to give the splendid mare a warm greeting. Flame seemed happy to see them. Ann carefully looked at her injured shoulder and was delighted to see that it had healed very well. Stormy constantly tried to get between Ann and Flame, making a pest of himself. He wanted all of the attention and sharing just didn't occur to him. Ann shooed him away while she looked Flame over.

The mountain grass had been good for the young mare. She looked terrific, her sorrel coat radiated health and gleamed in the afternoon sun. Her hair had grown over all the scrapes and injuries she received during the night of the flood. Her eyes were bright and her constant attention to Stormy indicated to Ann that she had recovered fully from that frightening night. "Flame, I think all four of us are lucky to be here today. I know what Buster and I went through on that terrible night, but only you hold the secret of your ordeal during that flood. Both you and Stormy have scars from the night of the flood, and only you know how Stormy received the injuries that caused the scars on his neck," Ann said, as she looked the mare over.

She climbed back in the saddle and continued inspecting the mares. Stormy pranced along beside Buster acting as if he had found a long lost friend. Buster enjoyed the company of the young stallion and would occasionally reach out in a playful nip toward the colt. Flame followed along for a few minutes, then lost interest and went back to grazing the long green grass on the hillside. When Ann was satisfied that the band was in good shape, she rode to where Flame was grazing. She sat on Buster and looked the sorrel mare over again. She watched her graze and noticed that every few minutes Flame would look up to check the whereabouts of her colt. "You really protect that little guy, don't you,

Flame?" Ann said with emotion and deep affection for the mare.

Reluctantly, Ann turned and started Buster moving in the direction of Dry Boulder Coulee and the trail leading out of the mountains toward the ranch. As they rode away, Stormy followed along. When they had gone a short distance from the band, they could hear Flame calling to the young colt. Stormy stopped and looked in the direction of the band. He looked back toward Ann and Buster making their way down the ridge. Whinnying loudly, he turned and took off at full speed toward Flame and the band of brood mares.

The next day, Ann was at the barn early enough to catch Casey before he left with the haying crew. "Hey, Case, what time are you getting back tonight?" she asked him.

"It will probably be about dark. Why, what's up?" he asked.

"I want to know if you're going to try to take in the Twin Forks rodeo on Labor Day?" she asked him.

"Maybe, but I haven't thought about it too much. We've been so busy that rodeoing hasn't been at the top of my list lately," he said.

"Well, think about it and maybe I'll see you tonight," Ann said.

Casey waved at her and said, "Okay."

Twin Forks was two hundred miles from High Valley and their rodeo always drew large crowds and more competitors than High Valley's rodeo. The Twin Forks rodeo was a premier event in Montana. Ann knew that if she could compete against Marsha Miller in the High Valley rodeo, she was sure she could compete and do well at the prestigious Twin Forks rodeo. The level of competition would be high and she knew this would be one event that Marsha would not miss. Ann was anxious to ride against Marsha again. She was hoping Casey would want to ride in the bareback event and would go to Twin Forks with her.

Ann kept busy with her ranch chores, but kept a lookout for Johnson. Occasionally, he came in from the fields to get some tools or a part for the machinery they were using. She saw his truck coming late in the afternoon and walked over when he pulled in. "Hi, Annie, how's it going?" he asked as he got out of the truck.

"Okay with me, how about you?" she asked.

"We're moving right along. We've just about got the first cutting baled. If it doesn't rain for a few more days we'll have it finished," he said.

"Well, that sure is good news. I know that will take a load off your mind," she said.

"Yes, it's always good to know your winter feed is put away," Johnson said.

"If you have a minute, I'd like to talk to you about something," Ann said.

Johnson said, "Sure, let's go to the office. That's where I'm headed anyway."

They walked into the barn and Ann asked Johnson about the Twin Forks rodeo. "I'm thinking about riding in the Twin Forks rodeo and thought I would check with you before I made any plans," she said.

"Ann, I have no objection to you riding in that rodeo. In fact, I think it might do you some good. That's a first class rodeo and you would be riding against the best in the state. That level of competition would be good for you. I think it's a great idea," Johnson said.

"Maybe we could all go. I know if Casey will ride, then Bill will want to go and I sure hope you'll go along too," Ann said.

"It's possible. Labor Day is always a slack time here on the ranch. All the hay has been put up and it's too early to bring the cows out of the hills. We most always have some spare time around then," Johnson said.

"School starts a week before the rodeo. I've been studying through the summer and I'm confident my teacher will give me the Friday off before the rodeo. That way, I can take Buster down a day ahead and he'll be rested for Saturday," Ann said.

"It sounds reasonable," Johnson said.

Johnson walked into his office and sat down. Ann noticed how tired he looked. They had been working hard from daylight to dark trying to get the hay put up before the weather turned bad. Johnson was a hard driver and Ann knew he would work harder than he would ever ask his crew. The long days were starting to catch up with him. "You know, Johnson, I got an "A" in my accounting course last year. I'll be a junior in high school this year and I'm taking some advanced courses like you suggested. I'll bet that I could do a lot of that paperwork for you," Ann said.

Johnson stared at Ann, then said, "That's an excellent idea. I wish I had thought of it myself. I'll bet you could handle it just fine and it's about time you became more involved in the way this ranch operates. Why don't you start by filing all these bills. Categorize them according to the various facets of our operations. Things such as, hay, cattle, horses, machinery, et cetera. Then take each category and add them separately, so we can see where our money is going," Johnson said as he pointed to a basket that was overflowing with invoices.

"I can do that easy enough. I'll start on it as soon as I'm done with my chores," she said.

She helped Johnson load his truck with boxes of baling twine for the balers they were using in the fields. "I've got to get right back. The baler James is running is getting low on twine and I don't want him to run out," Johnson said.

"I'll see you tonight," she said. Ann looked over the paperwork on Johnson's desk. There's nothing difficult here, just a lot of tedious work. I'll have this done before noon tomorrow, Ann thought. She left the office and headed for the corral where Buster was kept. She brought him into the barn and saddled him.

"Time for a little practice, Buster. It looks like we're going to go to Twin Forks and see if we can do better than we did at High Valley," Ann said to the horse. She loped Buster through the pattern several times and then stopped for a breather. She held Buster in a position to look over the course. Since losing her concentration at High Valley during their final run, Ann had schooled herself to put everything out of her mind except the actual execution of running the cloverleaf pattern of the barrels. She blamed herself for bumbling the first turn at High Valley and didn't want to ever let that happen again. Buster was pushing his upper limits, but she still felt they could improve and win at Twin Forks.

She walked Buster away from the finish line. She talked to him and his ears came back toward her. Ann had developed a system of conveying a warning to Buster that the next run would be at maximum effort. Her body movements such as settling down in the saddle and adjusting her boots position in the stirrups gave Buster the indications to prepare himself for a full run. Ann was a good trainer. She wanted there to be no doubt in the horse's mind that this time they were not going to walk, trot or lope through the pattern. They were going to run flat out.

Buster ran the course with no mistakes or miscues on Ann's part. It was a good fast run and Ann was pleased. She would have someone time their runs a few days before the rodeo. A time check would show how well they had improved. Buster was in good physical shape. Ann would hold him to light workouts until the last week before the rodeo. During the last week she would put more pressure on him to try and develop his top speed to an even higher level.

Because of the injuries Buster suffered on the ride down the cliff, they didn't have time to reach the high level of proficiency for the High Valley rodeo that they were now approaching. They were improving with each practice session and Ann developed new confidence in their ability. She was beginning to look forward to the pressure of competing at Twin Forks.

She unsaddled Buster and brushed him. She wanted to get her chores done before the men came back from haying. Ann wanted to talk to Casey before he went home for the day. She cleaned out all the stalls in the barn and spread fresh straw for bedding. Buster was the only animal using the barn now, but Ann liked to have the stalls clean and ready to use in case an injured cow or horse was brought in. She enjoyed the work and was soon finished. Ann went into the office and started on Johnson's paperwork.

She heard the trucks coming and went out to see Casey. Two pickups pulled in and parked near the barn. Casey and Bill were in one and Ann walked toward their truck. Casey saw Ann and waved as he reached into the back of the pickup and pulled out a box of tools. "Let me put these tools away and I'll meet you in Johnson's office," he said. Casey headed for the shop building with the tools. The men in the other truck waved to her and walked to their trucks to head home. They were temporary workers that Johnson hired when he needed extra help.

Bill walked with her back to the barn. "I'll walk back with you, Ann, I have to wait for Casey anyway," Bill said.

"I guess you've probably heard that I want to ride at Twin Forks during the Labor Day rodeo," Ann said.

"Yep, Casey told me about it. How are you and Buster doing, anyway?" he asked her.

"We're getting our rough edges smoothed out. I think there's gonna' be some surprises in store for the competition this time. I was a little green about running the barrels against that level of competition on the Fourth. I found out that you better not let anything bother you. Just concentrate on the job and don't let anyone distract you," Ann said.

Bill laughed and said, "I feel sorry for those girls at Twin Forks, I can't wait to get down there myself." Ann smiled. Bill had just given her Casey's answer. Bill wouldn't be going unless Casey was. Ann grinned at Bill. He couldn't figure out what she was grinning about.

Casey walked into the barn and saw them standing outside of Johnson's office. As he walked in their direction, he said, "I see the boss's truck, so he'll be here in a second." Ann was standing with a smile on her face and Casey wondered why. Ann didn't say a thing. She had her answer about Casey going to Twin Forks and that was the reason for her smile.

"By the way, Ann, today I scratched the silver buckle I won at the High Valley rodeo. So, I think I'll go on down to Twin Forks and win me another one, if Johnson can do without me that weekend," Casey said. Ann and Bill busted out laughing and Casey couldn't figure out what was so funny. It must be a private joke, he thought. They were laughing simply because of the way Casey decided to tell Ann he would be going to the rodeo.

Johnson walked in while Casey was talking and overheard his comment about the belt buckle. "If you win another one, then maybe you'll give me that old scratched up one," Johnson said.

"Well--wait a minute now. I need the old one to remember Moon Shot," Casey said with a grin. Everyone laughed and Johnson invited them into the office to discuss the day's happenings. They were winding up their baling operations for the first cutting of hay. On normal years the Bent Bar ranch would be able to harvest their hay fields in July and then again in August. This first cutting had gone well and they would be finished in a few days if the weather held.

"When we're done haying we can get on to other projects. We could use more pens and a big strong corral. I'd like to start building better horse handling facilities and maybe even some paddocks for keeping outside broodmares. In a few years we might need extra facilities. If Ann's stallion comes along like I think, I'm sure we'll be getting breeding requests from owners that would like to breed their mares to him," Johnson said.

"I see a strong market for a breeder who can breed and train performance horses. Horse shows and rodeo are becoming popular and people are always looking for a prospective horse they can buy and use for competition," Bill said.

"In order for a ranch like the Bent Bar to remain successful, we need to diversify. The price of cattle fluctuates and in bad years we've always been pinched for cash. This ranch needs to stabilize its cash flow. If we can develop a program of breeding and training outstanding performance horses, then I think we'll open a whole new area of successful operation. That will be a financial help when cattle prices are low. Some years I think we're just not going to make it. I juggle our money a hundred different ways trying to make ends meet. It would be nice to have something to fall back on during those years. I think the answer lies in good horseflesh," Johnson said.

There was a long silence as everyone tried to digest what they just heard. Ann began to grasp the enormity of what Johnson said. If he meant that the Bent Bar was going to pursue breeding and training horses in a commercial venture, she was all for it. Horses were her major interest. She always felt the Bent Bar could produce and train outstanding horses. Slowly, it began to dawn on Ann that this was really what she dreamed. She began to get excited about the prospect of the ranch branching out into a commercial horse facility. Ideas began to flash through her mind. They could build an indoor arena. They could stand several good stallions for breeding purposes, and they could hold horsemanship clinics. The possibilities were unlimited and Ann's excitement began to rise. Her thoughts were interrupted when Bill said, "There's a big market out there for good horses, it could sure carry this outfit in bad years and we have the people who can make a program like that work!!

"It's a wonderful idea and I know we can make it work. In two years when I start college, I plan on majoring in equine science. I've already decided that horses will be a major part of my life and a degree would go a long way in helping me achieve that goal," Ann said. Everyone watched the excitement building in Ann and listened to her comments with interest.

Johnson looked over at Casey and said, "Case, what do you think? Could we make a profit selling performance horses?"

Everyone looked at Casey, waiting for his answer. He stared back at them with a serious look on his face for a change. Long seconds passed and still he did not answer. Finally, Johnson said, "Well, Case, what do you think?"

Casey broke his pensive silence and said, "First, I'd like to tell you that, I for one, have always gotten along better with horses than I have with cows. Some of the horses I've known are a lot smarter than some of the people I've known, present company not included. The satisfaction I receive from breaking a good horse and then watching someone take that horse and use him for a good purpose is more compensation than any paycheck can give. I like the excitement of bringing a horse along and then watching him give you all he's got when you ask for it. That's what rodeo is all about. Performance. Athletic ability. Intelligence. Training. If this ranch pursued a program of developing these traits into its horses, I think we would see serious rodeo contenders asking for our stock. The ranch has always developed these traits in its horses. However, except for selling a few horses a year, we've always kept the good stock on the ranch. People in this area respect the Bent Bar for its horses. We don't raise enough horses to satisfy the demand for them. The simple fact that we always receive top dollar for our horses shows the high regard that people in our area hold for our horses. We've got a reputation locally, I think we can do it on a larger scale."

Casey wasn't through talking and everyone in the small office listened attentively as he continued. "We have some excellent seed stock here. Thanks to Johnson's desire over the years to only breed and raise the best of stock on his ranch, we now have a line of horses that's hard to beat. Just look at what we have out on the range right now. Even that old bay mare that gives the orders, is sharper and quicker than most horses you find competing in today's events. Look at her offspring. Take Flame for instance, she's probably one of the finest horses I've ever seen structurally, for a performance horse. She's built to do it. Her conformation says it all. The bottom line is progeny. Look at Stormy. We can see what he's going to develop into. A champion. Plain and simple. We have here on the Bent Bar ranch the foundation stock to develop outstanding horses that horsemen from all over the nation would be proud to own. I would be behind a program like that, one hundred and ten percent. To answer your question, boss, yes, I think we could show a profit breeding, breaking and training good horses."

The room was dead quiet when Casey finished. No one ever heard Casey talk so serious about a subject, or, for so long. They were all deep in their own thoughts, considering what Casey said. Ann listened to every word he said. Some of his statements had electrified her with excitement. A large scale horse operation on the Bent Bar would be a dream come true for her. With the combined knowledge of Johnson, Bill and Casey, she knew they could be successful.

Johnson brought everyone out of their deep thoughts. "Well, you all made some interesting observations about increasing our involvement with horses. I'm glad to hear that you're in favor of expanding our herd. I want you to think about it. Think about how we should go about getting started. What kind of facilities should we build? How should it be managed? What improvements can we make to our existing facilities? Just think about it for now and when we get our second cutting of hay put up, we'll have some extra time on our hands. Then, we can take a few steps in that direction. Our cattle operation is our main source of revenue and we'll continue to improve our herd. Any branch operations, like we just discussed, will be handled with the same amount of professionalism we show in our cattle. We'll get together again this fall and discuss any ideas or suggestions you may have about expanding into performance horses," Johnson said.

Ann and the others nodded. Plainly, what Johnson proposed had stirred deep thought amongst them. Ann was enthusiastic about expanding into performance horses. She knew Casey and Bill were all for the idea too. The future of the Bent Bar looked exciting. "There's one other thing, Ann. You'll need a travel permit from the brand inspector's office to haul Buster to the Twin Forks rodeo, since you'll be traveling out of your home county. Give Duke a call at his office and make arrangements for him to issue you a permit. I have friends in the Twin Forks area and I'll see about a place for you and Buster to stay while you're there," Johnson said.

"Oh, okay, I was wondering about that," Ann said.

I want everyone to know that I appreciate your input. I wouldn't attempt to go into a horse operation if it wasn't for having you around. Sometimes I think you people are half horse the way you handle them. I've got a lot of confidence in everyone here, and I think we can do a good job of it. Now, it's getting late and you better start for home. I'll see everyone tomorrow," Johnson said.

Bill and Casey filed out of the office. As they walked away, Ann heard Casey say to Bill, "That's the best news I've heard in a long time, partner."

Ann left Johnson alone in the office and walked toward the house. Johnson's proposal was welcome news. She had definite ideas about a successful breeding program and her colt, Stormy, played a major role in her plans. She often thought that she was capable of breeding and training barrel horses to supplement the ranch's income. With the right facilities and the professional help available right here on the ranch, she knew it could become a reality. She was often asked if Buster was for sale. There always seemed to be a market for well trained barrel horses. If they trained horses, she knew they would have no trouble selling them. It was a wonderful feeling to think they might be going into the horse business in a serious way.

She would be riding Stormy in a few years and if he performed in the barrels like she suspected, they would certainly have a winner on their hands. An accomplished barrel champion would be a big drawing card when they advertised his stallion services. Stormy was going to play a key role in their plans to enter the performance horse business.

Ann took care of Johnson's paperwork the following morning. She would gradually take more and more paperwork from Johnson. It would relieve him of the tedious task and give him more time for the important job of managing the ranch. She started working Buster harder on the barrels. He was getting plenty of exercise. Ann's ranch chores involved a lot of riding and Buster seemed to be on the go constantly. Between the ranch work and practicing the barrels, Buster's condition steadily improved.

Ann and Buster made their last trip into the mountains the week before school started. They didn't have to look far for the mares and their foals on this trip. The old bay mare had moved the band down into the lower elevations. Summer was about over and fall temperatures were descending upon the mountain country. The temperature was starting to drop below freezing at night in the higher elevations. There had probably been killing frosts up high and maybe the old bay had moved the band down lower to forage on the sweeter grass not yet nipped by frost, she thought. Ann was pleasantly surprised to find the band all the way down by Gunpowder Creek.

Stormy raced up to meet them. He was in the habit of looking for Buster and Ann when they rode out on their weekly check. He crossed the creek to meet them and then raced back through the water toward the band. The other foals raced with him but kept their distance when Stormy came up to Buster. He laid down the law with the other foals and they knew not to interfere with his friends or they would have to face his wrath. They respected Stormy's dominance and did not approach closer than a few lengths from Buster. Ann witnessed Stormy savagely attacking another colt that came too close.

They crossed the creek and rode into the band. Stormy ran to Flame and Ann saw the sorrel mare watching them approach. Flame looked sensational, Ann thought, as she rode toward her. Her bright coat was glistening and her superb muscular form radiated strength. "What a beautiful animal you are, Flame!" Ann said. She rode Buster right up to Flame and the two horses touched muzzles and exchanged greetings. Ann's gaze slowly moved over the mare's body. She could see no indication of stress or pain in the lovely mare's demeanor. She was completely healed. "I don't think we have to worry about you any longer, Flame. You look great," Ann said. "Next year you'll be able to raise another foal and I hope it will be just as good as Stormy."

Reluctantly, Ann turned Buster away from the band and rode higher into the mountains. She still had to check the cattle. Their rides into the mountains had built a great deal of stamina in Buster. All through the summer they made long rides into the higher elevations where the air was quite thin. Buster became accustomed to working in the clear, thin mountain air. His stamina increased remarkably and he could go all day without tiring. His muscles toned and he was the picture of a working cow horse. Ann had never seen him look so healthy. She had high hopes of improving their time around the barrels.

During the last week of summer, Ann started pushing Buster for high speed performance around the barrels. She worked him harder than ever before. The horse was in great shape, and the young trainer felt he was capable of lower times. Bill started timing their runs and Ann found that their work was starting to pay dividends. They were running consistently below sixteen seconds. Buster's interest in running the course remained high and he actually seemed to look forward to the workout when Ann saddled him and headed for the arena.

When school started, Ann was well prepared. She selected courses to help her with ranch management and accounting. There was no doubt in her mind that ranching would be her life. She wanted to be prepared for college with an arsenal of earned credits pertaining to agriculture and equine fields. Ann still had two years of high school left and she meant to make the most of it. She was a good student and studied hard through the summer. When she asked for the first Friday of the school week off to attend the rodeo in Twin Forks, her teacher granted the request.

That last week seemed to fly by. Ann worked Buster very lightly. On Thursday, she asked Bill to time them for one run. It would be the last time they practiced before riding in the actual event on Saturday. Everyone was anxious to see how they were doing and all the hands showed up to watch. They sat on the top rail of the fence and offered encouragement. Buster was never in better shape, or ran as well as he was running now. Ann worked on her mental control and concentration. She felt better about their performance than ever before. They reached a peak and Ann felt confident they would do well at Twin Forks.

Bill was in position. Ann rode over to the fence and asked, "How did you know we were getting ready to make a hard run with a timer?"

"A little bird flew over and said, "Buster's gonna' take Annie on a fast ride around the barrels, you better get up there and watch," Casey said. Everyone laughed.

"Annie, this is our last chance to watch before you leave for Twin Forks. We wouldn't miss it," James said.

"Thanks," Ann said.

She loped Buster down the arena and eased him into a fast gallop coming back to the starting line. She wanted Buster warmed up and to know what was on her mind. He was ready. She nodded to Bill and moved Buster into the same position they always used as a starting point. Repetition helps solve a lot of problems, Ann thought. She gave Buster the orders to go and he raced away. Buster went in a straight line to the left side of the barrel. He smoothly circled and raced for the second barrel. Again he executed a perfect turn and came out of number two heading exactly for their entry point for turn number three. It was a perfect run. They came out of three with Buster straining to reach top speed. They crossed the finish line at full speed. It was a great run and Ann knew they would have a good time. She was right. Bill looked at her and said loudly, "Great time! Fifteen and seventy-eight hundredths of a second!" The men on the fence cheered and clapped when they heard the time. It was Ann's best time ever.

"Annie, I think Marsha isn't going to be happy to see you and Buster show up on Saturday. You're really running good and you're gonna' be hard to beat," James called out.

"Thanks, James. We plan on making her earn her points this trip. I sure wish you'd come down and watch us one day," Ann said.

"Someday maybe I will, but somebody has to stay and look after things. I'll be rootin' for you just as hard as if I were there," James said.

"We're done with our haying for the year, the second cutting is baled and stored. Our feed is put up, so Bill and I will be down on Saturday," Johnson said.

"If you get down there tomorrow and find you've forgotten somethin', then give us a call and we'll bring it down Saturday," Bill added.

"Thanks. I'll be leaving early. I have a nine o'clock appointment with the brand inspector to get a travel permit for

Buster. Then we'll drive to Twin Forks and hopefully get there in the early afternoon," Ann said.

"I'll have my gear ready and meet you at Duke's office in the morning," Casey said.

CHAPTER 11

Ann felt guilty when she drove through town on Friday morning and saw the kids heading for school. She was excited. She wouldn't have to spend Friday in school. She was headed for Twin Forks and the thrill of competing in a first class rodeo against stiff competition. Ann tooted the horn and waved as she drove by school. She saw several of her friends wave back and heard someone yell, "Good luck, Annie, we'll be rooting for you!" Happily, she drove toward the brand inspector's office.

She was early, but Duke was in his office. There was no sign of Casey. She parked close to the office and walked inside. She flushed with pleasure when Duke greeted her and said, "Mornin', Annie, you really make this town proud of you. Taking on that competition down at Twin Forks at your age is quite an achievement. You're riding against some of the best in the state, and the best part is, I think you can beat them," Duke cheerfully said. Ann was too pleased with Duke's statement to say anything, she just smiled.

"Okay, let's get the paper work done for your travel permit. I need to see your bill of sale or proof of ownership for Buster. If you bred the horse yourself, I would like to see a detailed description of his markings," Duke said.

Ann handed Duke a description of Buster's markings and said, "My dad bred Buster on the ranch sixteen years ago. He was given to me when I was a baby. Buster and I are the same age. You've known Buster as long as I have, Duke. You know he belongs to me."

"I do remember Buster as a foal. However, I need to check him anyway. The law requires me to check every animal that comes through here, and that's what I intend to do. Now let's unload Buster and let me have a look," Duke said. Slightly embarrassed, Ann left the office and walked to the trailer.

She realized now that she should not have questioned Duke about inspecting Buster, even though he knew Buster belonged to her. Duke's reputation as a strict and just brand inspector was well known in the valley. Men like Duke were certainly an asset to the livestock industry, Ann thought, as she unlatched the gate to the stock trailer. Ann heard a loud noise and looked up to see Casey driving up in his old wreck. He parked and started to take his gear out of the back of his truck.

Ann backed Buster out of the trailer so Duke could inspect him. Casey threw his gear into the back of the Bent Bar truck and walked back to see Duke looking Buster over. Before anyone could even say "Hi," Casey said, "Hey, Duke, what in the world are you looking Buster over for? You know he belongs to Annie!"

Ann froze. Casey said the wrong thing, too. She looked at Duke to see what his reaction would be. Duke had been checking Ann's description of Buster's markings. He looked over at Casey. Ann could see his irritation. She was afraid to breathe. Hopefully Duke would overlook the remark.

Ann watched as Duke stared at Casey for what seemed an eternity. Then Duke looked at Ann and winked. He looked back at Casey and said, "Casey, I don't tell you how to ride them bucking horses, so don't tell me how to do my job, okay?"

Surprised, Casey said, "I'm sorry, Duke, I didn't mean any harm."

Duke smiled and said, "I know, Case, it's just part of the job." Casey smiled back and Ann felt a rush of relief. He had no way of knowing that Ann had just posed the same question. "Okay, kids, load him up. I guess he belongs to you," Duke said smiling. Duke handed Ann a form and said, "Here's your permit. You're all set. Now just make sure you drive careful going to Twin Forks and good luck to both of you at the rodeo. I'll be going down Sunday, so I hope the next time I see you, you'll both be wearing first place buckles."

Ann and Casey left for Twin Forks. They were in a festive mood, because they had the whole weekend ahead and were looking forward to the excitement of the rodeo. Casey talked most of the way and Ann enjoyed listening to some of his ideas about the horse operation Johnson had proposed. Ann had definite ideas of her own and was pleased to hear that Casey's perceptions of a successful operation followed closely with hers. "Like Johnson says, good horseflesh has a definite place on the Bent Bar. If we only breed the best, then we'll really have something to work with," Casey said.

They arrived at Twin Forks in the early afternoon and drove to the rodeo grounds. After registering and paying their entry fees, they walked around the grounds and looked over the arena. Ann planned on being back in the morning to get Buster acclimated to the new surroundings before their run. They stopped to let a shiny new pickup go by pulling a long trailer. When the trailer passed them it stopped, and they saw the driver's side window being rolled down. Marsha Miller leaned her head out and sweetly said, "Hi there, Casey, I was wondering if you were going to show up for this one. I'll be parked in the competitor's area. Stop by and see me when you have time." Casey waved and walked behind the trailer. Stunned that Marsha was so friendly to Casey, Ann stared at her. Marsha looked at Ann and said, "Oh, you're the girl from High Valley. I'm surprised to see you at a big rodeo like this." Then she rolled up her window and drove away, before Ann could respond.

Ann ran to catch up with Casey who was fast disappearing. When she caught up, she said, "Casey, I didn't know you were friends with her. Why did you take off so fast?"

"I don't know. We aren't exactly what you call good friends. She's pestered me since the night of the dance at the High Valley rodeo. I think she thinks we're better friends than we really are," Casey said. He seemed annoyed Marsha had stopped to talk to him. She felt a twinge of hurt when Marsha invited Casey to come see her.

Ann controlled her feelings. She schooled herself to remain in complete control of her emotions. She was determined to not let any distractions influence her ride this time. Changing the subject completely, Ann said, "Case, let's go take a look at the bucking chutes."

Relieved Ann wasn't going to make a big deal about Marsha, Casey said, "Great idea, let's go."

When they were satisfied they had seen all of the grounds, they walked back to the truck and trailer. Ann was anxious to get Buster to the ranch where they would be staying for the weekend. They drove the short distance out of town to the ranch. Johnson's friends made them welcome and got them situated for their stay. Ann put Buster in an empty corral and fed him a good ration of grain, and left his hay net full. Buster looked around the corral, then came back to the grain and started peacefully eating. He looked up at Ann and she laughed. She thought Buster had given her a look of resignation, as if to say, I guess, if this is where I'll have to stay tonight, then I'll just have to make the best of it. Ann watched Buster and thought how much a horse's feelings were like a person's. They always felt uncomfortable when they were in a strange place. Buster would tolerate this place but he would rather be at home in his own corral.

The next morning Ann was up early checking Buster. He gave her a friendly nicker when he saw her coming. Buster met her at the gate, waiting for attention. She rubbed his neck and chest and then gave him a few affectionate slaps on the rump. Ann went to her trailer and portioned out some grain in a tub. While she was feeding Buster, Casey walked up and climbed to the top rail of the corral. "Good morning, Ann, how's he look?" he asked.

"Mornin', Case, he's okay, just a little lonely. Buster never likes to be away from home. He was glad to see me this morning," she said.

Ann looked up toward Casey and saw him yawning. "You look tired, Casey, how did you sleep last night?" Ann asked.

"Oh, I'm okay. I was restless all night. I guess I'm a little like Buster, I'd rather sleep in my own bed," he said.

"We should leave here in about an hour, so we can get a good parking place and get Buster used to the crowds and noise," Ann said.

"Okay, I'm going to check out my bareback equipment and I'll be ready to roll whenever you are," he said.

They left the ranch and Casey drove to the rodeo grounds. After parking, they unloaded Buster. He looked around when he backed out of the trailer. Ann watched as Buster perked up and looked over the rodeo parking area. He knew the scene. They were going to ride here today. He had been bored for the last two days. The thought of doing something enthused him. He looked forward to whatever action Ann had in store. Buster's whole attitude changed when he saw the other horses and realized he wouldn't have to loaf around a strange corral all day. He whinnied and pawed the ground in anticipation. Casey looked at Ann and smiled. "I think Buster is ready to rock and roll. He's fired up and ready to go. You better hang on to that saddle horn today, girl, Buster is ready to race," Casey said.

"He sure looks ready. I hope he feels the same way in a few hours," Ann said.

"I'll see you before you run, I'm gonna' go and see what horse I drew and talk to some friends. If you need anything, look for me by the bucking chutes," Casey said.

Casey walked away and Ann secretly hoped that he wasn't going to see Marsha. I shouldn't worry about it. Casey is a big boy and he can do what he wants, Ann thought. She put Marsha out of her mind and started taking care of the small chores that were part of preparing for a barrel race. She brushed and curried Buster. When she was finished, she stepped back and looked at him. He was in positively splendid condition. His coat gleamed in the late morning sun. Ann was satisfied with what she saw. A gratifying feeling of confidence settled upon her. They were both ready.

Ann saddled Buster and left him tied to the trailer. She was pleased to see Johnson and Bill making their way toward her. They spotted the Bent Bar trailer and were happy to see Ann and Buster. "Is everything going okay?" Johnson asked.

"Everything is fine, we're all set, and Casey is over at the chutes," she said.

Bill looked Buster over and said, "I don't think I've ever seen this old boy in such good shape. You've really done a great job with him, Annie."

"Thanks, Bill, I think he's ready to go. We'll be riding in the Grand Entry shortly and then I plan on some light warm up exercises before our event," Ann said.

"Best of luck to you. We'll be watching," Johnson said.

"Let's head over to the chutes and see if we can find Casey," Bill said. They left and Ann spent the remaining time talking with her neighbors.

The Grand Entry Parade at Twin Forks was much bigger and had many more riders than the rodeo at High Valley. This was the biggest rodeo Ann had ever competed in and she was awed by the size of the crowd. She was thrilled to see a girl she knew. They quickly struck up a conversation while waiting for the Grand Entry to start. Her name was Beth and Ann had known her for several years. They competed in other barrel races and always liked each other. They rode together through the Grand Entry and Ann was glad to have a companion to talk to.

After the parade Ann and Beth rode out of the parking area side by side talking about the upcoming race. "I don't care if I win today. I just want to beat Marsha. She's really conceited and I'd like to take her down a notch," Beth said.

Ann laughed and said, "She really aggravated me at High Valley, so I sure hope one of us can beat her this weekend."

"Well, Annie, let's try as hard as we can and maybe one of us will beat Miss Fancy Pants," Beth said. Ann laughed. She reached over and slapped her hand together with Beth's. Ann was happy to have a confidant in Beth as she related how Marsha caused her to lose concentration at High Valley.

"That's one of her favorite tricks, you'll learn not to let her bother you," Beth said.

The girls split up to work their horses separately. Their event would be starting soon and they both wanted to have their horses warmed up before they entered the arena. "See you in the alleyway," Beth said as she loped away. Ann waved at Beth and then turned her attention toward Buster.

It was time to concentrate on the run. She trotted Buster toward the arena entrance. Ann could see several girls waiting for the event to start. She didn't want Buster to stand inactive waiting for their run, so she walked him around to keep him warmed up.

Close to two hundred miles north of the Twin Forks rodeo grounds, along a remote range of the Rockies, a beat up old pickup was winding its way down out of the hills. Two hard looking men were in the truck. They were covered in dust and looked like they hadn't seen a bath in months. Both men had at least a week's growth of beard and their clothes looked like they had been sleeping in them. Dried mud was encrusted along the sides of the truck and horse trailer they were towing. They had been driving the back roads that ran north and south along the west side of High Valley. The men were in the back country several days, camping at night beside their old truck and trailer. Now, they were almost out of gas and their groceries were gone.

Camping in the back country wasn't in their plans. For two days they were stuck on an almost impassable road when their pickup slid off the road. Both men were mad at one another and blamed each other for the mishap. They worked for a full day without success trying to get their rig back on the road. Their whiskey ran out two days ago, and they were in a foul mood. Last night, the short one took a Winchester saddle gun and shot a doe deer for fresh meat. He saw the doe and her two fawns in a meadow near where they camped beside the truck and trailer. He butchered the deer and removed only the choice tenderloins. He left the rest of the meat to rot. The two terrified fawns watched him butcher their mother from the dense cover they ran into when the shot exploded upon their peaceful glen. He saw the fawns but felt no regret for taking their mother, knowing they would not survive the coming winter without her. He wanted to have something different to eat than the beans he had been eating since they became stuck. The fawns he orphaned meant nothing to him.

The men cooked the meat over an open fire. They ate their fill and then slept until daylight. The sun woke them, shining through the tall fir trees where their forced camp was located. Deprived of whiskey for two days, both men reached a stage of sobriety, which neither had experienced in many years. They were able to think more clearly and soon figured out how to get their truck and trailer back on the road. Now their only concern was to get to the nearest town as quickly as possible. They wanted more whiskey and a store bought meal. The nearest town was High Valley. When they got out of the hills and hit a good county road, they headed straight for town.

Glad to be out of their predicament, they began to feel a lot better. They started talking to each other again and even acted a little friendlier than they had since becoming stuck. "Shorty, maybe from now on you'll start listening a little closer when I try to tell you somethin'," the taller one said.

"I ain't in no mood to hear no sermon," Shorty said.

"I aint givin' you no sermon. But we wouldn't a' been stuck up there all those days if you hadda' listened to me," the tall man said.

"We needed to git up high to find somethin'," Shorty said.

"Git up high, the heck. Cattle and horses don't eat trees and rocks, and that's all that's up in that country. All the stock's down here in the foothills and valleys, working on good grass. Any idiot knows that," the tall man said.

"That momma' deer you ate last night wasn't eatin' trees or rocks when I shot her, so quit callin' me a idiot," Shorty said.

"I ain't callin' you no idiot, you jackass, but if we're gonna' fill that trailer back there, it's gonna' have to be down here," the tall one said.

"Look, Chester, down here a man can get caught. There's too many eyes that can see you pickin' up stock. You ever thought of that?" Shorty said.

"Sure, but we're runnin' low on cash, so we might have to take a chance," Chester said.

The county road they were on followed along the edge of the valley. It passed through the Bent Bar ranch on its way to High Valley. The winding road followed along the base of the foothills. Soon, Shorty and Chester were driving beside

Gunpowder Creek. A heavy line of cottonwood trees blocked their view of the creek, but they knew there was a stream of some sort on the west side of the road. Cottonwood trees and heavy willows were a sure sign of water. Neither of them knew the name of the creek or exactly where they were. The only thing they knew for sure was that, the quicker they got to town, the quicker they could get a drink.

Shorty and his partner, Chester, had been scraping out an existence for the last two years dealing in stray stock. Neither one was overly ambitious and their thieving lifestyle seemed to suit them. Chester liked to call their profession an "honorable" one. "Look at it this way, Shorty. We go around the country cleaning up all the loose and unbranded stock. Well, if it wasn't for us, them animals would be wandering all over the country, gettin' on the roads and such. So, you see, we're doin' the country a service. Just cause once in a while some of the animals we pick up are inside a fence, don't mean nothin'. We probably need the money more than its owner does. Besides, if they're too lazy to brand their stock, then I'm not against doin' it for them. With my own brandin' irons, of course," Chester was fond of saying.

Shorty heard Chester's theory on their lifestyle a hundred times. Every time Chester told it, he always got a good laugh from Shorty. When he got to the part of using his own branding irons on someone else's stock, Shorty would erupt in laughter. When he did, he would almost always guffaw so hard that he sprayed the inside of the windshield with his chewing tobacco. Chester would cuss him out for making a mess and Shorty would grin back with brown juice dribbling down his chin. His smile was something to see. He was missing most of his upper teeth and the few that were left were the color of what you might find in a barnyard.

They were nothing but downright, thieving, modern day rustlers. They managed to stay one short step ahead of the law. By accident they fell on a scheme that, so far, had kept them out of the jail cell where they belonged. They had been in a brand inspector's office at a stock yard trying to sell stolen cattle. The inspector was called out of the office to verify a brand. He made the mistake of leaving the two thieves in his office alone. Shorty was half drunk at the time and had his courage up. The whiskey inspired him and he stepped behind the counter as a sort of joke and said to Chester, "Haw-Haw, I'm the brand cop, now let me see your papers on them cows, mister!" They both got a good laugh out of his prank. Then Shorty happened to glance to the shelf below the counter and saw a stack of books. He stole one containing the brand inspection forms and one for travel permits. He shoved both receipt books inside his shirt and got out from behind the counter before the unsuspecting brand inspector returned. They now had the necessary legal paperwork to transport and sell all the horses and cattle that they managed to steal. All they had to do was forge both documents. They would simply write in the description of the animals they wanted to sell and scribble in an unintelligible signature.

The strategy worked so well that they would steal more forms every five or six months to prevent them from being traced by the numbers on the stolen forms. By the time the forms were discovered missing, and an alert was issued to look for them, Shorty and Chester were already using different forms. It was an easy charade for them to lure an inspector out of his office while one stayed behind and pilfered the forms. So far they managed to keep themselves in groceries and whiskey with their illegal activities. They only operated when they were short on money and changed their territory often so as not to draw attention to themselves.

Shorty looked ahead as the road turned away from the foothills. He drove slowly and when the road turned back toward the mountains, he could see a small herd of cattle grazing on the hillside. He let the old truck slow down to a stop. Chester was daydreaming and looked over at his partner to see why he was stopping. "Are we running out of gas?" Chester asked.

"Nope, just look up at that hillside above them cottonwoods," Shorty said. Chester followed his gaze and saw the cattle.

"Them are too far away. How would we get em' down here? Besides, it's too late in the day. We need gas and groceries and I need a drink," Chester said.

Shorty didn't answer Chester right away, he kept watching the cows. "Hand me them binoculars," Shorty said. Chester reached in the glove compartment and took out the old pair of field glasses.

He handed them to Shorty and said, "Quit wastin' time. I want to get to town. Them cows are too far away I told you."

"Chester, will you just shutup for a while," Shorty said. Shorty looked through the field glasses for a few minutes. Then he turned toward Chester and gave him the best toothless smile he could muster.

Shorty started the truck moving again and said, "I've got a plan." He started laughing and Chester cringed when he saw Shorty spray the inside of the windshield with tobacco juice that escaped through the gaps of his missing teeth.

"I'll tell you, Shorty, your plan better be to get this rig into town as quick as you can. I'm thirsty and hungry for some real food, so get rolling," Chester said irritably.

"Settle down, Chester, I'm headed for town but here's what we're gonna' do", Shorty said. "We're gonna' go to town and get the stuff we need to last a few more days, then we'll head back out here. We'll cut the bob' wire fence and drive down into them trees and camp out of sight in them cottonwoods. There's got to be a crick' running through them woods, so we can have runnin' water for a change. I could see through the binoculars a good trail coming off the hill where them cows are grazing. I'll bet that bunch of cows are coming down into them cottonwoods to bed down at night. The trail I saw looks like it's been used pretty regular. If they're beddin' down in them trees, it should be easy to check and see if any calves haven't been branded. We still have some grain left in the trailer. Maybe we can draw em' in with the grain close enough to get a rope on a couple of em'. The best part is that nobody will be able to see us down in them woods, so we can take our time," Shorty said.

Chester looked over at Shorty and said with a wicked grin on his ugly face, "Shorty, sometimes you amaze me with your crooked schemes." They both laughed and the windshield acquired another bath of tobacco juice.

Ann was on Buster waiting in the alleyway before the start of the event. There were a few other girls waiting with her. She had been watching for Beth to ride in, but so far there was no sign of her friend. She saw Casey walking her way and heard one of the other girls say, "Here comes that handsome bronc rider. I'd like to know him a little better." Ann looked at the girl and giggled.

Casey walked up to Buster and said, "Buster, I'm gonna' give you a good ol' rub on your neck to pass some of my luck on to you." Casey started rubbing Buster's neck. The girls curiously watched. Then Casey looked up at Ann and said, "Now it's your turn, Annie, bend down here and let me rub some luck into that cute little head of yours." The girls laughed and Ann dutifully pulled her hat off and bent toward Casey. He playfully rubbed the top of her head and said, "You'll for sure win now. There's no sense in the rest of you girls even riding today." The girls laughed again.

The girl who said she would like to know Casey, called out to him, "Hey, cowboy, I'll take a little of that luck myself." Ann laughed out loud, because she knew what was coming. Casey hated to be called a cowboy.

Casey looked in the girl's direction and very seriously said, "Young lady, I am not a cowboy, I am a cowman. If you'd like to see a real cowman in action, just watch the bareback bronc riding. My number is thirty six, and I'll be riding Smoky Joe out of chute number four. Cowboys belong with their momma's, so please don't confuse me with them, thank you."

"Well, I'm sorry, Mister Bronc Rider. I won't let it happen again," the girl said good naturedly. Everyone laughed.

Casey walked over to where the girl was sitting her horse and said, "My name is Casey and I'm from High Valley.

"Glad to meet you, Casey, I'm Jill, and I'm from right here in Twin Forks," she said. Jill didn't have a chance to continue the conversation. They looked up when Marsha Miller rode up on her buckskin and called out to Casey.

"Hey, Casey, I missed you today, but I'll be looking forward to seeing you in town tonight," she said. The pleasant atmosphere that surrounded the girls with Casey's good natured joking evaporated with Marsha's arrival.

Embarrassed, Casey said, "Hello, Marsha, I'll probably be in town tonight, but I'm not sure where my partner Bill wants to go. So no telling where we'll end up," Casey cut his answer short and walked back and quietly said to Ann, "Good luck, Ann, I'm behind you all the way." With that, Casey turned and walked away. Ann watched Casey. She felt a twinge of emotion for poor old Casey. The girls were always after him and sometimes he just plain got tired of it.

The arena judge called for the girls to line up and be ready to move into position. He reminded them of the thirty second rule. Ann looked around and was relieved to see Beth riding up. Beth rode into the group and Ann said, "I was beginning to worry about you."

"Just doin' a little serious preparation," Beth answered.

The first rider was called into the arena and the next girl up moved "on deck." The first rider ran through the pattern with a flawless performance. The crowd gave resounding applause when she raced across the finish line. It was an outstanding run. Beth looked at Ann and said, "She's really giving us something to shoot for, that was a good run." Ann felt Buster's impatience and secretly hoped they could turn in a run like they were doing in practice. I must concentrate on why we're here today and focus solely on running those barrels like we are capable of doing, Ann thought.

Beth moved into the arena for her run and Marsha moved "on deck". Ann watched as Beth kicked her horse into a run and urged him toward the first barrel. Ann saw they were going to cut the first turn too close and prayed they wouldn't knock the barrel over. She knew how badly Beth wanted a good run and was anxious for her friend to do well. Beth rounded the barrel too close. Her horse tried to correct himself, but was too late. Beth's knee hit the barrel and it tipped precariously as they ran toward the second barrel. It teetered on the verge of falling, and seemed as if it were challenging the law of gravity. The crowd was screaming for the barrel to remain upright in hopes the rider wouldn't suffer a penalty.

Ann heard Marsha Miller yell, "Fall! Fall!" The barrel oscillated, but remained in its upright position. The crowd screamed in delight. Beth continued around the pattern in good time.

Ann looked at Marsha and wondered what type of person would actually wish bad luck on a fellow competitor. She probably didn't care if she won fair and square, just as long as she won. Winning wouldn't mean a thing if I won only because someone else had a misfortune, Ann thought. Beth came flying across the finish line and stopped in a spray of dirt and dust. She looked flushed and Ann yelled encouragement. "Good run, Beth." Her time was read at sixteen point zero nine seconds. A good run that put her in the lead. Marsha was next and moved into the arena. Ann moved into the next up spot and watched her make her run.

Marsha may be a miserable person, but she was very striking riding into the arena on the muscular buckskin. Her clothes were beautiful and she certainly rode well, Ann thought. Marsha got the nod from the judge and raced away into the cloverleaf pattern. Ann watched as Marsha and the buckskin sped around the barrels in what obviously was going to be a great ride. Marsha was good. She came charging out of the last barrel whipping the buckskin hard in an effort to capture the lead. It was an exceptional run and Marsha took the lead with a time of fifteen point nine eight seconds. Ann moved into the arena. She felt confident that Buster could beat Marsha's time. They made faster runs in practice. If she kept her attention focused on guiding Buster in the right moves, she knew they could gain the lead. Ann wanted to win. She felt Buster's eagerness and a firm resolve settled upon her. She lined up and studied the course. A growing feeling of confidence filled her as she heard the crowd cheering. "We can win this one, Buster," she said aloud. Buster was excited and Ann seemed to transfer her determination to the fired up gelding. She released Buster and urged him to top speed.

Total concentration. One barrel at a time. Three barrels to maneuver around at high speed. No mistakes. Push as hard as you can, only as long as it feels right. There is no room for foolishness. Precision riding, don't cut any corners. Her self taught discipline flashed through her mind as Buster approached the first barrel. Around perfectly, and away they raced toward number two. Concentrate on number two before you even think of number three. Halfway around start looking for three. Get there in the right position as fast as you can. Ann's tunnel vision took over. It was as if they were alone in a void. Nothing existed except three steel barrels and the desperate need to race around them at the highest possible speed. There was no arena. She could not hear the noise of a thousand cheering spectators. The sound of the band seemed to fade remotely into the background. She was aware only of the straining animal under her and his desire to follow her every command, whether it was right or wrong. Ann Olsen achieved the total mind set of functioning only for the task at hand. Her task was to communicate only the right moves to her horse and not be too anxious to correct him. Buster had a well functioning mind, and he knew where they wanted to end up and how he had to travel to get there. Ann must not give bad commands. Her concentration was complete and they went around the last barrel in a blur of speed. Buster went across the finish line still straining to gain more speed. They were almost in the alleyway before Ann pulled him up and then and only then did she hear the roar of the crowd as they applauded her run.

She easily took the lead with a time of fifteen point eight six seconds. She was twelve-hundredths of a second ahead of the nearest competitor. Ann was elated. If they could hold the lead for the rest of the event, they would finish the day in first place.

"Way to go, Annie, you blistered them! You beat Marsha by a good spread," Beth yelled. Beth walked her horse beside them while Ann walked Buster around till he calmed down.

Ann looked around, she was slowly coming out of her concentration. Other things came into focus. She saw Marsha on her horse watching both her and Beth ride by. Ann waved and said, "Hello, Marsha." Marsha ignored her.

Beth looked at Ann and asked, "Are you feeling okay?" Ann laughed and said, "Yes, I feel wonderful."

When Buster's breathing returned to normal, the girls tied their horses to the fence and walked back to the arena to watch the rest of the racers make their runs. The event moved rapidly. When the results were announced, Ann captured first place. Marsha finished second and Beth third. When Beth heard the results she laughed and said, "Marsha's in trouble now, you're in first, and I'm in third place. She's second, and that means we've got her surrounded." They both laughed and walked back to their horses.

"Let's put our horses away and get back here so we can watch Casey ride his bronc," Beth said.

"Sounds great," Ann said, and then thought, Casey's captured another admirer.

Johnson and Bill watched from the stands when Ann made her first place run. They were both pleased she had taken the lead on Buster. Bill remarked to Johnson that Buster was doing a heck of a job considering his age. He was old enough to be a great grandfather to some of the horses he was competing against. "That doesn't surprise me. He's got some awful good breeding behind him. Look at his mother. I rode her until she was better than twenty years old. She's probably roped more cows in her lifetime than most horses ever see. She was a good working horse right up until I turned her out to enjoy a peaceful retirement. Then she stepped in and took over the band and has been keeping them out of trouble ever since. That old bay mare is quite a horse and Buster shows a lot of her in the heart he has," Johnson said.

"I remember when I was a little boy watching you rope on her. She was really something. She still has what it takes. You can't ride into the hills looking for the horses without her finding you first. I've never found the band without finding Rosie already watching our approach," Bill said.

"Yep, she's been one of them horses that takes over a special spot in your heart," Johnson said.

"Well, look who's coming," Bill said. They watched Casey making his way up into the stands.

Casey never gave them a chance to say Hi, how are you, or nothing. He started right in on Bill for making him have to come look for him. "Bill, you know bronc riding is coming up quick, you need to be down helping me, not making me spend time looking for you. Now, come on, let's get going. How ya' doin', Johnson? Come on, Bill, let's go," Casey said all in one breath.

"I'm doin' okay," Johnson said.

"Huh," Casey said.

"I said, I'm doin' okay. You asked me how I was doin' and I answered you, Casey," Johnson said. Bill busted out laughing and Casey looked at Bill with a perplexed look.

"What are you laughing at?" Casey asked.

"Nothin', come on, let's get going if you're in such a big hurry. How ya' doin', Johnson? I'll see you after I help Casey with his bronc," Bill said.

Johnson laughed and Casey looked at them and said, "You two sure talk in circles sometimes."

Ann and Beth were in the stands watching when Casey came out of chute number four, spurring hard on Smoky Joe. Casey didn't have to worry much about a good ride. Joe was a good horse and seemed to enjoy bucking. He liked the challenge of throwing a rider as fast as he could. Bells or horns or eight seconds didn't mean a thing to Smoky Joe. He was all horse and it showed. He came busting out and bucking hard. He spun, twisted and sunfished in obvious enjoyment. He liked his profession and he intended to earn his keep. Joe was a talented performer. He wanted to show everybody how good he was. Casey stuck to him like glue. When the horn went off, Casey easily slid across onto the pick up rider's horse and in one graceful movement transferred to the ground. The crowd cheered him for a good ride.

Smoky Joe felt the rider's departure and without the extra weight on his back, really cranked up the bucking. He started putting on a show that brought the crowd to their feet. The pick up riders were trying to catch him to release the flank strap that made him buck. Old Joe wasn't through yet and he continued to perform. He was what you might call a show-off and didn't want his moment of glory to end quite so soon. He bucked high and wide as he passed in front of the stands. The crowd gave him a standing ovation and the pick up riders decided to let him finish his performance. In one last burst of professionalism, Smoky came bucking past the stands throwing his hind legs high toward the sky. When he showed everybody what a good bucking horse looked like, he slowed and came to a full standing stop in front of the cheering crowd. The pick up rider rode up and released his flank strap. When Smoky felt the pressure come off, he turned and gracefully trotted toward the holding pens at the end of the arena.

The crowd loved the performance. The announcer spotted Casey walking toward the chutes. "That was one heck of a ride. Nothing against you, number thirty-six, but Smoky Joe was the star of the show on that go around," the announcer said and the crowd roared in laughter. Casey laughed hard with everyone else. He had to agree. Smoky Joe paid Casey well. His score was announced as a good seventy-eight. That put Casey in the lead for the day and in a very good mood.

The two Bent Bar riders were through for the day. Each led in their events. Johnson told Bill that he thought Casey could surely win tomorrow and he was hoping Ann could turn in another winning ride as well. "She's rode good enough in practice to win here. If she performs tomorrow like she did today, then she might do it," Bill said.

"Let's keep our fingers crossed. Now let's go see if we can find them. I might spring for dinner tonight," Johnson said.

Shorty and Chester bought enough groceries to last a few days. They gassed up their old truck and stopped by the liquor store. Chester came out with a dirty grin on his face and held up two big bottles of whiskey. He got in the truck and Shorty drove around to a side street and stopped. They opened a bottle and each took a couple of swigs of the dark liquid. When they temporarily quenched their thirst for alcohol, Shorty drove to Molly's restaurant. They ordered a big meal. When Molly served them their food, they dug in with noisy gusto. Molly and the rest of the patrons were glad to see them go when they finished. They were sure a dirty pair, Molly thought.

Shorty drove out of town and headed up the valley where he saw the cows on the hillside. They took turns sipping whiskey out of one of the bottles as they drove past the Bent Bar. "Them cows probably belong to that there outfit. It looks like a prosperous ranch, so it won't hurt them to come up a few calves short when they gather them up this fall," Shorty said.

Chester belched and fumes of the whiskey engulfed the cab of the truck. "What do ya' mean -- a few calves --, let's cram as many in there as we can git'. They ain't gonna' miss em' for a while and nobody's gonna' see us down in them woods. You come up with a foolproof plan this time, Shorty. How about another snort?" Chester said and handed the bottle to Shorty. Shorty didn't decline the offer. Chester threw the cap away when they left town, so all Shorty had to do was tip the bottle up and guzzle the fiery liquid. He took a long swig and handed the bottle back to Chester.

By the time they reached the area along Gunpowder Creek, Shorty and Chester were feeling the affects of the alcohol and were getting back to their usual style of drunken incompetence. By now, it was late afternoon. Shorty was anxious to get their rig hidden in the trees and stop driving for the day. He planned on doing some serious drinking once they were hidden from sight. The last few days had been hard on him, being stuck up in the mountains without any of his usual nourishment from the whiskey bottle. He had ideas of making up for the last few days once they were settled amongst the trees.

"Chester, let's look for a good level place to cut this fence where we can drive down into them trees without getting stuck again," Shorty said.

Chester took a nip from the bottle and said, "I'm lookin'."

"Set that bottle down and get your wire cutters out. See up ahead? It looks like maybe the ground's good and hard and the shoulder's not too steep to drive off of," Shorty said.

"Yeah, I'll cut the wires and you drive through. I'm gonna hang the wires back up once you're through, so maybe nobody'll notice they been cut. Then we'll come out the same way tomorrow," Chester said. Chester started rummaging under the seat looking for the wire cutters. He was holding the whiskey bottle in one hand and groping under the seat with his other.

"Chester, hurry up. We're almost there. Set that bottle down so you can use both hands!" Shorty yelled.

"Shut up, Shorty, I can't set the bottle down. I threw the cap away like you told me when we left town," Chester said.

"Then hand it over and I'll take care of it while you find them cutters," Shorty said and laughed. Tobacco juice sprayed over the instrument panel. Chester grinned and handed the bottle to Shorty.

Chester found the cutters and held them up for Shorty to see. "Time to go to work," he laughed.

Shorty pulled up to a level spot and looked it over. He looked in the rear view mirror to make sure no one was coming behind them. From the fence over to the trees was about a quarter of a mile and the ground looked level with just a little brush mixed in with the grass. It looked like they could drive into the trees without any problem once they cut the five strands of barb wire. He couldn't see anyone coming in either direction. He looked for the telltale sign of dust that a vehicle would make driving on the dry dirt road. Shorty couldn't see any dust in the distance. No one was within miles of where they stopped to cut the fence.

"Go ahead, Chester, and hurry up about it," Shorty said. Chester jumped out of the truck and immediately fell flat on his face. He drank a good portion of whiskey on the drive out to the creek. His equilibrium was thrown out of kilter by the whiskey, it didn't adjust quick enough when he jumped out. Shorty laughed hard at his partner's misfortune and Chester sent a few nasty words in his direction. Chester picked himself up and headed over to the fence.

He cut through all five strands of the fence and pulled the wires back out of the way so Shorty could drive through. Shorty eased the truck and trailer off the road and slowly drove the rig through the opening. Shorty waited while Chester tried to hook the loose wires back around the fence post. Chester was having a hard time reconnecting the wires. After being cut, they weren't long enough to reach back around the post. Shorty saw the problem, and got out of the truck to help. He wanted to get down into the trees as quickly as they could before anybody saw them.

Chester was fumbling with the wires trying to stretch them back to the post. "Forget it, Chester, let's just pull them back out of the way. Maybe nobody'll notice there ain't no wires on this one span. It's gonna' be dark pretty soon and we'll leave early mornin'. Probably nobody will even come by anyway," Shorty said. Chester agreed. They pulled the five strands of barb wire back along the fence out of the way. They hooked the strands to make them as inconspicuous as possible and stepped back to look at their handywork. "From a distance, you'd never know them wires were missin' from between them posts, would you?" Shorty asked Chester.

"Nope, not unless you were starin' right at it," Chester said.

They drove through the field toward the cottonwood trees along Gunpowder Creek. Shorty found a faint trace of a road and followed it. It turned into the trees and wound along until it came to the creek. There was a small clearing beside the creek and Shorty stopped and turned off the motor. "Hot Dog! If this ain't perfect, I ain't never seen perfect," Chester said.

"This sure looks good for what we need to do. I can even see some cows up on that hill from here," Shorty said.

"Shorty, look at all the manure around here, and look at all the places you can see where the cows have been beddin' down at night. You sure were right about this spot. We ought'a be able to snatch enough beef to make a reasonable profit out of this trip," Chester happily said. There were also fresh horse droppings scattered around the clearing that Chester hadn't seen.

Shorty looked at Chester and smiled. His remaining upper teeth stuck out over his lower lip. They looked like two brown snags, and tobacco juice dipped off the ends onto the week old growth of beard on his chin. "Well then, maybe we ought'a drink to our good luck," he said and laughed.

"Sounds good. But you know me, I'll drink to anything," Chester said and laughed along with Shorty.

They got out of the truck and each one took a long pull on the bottle. Chester and Shorty looked around the area and Shorty commented on how much the cows had been using this clearing. "They probably won't come right into the clearing tonight with us here, but they'll most likely bed down close by. If we get up at daylight before they leave, then it should be easy enough to spread that grain out and keep the momma' cows occupied while we kidnap a few of their babies," Shorty said.

"And the best part is that we don't have to do a thing until mornin', so we can relax for the rest of the day," Chester said.

Shorty started pulling gear out of the back of the truck. Chester helped and they set up a temporary camp. Shorty bought bread and sandwich meat with the groceries in town. His plan called for camping in the woods without a fire. Smoke from a campfire could give away their location, so he bought the kind of groceries that didn't need cooking. They could get along in a cold camp for one night and wouldn't have to worry about someone riding up to check on the smoke a fire would create.

When they finished setting up their camp, both men walked down to the creek to look around. They could see the herd of cows grazing on the hillside in the late afternoon light. "You know, Chester, we've had a rough couple of days. Whadd'ya say we just relax and spend the rest of the day enjoyin' ourselves for a change," Shorty said.

"Suits me just fine, let's go back to camp and have a drink," Chester said.

Shorty laughed and said, "How about four or five drinks!"

CHAPTER 12

Sunday, the final day of the Twin Forks rodeo dawned bright and beautiful. It would prove to a be fateful September day. Casey awoke early. He showered, dressed and then walked out to the corral where Buster was nosing into fresh hay. "Morning, Buster, you fine looking steed. Are you ready to race today?" Casey questioned. Buster kept eating and didn't pay any attention to Casey. "Well, if you won't answer me, then point in the direction of where your pretty little owner is."

Casey heard giggling and turned to see Ann walking up with Buster's halter in her hand. "Buster is a great horse, but the last I heard, he hadn't learned how to talk," she said.

"Never underestimate the power of a good horse," Casey said, and laughed.

"Annie, I feel like I could ride the worst demon in the world today. Have you ever seen a better morning?" Casey asked Ann.

"I'm glad to see you in such high spirits. I'd bet a bucket of oats that you'll win easy today, Casey," Ann said and smiled.

"I do feel good and you know attitude means a lot on how you perform. You gotta' feel positive. Remember that and maybe you'll win today," Casey said.

"Yes sir, I will. Now, can you give me a hand getting Buster loaded?" Ann asked.

"Sure thing, we don't want to be late getting back to town. Let's get going and I'll buy you breakfast somewhere," Casey said.

They loaded Buster into the trailer and Casey jumped into the driver's seat. Ann got in and they started for town. Casey drove slowly. When they reached the outskirts of Twin Forks, they saw Johnson's truck parked in front of a cafe. Casey pulled over and parked. Ann checked Buster, and then followed Casey inside.

It looked like "Old Cronies" day in the restaurant. Johnson and Bill sat surrounded by a lot of their old friends. Sam and Duke were there and other people whom Ann didn't immediately recognize. She saw her friends, Beth and Jill, and waved. There were several other competitors sitting around the small cafe and it was obvious that this restaurant was a favorite spot for the rodeo contestants. Everyone was in a cheerful mood and the chatter was friendly and light.

Bill stood up and waved to Casey when he saw them walk in. The group quickly made room at the table for Ann and Casey. Johnson smiled at his two Bent Bar riders and introduced them to the people sitting around their table. "Here are the two that Bill and I have been bragging about. Casey here sticks on a bronc like a fly on a piece of new flypaper and this young lady is on her way to becoming one of the top barrel racers and, I might add, trainers in the state," Johnson proudly said. Everyone introduced themselves. Ann and Casey were shy at first, but soon felt right at home with their new acquaintances.

Duke looked fondly at Ann and said, "Ann doesn't like to talk about it, but she is the young lady that rode her horse off the top of a high ravine after lightning exploded behind her horse and spooked him off the edge. You might've read something about it in the papers last spring." Ann turned red and looked across at Duke. She always hated to be recognized as the one who made that impossible ride. The table became quiet and everyone looked in Ann's direction.

Beth heard Duke's comment and from across the small dining room she said, "Annie, was that you? I had no idea that article was about you. You have to tell me all about it today." Ann smiled across the room at Beth and nodded her head.

Bill recognized Ann's embarrassment and came to her rescue. "That was Annie, and you'll get a chance today to see the horse she rode off the cliff. She's riding him in the barrels. She rode to first place yesterday," he said. Ann was glad Bill changed the subject to Buster. She looked across to Bill and silently thanked him.

Beth came over and asked Ann to come sit with her and Jill. She said, "Okay," and thankfully slipped away from any other conversation of that stormy night.

As Ann moved over to Beth's table she heard someone say, "How in the world did they survive that ride. What kind of shape is the horse in now?"

"Good shape, you'll see him run in just a few hours," she heard Sam say.

"He must be one heck of a horse," the same person said.

"The Bent Bar breeds and trains outstanding stock and that horse came from one of their best mares," Duke said.

Ann enjoyed being in the company of her friends. The girls were excited about the final day of the rodeo. They talked about yesterday's results. They made Ann feel like a celebrity with her first place lead. The conversation turned to Marsha Miller and the fact that she always seemed to do well on the final day. "She's good, so don't ever underestimate her. Ride as hard as you can, because I'll guarantee you that Marsha will be riding to win," Beth said. The girls solemnly nodded in agreement. The table was quiet as each girl fell into silent contemplation of Beth's advice.

When Casey finished his breakfast, he excused himself from the table and made his way to the girl's table. "Look who's coming," Jill said.

In a whisper, Beth said, "It's the cowboy." All three girls burst out laughing.

Casey walked up and said, "Okay, what are you laughing about now?" His question caused the girls to laugh even harder at their private joke. Casey looked perplexed and said, "I'll never understand women." He sat down next to Ann and shook his head in dismay. When the girls saw the look on his face they giggled even more. Finally he said, "When you get through with your private joke, then maybe we should head out to the rodeo grounds. I'm supposed to ride there today. I don't know about you three." Casey stood up and reached over Ann and picked up the check for her breakfast.

Still giggling, Beth picked up her check and held it out toward Casey. "Here, Casey, how about paying for mine too!" she said.

Before Casey could say a thing, Jill picked up her check and held it toward the bewildered bronc rider. Casey looked around the restaurant. It became very quiet in the dining room. He saw everyone watching him with good natured smiles on their faces in anticipation of what he would do. With everyone watching, Casey knew that he would lose face if he refused to pay their bills. Summoning up all the chivalry he could, he said loud enough for everyone to hear, "Ladies, it would be my great pleasure to treat you all to breakfast." He reached across the table and snatched the checks out of Beth and Jill's extended hands.

Everyone in the restaurant enjoyed the episode and began to laugh. Some clapped and made comments about what a gentleman Casey was. Others held out their checks and said, "Here, Casey, you can get mine too."

Casey went right along with the fun, but knew he better get out of the restaurant before things got too far out of hand. With a dramatic flourish, Casey swept his hat off and placed it over his heart. "Ma'am, we better hit the trail. The Twin Forks rodeo awaits," he said to Ann loud enough for everyone to hear.

Farther north, along the banks of Gunpowder Creek, Shorty was trying to awaken. He was lying in his filthy sleeping bag on the bare ground beside the truck. His head was throbbing, and felt like someone was using it for a drum. Sunlight was filtering through the cottonwoods and penetrating his closed eyes. It was as if a bright red light was shining in his eyes. His mouth was dry and his lips felt cracked and brittle. Slowly, the throbbing in his head and the bright sun were bringing him back to consciousness. His stomach was upset and he needed to relieve himself. He felt terrible and almost wished he were dead. He drank way too much whiskey last night and was paying for it now.

The discomfort Shorty was feeling finally roused him. He lay there not wanting to move. He wondered why he drank so much. He always felt this bad after a long bout with the bottle and promised himself a thousand times he wouldn't do it again. He only made that promise on the morning after one of these terrible drinking sprees, but before the day was very far along, he always seemed to forget and was soon drinking again.

Shorty forced himself to crawl out of the sleeping bag. He stood upright and the pounding in his head increased to the point that it seemed as if a bomb had gone off inside his skull. He leaned against the truck and tried to clear his head. He needed to find the jar of aspirin he kept in the truck for this kind of emergency. Shorty opened the door and looked in the glove compartment. He found what he was looking for and walked unsteadily to the creek for some water to wash the pills down. He splashed the cold water on his face, and threw a few of the white pills into his mouth. He washed them down with water cupped in his grubby hands. Shorty stood up and walked over to a cottonwood tree, and leaned there waiting for his head to clear.

There was a lot of activity going on at the rodeo grounds when Casey pulled into the parking area. He found a good spot and parked the rig. They unloaded Buster and laughed when he backed out of the trailer, looked around and then snorted. It was as if he was saying, "I've been here before!"

Buster was showing a lot of spirit this morning and started pawing the ground when Ann hooked his lead to the trailer. "Looks like your pony is ready to race again today," Casey said.

Ann looked admiringly at Buster and said, "I feel very fortunate to own a horse like Buster." She didn't have to explain anything more. He knew all about the bond that developed between a good horse and its owner.

Casey thought about the strong bond that existed between Johnson and his old mare, Montana Rose. They had been quite a pair when she was Johnson's number one riding horse. They could outrun and out rope anyone in the valley. Johnson showed such high respect and devotion to the old girl that people often joked about their relationship. Someone once asked him if they slept in the same stall together. Johnson laughed and answered, "Only when she's lonely!"

Casey slapped Buster on the rump and said, "Annie, you've got it all under control, so I'll go see what wild critter' I drew for today's ride."

"Okay, Casey, and thanks for buying breakfast," Ann said and laughed. She got a kick out of the fun they had in the cafe.

Casey raised his eyebrows and shook his head. "I'm glad somebody enjoyed it," he said, then turned and walked away muttering to himself. Ann laughed at Casey's good humor, but then turned her attention to the serious task of preparing for the final day of the rodeo.

Shorty had been leaning against the tree trying to get himself under control. He had a bad hangover from the whiskey and it was taking him awhile to get started. He heard a loud splashing noise coming from upstream. He looked in that direction and saw a cow and her calf crossing the stream. Shorty looked across the stream toward the hillside and saw several cow-calf pairs making their way toward the hill. It suddenly dawned on him that he overslept and all the cattle were leaving the sanctuary of the cottonwoods and heading into the hills to graze.

Angrily, he turned and stomped toward the truck and trailer. He could see that most of the cattle already left the trees and were across the creek. They would never be able to stop the remaining cows from crossing the stream and heading into the hills. He and Chester laughed in joy last night when they watched the wary cattle cross to their side of the creek and stop to stare at them just before dark. The cattle moved upstream and settled in for the night close enough for Shorty and Chester to feel confident about stealing a trailer load of calves in the morning. All of their good plans were going to waste because they got drunk and overslept. Shorty vowed to quit drinking. This time he told himself, he meant it. Shorty stomped up to where Chester lay snoring. He yelled at Chester to wake up and started kicking at the hump made by Chester's body in his grimy sleeping bag. Chester grunted and then cussed when he realized Shorty was kicking him awake.

It was time to go. Ann heard the band warming up. She brushed Buster's back one last time and then carefully placed his saddle pad in place. She positioned it a little farther up on his back than it should be and then slid it back down in the proper spot. She was making sure all of Buster's hair followed the natural alignment and wasn't forced out of place by the saddle pad. Sliding it down in place was like passing a big brush down his back. All the hair lined up the way it should be. No sense taking a chance on irritating his back because his hair was forced and held out of place by a poorly placed pad, she thought, as she carefully slipped the bridle over his head and slid the bit in place. Everything looked good, so she mounted and rode toward the arena.

Casey was in the holding pens behind the bucking chutes looking over the stock. "How'd you draw, Casey?" Don Smith, another bronc rider asked.

"Fair, Don, fair. I'm on Black Magic today. How about you, Don, who are you on?" Casey asked.

"Well, I'll be pushin' you hard today, Casey. I drew the horse that gave you such a great ride at High Valley. A critter' named Moon Shot," Don said and grinned.

Casey smiled and said, "He'll sure give you a ride. I almost didn't ride him to the horn at High Valley. You just have to know how to start his motor." Don looked quizzically at Casey and wondered what he meant.

"Come on, Don, we've got some time. I'll let you buy me a cold drink at the concession stand," Casey said.

"You're all heart, Casey, but I'll take you up on it," Don said. They left the pens and wandered over to the midway. The band was starting to play and Casey wanted to watch the Grand Entry. He and Don got their drinks and found a spot where they could watch the riders when they raced into the arena.

Casey wanted to be around the stands to watch for Bill. Sometimes Bill didn't come early enough to suit Casey. He suspected Bill liked to aggravate him and wait until the last minute to show up to help him get settled on his horse. I'd be lost without Bill, and I think he knows it, Casey fondly thought. "I'm gonna' stick around here and see if I can spot Bill," Casey said.

"I've got some time, I'll stick around with you. Maybe some of your luck will rub off on me," Don said and laughed.

Casey felt someone tapping him on the shoulder and turned to see Bill grinning at him. "Hey, Case, have you got both of your spurs today?" Bill asked.

"You better ask Don that question, he drew Moon Shot today," Casey said.

"What are you two talking about?" Don asked. Casey and Bill laughed. Don looked at them and shook his head in exasperation.

Ann was Saturday's leader, so she was the first rider up today. She was waiting in the alleyway for the announcer to call her into the arena. Things had been tense while the girls waited. Marsha rode her buckskin into the alleyway and saw Ann waiting with a few other girls. She rode right up to them and said sarcastically to Ann, "Isn't that horse too old to be riding in these events?"

Before Ann could react to the callous statement, Jill said to Marsha, "Go blow your horn somewhere else, Marsha, Buster was young enough to beat you and your fancy buckskin yesterday."

Ann started to say something nasty, but realized Marsha was attempting to distract her from the coming event. Instead she politely said, "Buster's up there in years, but he still does a good job." Ann wasn't going to let Marsha distract her again. Ann felt a warmth toward Jill for defending her. It was nice to have good friends, she thought. Ann heard the announcer call her name. It was time to go, Marsha's ploy failed this time. Ann entered the arena in a good frame of mind and felt Buster's eagerness under her. They were a team and were ready to ride.

Along the banks of Gunpowder Creek, the two rustlers were in a foul frame of mind. Chester jumped out of his sleeping bag and took a swing at Shorty for kicking him while he slept. Chester hated for someone to wake him in the morning. Even worse, was for someone to kick at him while he was still asleep. Chester's wild swing missed, because he was still half asleep and didn't quite have all of his faculties about him. The force of his swing going past Shorty's jaw carried him fully around. Off balance, he fell back to the ground in a heap. Shorty regretted kicking him now. Chester was a lot bigger than Shorty and could do a lot of damage if he ever lost his temper. Shorty had more intelligence than Chester and usually gave the orders. He controlled the taller man with reasoning.

Shorty backed off and said, "Aw' come on, Chester, I was just trying to get you up. You were snorin' so loud, that I thought I had to tap on you, to git' you awake. Don't be mad now, we gotta' git goin'. It's late and all the cows have already left the crick'."

Chester looked up at Shorty and let his words sink in. Chester felt like he had been run over by a dump truck. His head hurt and he had a bad hangover. "You mean all them calves are gone?" he finally said.

"That's a fact. We slept too late and they all headed out already," Shorty said.

Chester sadly shook his head and staggered to his feet. He leaned against the pickup to steady himself. "Well, what are we gonna' do now, Shorty?" he asked.

"The way I feel, I want to go back to bed," Shorty said.

"That's a good idea," Chester said and started over to his dirty sleeping bag.

"Now hold on, Chester, don't go back to sleep. Let's just take it easy for a minute, then maybe we can think of something else. Otherwise, we have to stay here another night and wait for them cows to come back," Shorty said.

"Look, Shorty, I'm sure as heck getting tired of sleeping on the ground. I don't want to stay here another night. I'm ready to head home to Wyoming and sleep in a real bed for a change. That cabin in them hills sounds pretty good to me right about now," Chester mournfully said.

"I could stand a little rest down there myself, but we're gettin' awful low on money so we're just gonna' have to find something to sell somewhere. And we got to do it before we head home," Shorty said.

Both men heard a splashing noise and turned to see a bright sorrel colt in the middle of the creek, pawing the water. He was playfully splashing water in all directions. He seemed to be enjoying the fun and the men watched in amusement. An old bay mare came into sight upstream from the colt. The men watched as the old horse looked downstream where they were standing beside their truck. She raised her head high when she spotted them and her ears flicked quickly in their direction. She turned her head and looked behind her in the direction she had come. She looked forward again, toward the colt playing in the creek, then focused her full attention on the men. She didn't like what she saw.

The old mare was gray around the muzzle but she showed a surprising quickness when she raced down the bank and stopped by the colt. Shorty and Chester watched as the mare started urgently whinnying at the youngster. She was obviously not happy about seeing the strange men. She seemed to be urging the young sorrel colt to come out of the creek and follow her away. The men heard the sound of racing hooves and looked above the old mare in time to see a beautiful sorrel mare come running into their sight over a small rise. Other horses soon came into view, but they stopped on top of the rise above the bank of the creek. The sorrel mare raced down the hill where the old bay was standing whinnying toward the colt in the water. The sorrel was obviously the colt's mother and had run to find the colt when she heard the old bay mare urgently whinnying an alarm.

Shorty and Chester were afraid to breathe for fear of spooking the horses. They were completely surprised by the appearance of the band of horses. Larcenous thoughts raced through their minds as they watched the horses on the other side of the creek. They were evil men and amusing thoughts of the playful colt splashing water, were soon replaced in their black hearts, by wicked ones. Very slowly, Shorty turned his head toward Chester and in an almost whisper, said, "Chester, maybe we won't have to sleep on the ground tonight, after all."

They were running well. Ann knew they had one of their best runs going when they came around the second barrel and Buster accelerated so swiftly that she almost rode up on the cantle of her saddle. Confidence built in the horse and rider as they approached the last barrel in perfect position. Buster attained a high velocity in the stretch toward the last barrel. Ann felt an underlying urge to push Buster even harder to try and ensure the win. He was running better than he ever ran before. Everything felt good. She decided to go for it. She slacked up slightly on the reins to give the horse the okay to go for more speed if he could. Buster acknowledged the cue and entered the third barrel at a greater speed than normal. He carried that speed a little longer before checking himself, as they entered the turn. He made an outstanding turn and kept an excellent pocket as they circled the barrel.

Ann's elation grew as they executed the last turn. This was going to be a great ride if they could finish with a hard run to the finish line, she thought. Straightening out, Buster started digging hard with his powerful hind quarters to accelerate to top speed for the final dash.

Ann gasped in surprise when she felt Buster's right rear leg lose traction under the force of his driving push. She realized what happened. They carried too much speed into the turn and that tremendous momentum caught up with them as they came around the barrel. His hindquarters moved slightly over their center of gravity as they made that last turn. With the weight of his hind end not quite where it should be when he drove out, the loss of traction on that leg was inevitable.

Buster instinctively corrected the loss of balance and adjusted his gait. He was back in control and running hard for the finish line with a minimum of lost time. It was a slight mistake, but that one little slip would cost them dearly. They flashed across the finish line and slid to a stop in the alleyway. It was still a good run and Ann anxiously waited for the announcer to read their time.

It seemed like an eternity before the announcer read the time called up to him by the line judge. Fifteen point nine five seconds. That's okay, Ann thought. Not as good as yesterday, but still a good run. Maybe it would hold. With their twelve-hundredths of a second lead from yesterday, they were still in a good position to take the overall win. Time would tell, she thought. I'm the first rider, everyone's got something to shoot for now. She rode out of the alleyway and decided to walk Buster down and not watch Marsha make her run. Beth passed her on her way to the "on deck" position. Beth waved and said, "Good run, Annie."

Ann smiled and waved back. "Good luck, Beth," Ann said.

Marsha knew she had to make up some time if she was going to take the overall win. She needed the win to help in her quest to be the number one barrel racer in the state. The points she would earn with a first place overall would go a long way toward putting her in the lead. This run was important and she intended to push extra hard to gain the lead. The buckskin was ready and showing impatience. He was in an ideal frame of mind to turn in an outstanding race. He wanted to run and Marsha intended to let him have his way. She was confident she could easily take the lead away from the girl from High Valley. The Olsen girl's run had not been that great and if no one else turned in a higher time, Marsha felt she could gain and hold the overall lead.

The judge indicated to Marsha that she could start whenever she was ready. She roughly positioned the buckskin and jabbed her spurs in his sides to excite him. The horse didn't like the feel of the spurs and pranced sideways trying to escape the pain. When Marsha felt she had him worked up to the point where he wanted to run away from the spurs, she gave him his head and he bolted toward the first barrel. His speed was impressive. It seemed as if the horse reached the barrel and was running for the second before the spectators even realized Marsha started her run. They were going flat out when the buckskin checked his speed and cut around the last barrel. Marsha lashed him from side to side with her whip as he raced for the finish. They were good and their time proved it. Marsha turned in a fifteen point eight second run and nudged Ann out of first place by a mere three one-hundredths of a second when their scores for both days were tallied.

Shorty watched the colt. He began to form a plan in the corridors of his wicked mind. He knew the colt held the key to success in luring the band of horses across the creek. They had to get close enough for Chester to get a rope on them. Once they roped one horse, he knew the others would spook and they wouldn't have time to rope another before they ran. They needed more than one horse to make a decent profit for their trouble. If they worked it right, they could get two horses and then it would pay, Shorty thought. He studied the colt. He couldn't see a brand anywhere on the young horse. Shorty knew that if the horse had been branded, it would have been recently because of his young age. The brand would not be completely healed and his hair would not have had time to grow over or hide the scars from the branding irons. Shorty couldn't believe their luck.

"Do you see a brand anywhere on that colt?" Shorty asked Chester in a low voice.

"Nowhere, and at his age, if he was branded, it wouldn't a' healed yet and we'd see it easy," Chester whispered.

"How bout' them mares," Shorty whispered.

"Nothin'," Chester answered.

"We gotta' be real careful and try not to spook em'. If we can get that colt over here, then his momma' will come after him and maybe we can get two of em'," Shorty whispered.

"Tell me how ya' wanna' do it," Chester said.

"Only one of us move at a time. You get the grain, move slow and try to act as natural as you can. You know how horses can read your actions. They can tell if you're up to no good, or nervous, or just plain ignorant. So try to act like you're doing somethin' that you just naturally oughta' be doin'. Take the grain down to the crick' and make a few small piles leadin' up toward the trailer. If we get him across, them mares will follow. When he comes over, I'll slip up to the trailer and snake a rope through the front and tie it off. If you can rope him at the back of the trailer, I think we could drag and push him all the way in. We'll tie him off tight in front and use him for bait, then I think maybe his mother might be easy to get inside too. Slam the door on her and away we go. At least that's what I'm thinking anyway," Shorty said.

"That just might work, Shorty, I think that might work good. When do you want me to do it?" Chester asked.

"Right now, idiot. They ain't gonna' stay there forever. Git' movin' and act slow an' natural," Shorty said irritably. Chester looked at the colt again, then turned and started toward the trailer. He was unsteady and tripped on his own feet. He fell with a thump and hit the ground.

Chester heard Shorty cuss and say, "Quiet, you jerk!" He jumped up and looked across the creek. All the horses were watching him. He settled down and ambled to the front of the trailer. Chester opened the small door to the tack compartment. There was so much junk inside that he had to rustle around a little to find the grain bag. Chester swept old sacks and empty beer cans out of the way and finally saw the bag of grain. There wasn't much there, so he knew he better not waste any. He had to save some to make a pile right at the back of the trailer to get the colt close enough. I better do this right or Shorty will blame me if it don't work out just like he's got it planned, Chester told himself.

Chester got the grain bag out of the trailer and untied the piece of baling twine holding it closed. He walked slowly down to the creek holding the bag in front of him. He watched the horses. They were watching him. The colt stopped splashing and focused his full attention on the approaching stranger. Chester changed his direction slightly and headed a little higher on the bank. He didn't want to walk directly toward the colt. He wanted the colt to think that he wasn't the least bit interested in him. Chester knew the old horses would be the ones to watch closely. That old bay mare seemed to be the boss and she might spook and take the rest with her. "I better take it real easy," Chester told himself. He heard the old horse nickering to the colt. She don't like this at all, I better keep my eye on her, Chester thought.

Ann felt disappointed when she heard Marsha's time and realized Marsha moved into first place. That one little slip coming around the third barrel cost them the win. They probably lost a full tenth of a second when Buster's hind leg lost traction and slipped in the turn. Still, she felt good about her performance. After all, Marsha was one of the best in the state and Ann made her ride hard to capture the lead. Running second in this league isn't that bad. I'll improve and my horses will get better. Someday, I'll be in first place. I'll just have to settle for second place this weekend, Ann cheerfully thought. She walked Buster through the parking area and tied him off to the trailer. She unsaddled and brushed him down. When Buster was settled in at the trailer with some good grass hay to work on, she walked back to the arena to watch the rest of the rodeo.

Bill and Casey were getting ready in the chutes when Casey tapped Bill on the shoulder and said, " Look, Don's up on Moon Shot, let's see how he does." Bill smiled and nodded at Casey. "I told him earlier, that he had to know how to start Moon Shot's motor to get a decent ride out of him," Casey said and smiled. Bill grinned at his friend and they waited for Don to come out on Moon Shot.

Don nodded that he was ready, and the judge gave the okay to the men working the gates. The gate swung open and Moon Shot charged straight out. He made three hard jumps into the arena and then slammed down in a stiff legged stop. He spun around and bucked half heartedly back toward the chutes. Don was spurring hard down both sides trying to instigate a better performance out of the strong horse. Moon Shot would have none of it. He raced to the center of the arena in a half crow hopping, half bucking action that disappointed the rider. Moon Shot wasn't giving Don the kind of ride the bronc rider needed to rate a high score. He made a few more easy bucks before the eight second horn sounded. He was bucking so easy when the horn sounded that Don easily stepped off to the ground and let the horse run on by himself. Don hadn't even lost his hat. He started walking back to the chutes. The announcer read his score. It was a disappointing sixty-eight. Don shook his head in disgust. He remembered how good the horse bucked at High Valley and couldn't understand why he hardly bucked at all today.

Back at the chutes, Casey looked at Bill and said, "I guess Don didn't know how to crank up Moon Shot's motor."

Bill smiled and said, "Looks that way, don't it."

Casey's horse was moved into the chute and they switched their attention to getting the bucking horse rigged up for Casey's ride. Don got back to the chutes and yelled up to Casey, "I got robbed!"

Black Magic, the horse Casey rode on Sunday, gave him all he needed to win the bareback bronc championship at Twin Forks. The stringy looking black horse was all wiry muscle. He was a straight forward, no nonsense bucking horse. He came out of the chute like he was launched from a bazooka. He was honest about his bucking and didn't waste any time trying to fool the rider. He just bucked as hard as he could. Casey had to pay attention, and when the horn sounded he was still on top of the wiry horse and looking for the pick up rider. He was ready to get off. It was a good enough ride to win the top award.

Ann placed well in the two rodeos she competed in during the summer and earned some points toward qualifying her to compete in the state finals. However, her overall total was not enough to place her on the list of finalists to ride for the state championship. She would have to compete in more rodeos throughout the year to earn enough points to qualify. After today's second place finish against Marsha, who was currently leading the state, Ann felt confident that she would be able to qualify in the future. She was satisfied with her results at Twin Forks.

On the drive back to High Valley, Casey talked up a storm. He was tickled with his first place finish. He talked about entering bigger rodeos and trying his luck against stronger riders. He wanted to compete in more championship rodeos. "The challenge of that arena and trying to stay on a horse that doesn't want me there has a powerful attraction to me," Casey told Ann.

Ann talked about her desire to win a state championship. She told Casey how badly she wanted to be offered a scholarship and be part of the college rodeo team. "I've got two years to go and I think I can do it. By then, I'll be working Stormy. With his potential, who knows how far we can go!" she said.

CHAPTER 13

There was a lot depending on what he did next, so Chester was careful how he moved. He eased down the bank until he was opposite Stormy. Chester stopped and looked at the colt. He didn't see any alarm in the young horse's eyes. Chester looked back at the mares. Their ears were at attention and they were watching every move he made. He untied the twine and opened the grain bag. The colt still showed no concern about his actions. Chester walked down the slope toward the creek. Stormy stopped splashing and watched the man closely. He raised his muzzle in the air when the strong unpleasant scent of the man reached him.

Chester casually walked to within five feet of the water's edge. So far, so good, none of the horses had made a move to leave the creek bottom, he thought. He knew the longer he stayed near the water and the colt, the greater the danger of the older horses bolting and taking the colt with them. Chester bent down by the water's edge and let a few pounds of grain trickle out of the bag. He slowly stood and walked quietly toward the trailer. He stopped halfway and turned to see how the horses were reacting to the grain.

Chester couldn't have been more pleased. The colt had crossed the creek and was eagerly eating the grain he spread. The older horses had taken their attention from the men and were inquisitively watching Stormy. Chester turned his head and looked at Shorty. Shorty gave him a "thumbs up" sign and Chester watched as Shorty pulled a rope from the back of the pickup. Chester spread more grain on the ground and made sure all the horses saw it. Timing was important now, Chester cautioned himself. He watched as Shorty walked to the back of the trailer and opened the big door. Still holding the rope, Shorty stepped into the trailer.

Shorty opened a little vent door at the front of the trailer and passed the end of the rope through the opening. He went to the back of the trailer and neatly placed the coiled rope on the edge of the trailer floor. He stepped out and walked around the blind side of the trailer from the horses and tied the end of the rope to the truck. The rope was ready for Chester to throw a loop over the colt's head. Shorty was starting to feel good about their plan. The colt came to the grain and if he approached the trailer, then Chester could easily rope him.

About the only thing Chester was good at was roping. Shorty could never figure out why Chester was such a good roper. He was clumsy at everything else he tried, but in his sober years had always been able to pick up extra cash at jackpot ropings around the country. Chester bummed around the rodeo circuits and made a name for himself as a calf roper. He could have gone on to win a few championships, if the booze hadn't got the best of him. The more ropings Chester won, the more he drank. He won fairly regular and usually had the money spent on whiskey and women before the weekend was over.

Chester spent years traveling around the country, roping in small time events. Age and whiskey took their toll and he gradually started losing to younger ropers. His roping wasn't the problem. He seemed to be able to throw a good loop during the competitions. It was his riding that went downhill. He lost his ability to put the horse in the right place at the right time. More and more often, he was forced to make longer throws at the calf. He could throw an accurate loop but started having trouble bailing off the horse and running in to tie the calf.

His horsemanship became so bad that he started having bad wrecks when he tried to dismount at high speed during the ropings. He forced himself into an early retirement from the rodeo circuit after one cold winter night. He showed up drunk for the calf roping event. The calf came out of the chute and Chester was late giving his horse the go ahead out of the box. The calf got a good lead on Chester's horse and Chester spurred hard trying to catch up. Chester was confident in his roping ability and when the calf was barely within range, he threw, and the loop settled over the calf's head. He threw his slack away like a pro and the calf was firmly caught.

That's when the trouble started. He tried to make a fast dismount and lost his balance. When he hit the ground his legs didn't keep up with his direction of travel and he fell. Calf roping is a timed event. The fastest time wins the money. Chester knew he was losing time, so he jumped up and raced down the rope for the calf. When he fell coming off the horse, he injured his left leg and now it gave way and he fell again. Embarrassed, he got up and in a running limp, made it to the calf. He was a big man. He flanked the calf, lifted it high into the air, and then slammed it down hard to wrap and tie its legs.

The calf wasn't happy about being roped and the added insult of being jerked off the ground, then slammed down on its side was too much to take. The calf started kicking and put up quite a fight when Chester tried to wrap and tie it. Chester lost a lot of time. Now he tried to make up time and took a short cut tying the calf's legs. The calf was enraged about the treatment he was receiving and fought for all he was worth. Chester skipped a wrap trying to save time and then threw a sloppy half hitch around the calf's legs. The calf wasn't cooperating and struggled to escape.

Before Chester could raise his arms in the "all done" signal, his short wraps and loose tie lost out to the wildly kicking calf. Its legs came loose. Free from the restraint of the piggin' string, the calf made a tremendous kick with its hinds legs. Unfortunately for Chester, one of those powerful hind legs connected squarely with his jaw. The force of the kick knocked Chester clear over on his back. It also broke his jaw.

Chester was knocked out cold, lying in the middle of the arena. The spectators got a kick out of the calf winning the contest. They cheered when the calf jumped up and trotted toward the end of the arena leading Chester's horse, who was still connected to the calf by the rope. It seemed like the horse and calf teamed up and neither one wanted any more to do with the unconscious man lying in the arena. Chester ended up spending months with his jaw wired shut and had to quit chewing tobacco. He decided he didn't want any more baby calves humiliating him like the last one did, so he quit roping for a living. That's when he met Shorty. Chester needed money and when Shorty offered to take him in as a full partner in his livestock operation, he gladly accepted.

Shorty stayed by the back of the truck and watched the horses. Happily, he saw the colt finish the pile of grain by the creek and move up the bank to another pile. The colt stopped and started cleaning up the grain in the second pile. The sorrel mare raised her muzzle and sniffed the air. The aroma of the sweet feed came across to her and she started across the creek. The bay mare stood her ground and nickered a warning to the young mare to be careful. Flame warily crossed the creek and moved toward her colt. Stormy was going through the grain like a vacuum cleaner and showed no concern for the men. Flame walked up the bank where Stormy was eating the grain in the small pile.

Chester walked to the back of the trailer and waited for the colt to finish the grain before dumping any more out. With the mare helping the colt eat the grain, Chester knew it wouldn't take long for it to be gone. The horses were getting a good taste and when the small pile was gone, would be eager for more. He would wait for them to finish before pouring another portion out, so they would be within roping range, at the back of the trailer.

Hidden at the back of the pickup, Shorty hardly moved as he watched Chester luring the horses in range. For once, Chester was following their plan to perfection. He was dumping out just the right amount of grain. Chester was being stingy with the grain and let it trickle out of the bag. He was teasing the horses with the small amounts he dropped. Chester didn't want the horses to spend too much time at any one pile. Too much grain would cause their desire for more to diminish and they might not want to chance coming right up to the back of the strange trailer. He's just whetting their appetite, Shorty thought, as he watched Chester move to the back of the trailer.

Shorty kept a close eye on the old mare across the creek. She was rigid. Her full attention was focused on the two younger horses. Occasionally she darted a quick suspicious look at the men near the trailer. We'll have to watch that one real close, Shorty thought. It seemed as if Rose was reading the evil men's minds. She whinnied to the horses on the other side of the creek and started prancing nervously back and forth along the water's edge. She didn't like the looks of the men, or their foul odor wafting across the creek, mixed in with the sweet smell of grain. She's getting awful nervous, Shorty thought as he watched the old mare begin to prance back and forth.

Chester realized the old mare was becoming more and more uneasy about the situation. He knew they would have to act soon, before the old horse succeeded in calling the colt and his mother back across the creek. They had just about eaten all of the grain from the last pile. Chester watched them and decided it was now or never. He coughed lightly to draw the horse's attention. The two horses looked toward him. Chester held the bag up high and let the remainder of the grain trickle out to the ground. Both horses watched as the feed fell from the bag. They knew what it was and how much better it tasted than the fall grass. The first frost had burned the grass and given it a stale taste. The sweet grain was a delicious treat.

When the last of the grain fell from the bag, Chester reached into the trailer and picked up the coiled rope. He stepped back around the side of the trailer and out of sight of the horses. He shook out a loop. Their plan was in place, now it was up to the horses to fall for the bait, Chester thought, as he looked back at Shorty. Shorty grinned and nodded approval at the way Chester had handled the grain. Chester couldn't see the horses from where he was standing behind the trailer. He mouthed the words to Shorty, "Let me know." He wanted to know when the horses came within roping range. Shorty nodded an "okay" back to him. They waited for the horses to make the next move.

Stormy didn't keep them waiting long. He watched Chester pour the grain behind the trailer. There wasn't much left where he was, so he walked toward the back of the trailer where he could see more of the sweet feed on the ground. Flame liked the grain, but she wasn't quite sure that Stormy should move so close to the strangers. She had never seen these men before and she didn't like their smell. She nickered softly to Stormy as he walked toward the trailer. Stormy stopped and looked back at his mother. He had never been harmed by anyone. He had no reason to fear these men. He walked right up to the grain near the rear of the stock trailer.

Chester couldn't see Stormy approaching. He watched Shorty, waiting for him to tell him when the horse was in roping range. Chester watched Shorty's eyes and saw them following the colt to the back of the trailer. He knew the horse must be close. Shorty turned his head to Chester and nodded. Chester stepped out from behind the trailer and in one smooth sidearm motion sent a loop singing toward the colt. Stormy was surprised by the sudden appearance of the stranger and when he saw the rope sailing through the air toward him, he bolted toward his mother.

Chester was a natural roper and he figured the colt would probably bolt away at the sight of him. He compensated for the colt's quick move when he threw the rope. Stormy actually ran into the loop as he turned and bolted in alarm. The noose pulled tight, and when the colt hit the end of the rope it flipped him over backwards. Shocked and terrified by the suddenness of the rope, Stormy jumped up and tried to run. Again, he hit the end with enough force to throw him back to the ground. Shorty and Chester jumped into action when they saw the colt was caught. Shorty started pulling on the end of the rope where it came through the front of the trailer. Chester ran behind the colt and started kicking and yelling at him in an attempt to spook him into the trailer. In panic, Stormy jumped away from the man and Shorty quickly pulled the slack out of the rope. Swiftly, the men pulled and spooked the frantic colt into the trailer.

These men had a lot of practice when it came to loading unwilling stock. They used a combination of force and fear to get the job done in a hurry. In a matter of seconds, the terrified colt was pulled all the way to the front of the trailer and Shorty quickly retied the rope. Chester raced around the trailer and pulled another rope from the back of the truck and quickly formed a loop to try and catch the sorrel mare. He ran to the back side of the trailer to get in position for another throw. Stormy was screaming frantically in great fear. He had never been treated so brutally by anyone and he called out in terror for his mother to rescue him from this nightmare.

Flame watched Chester step out from the trailer and send the rope streaking toward Stormy. The enormity of the act took her by surprise. She was confused and it took a few seconds for her to realize the danger to her colt. The men tied the colt in the trailer so swiftly that Flame didn't react until she heard the terrified screams of Stormy echoing off the metal sides of the trailer. Stormy's screams galvanized her into action.

In three great bounds, she was at the rear of the trailer. She saw Stormy fighting the rope that held him. He was thrashing his head and whinnying in great fright. Flame reared up and crashed her hooves down onto the lip of the trailer floor. She backed away and reared again in frustration. She could see her colt, but felt helpless to free him. She caught Chester's movement when he came from the side of the trailer in an attempt to throw a loop on her. She whirled away to the opposite side of the trailer and reared high again, bringing her hooves crashing down into the side of the trailer. She left huge dents in the lower edge of the roof where her hooves struck. The force of her fury rocked the trailer. Stormy screamed in terror when he saw Flame through the trailer vents, reared high in the air, bellowing her anger at the men. She came crashing down on the trailer rocking it again with the force of her blows.

Her fury scared Chester and he hesitated to follow her to the other side. Shorty screamed, "Get a rope on her before she wrecks our whole outfit!" Chester stepped out from behind the trailer and started to swing the rope. Flame saw him and immediately turned to vent her anger on him. She stood on her hind legs and pawed the air above the frightened rustler. She screamed out in rage and struck at the man with her front legs. "Hurry, Chester, Hurry!" Shorty yelled. Chester threw the rope at her, more in defense than in an attempt to catch her. The leading edge of the loop slapped against her neck and the back of the loop cartwheeled over her head. Chester instinctively pulled the slack and Flame felt the loop tighten.

Now Flame's rage exploded and she turned her violent wrath full force on Chester. Chester dropped the rope. He turned and tried to flee from the crazed mare. Flame struck out at the fleeing man and caught him with her powerful front hooves. She knocked him to the ground and reared over him. Chester tried to rise, but Flame savagely lashed out again and smashed him back down, crushing his shoulder. She reared again to deliver another blow. Chester screamed out in panic, "Shorty! Shoot her! Shoot her before she kills me!" Shorty was frozen in wide eyed amazement at the mare's savage attack. Chester's screams brought him out of his daze. He jerked open the truck door and snatched the saddle gun from the rack behind the seat.

He turned in time to see Flame rear high in the air, ready to deliver another crushing blow. Flame let out a bloodcurdling scream as she prepared to destroy Chester. Chester cried out in agony for Shorty to hurry. The sight of the enraged mare, rearing high over Chester, screaming out her fury with the rope still hanging from her neck, sent tendrils of fear racing through Shorty's body. He levered a shell into the chamber and raised the rifle toward the awesome sight of the savage horse.

Chester screamed as the mare started down to pound him into the dirt. Shorty quickly fired at the fearsome horse. At the same time, Chester rolled toward the trailer in an attempt to protect himself. The 150 grain soft point bullet hit dead center on the rope hanging from the mare's neck and cut it cleanly in two. The bullet entered her chest, and its trajectory took it into her shoulder. The concussion of the bullet smashing into her, knocked her to the side. In a rage, she turned back toward the source of the explosion and saw Shorty. Without hesitation, she reared up and pawed the air with her good front leg and started after him while blood pumped out of the hole made by the bullet.

Now driven by overwhelming fear, Shorty levered another shell into the chamber as he raised the rifle to his shoulder and fired again. The bullet struck her head, knocking the sorrel mare over backwards. She crashed down on her back. Shorty ran to get Chester. He was met by the sound of pounding hooves and looked up to see the old bay mare charging straight at him in wild eyed rage.

Johnson's old bay mare, Montana Rose, had watched in fear as Chester threw the rope over Stormy's head and then forced him into the trailer. She saw her daughter, Flame, charge to the young colt's rescue. Greatly alarmed, she watched the battle between Flame and the tall man. She felt helpless and whinnied in dismay when she saw the rope fly over Flame's head. When Flame knocked the man down, Rose started across the creek to help the young mare in her fight. The sound of the first shot stopped her in her tracks with its unexpected, exploding noise. Then she heard the second shot and watched as Flame went over on her back with blood gushing out of the wound in her chest. Instantly she was at a full run toward the predators attacking Flame and her colt.

Shorty raised the gun again and rapidly fired twice at the charging mare. The bullets slammed low into Rose's chest. The first bullet burst through her breast bone and entered her chest cavity. It lost its velocity and lodged deep in her heart. The second bullet followed nearly the same path. It cut a swath through her lungs as it expended its energy. Rose's great forward motion carried her nearly to the trailer and Shorty jumped back in fright. The great mare died in mid stride. She was dead before she hit the ground. Chester tried to scramble away in panic but was blocked by the body of the sorrel mare where she had fallen.

Stunned by the attack of the two horses, Shorty stepped away and looked at the two fallen mares. His great fear gradually gave way to loss. Shorty thought of what the horses would have been worth if he hadn't shot them. Angrily, he looked down at Chester and said, "Let's get out of here before somebody comes to investigate them shots!" It was then that he saw how badly his partner was hurt.

In a pain wracked voice, Chester sobbed, "Please help me, Shorty, I'm hurt bad!"

Shorty set the gun down on the fender of the truck. He was apprehensive about helping the wounded man. He didn't want to get Chester's blood on him. If he's gonna' die, I'd be better off to leave him here with the dead horses and clear out of the country myself, Shorty thought. He cautiously approached Chester where he was lying between the trailer and the fallen sorrel mare. "How bad are ya'?" Shorty asked.

"Bad, my shoulder is smashed and I think some of my ribs might be broke. You gotta' get me to a hospital," Chester moaned.

"You ain't gonna' die then?" Shorty asked.

"I don't know, hurry and git' me outta' here," Chester pleaded.

Shorty ran around the truck and opened the passenger door. He went back and as gently as he could, lifted Chester to his feet. Chester cried out in pain and Shorty could see blood coming from his mouth. They struggled around the front of the truck and managed to get Chester into the cab. Shorty felt one short flash of compassion when he saw pain and tears in Chester's eyes. It didn't last long and he ran back to the driver's side and jumped in the truck. He started the motor and began to pull away when he heard the frantic whinnying of the colt in the trailer.

He stopped and jumped out of the truck. He was confused about what to do with the colt. Shorty saw the rifle still lying on the fender. He forgot he set it there when he helped Chester into the truck. I better settle down and get myself under control, Shorty thought. He picked up the rifle and looked at the two mares lying in the dirt. He could see that the old mare was dead. Blood was everywhere and the pungent odor of death was in the air. The sorrel mare was still breathing. Blood pumped out of the bullet hole in her chest with each weak beat of her heart. She was still alive, but just barely. He could see the red goove of the second bullet's path, where it had traveled up the side of her head below her ear. I just grazed her head on that second shot, luckily it stopped her though, Shorty thought. Shorty decided to put her out of her misery with another shot. He cocked the gun and raised it to fire. Then he thought, she's gonna' die anyway, besides, what do I care if she suffers. Look what she did to poor Chester. Somebody might even hear another shot. Best we just clear out of here as fast as we can. He lowered the hammer on the rifle. Now, I gotta' figure out what to do with this screamin' colt. I should shoot him too, for all the trouble he's caused.

Shorty walked around Flame, he could see her chest barely rise when she struggled for a shallow breath. She won't be in this world much longer, Shorty thought. He looked into the back of the trailer at the colt still struggling to get free. I've got to settle down and start thinkin'. I almost drove away with the gun lyin' on the fender and the door to the trailer wide open, where anyone could see that colt tied inside, Shorty thought. We need to get out of here fast. If I turn the colt loose, I won't have any way of gettin' the loop off his neck and we'll lose a good rope. I could shoot him and then take the rope off, but that would waste another shell and make more noise. If we take him with us, we'd have to haul him all the way to Wyoming and turn him loose in our corrals or just let him go out in the hills. Maybe the best thing to do is to get started out of here and worry about the colt later, Shorty thought.

Shorty closed and latched the trailer door. At least no one will be able to see the little horse in there, Shorty thought. He made a quick sweep around the area to make sure they weren't leaving anything lying around that could link them to the killing of the two mares and the disappearance of the colt. Satisfied they weren't leaving any clues, Shorty got back in the truck and drove out of the cottonwoods toward the county road.

He drove slowly across the field toward the hole in the fence where they cut the wires. The truck bounced over a rough spot and Chester moaned in pain. Shorty pulled through the opening in the fence and told Chester to grit his teeth until they got back on the road. He gunned the engine to climb up the shoulder. The truck lurched up onto the gravel road and the rear wheels started spinning, trying to gain traction pulling the load of the trailer up the short incline. Chester cried out again when the truck bumped hard going up the shoulder. They made it safely and Shorty accelerated the old truck toward town and away from the slaughter on Gunpowder Creek.

"Chester, can you hear me?" Shorty asked.

"Yeah, but I hurt bad, Shorty," Chester said.

"Listen, Chester, you're gonna' have to hold on for awhile. We can't go to no doctor anywhere around here. When they find those horses, they'll remember us and tie us in to the killin' of them. We're gonna' have to drive clear out of this country before we try and find you some help. Can you hang on that long?" Shorty asked.

"I'll try," Chester moaned.

Shorty reached under the seat and felt around till he found the whiskey bottle he put there last night. He pulled it out and looked at it. It was still half full. He handed it across to Chester and said, "Take a big swig of this and maybe it won't hurt so bad, Chester." Chester looked at him in complete misery. He slowly reached out with his good arm and took the bottle. Shorty was hoping Chester would drink enough whiskey to kill the pain. Chester took a swallow and passed the bottle back to Shorty. I hate to see a man drink alone, Shorty thought. He tipped the bottle up and drank deeply.

CHAPTER 14

Ann raced out of the house and headed for the barn at a high lope. She was late and wanted to drop the envelope on Johnson's desk before she ran for the school bus. They arrived back at the ranch from Twin Forks last night and by the time she took care of Buster it was very late. She overslept, but if she hustled, she thought she could make it to the road before the bus came.

She ran into the barn and was relieved to see no one around. She went into the office and placed the white envelope in the middle of Johnson's desk. There, she thought, that's done. She stepped back and looked at the envelope lying there. He sure can't miss seeing it when he comes in today, she thought. She turned and raced out of the office and headed down the lane to the county road. She could see the bus coming and knew she would be there before it arrived. Things were working out just right. Ann left her final payment for the purchase of Stormy on Johnson's desk.

She worked all summer for this day. Stormy was hers now. She paid her debt to the ranch and felt wonderful about keeping her promise to Johnson, to finish paying for the colt by the end of the summer. It was a satisfying feeling to pay your debts on time, she thought. She beat the school bus to the stop by thirty seconds and was breathing hard when she climbed on for the ride to school. Her thoughts turned to what was ahead during the school year. It's time to buckle down. I've got to concentrate on school and devote more time to studying, she thought.

Ann skipped school on Friday to compete at twin Forks, so she had a lot to make up today. She dug right in and devoted the day to school work. During lunch, she went over the weekend activities with her friends and told them about the excitement of competing in a big rodeo. Everyone thought it was wonderful that she placed second in such a large event. "I hope to win those big events someday. I've got a colt coming along that is going to help me get there, too," she told her friends.

"Ease up on him a little," Johnson told Bill. Bill loosened up on the rope and the colt backed up and stopped when the rope came tight again.

"We're gainin' on him," Bill said.

"He's got different ideas than we do about what he ought to be doin'. He'll come around to our way of thinkin' when he figures out we don't plan on hurtin' him none, but that he has to do it our way," Johnson said. Johnson was helping Bill work a two year old colt that was giving him trouble. "Sometimes just the sight and feel of two people working a horse intimidates them a little and maybe they feel outnumbered. I don't know, but it sure can speed things along with an uncooperative horse," Johnson told Bill years ago.

"He's hardly fighting the rope now, so I'll take him from here," Bill said.

Johnson stepped back and looked the dark bay colt over. "You were right about this one, Bill, he's worth keepin'. He's as smart as a whip and built with that good cow horse frame. I like him, and when he figures out what his job in life is supposed to be, he'll make a top horse, no matter what he's trained to do," Johnson said.

"He's gonna' be a good one all right, look at his eyes, he doesn't miss a thing. He keeps track of what's goin' on around him. This is the kind of horse that can keep you out of trouble," Bill said. Bill moved around to the side of the colt and tightened up on the lead rope snapped to the colt's halter. The colt immediately turned and took one step toward Bill, facing him.

"He's catching on quick now," Johnson observed.

"Thanks for the help. I'll keep workin' with him for a while before I turn him loose," Bill said.

"Okay, I'll be at my desk if you need any more help," Johnson said.

It was still early morning and Johnson hoped to get some paper work done before the day got too far along. He walked into the barn and down the wide alleyway toward his office. He opened the door and walked in. He saw the white envelope sitting in plain sight on his desk. He picked it up and smiled when he saw the drawing of a smiling face on the front of the envelope. I bet I know who this is from, he thought. He opened it and counted out the exact amount of money Ann owed to pay her debt for Stormy. He read the enclosed note. It said, Final payment for Stormy, future world champion barrel horse. Johnson smiled and studied the note. It wouldn't surprise me if she turned that horse into a world champion, they both have what it takes, he pleasantly thought.

He entered her payment in the accounts ledger and got started on the paperwork he had been putting off for days. The ranch did well this year and he wanted to figure a way to utilize the profits to the best benefit of the ranch. When we bring the cattle out of the hills this fall and sell the calves, we're going to have an excess amount of cash in the bank. Even after we pay all the bills, we're still going to be in good shape, Johnson thought. He planned on working out a cautious approach to upgrading their horse handling facilities. If he could justify it, he wanted to use some of this year's profits to build an indoor arena. That would give them the ability to carry on a training program during the long mountain winters when the weather was too nasty to work outside.

Johnson was jolted out of his concentration. He sat straight up in his chair as he heard the sound of a horse's hoofs pounding hard and fast coming up the lane from the county road. It was so unusual for anyone to run a horse that hard coming into the ranch that he jumped up and ran out to see what was going on.

Apprehension gripped him when he saw James coming at a full run up the driveway. Something must be awfully wrong for James to run his horse like that, Johnson thought. Bill heard the horse running too, and ran up beside Johnson and said, "We must have trouble!"

James came on hard and when he neared the men he slid his horse to a stop and jumped off. His face was twisted and covered with deep anguish. The men were shocked by James' appearance and Johnson shouted, "James, what has happened?"

"God--Johnson! Someone has shot our horses!" James cried in distress.

"What?" Johnson shouted incredulously and grabbed James by the arm to steady him.

Bill grabbed the reins of the horse and shouted, "Where?"

"The clearing in the cottonwoods below Dry Boulder, on the crick', Flame's still alive, but barely breathing. She's shot bad and there's blood everywhere. We need to call Doc Brown in a hurry!" James sobbed.

Bill ran to the barn to call the veterinarian and Johnson called out after him, "Call the sheriff too!"

Johnson was still holding James by the arm and he looked into his stricken face. He could see tears starting to form. A cold shiver went through Johnson as he realized James had not yet told him the worst. He was afraid to ask for fear of what else he might hear. He stared deep into James' eyes and saw both grief and anger. A sob escaped James as he kneeled on the ground and dropped his head into his hands. His body shook in light tremors. Johnson knew a catastrophe of monstrous proportions had occurred in order to affect this stouthearted man so deeply.

Johnson stooped down beside James' stocky form and put his arm on his shoulders. He felt James shudder, and was deeply moved. He said nothing, and waited in an effort to console him. What more could have happened? Johnson wondered. Bill came running out of the barn and saw the two men bent down on the ground. He stopped and a growing feeling of dread began to sweep over him as he watched the two men and saw James body wracked with sobs. Something more terrible than I can imagine has happened, Bill thought.

James began to gain control of his emotions. He removed his glasses and wiped his eyes. The sobs lessened and Johnson rubbed his hand at the base of James' neck and said,

"James, whatever's happened, we'll get it worked out." Bill remained standing near the barn. He was hesitant to approach until the painful moment for James passed.

James finally looked up into Johnson's eyes and said, "We got to hurry and try to help Flame, we might save her." He paused and a light sob escaped. He looked into Johnson's eyes and softly said, "Johnson--the worst part is--(his body shook and a soft cry slipped from his lips)--Rose is shot dead--lying right next to Flame."

The impact of James words rocked Johnson back on his heels. He emitted a choking noise from deep in his body. "Aaaw--Aaaw--No!" he cried out. Bill ran for Johnson to see what terrible thing caused that reaction. Johnson rose to his feet and a terrible rage overcame him.

Bill ran up and shouted, "What's happened? Tell me!"

Johnson turned to Bill and Bill could see rage in his eyes. "Somebody has killed Rose!" Johnson shouted.

"Oh no," Bill said in a barely audible whisper. Then Bill said, "Okay, Johnson, we need to hurry down there to help Flame if we can. Let's get moving right now!" Bill knew the trauma of Rose's death was a crippling blow to Johnson. He had to shock him into action to lessen the pain. They couldn't help Rose now, but Flame was in desperate need of their help. Bill knew he must bolster both Johnson's and James' spirit if they were going to save Flame.

He took control and started issuing orders to each of the grief stricken men. "James, you've seen her wound, get what we need from the medicine box. Grab bandages, antiseptic and anything else we'll need. Johnson, get the truck and throw towels, a bucket and sponges in it. Doc Brown is on his way, he knows the spot where the horses are. He'll call for the sheriff to meet us there. Now, let's get moving!" Bill said in a commanding voice.

Johnson looked at Bill and said, "I will not rest until I catch the people responsible for this." Then he turned and ran for the truck.

Bill spun around and ran back to the barn to help James. He saw him going through the medical supplies. "Are you okay?" Bill asked.

"As good as I can be, after what I found down there. It's really bad, Bill," James said. They heard Johnson gunning the engine on the truck. James hurried out with the medical supplies. Bill grabbed a large folded canvas and hurried after him. They jumped in the truck and Johnson roared toward Gunpowder Creek.

The bell ending Ann's last class of the day finally rang. She put a lot of effort into today's studies and was glad to hear the bell ring. She gathered her books and walked out of school toward the bus that would take her home. On the way to the bus, she was surprised to see Johnson's truck parked along the curb in front of school. Delighted to see him, she ran down the walk to his truck. She could see a grim look on his face. "Johnson, what are you doing here?" she asked.

Startled from deep thoughts, Johnson looked up in surprise. "I came to pick you up and give you a ride back to the ranch," he said in an emotionless tone. He must have already been in town, Ann thought.

She jumped in and asked, "Did you find my final payment for Stormy on your desk this morning?"

Johnson turned and looked at her. She was shocked by the look on his face. "Yeah, I found it," he said. Ann felt strange about Johnson's lack of emotion. Paying off Stormy was a big event for her, Johnson could at least make a nice remark, she thought. She decided to wait for him to carry the conversation further.

He didn't keep her waiting long. Under great strain, Johnson shattered Ann's dreams for the future. "Annie, something terrible happened at the ranch yesterday while we were at the rodeo in Twin Forks," Johnson solemnly said.

Ann turned in alarm to look at Johnson. "What happened?" she asked apprehensively.

"This is tough. (He paused for a few seconds and then continued.) Someone cut the fence and drove down into the woods along Gunpowder, near where Dry Boulder comes in," he said. Ann listened with a rising sense of foreboding. She waited for him to continue. "Do you know the spot where the cattle and horses have been bedding down lately?" he asked.

"Yes. What did they do there?" she asked quickly.

Johnson cleared his throat and with great pain in his voice said, "They shot and killed Rose and they shot Flame too. She is lying near death, in the clearing by the creek."

At first, Ann couldn't believe what she heard. She went numb. She turned and looked at Johnson. When she saw his agonized look, she knew it must be true. She felt as if some dreadful mistake had been made. Johnson's grief was real. It really happened. She screamed and then shouted in horror at Johnson, "Who did that? How could anyone shoot our horses?"

"We don't know. Doc Brown worked on Flame all morning trying to stabilize her. Poor Rose was dead when James found them this morning. Duke and the sheriff combed the area looking for clues and think they may have a few leads. They found an empty whiskey bottle in the brush and a rope that had been shot in two. Someone camped overnight in the clearing with a pickup. They were pulling a trailer. Bill and James are with Flame now. Duke was still there when I left to come for you," Johnson solemnly told Ann.

The horror of the act descended on Ann and she felt great pity for Johnson. She knew what Rose meant to him. The bay mare was part of Ann's life, too. She could remember the wonderful mare from her earliest childhood memories. Rose had always been a part of the Bent Bar. Flame was special too. She was a spectacular mare and they wanted her breeding and great ability to be the foundation of their future plans. Flame was also the dam of Stormy, Ann thought.

Then the thought of Stormy fell full force on her. "Stormy! Where is he? Was he hurt too?" she cried out.

Johnson looked at her with hurt in his eyes and said softly, "We can't find Stormy."

A dread fell over Ann. The thought of losing Stormy was almost too much for her to bear. Johnson could see tears forming. Losing the colt would devastate her. "Casey rode into the hills and found the band of mares. Stormy wasn't with them," he added.

"Take me there. Take me to Flame," Ann said firmly. Relief flooded Johnson. Ann was maintaining her composure and wasn't falling to pieces. She's going to control herself and try to find Stormy, Johnson thought. "If Stormy is not with Flame, then there is a good possibility that he's still alive. He must be somewhere and I'll find him, wherever he is, I'll find him!" Ann said.

Johnson related the details as he drove to the clearing on Gunpowder Creek where Flame was fighting valiantly for her life. "James started into the hills to check the stock early this morning. He rode down the county road and was planning on climbing the steep ravine that you and Buster rode down. He came to a spot where someone cut the fence and drove to the creek. When he investigated, he found Flame and Rose lying in the clearing. Poor Rose was dead and Flame was barely clinging to life. He raced back to the ranch for help. We called Doc Brown and he came right away," Johnson said.

Ann listened quietly as Johnson spoke. Johnson felt hurt when she began sobbing. He drove to the ranch and turned off on the road that led to the clearing where the killing had taken place. She could see Casey, James, Bill and the brand inspector, Duke, standing over Flame. An olive drab canvas was covering Rose. Ann's legs felt weak and she hesitated to get out of the truck. The morbid sight of the covered remains of Rose, lying dead under the canvas, and Flame lying next to her, near death, was too much for her to bear. Ann broke down into uncontrollable sobbing.

Everyone gave Ann time to regain her composure. Finally, Casey walked over to the truck and opened her door. "Come on, Ann. We're going to have to work together to find these people. I think they took Stormy with them," he said. At the sound of Stormy's name, Ann stepped out of the truck and a determined look replaced the sorrow on her face. She walked over to Flame.

"How is Flame?" she asked.

"She's hanging on. Doc removed the bullet and cleaned the wound. She's full of antibiotics and her breathing has improved slightly since James found her. She's still unconscious, but Doc said that if she can make it through another night, she might have a chance. He found rope fibers in the wound. That explains the rope we found cut in two. Doc says the rope probably saved her life by absorbing a good portion of the bullet's impact. That's about the only good thing I can say about the whole affair," Bill said.

"We've found a few things that may help us find the culprits responsible for this," Duke said.

"Anything more since I left, Duke?" Johnson asked.

"A few things. We found a large chip of paint imbedded in one of Flame's front shoes. A paper bag with a receipt from the High Valley grocery store and, of course, the empty whiskey bottle that should produce some good fingerprints. Whoever did this also chewed tobacco. There's tobacco juice everywhere," Duke said.

Casey said, "Sheriff took the paint chip and the other things we found to be analyzed at the state crime lab. He thinks they'll be able to lift a good set of prints from the bottle. He's also checking the grocery receipt at the store to see if they can recall any one who made that purchase. It was dated Saturday. He said he would talk to all the store clerks for leads and see if anyone can remember selling that brand of whiskey to anyone recently."

"The tracks around the area indicate there were two men involved," Duke said.

"I've found tracks that are most likely Stormy's. A colt came across the creek into this area where you can see they were parked. There's bits of grain lying around here too. They probably used grain to get the horses to come in close. I haven't been able to find any colt tracks leaving the clearing," Casey added.

"It looks like they took the colt. Maybe they were trying to get Flame in the trailer too, when they ran into trouble. The mares must have put up a fight for the colt, and the men ended up shooting them. I'll put out a bulletin with Stormy's description to every livestock inspector's office in the state. If any one tries to sell that colt, we'll catch them," Duke said.

"I wish now that I had branded our horses. From now on, every Bent Bar horse will carry our brand," Johnson said.

"We can't move Flame. I'll camp here with her, so I can keep an eye on her," James said.

"I'll run back to the ranch and get some gear and stay with you," Casey said.

"Thanks, Case," James said.

Ann saw Johnson look down at the covered body of Rose and watched as his face tightened in agony. He said, "I'll be back shortly after daylight and take care of Rose. She was the best saddle horse I ever owned."

Ann walked to Johnson's side and placed her hand on his arm in support. In a loud firm voice, she said, "We will catch these men. Don't anyone ever doubt it!"

Early the next morning, Ann left the house and heard the low rumble of a piece of heavy equipment. She followed the sound and found Johnson warming up the backhoe. He stepped off the machine when he saw her coming. "Good morning, Ann," he said.

"Morning, Johnson. Would it be okay for me to take a pickup to school today?" she asked.

"That would be fine," he said.

"During my lunch hour, I want to run some errands that may help us find Stormy and the people that took him," she said.

"Any way I can help?" he asked.

"Just let me start using the truck," she said.

"It's all yours," Johnson said.

Johnson drove the backhoe down the road and turned toward the creek where Rose was lying. James and Casey heard him coming. Johnson maneuvered the machine into the clearing. He set the brakes and pulled the throttle back to the idle position. He stepped off and walked over to the men standing by Flame. He handed James a thermos of coffee and said, "Here, James, I know how you like your morning cup of coffee. How is she?"

"Improved. Her breathing is slightly better and she has started blinking her eyes. The bleeding has completely stopped. Thanks for the coffee," James said. Johnson bent down and placed his hand on Flame. He could feel a definite improvement in the strength of her breathing.

"Doc called last night and said that if any horse could survive that injury, it would be Flame. If she regains consciousness, Doc feels she'll recover. He said we'd never be able to use her hard again. The bullet caused a lot of damage to her shoulder and she may carry a limp for the rest of her life. She lost a lot of blood and Doc said he'd be back today to give her another I.V."

"I'll stay with her," James said.

"Well, you two know what I'm here to do, so I'll get to it," Johnson said.

Johnson climbed on the backhoe and revved the engine. He drove the machine across the clearing to a spot near the creek. High on the bank, near a large beautiful cottonwood tree, he started digging a grave for his beloved Rose. Casey watched Johnson work. He cleared the brush from the area and started digging with the powerful machine. Casey walked over where Johnson was working. He intended to offer his help. He stood off to the side of the machine to get Johnson's attention. Soon, Johnson saw Casey out of the corner of his eye and turned to look at him. Casey could clearly see a trail of tears streaming down the wrinkled face. In respect, Casey turned and walked back where James was drinking his morning coffee.

Johnson worked quickly. When he was satisfied with the grave, he backed the machine away and idled it down. He got off and walked over where Rose lay covered by the canvas. He removed the canvas and took it to the grave. Neatly, he covered the bottom and sides of the grave. Johnson eased the machine around and as gently as possible, connected Rose to the long boom and moved her to the grave. With the grace of a ballet dancer, Johnson manipulated the controls and gently lowered his old friend into the canvas lined grave. He stopped the machine and climbed into the grave. He pulled the top sides of the canvas over Rose.

Satisfied with the covering, he started to pull the last corner across her head. He paused and looked down at the old mare. He rubbed his hand on her forehead as he had done a thousand times in the past when he was praising her for a job well done. "Old girl, you were more horse than any one man deserved. I was lucky to know you and even luckier to have spent these last twenty years and more in your company. I know we'll ride together again someday, somewhere. Then I'll tell you that I caught up with, and punished, those that did this, Goodbye, Rose." Tears flowed down Johnson's face as he pulled the cover over her head and climbed out of the grave.

He covered the grave with the rich, creek bottom soil and dug a huge boulder that eroded out of the bank during the spring flood. Using the powerful hydraulic system, he moved the boulder up the bank and positioned it on the grave of his mare, Montana Rose.

Ann organized a team of classmates and teachers to help her in the search for Stormy. They used the school's printing machine and made flyers with the colt's description and the circumstances of his disappearance. During the lunch break, she went to Duke's office and got a list of all the stockyards in Montana. He gave her a list of every brand inspection office and supplied her with addresses of every livestock company in the state. They mailed notices to every possible place a horse could be taken and sold. They called the newspaper and reported the evildoing to the editor. He promised to publish a story about the crime on Gunpowder Creek. Everyone was outraged about the shooting of the horses and promised their full cooperation in finding the criminals.

That evening the High Valley sheriff came to the ranch and gave a report on the progress of his investigation. He described the two strangers that the clerk remembered buying the groceries listed on the receipt. "They were also in Molly's Saturday evening. They ate and left. She watched them go. They were driving an old mud covered blue pickup. She had seen them once before, and said they caused trouble with Sam, and you'd probably remember them. Both were dirty. There was a tall one and a short one. The short one had a few upper front teeth missing. Also, a man fitting the description of the tall stranger bought two bottles of whiskey at the liquor store on Saturday. They were the same brand as the bottle we found at the scene. The state crime lab is running tests on the evidence. Hopefully we'll get more help from their results. Duke has issued a bulletin to every state livestock inspector. Stormy has been put on the "stray list" and hopefully will be found soon," he said.

"I remember those two men in Molly's. Duke will remember them too. He was suspicious of them last spring when they brought in two horses to sell at the stock yards. I remember him saying he didn't like the looks of them, but all their paperwork was in order so he had to okay the brand inspection," Johnson said.

"Okay, I'll check with Duke. In the meantime, keep your hopes up of finding Stormy. We're going to do our best to find these men and prosecute them. If you think of anything else that would help, call my office right away," the sheriff said.

CHAPTER 15

Stormy's mouth was dry and he was hungry. He was becoming dehydrated. He hadn't eaten or had anything to drink since being forced into the trailer. Weary and weak, he continually called out for his mother. As time in the trailer passed, his whinnying grew less and less. He spent more and more time leaning against the side of the trailer in a delirious state. He was confused and outraged about being treated so cruel by the men that took him. He simply did not understand why he was imprisoned without food or water, and why Flame did not come for him.

Shorty drove straight through the night. He dropped Chester off at a Wyoming hospital early the day after Flame smashed his shoulder. They told the doctor that Chester was thrown and stomped by a horse he had been breaking. Chester's injuries were serious and he needed surgery. The doctor told Shorty that Chester would have to stay in the hospital under their care for four or five days. He left Chester and drove to their cabin high in the mountains of a remote Wyoming wilderness area. Shorty wanted to get as far away from where he shot the horses as he could.

It was almost noon when he stopped to open the dilapidated gate that blocked the road leading to his ramshackle cabin. He drove through and stopped and closed the gate. He drove to the cabin hidden in the trees. There was a series of corrals winding around through the trees near one side of the cabin. Shorty used the corrals to hold stolen livestock until he decided where the safest place would be to take them to sell without drawing suspicion. He pulled in and parked near the corrals.

Shorty got out and stretched. His neck and back ached and standing felt good. He was tired. He had been going hard without sleep for over twenty-four hours. Shorty looked back at the trailer that held the young colt. He walked back to the front of the trailer and opened the small door above the feed tray. He reached in and untied the rope holding the colt. The loop was still around the colt's neck. Shorty reached in the side of the trailer and managed to grab the loop and pull it off the colt's head. I should unload that troublemakin' colt, but right now, alls I want to do is sleep. He can just rot in there for awhile, for all I care. Maybe he'll be easier to handle if I leave him cooped up in the trailer for a few days, Shorty thought.

He split a stream of tobacco juice to the ground and walked toward the cabin. He unlocked a padlock on the door and went inside. The cabin had a stale smell and reeked of tobacco. Shorty didn't even notice. He went over to one of the bunks against a wall and flopped down. Within minutes, with his clothes and dirty boots still on, he fell into a deep, snoring sleep, almost five hundred miles southeast of Gunpowder Creek.

Shorty slept clear into the next day. When he awoke, it took him a while to figure out where he was. Slowly the cabin's familiar appearance started to penetrate the recesses of his mind. He got up and walked outside. It felt good to be back here, where no one ever bothered him. He looked toward the truck and when he saw the trailer still hooked up, he began to remember all that happened in the last few days. Shorty walked over to the trailer. The dazed colt came awake. He spooked and crashed against the inside of the trailer. It startled Shorty and he jumped back in surprise. "Well, I'll be, I forgot about that little horse in there. Chester too, I wonder how he's doing," Shorty thought.

Stormy had been in the trailer for over two days and had fallen into a lethargic daze. Shorty's sudden appearance surprised him. The sight and smell of the rustler caused him to bolt. He watched as Shorty looked in one of the side vents. "You settled down any, colt? When you do, I'll let you out to the corrals," Shorty said. Stormy nervously watched and listened to the foul smelling man's words. Stormy watched through the vents as Shorty walked away and went into a weather beaten outhouse.

When Shorty came out, he looked again at the trailer and said, "You can stay there a while longer, colt. You don't know how close you came to getting a bullet right through that little white spot on your forehead." He walked back into the cabin and built a fire in the wood stove to make something to eat. In a few minutes, Stormy smelled smoke and saw a bluish white column of smoke rising out of the stove pipe on the cabin's roof. The young horse saw Shorty again late that evening, when he came out of the cabin. This time Shorty paid no attention to the trailer. He made a trip to the outhouse and returned straight to the cabin. Stormy leaned against the side of the trailer and fell into a half sleep.

Midmorning on Stormy's third day in the trailer, he heard the cabin door open and twisted his head around to look toward the door. He watched as Shorty came out and made his ritual trip to the dilapidated outhouse. When Shorty finally came out of the small shack, he walked to the trailer. Stormy stood rigid and watched him approach. "Today's your lucky day, horse. I gotta' unhook the trailer, so's I can go to town. I'm gonna' check on Chester and get some groceries and libations for myself and you're going into them corrals," he said.

Shorty got in the truck and cranked the engine until it finally coughed and started in a cloud of blue smoke. He revved the engine trying to warm it quickly. After a few minutes, Shorty jerked the old truck into gear and backed toward the corrals. Stormy braced himself against the jolting movements of the trailer. He became alert as he realized that a change was taking place. Shorty backed the trailer into a narrow alleyway leading to the corral. He stopped when he was close enough to the corral fence to open the door on the trailer so it would block the colt from escaping when he let him out.

Shorty got out of the truck and opened the alleyway gate. Satisfied the colt couldn't escape, he opened the rear door and climbed out of the alleyway to watch the colt come out. Stormy twisted his head around to watch when Shorty opened the door. He saw freedom and rocketed out. Shorty was surprised the colt still had so much energy after spending three days in the trailer without food or water.

The colt raced around the small corral looking for a way out. Shorty climbed back into the alleyway and closed the gate. Stormy quickly saw that the only escape from the corral was through one of the gates and they were all closed. The rails and boards making up the corral were too high to jump, so Stormy slowed to a trot and finally stopped on the far side of the corral where there was a water trough. Water was dripping into an old bathtub from a pipe running to a small creek behind the cabin. An overflow ran out into the woods. Stormy drank deeply trying to quench his three day thirst. He took several deep draughts of water and looked back at Shorty.

Shorty watched the colt race around the small corral. When Stormy stopped at the water trough, Shorty got back in the truck and pulled the trailer out of the alleyway. He unhooked it from the truck and drove over to the front of the cabin. Stormy watched Shorty walk to the back side of the corral where there was a stack of old hay. He opened a bale of moldy hay and threw two or three flakes of the rank stuff into the corral. Stormy kept his distance from the hay and kept a close eye on Shorty. Shorty went into the cabin. About an hour later, he came out, got into the pickup and drove away.

Relieved that the foul smelling man was gone and glad to be out of the trailer, Stormy walked over and investigated the old hay. It smelled bad, but the colt needed nourishment and started nibbling at the moldy hay. It tasted terrible, but after picking through it and trying to separate out the worst of it, he began eating. It would keep him alive. The more he ate the more he became accustomed to the bad taste and soon was indiscriminately munching on the poor feed. Stormy ate his fill, trying to make up for the long period without anything to eat. When he had eaten all he wanted, he went back to the water trough and drank again. The long ordeal had exhausted him. Now, with his thirst quenched and food in his belly, he settled down on the ground and fell into a deep sleep.

Stormy slept undisturbed until dark. He awoke refreshed and rose from the ground. He looked around and noticed the truck had not returned. He walked to the water trough and drank. He nosed around and found bits of the old hay. He picked on the remaining pieces trying to satisfy his hunger. When he cleaned up the last of the hay, he walked around the perimeter of the corral inspecting the gates and walls of the enclosure. He was hungry and lonely. A sudden overwhelming feeling of depression passed through the colt. His good life with the band of horses on the Bent Bar ranch was gone. He was all alone in a strange place and had only a few pounds of moldy hay to eat in over three days. A plaintive loud whinny escaped from the colt. He was desperately calling for his lost companions. Only silence answered him. Then, as if in sympathy for the mournful call of the colt, a coyote wailed a long sorrowful howl from a far off ridge.

There was no help for the colt. No horses answered the young stallion's calls. The man was gone and the only sign of life was the cold, distant call of the coyote. Stormy paced around the corral in the black night looking for a way out. His deep depression lifted slightly as he carefully walked the corral with the thought of escape on his mind. He thought of Flame and the band of horses. They were not nearby, or they would have come to his calls. He would have to find them, but first he had to break out from the confines of this dingy corral. For hours the colt paced around looking for a weak spot in the fence. The boards and rails were nailed high and tight. He found no way out. After hours of circling and testing the strength of the fence, Stormy began to realize the only escape from this corral would be the way he came in. Through the gate. Dejected again, he laid on the ground to await his fate.

Pale shafts of light filtering through the tall trees surrounding the corral spoke of a dawn still trying to scale the high peaks that blocked its arrival at Shorty's hideout. Stormy awoke on his fourth day of captivity to find he was still in a nightmare, far from home, in a strange place. He rose and moved to the water trough. He quenched his thirst and looked over the corral. He came alert when he heard the far off sound of a truck winding its way up the narrow road leading to the cabin. Fear flashed through him when he realized the man was returning. Gradually the sound came closer and soon Stormy recognized the familiar sound of the same truck he listened to during the long journey from the banks of Gunpowder Creek.

The full light of dawn flooded through the trees when Shorty pulled in and parked the old truck in front of the cabin. Stormy backed against the far side of the corral when the truck came through the gate. The colt watched as Shorty got out and slammed the door. The sound of the metal door slamming shut sounded like an explosion in the quiet of the early morning light. Stormy remained stock still as he watched Shorty look around the small clearing in front of the cabin.

Shorty emitted a loud belch and reached inside the open window of the truck. "No sense leaving ya' in there," he said. He came out holding a half empty whiskey bottle. Shorty went to town for groceries and spent most of the day and night in a saloon. He became very drunk. Before the saloon closed in the wee hours of the morning, Shorty bought a few bottles of whiskey and started back to his cabin. He tipped the bottle high and filled his mouth with booze. He gargled it around noisily and then swallowed. He belched again and looked toward the corrals.

Stormy focused his full attention on the man and didn't move a muscle when he saw Shorty look his direction. "Well, look who's still alive. I wonder if you know how much trouble you caused me an' Chester," the drunken man said. Stormy stood on the far side of the corral and watched the man walk unsteadily toward the corral. Tendrils of fear shot through his body when he caught the odor of the man and was reminded of the terror of being forced into the trailer on Gunpowder Creek.

Shorty walked into the alleyway and leaned against the corral gate for support. "You cost us a lot of money and time. Now, we're gonna' have to pay a big bill to get Chester out of the hospital. I wish we'd never of run into you up there in Montana," Shorty yelled at the colt. Alarmed, but far from panic, Stormy watched the man without moving. Shorty bent down to the ground and picked up a few rocks. He threw a rock at Stormy and missed the colt by several yards. Stormy didn't move. Shorty threw again and came a little closer. Increasing alarm caused Stormy to whinny and move nervously in place. Shorty threw another rock. His aim was poor and he missed again. Stormy remained in the same place and nickered in fear at the drunken man. Shorty picked up more rocks and flustered because he kept missing, started wildly throwing rocks at the colt.

Stormy spun around and ran to the end of the corral to escape the flying rocks. Shorty was working himself into a state of high agitation. The fact that his aim was so bad that he couldn't hit the colt with the rocks was starting to irritate him, and now Stormy moved further away. "Maybe it's about time I taught you a lesson. You need to learn some manners and show a little respect for the people that feed you," Shorty yelled. Stormy's fear increased when the man started yelling at him. Stormy watched in nervous concern from the far end of the corral as Shorty spun around and started to pick up more rocks. Suddenly, Shorty spotted a broken piece of fence rail that had been discarded near the alleyway. He picked up the piece of railing and turned and waved it in the air at the colt. "A few good hard licks with this rail and maybe you'll show me a little more respect," Shorty yelled.

Stormy watched in rising alarm when Shorty waved the rail and yelled in his direction. He knew the man was going to come after him. Shorty waved the rail in the air again and walked directly to the gate leading into the corral. He set the rail down and unlatched the gate. Shorty pushed the gate open. He picked the rail up and started waving it in the air again. He walked through the open gate holding the rail above his head in a threatening gesture. In a drunken fog, Shorty ran for the colt swinging the broken rail. Stormy, in great fear now, raced around Shorty to the other end of the corral. Shorty swung the rail at the horse as he ran around him but hit nothing but air. Stormy easily evaded the lurching drunk. Shorty's anger toward the innocent colt was quickly mounting. Brandishing the rail as a threatening weapon, he again started after the frightened colt.

"You're gonna' have some welts on your miserable hide before this is over, you worthless cayuse," Shorty screamed in anger. Stormy was trapped in the small corral with Shorty. He knew it was only a matter of time before the enraged drunk landed a blow with the long wooden rail. Holding the rail high, Shorty closed half the distance to the colt. Trembling, Stormy watched him approach. Suddenly, Shorty stopped and looked at the alleyway. He forgot to close the corral gate. The rustler quickly looked back at the colt to see if he realized the gate was wide open. Shorty cussed when he realized his mistake. He threw the rail down and sprang for the gate to slam it shut before the colt could escape.

Stormy was focusing his full attention on the man who was trying to harm him. He hadn't realized the drunk had forgotten to close the gate. He spent hours last night looking for an escape. Stormy knew the only way out was through the gate. He watched Shorty scramble toward the open gate, and the freedom it offered. Now, he realized Shorty had not closed it. Shorty was one pace away from reaching the gate, when Stormy exploded into action.

The small colt burst into a full speed run directly for the man now reaching for the open gate. Stormy slammed into Shorty, knocking him away from the gate. The force of the collision between the young stallion and the old drunk knocked them both to the ground in a tangle of legs and hooves. Escape was on the colt's mind. He bolted up and was away before Shorty could regain his feet. Stormy raced past the cabin and turned into the cover of the forest. He could hear Shorty screaming a string of oaths from the corral as he raced to freedom.

Stormy ran through the woods at great speed. He ducked low branches and twisted back and forth avoiding the trees as he raced headlong into the heavy woods. He turned uphill and ran at an unbelievable pace up the steep mountainside. The old bay mare always ran for higher ground when she felt threatened, and now Stormy followed her teachings. He drove hard for twenty minutes before slowing his pace. He came to a small meadow and crossed it. He entered the woods on the far side. Feeling safe in the heavy cover, he stopped and watched his back trail.

Hidden in the heavy brush, Stormy rested and let his breath return to normal. He had exerted tremendous effort racing up the mountain in the heavy timber. He rested until his pounding heart slowed. No one followed. He had escaped from Shorty. He heard the sound of water gurgling over rocks deeper in the woods. He moved in that direction and came to another small clearing with a clear stream of running water. There was green grass in the meadow. Hungry, he began feeding on the first real food he had seen in days.

Stormy stayed hidden near the small meadow for a few weeks. He felt safe in the heavy cover. Occasionally, deer or elk came through his sanctuary, but he knew they posed no threat to his safety. He moved away from the meadow when he grazed off all the grass it had to offer. Cautiously he began exploring the mountain range. It was a remote area and feed was plentiful. He recovered from his ordeal with Shorty and Chester but did not forget the terror they caused. Stormy stayed far from the roads low on the mountain and avoided all civilization. He did not want to risk an encounter with the two cruel men who took him from his mother and caused so much pain.

Stormy began to feel at home in this new place. The elk and deer that grazed the high parks and meadows soon became accustomed to the young colt. They tolerated him when he wandered into an area where they were feeding. Loneliness was his constant companion and he began roaming great distances looking for his lost band. Fear kept him high in the mountains. He wouldn't risk going into the valleys below. Shorty left an imprint of fear on the young horse and that fear kept him hidden in the high country.

His first winter in that remote range of mountains in northern Wyoming was relatively mild. The snows were light and all of the animals living on those high slopes fared well. Forage was not easy, but could be found. Stormy prospered and grew. When the heavy snows of spring fell on the mountains, Stormy followed the herds of elk and learned their ways of survival. He pawed deep into the snow and uncovered feed hidden all winter. The elk kept moving and foraging and Stormy followed them. He learned to pick his way on the high ridges and look for feed on the windward side of the mountains, where the wind had blown the ground clear of snow.

The young stallion worked hard to survive that winter. He was constantly on the move. He ranged across the high country looking for familiar ground. Stormy found nothing he recognized and gradually, memories of the Bent Bar ranch and its familiar surroundings began to fade. He avoided any contact with humans. His experience with Shorty and Chester robbed him of any trust of people. He desperately wanted the company of other horses. Occasionally he would see horsemen and sometimes even pack strings of many horses along the lower slopes. The horses he saw always had people with them. He would move into the deeper thickets and hide until they moved out of his range. He was not ready to chance being captured again.

The mild winter slowly gave way to a magnificent spring. The snows gently softened and made their way downhill in a life sustaining liquid that cascaded off the slopes on their unstoppable downhill journey. New grass began to make its appearance. Large and small animals alike welcomed this promise of easier times. Anticipation of summer's bounty was in the air when Stormy reached his first year of life. Nutritious mountain feed and the constant work of simply surviving a mountain winter had developed the young stallion's body more than if he spent the winter being fed in a pasture or corral on his home ranch.

Early spring of his first year found the stallion developing into a magnificent creature. His survival depended on quick action. He was always alert and an aura of intelligence surrounded his every move. His body was developing into a superb structure that could endure extreme hardship and still function perfectly. He could run straight uphill and sustain blinding speeds without tiring. His inherited athletic abilities enabled him to fly down mountainsides turning and jumping around and across obstacles at speeds that were astounding.

Standing on a high wind whipped ridge, his flaxen mane and tail whipped hard in the heavy breeze. The copper colored young stallion appeared to have been chiseled from bronze by a master craftsman. His developing muscles bulged against his copper coat and pushed hard against blood vessels corded across the surface of his magnificent structure. Far from his home range, and alone on this high ridge, Stormy welcomed the second spring of his tumultuous life.

CHAPTER 16

The pleasant smell of newness greeted Ann when she entered the large structure. The building was finished and its size was awesome. A huge indoor arena with chutes, stalls and seating for spectators had been constructed adjacent to the barn on the Bent Bar Ranch. Profits from last year's cattle and horse sales financed the impressive building. Johnson had said, "If we're going to build it, let's build it right." Now completed, the building was definitely "right." It was large enough for breaking and training horses in. It was even large enough to hold a rodeo and horse sale if they wanted to. There was a large office for Johnson in the rear of the building. He never used it though and Ann asked him if there was something wrong with it. He answered, "No, nothing's wrong with it. I'm just more comfortable with my old office." So Ann started using the new office herself.

The best part, Ann thought, is that now they could continue their training through the long winter in the comfort of the large indoor building. It was the ranch's first step toward developing a professional horse breeding and training program. Excitement mounted as the building neared completion. The contractors barely pulled their equipment off the ranch when Ann was inside the building measuring distances and setting up her barrels. The loss of Stormy and death of Rose was devastating to everyone. However, construction of the indoor arena helped ease the pain of the terrible loss. Ann devoted all of her spare time helping with the new arena and working with the colts they would offer for sale this year. She tried to stay fully occupied to prevent herself from thinking of her lost colt.

Ann threw her heart and soul into finding the stolen colt. Months passed without a clue to Stormy's whereabouts.

She enlisted the aid of the entire school in attempting to locate the horse. They alerted every livestock yard and brand inspector's office in three states and still there were no leads. Almost seven months passed since that awful day on Gunpowder Creek. She still felt that someday a clue to Stormy's disappearance would surface. She continued to mail out inquiries and check with law enforcement agencies about the colt. After all these long months since his loss, she was still determined in her search for the sorrel colt.

She led a dark bay horse into the building. He was an impressive gelding and stood tall and alert. He was young and had the inquisitive nature that good horses show. He looked around the arena but dutifully followed the young trainer closely without letting his lead rope come tight. He was a prospect and Ann intended to bring the best out of him to see if he had what it takes to become a champion. He showed a lot of spirit and had taken more time than normal to come around to a people's way of thinking. Bill started him as a colt and thought he had a tremendous amount of potential. When he finally decided to cooperate, he showed an exceptional amount of intelligence and ability. Ann was starting his training as a barrel horse but felt he would do good at whatever he was trained for.

On his right hip was the brand of the Bent Bar Ranch. A solid bar with two opposite bends in the middle of its span.

THE BENT BAR BRAND

The Bent Bar always branded its cattle, but until the tragedy on Gunpowder, they never branded their horses. Johnson made a firm new policy of branding all horses in an attempt to prevent another catastrophe. Duke's warning that the sight of a good brand was a deterrent to rustlers, and the loss of Stormy, prompted Johnson's decision. The dark bay colt was one of the first to be branded.

Ann mounted the horse and walked him around the perimeter of the arena. After a few circuits she jogged and then loped him until he loosened up. When she felt satisfied with his mental attitude, she began walking him repetitively through the cloverleaf pattern of the barrels. It was boring work, but she was instilling a definite mind set in the young horse. He would only be allowed to traverse the pattern in one way and one way only. Any deviation from that pattern would be corrected immediately. She worked him for a little over an hour. When the colt started to show the beginning of lack of attention to her commands, she stopped. She knew too much training was worse than not enough.

She rode the colt out the big doors at the end of the arena and through a long alleyway that bisected a set of corrals and holding pens built to accommodate the stock that would be worked or shown inside the new arena. At the end of the alleyway she opened a gate and rode across a parking area to the barn. She unsaddled the colt and brushed him down. Ann brought Buster out of his stall and brushed and then saddled him. She rode him to the arena and warmed him up.

Ann scheduled a busy summer for her and Buster. Since the loss of Stormy, she decided to push hard with Buster for a few more years in the barrel racing circuit. She needed to accumulate wins and score a large number of points to qualify as a finalist in the competition for the state championship. She would be finishing her junior year in high school this year. If she didn't qualify for the state finals this year, that only left one year, her senior year, to try and gain state recognition as a barrel racer. Hopefully, if she was able to place high in the state standings, then maybe she would be offered a rodeo scholarship from the university. Buster was good but his age was a big factor. Ann could only hope that his speed would hold up for a few more years.

"You've still got it, Buster. If we work hard and train smart, I know we can get to the state finals," she said. She ran Buster through the pattern at a medium fast pace several times and then walked him around the perimeter of the arena. She gave him a ten minute rest and then trotted him toward the starting line again. She gave him imperceptible cues, alerting him to be ready for a full speed run. Buster received the cues and prepared himself mentally for a hard run.

Ann gave him his head and urged him to a fast run. They flew around the barrels with the precision of a well trained team. Each knew what the other was going to do. They ran a fast time and Ann was satisfied with the workout. She gave Buster a few loving pats on the side of his neck and rode him out of the arena. She rode back to the barn and turned Buster loose. When she finished, she walked to Johnson's office and found him working at his desk. She was pleased to see Bill sitting beside the desk going over some paperwork with him.

Ann politely tapped on the doorway to the office before entering. Johnson looked up and said, "Come in, Ann. We're just going over a breeding program for the mares this spring."

"I hope you're going to use the same stallion on Flame this year that we used to breed Stormy," she said.

"Flame's recovered fairly well, but she's still not a hundred percent," Johnson said.

"I know, and I almost cry every time I see her hobble across the corral. When I look into her eyes, I can see the deep pain and loss she is suffering," Ann said.

"I think she'll be well enough to breed this spring. By the time her foal comes next year, she should be healthy enough to raise another youngster," Johnson said.

"I'm just glad she survived. It was sure touch and go there for awhile," Bill said.

"My fervent prayer is to someday have the privilege of getting my hands on the men who shot her and Rose and stole Stormy," Johnson said. There was quiet for a few minutes, while everyone remembered that fatal day.

Changing to a lighter subject, Bill asked Ann, "How's Thorny doing?"

"Oh Bill, I wish you wouldn't call him Thorny. That's not a good name for a horse," Ann said.

"Sure it is. He was sure a thorn in my side when I was breaking him last fall. That darn colt was hardheaded and didn't want to do things my way at all. He's smart as a whip and I guess he figured he was smarter than me and we should'a been doing things his way. It took me forever to get him to come around to my way of thinking. That's why I started calling him Rose's Thorn and I guess the name just stuck," Bill said.

Johnson laughed at Bill's reason for naming the bay colt, Thorny. "He's a fine horse now, and I know Rose would be proud of her last son if she was still around," Johnson said with a warm smile.

Ann smiled and said, "Well, Bill, Thorny is doing just fine. I started some basic work on the barrels with him today. It was slow going and he got bored after an hour or so. He's got a lot of go in him and he likes a faster pace than I was giving him. He's got to learn the basics first, then I'll kick him up faster. He doesn't have a mean bone in his body and I think he's just a great colt."

"He's contender potential. You might consider keeping him to compete on, now that you don't have Stormy to replace Buster," Johnson said, and immediately regretted the statement.

"Mr. Johnson, I have not given up on finding Stormy. That colt is out there somewhere and I know deep down that someday I'll find him. I'm still sending flyers out once a month to remind all the stockyards and brand inspectors. I'm keeping Stormy's description fresh on everyone's mind, in case he shows up somewhere. If you would go in the new office, you would see the campaign I have been running, trying to locate that horse. I have descriptions and drawings of the men we suspect and detailed lists of all the clues found at the scene. I've made that information available to hundreds of stock yards and dozens of agencies over a three state area. I'm confident he will show up someday. Thorny is an awful good horse, but right now I am not looking for a replacement for Stormy," Ann said with strong conviction. Embarrassed, Johnson said no more.

Ann and Buster competed hard all summer. Ann trailered Buster over a four county area competing in different rodeos and county fairs. She collected trophies and buckles when they won and ribbons when they placed. They worked hard and the points they earned slowly accumulated and gave the young rider hope that she would qualify for the state finals. Buster held up well under the heavy schedule. It seemed like every weekend Ann was loading him in the trailer and traveling somewhere to a barrel race. Occasionally, Casey would go along and ride with success in the bareback bronc riding event. Casey was getting where he wanted to go. He was winning consistently and his wins were qualifying him for bigger rodeos.

That fall, Ann started her last year of high school. She entered the Twin Forks rodeo again and sadly remembered that it had been a full year since Stormy disappeared. There were somber thoughts around the ranch as the time neared to leave for Twin Forks. Everyone remembered what happened last year while they were away. James promised Ann and Johnson that nothing would happen this year. He planned on riding steady until they returned. "If I even see a strange jack rabbit on the Bent Bar, I'll stop him and ask for his I.D., so don't worry about a thing. Just come home and tell me you won down there at Twin Forks," James said.

Ann and Buster rode hard and placed on both days. They came in third overall. Marsha Miller repeated her win on her buckskin horse and Ann's friend, Beth, pushed Marsha hard and finished a close second. Casey rode a jug headed horse on Saturday and scored in the high seventies. His draw on Sunday gave him all he wanted and threw him, just as the horn sounded. The judge ruled it a ride, and with that high score, Casey squeaked by to win the event for the second year in a row. "I sure must be living right. That crazy horse threw me sky high just as the buzzer sounded. I didn't think I rode him until the judge signaled that I did. That was a lucky ride," Casey said.

"Every one of your rides are lucky," Bill quipped.

Ann spent the rest of that year trying to win enough points for the state finals. Fall moved toward winter and there were less and less events to compete in as the racing year came to a close. In November, she tallied up her points and came up short. She was close, but not close enough. She needed a few more wins through the year to have qualified, she thought. She read the results of the state finals. Marsha Miller rode hard and pushed her buckskin horse to the state championship. Marsha may be a miserable person and I don't really like the way she treats her horse, but I will admit that she is a tough competitor, Ann thought, after reading about Marsha's victory.

With another year of experience behind her, Ann reflected on what she learned over the past year of competition. She realized that the dream of a state championship would take more effort than she had put forth so far. I have to enter more rodeos, she told herself. The more I compete, the more I'll win and the more I win, the more points I'll earn. Next year, if we ride in as many events as we possibly can, I believe Buster and I can qualify and end up in Billings, riding for a state title.

With the racing season behind her, Ann concentrated on her senior year and training horses. She spent more time than ever before working the young horses in their new arena. Thorny learned fast and before long was turning in a respectable performance around the barrels. Ann felt that in another year, and with experience behind him, he would develop into a champion. There were other colts to work, and with Bill's help they began to mold the young horses into well trained animals. They worked on discipline first, then reining and stopping. Good stops were a must for an arena horse and a lot of time was spent developing technique into the colts as second nature to the commands they were trained to follow. It was worthwhile work and Ann always came away with a feeling of satisfaction and accomplishment after a young horse started responding to her training.

Stormy was still on Ann's mind and hardly a day went by that she didn't think about the lost colt and wonder what else she could possibly do to find him. She staunchly adhered to her monthly schedule of mailing flyers to anyone who she thought might be in a position to help in her search. More than a year had gone by without any word. It was hard to believe that no one had even seen the colt in that length of time. She began to wonder if possibly Stormy had suffered a fate similar to Johnson's beloved mare, Rose.

CHAPTER 17

A few flakes of new snow drifted by on the light breeze. The morning dawned cold. The temperature, combined with moisture laden clouds, began to produce the first snowfall of the coming winter. The crisp smell of new snow was refreshing. A change was coming and it was not altogether unwelcome. The summer had been hot and this first frosty hint of winter was invigorating. From high above, Stormy was watching a rider on a grullo horse pushing cows down out of the high country. The shouts of the rider, urging the cows on, drifted up. The smoky colored horse moved back and forth behind the cows, nipping at the laggards. Remorse settled on Stormy as he watched the other horse. He craved company and the loneliness of living alone in these remote mountains had brought him north along the mountain range searching for companionship.

Sadly, Stormy watched the horse and rider go out of sight when they pushed the small bunch of cattle into a timbered draw. For over a year now the growing colt wandered along this range of mountains looking for other horses. Occasionally, he saw horses, but they were always with riders. Caution kept Stormy from trying to join them, as long as there were people with the horses. As he grew older and started maturing, the young stallion felt a stronger urge to find and live amongst his own kind. Fear of people kept him from traveling into the low country where he saw other horses.

Stormy felt comfortable and safe in the high meadows and forests below timberline. Faintly, he remembered the terror caused by the two men and that thought kept him out of sight and high in the mountains. He enjoyed virgin grass and clean, clear water along the length of this mountain range. All of life's necessities were here, except for the burning desire of all herd animals to be with a group of their own kind. The colt wandered for hundreds of miles. His body became incredibly tough and strong, traveling long distances across the steep terrain in the thin air of the high altitudes. His endurance was remarkable. The young horse could cover miles across rigorous country swiftly, and with the deftness of a mountain goat.

Stormy looked down on the draw where the horse and rider had disappeared. He could still hear shouts of the rider and bawling cattle. Reluctantly, he turned and looked back to the south in the direction from which he came. He looked again toward the draw below. A low nicker of loss escaped from deep within. Suddenly, an urgent need to see that cow horse again overpowered him. He erupted into a downhill flight that would have been frightening for an average horse. He raced headlong, straight down the steep mountainside toward the timbered draw.

With the beauty of coordination and power, the colt coiled and uncoiled his powerful legs in great leaps down the steep slope. His front legs seemed to glide and dance as they guided him around boulders, trees and fallen timber, while his mighty rear legs provided an awesome driving force behind his scorching run. He came onto an open plain leading to the draw and stretched out into a full run. The exertion was stimulating and he surged ahead directing his full energies into attaining his highest possible speed to reach the rim of the draw quickly. Soon he slowed and raced along the rim trying to spot the horse and rider below. He screamed out as he ran along the rim looking into the draw.

From the timber below, he heard the sound of another horse. A loud questioning whinny echoed off the walls of the small canyon. The grullo answered his calls, wondering what strange horse was above. Excited by the sound of another horse, Stormy sat back on his hind quarters and threw his front legs out straight in front, in a swift, jarring stop. With the full force of his huge lung capacity, he cried out again to the horse below.

Stormy heard the sound of the horse coming fast out of the timber. Eagerly, he looked over the rim of the draw anticipating the sight of one of his kind. He caught glimpses of the horse coming through the trees toward his side of the draw. The grullo broke out of the timber into an open area along the sides of the canyon. The sight of the rider on the grullo's back alarmed the young stallion and he called out in disappointment to the horse. Stormy watched as they heard his call and looked up. The rider pulled the grullo into a quick stop when he caught sight of the muscled young stallion above.

Shocked, and in wonder of the magnificent sight of the deep copper colored horse, the rider stared in awe with his mouth opened in astonishment. Alarmed, but with the intuition of safety afforded by his position high above, Stormy held his ground and called out again. Below him, the horse and rider stared back in surprise. Only the sound of the cattle still making their way down the draw answered Stormy's last call.

The rider looked the strange horse over carefully, with the eye of an experienced horseman. He could see that this strange animal was a superb creature. From far below he saw the muscles in Stormy's body. They were magnified by his run down the mountain, and stood out prominently. "What a good lookin' animal that one is. Where do you figure he came from, Mouse?" he said to his horse. The grullo pranced nervously but kept his eyes alertly on the stallion above. "Do you reckon we could get him to follow us home or get close enough to get a rope on him. I would sure be proud to own an animal as wondrous as that," the rider said. He began to try and figure out a way to capture the animal on the rim of the canyon.

The rider talked to his horse very softly. The horse nickered and flicked his ears back toward the man on his back. This was an unexpected turn of events for the horse and he was still trying to figure out who the stranger was. He wasn't sure if he should be alarmed, and wondered if the horse was friendly. The sound of the rider's voice was comforting to him and he waited for his instructions. "Okay, Mouse, we're gonna' try and get him to follow us down to that first fenced pasture. If it don't look like he'll do it, then we'll try and rope him. I hope he follows us, cause if he don't, I got a sneakin' suspicion that you might have a hard time catching up with him, to get me close enough to get a loop on him. No offense, Mouse, but he looks pretty fast," the rider said congenially to his horse.

Up above, Stormy watched the two and heard the low murmurings of the rider. He heard the grullo nicker and the sound seemed friendly even though there was a man on the horse's back. "Now listen, Mouse, we're going to act like that horse up there don't interest us at all. You keep talking to him and we'll ride back to the cows real slow. Maybe if we act like we have no interest in him he'll feel safe and follow us," the rider said. The rider touched his heel on Mouse's right side and the horse turned to the left and walked back into the woods. Stormy watched in disappointment as the horse faded from his sight. The stallion whinnied and heard the departing horse answer from the thick timber below. Stormy ran along the top of the draw calling out to the first horse he had contact with in over a year. He heard no answer to his calls.

The young stallion felt no immediate danger from the rider on the horse's back. He showed no interest in him and had ridden away. Undecided as to what to do, Stormy galloped back and forth along the rim of the small canyon. He stopped and called out again to the unseen horse. Minutes passed and Stormy heard no answer to his last loud whinny. He did not want to lose contact with the friendly animal. Muffled by the trees and sounding far off, Stormy heard the horse again. Afraid of losing him, Stormy jumped straight off the rim of the canyon in a desperate move to catch up with the vanishing horse.

He crashed down the steep walls of the draw using his front legs as brakes and controlling the speed of his descent. Within seconds he was in the bottom of the draw and used his highly developed sense of smell to follow the horse's trail. He moved swiftly through the black timber with the scent of the horse, mingled with the man odors strong in his nostrils. Ahead, he saw a small clearing. At the far end, stood a horse and rider looking straight back at his approach. The stallion hesitated. The rider made no threatening moves. Stormy stepped out of the timber into the clearing and stopped. The horse and rider at the far end of the clearing turned and rode into the woods again.

Stormy followed along behind them for close to an hour. Occasionally the horse and rider would stop and watch him. Intermittent calls from the grullo kept Stormy in a state of high anticipation and he eagerly followed them. Gradually, the distance closed and soon Stormy followed a short distance behind them. The rider was happily thinking that his plan was working well and that the magnificent stallion behind him would follow them all the way home. They came out of the draw into the lower country and the land leveled out and opened up into fenced pasture land. The rider and grullo horse started working the cows through an open gate into a fenced pasture. Stormy stopped well back from the fence and watched them work. He didn't like the looks of the small opening with fence posts and strands of wire on both sides of it.

The last of the cows moved through the opening and the horse and rider followed them into the pasture. Mouse kept moving behind the cows and soon they were almost a quarter of a mile inside the fence. The rider stopped the horse and looked back for the stallion. He saw Stormy far back and standing stock still looking toward him. The stallion had not followed them through the gate. Disappointment passed through the man. "He don't like fences," the man said softly. He sat on his horse and waited, facing the stallion, hoping he would come through the gate after them.

Stormy stopped at the fence. He desperately wanted to follow the smoke colored horse into the pasture. The fear of the fence was greater than his desire to follow the horse, so he remained outside and whinnied. "It looks like he ain't gonna' come in here, Mouse. I hope you ate your Wheaties this morning, cause I think we're going to have to go after him," the rider said. The cows kept making their way toward the home ranch while the horse and rider waited patiently for Stormy to come through the gate.

A half hour passed and Stormy remained outside the fence. "Okay, super horse, I guess it's up to you now," the rider said to Mouse. He touched his heels to the horse's sides and they moved back to the opening in the fence. The rider slowly slipped the thin piece of latigo leather, holding his catch rope to the saddle, loose from the saddle horn. Out of Stormy's sight, on Mouse's side, the rider shook out a large loop and took a couple of dallys around the horn with the end of the rope.

Stormy watched them start back to him and the open gate. He backed a few lengths and whinnied in expectation. The sly horseman stopped Mouse and watched the stallion. He wanted to give the impression they were just friends and meant no harm. Stormy felt disappointment when they stopped. He watched but didn't move as they started for the gate again. He felt elation at the sight of another horse after so long being alone. Nervously, he nickered to Mouse and the grullo picked up the nervousness in the strange stallion's voice. In turn he became apprehensive and relayed that slight fear back to Stormy. Stormy backed off a few more lengths.

The rider moved Mouse through the gate and angled toward Stormy. He saw indecision in the sorrel stallion's eyes, and not wanting to spook him away after getting this close, stopped his horse facing him. Stormy held his ground but came no closer. The rider was close enough to see how magnificent this strange horse was built. His hand holding the rope became sweaty as he looked the great creature over. He had never seen a horse with such remarkable conformation as this animal displayed. Now, the rider's excitement grew as the thought of owning such a horse entered his mind. He moved Mouse a few more steps toward the stallion and stopped again.

The rider carefully played his hand out, attempting to get within roping range of Stormy. For over an hour, he eased Mouse closer and closer. Not quite satisfied with the rider on the horse's back, Stormy moved away when they came too close to him. He wanted the other horse's company, but wasn't quite ready to accept the rider. He continually moved away, keeping a safe distance. The rider understood the horse's reluctance, and didn't force himself on the nervous stallion. Gradually, the stallion allowed them to come a few lengths closer.

Time passed and Stormy allowed them to get within roping range. He wanted to touch muzzles and greet this horse as a friend. The rider was feeling confident and gripped the rope hard in his sweaty hand. He felt butterflies in his stomach and knew that they were within minutes of roping this magnificent creature. Stormy took a step toward Mouse and the rider knew the time had come.

He watched the horse take his eyes off him and direct his full attention on Mouse. Swiftly, the rider snapped the rope above his head and sent it flying toward the tense stallion. Stormy caught the movement and flashbacks of grain, terror, gunshots and another rope flying through the air, blazed across his consciousness. Only a microsecond had passed since the rope started toward him but Stormy recognized it for what it had done to him in the past. He spun around to flee and the rope soared above his head. He ducked away and heard the rider cry out in disappointment as the rope missed and flew harmlessly to the side of his head.

Stormy was away, running in full flight from the threat of the rider and his rope. He could hear Mouse pounding after him and the rider urging his mount. The rider was frantically coiling the trailing rope to ready it for another attempt, if Mouse could put him within range again. Stormy would never allow them to close on him again. He felt betrayed and cold determination settled on him as he raced away. He directed tremendous energy into his muscular legs and they responded with a speed that left Mouse far behind in just a few lengths. Stormy rocketed away so fast that by the time he reached the end of the small clearing and entered the timber, poor Mouse was twenty lengths behind and out of the race for good. The rider pulled Mouse up before they entered the timber and said to the blowing horse, "Hold up, Mouse, there ain't no use. That horse took off like a jet airplane. I ain't never seen such speed in my life. We'd never catch him in a hundred years!"

Mouse was breathing hard and still excited, as the rider threw his coiled rope over the saddle horn and stepped out of the saddle. He held the reins and stood beside the blowing horse. "Now don't be embarrassed about getting outrun so bad, Mouse. That was some kind of special horse. I'm not mad at you cause' he run off from us like he did. That red horse was like a ghost horse, he ran so fast. I might even think all this was just a dream if you weren't standing here breathing so hard from that chase. You're a fast horse, Mouse, so don't feel bad. Maybe some day we'll see him again," the forlorn rider said.

Stormy outran Mouse with ease. He simply decided to run hard and turned all his energy to gaining great speed. His exceptional breeding and rugged lifestyle had developed him into a superior horse and few could match the speed the young stallion could instantly achieve. Stormy raced through the timber and ran back up the draw, in the direction he came earlier. He was dejected and disappointed. He thought he had finally found the company of another horse, but the sight of the rope sailing toward him brought back the fear of man and his menacing rope.

The colt associated danger, captivity and terror with a rope. He had been imprinted to flee at the sight of a rope, to escape as far from the danger as possible. He ran up the draw to the place he had first seen the grullo horse and his lanky rider. He lunged up the steep bank and rapidly gained the top. Stormy paused on the rim of the draw and looked down into the lowlands. Far off in the distance, he could see the horse and rider making their way back across the fenced pasture, toward their cattle, still trailing for home. Stormy turned and headed to the safety of the high country. In light snow, he traveled south, back into the more remote regions of the mountain range, in the direction he had come.

The snow continued for days and increased in intensity. Stormy worked his way along the range, foraging in meadows and sometimes sharing the same clearings with bands of elk. He was a familiar sight to many of the animals. The old cows who led the bands never sounded an alarm when they saw the colt entering their grounds. The winter continued with an unusual amount of snowfall, causing all of the animals to work harder searching for food. Stormy fared well, but as the long months of winter continued, he found himself more and more dependent on following bands of elk. He foraged in areas cleared by herds, pawing through the snow, in their search for food.

In late winter, the accumulation of deep snow made foraging difficult. High winds caused huge snowdrifts. Feed in the high country was becoming scarce. Without the elk, the colt would never have been able to survive. With their numbers, they broke through the deep drifts, making travel possible for other animals and exposing scarce feed. The colt followed behind them as they moved along the range, cleaning up any feed they left. It was a hard winter and the lack of nourishment began to show on the colt as spring approached.

Stormy was down to hard muscle. He had been struggling to survive the deep snows of the long winter. He carried no extra weight and his ribs and hipbones stuck out from his frame. Spring storms brought more snow. Pressure systems continually pushed through from the west, deepening the snow in the high Rockies. It accumulated to the point where even elk were struggling to survive. Stormy's strength deteriorated and he struggled harder, using more precious energy to survive.

Weakened now, the stallion realized he could no longer survive in the deep snow of the high mountains. He had to escape the strangling grip of the deep spring drifts and move into the lower elevations. Hungry and weak, Stormy worked his way lower. He found little food and his condition weakened more as fought his way down to the valleys. His hunger forced him lower, and soon, memories became faint of the dangers of men and their ropes. The snow lessened and he was able to paw through and find enough feed to keep alive.

He travelled on the fringe of the valleys and worked his way along fence lines, feeding on whatever he could find. He would move into the timber during the day and feed only under the safety of darkness at night. The colt felt uneasy in the lower country. He spent most of his young life in the high mountains. He was only six months old when he escaped from Shorty. Now, at almost two years of age, deep spring snows forced him back into the valley he fled from, so long ago.

He came upon Shorty's cabin early one evening, while he was making his way out of the timber. He had been bedded down all day under the protection of the tall trees. He awoke hungry and moved out to the edge of the forest. He caught the faint odor of smoke. Curious, he eased along into the wind looking for the source of the smell. Just before dark, he came out on a small ridge and looked down onto the old set of corrals. Wood smoke was coming out of the chimney of the cabin and the old blue pickup truck was parked nearby.

Stormy remembered the place and the man he had escaped from. He could see another horse in the corrals feeding on hay scattered on the ground. He could smell the hay and it was not an unpleasant aroma that drifted up to him. It had been a long time since he had eaten his fill. Hunger eased his fear of the dangers that existed in these lower valleys. Stormy saw a small stack of hay on the outside of the corrals. The bales were stacked just inside the trees and close to the corrals. Shorty had been feeding the old horse in the corral for a few months and loose hay was scattered across the ground between the hay stack and the pen. Stormy moved closer to the corrals and watched from the safety of the trees.

Long after dark, with hunger pains kindling his courage, Stormy moved out of the woods and walked toward the hay stacked near the corrals. Cautiously, he approached the hay. The smell of the feed was strong and overpowered his fear. He heard the horse in the corral offer a low curious nicker. Apprehensive about being where he was, Stormy did not return the greeting.

The colt stopped near the hay, pausing to see if anyone would come out of the cabin. He saw no movement. He stretched out and pulled a full mouthful of hay from one of the bales in the stack. The taste of the grass hay was a wonderful sensation and he began devouring the feed. The old horse in the corral was wary about the stranger and offered no further greetings. Stormy worked steadily on the hay trying to satisfy his profound hunger. He spent months pawing through deep snow trying to find enough nourishment to simply stay alive. Now, here was feed in abundance and he gorged himself.

The night deepened and Stormy fed on the hay stack until he began to feel a fullness in his stomach. He retreated into the woods and moved several miles away from the cabin. He had eaten his fill for the first time in many long months. His system was not accustomed to the great amount of feed he had ingested. He felt uncomfortable and slightly dizzy. The young stallion found a brushy spot in the deep woods and feeling safe, bedded down amongst the safety of the heavy cover.

Stormy returned night after night to the hay stack. He began to feel stronger and his lean frame started filling out again. Soon, he became accustomed to the old horse in the corral. One night, he went up to the edge of the corral and touched muzzles with the old captive horse. The contact was pleasing and thereafter Stormy would always greet the old horse when he arrived late in the night. Neither Shorty nor Chester noticed the signs of a horse feeding on the back of the haystack. They only threw hay to the old fellow in the corral every few days, so it was a few weeks after Stormy began feeding on the rear of the stack that Shorty finally noticed the missing hay.

Shorty went out to feed the horse they had stolen a few months before. He pulled a bale off the top of the small stack and was surprised to see that the rear of the stack was almost demolished. He walked around to the rear and saw that something had been feeding on their hay. He saw that it had been a horse. The bales at the back had been eaten and hay was scattered and tramped into the packed snow. There were horse droppings covering the area and the snow showed tracks of a horse. Shorty saw a trail coming out of the woods where the horse had been traveling back and forth. Tickled by what he found, Shorty went back to the cabin to tell Chester of their good fortune.

"We got us an easy one, Chester," Shorty said when he entered the cabin. Chester was sitting at a small wooden table smoking a cigarette when Shorty barged into the cabin.

"What do you mean by that?" Chester asked.

"There's been a stray horse feeding on the back of our hay stack and it ain't that old bag of bones we got in the corral," Shorty said gleefully. Chester looked up in disbelief. He knew it was true, when he saw the look on Shorty's face. Shorty had a grin of genuine happiness on his whisker stubbled face. He was smiling wide and Chester could see a gob of juicy tobacco ready to escape through the gap caused by his missing teeth. Shorty started to giggle in happiness and Chester jumped up and moved out of his line of fire.

Chester got out of range and asked, "What do we do? Is he there now?"

"No! He ain't there now, he's been coming in at night, when we can't see him," Shorty said, still grinning.

"Well, how do we get him, rope him?" Chester asked.

"No, we don't have to rope him. We'll catch him easy as pie," Shorty said.

"Well, darn it, tell me how," Chester said.

"Easy! There ain't much hay left in that stack. We'll move what's left into the corral and put that old horse in the pen next to it, so he can't get away, or get to the hay we stack in the corral. We pull some rails off the back of the corral so the stray horse can get in the corral to feed on the hay. We let him feed on it for a few nights to get used to going in the open corral. When he gets comfortable about going in there, we gradually move the hay a little further in, away from the opening we made to let him in. We keep moving the hay in, until it's against the far wall of the corral and he's feeding clear inside. When everything looks right, we sneak up and close the hole in the fence and we got him trapped! That's all there is to it!" Shorty said and looked proudly at Chester.

Chester grinned and said, "Let's get started moving the hay."

Stormy knew something was different. He stopped and studied the place where the hay had been. In the darkness he could sense that a change had taken place. His eyes were accustomed to the black night and he saw that the hay was gone. From a distance and in the safety of the trees, he surveyed the area. He saw a difference in the corral and realized that it now had an opening in it. Inside the opening he saw a few bales of hay laying haphazardly on the ground. He didn't like the change and moved away and back into the deep woods.

Stormy stayed clear of the cabin for a few days. He foraged around the base of the large conifer trees in the woods, but found little to eat. He pushed through the snow and moved back higher in the mountains. The small meadows he probed, still held deep snow and offered very little browse to satisfy his growing hunger. Recalling the easy feed by the cabin, he returned late one night to see if the hay was still there. He moved close to the corrals and nickered to the old horse now confined in another pen.

He was gratified to hear the familiar sound of the old horse returning his greeting. He moved right up to the corral and looked through the opening. He saw the hay lying just inside the corral. Stormy walked through the opening and started eating the hay. Uneasy, he kept looking at the cabin to be sure no one was coming. He ate quickly, and before he had his fill, apprehension forced him out of the corral and back to the safety of the deep woods. He returned the next night, and still not challenged by any danger, stayed longer and ate his fill. When he returned the next night, the pile of hay in the corral had been replenished and was scattered a little further inside the enclosure.

A week passed. Stormy returned every night and was now complacent about entering the corral. On this dark windy night, he found new hay piled high against the rail fence on the far side of the corral. Stormy moved across the corral and greeted the old horse in the next pen. The horse nickered back and Stormy boldly began feeding on the pile of hay.

Hours passed and Stormy was beginning to satisfy his hunger. The wind increased and noisily whistled through the trees. Downwind and under cover of darkness, Shorty and Chester used the roar of the wind to hide their approach to the opening in the corral. Stormy heard the clump of wood hitting wood and jerked his head up in time to see the two outlaws hurriedly closing the opening.

CHAPTER 18

Johnson heard the phone ringing in his office. It rang for quite a while and he was convinced that, as soon as he turned the foal loose to run for the phone, the caller would hang up. He had just slipped a halter on the filly's head for the very first time and didn't want to lose her attention by leaving to answer the phone. Flame foaled a beautiful sorrel filly and Johnson had just started the youngster's education. The filly had been attentive and more than a little curious while Johnson introduced her to her first encounter with a halter.

The persistent ringing continued. "Whoever that is, is sure determined," he thought. Reluctantly, Johnson moved away from the filly and started for the phone. When he closed the gate to Flame's stall, Johnson started running. If they hang up now, I'll sure feel foolish, he thought as he raced for the phone. He entered the office and hastily jerked the receiver out of its cradle.

"Bent Bar Ranch," Johnson said into the mouthpiece.

"Johnson, this is Duke. Listen to me closely. I think we may have finally found Ann's colt and the men who shot the mares. There are two men trying to sell a two year old that matches Stormy's description!" Duke shouted from the other end of the phone line. Stunned by what he heard, Johnson didn't immediately answer as he tried to comprehend what Duke said. "Johnson! Did you hear me?" Duke anxiously asked.

"Yes! Yes! I heard you, Duke. Where are they? Where is Stormy?" He shouted back into the phone.

"South Dakota! The inspector is trying to stall them for me," Duke answered. The full impact of what Duke said was dawning on Johnson. Questions flashed through his mind and suddenly he started asking for all the details. Duke waited until Johnson stopped asking nonstop questions. In a precise manner, he began giving Johnson all the details from a phone call he received from a brand inspector at a small South Dakota stock yard.

"Just ten minutes ago, I received a call from a brand inspector in a small town just across the Wyoming border, in South Dakota. Two questionable characters brought in two horses to sell. He became suspicious when he went into the pen where the horses had been unloaded. One of the horses was an old worn out animal, while the other one was a young stallion. The stallion really caught his attention. He saw that it was an exceptional horse and couldn't understand why these two grubby characters would want to sell such a fine animal as a canner. Neither animal had a brand, but the men produced ownership papers and a travel permit for them."

"He said that he kept wondering about the younger horse. Their papers were in order so he started filling out the brand inspection report. While he was filling in the description of the young stallion, he remembered a notice he received concerning a horse stolen in Montana that seemed to fit this animal's description. He found the flyer. It must have been one that Ann's been sending out. He compared the stolen horse, described on the flyer, to the stallion in the pen. The markings were the same and the age of the stallion was about right compared to the weanling stolen a year and a half ago. The description of the men suspected of stealing the colt and shooting two mares seemed to fit the two bums that brought these horses in."

In rising excitement, Johnson interrupted and said, "Duke, how far is that stockyard from here?"

"It's six hundred miles and it will take all night to get there, if we hurry," Duke said.

"Well, let's get going!" Johnson said.

"Now slow down a little, Johnson, there's more. The inspector said the horses wouldn't be sold till tomorrow during their weekly horse sale. That gives us enough time to get over there and look for ourselves to see if it really is Annie's colt. However, the paperwork for the stallion shows the men own him, so legally the inspector has to okay the sale. I told him there is a possibility that the paperwork could be a forgery on stolen forms. He said if we could identify the colt, then he would delay the sale of the stallion until we proved ownership. If we're not there before the sale, then the stallion will legally be sold to the highest bidder and the two men can claim their check and leave," Duke said.

The thought of finding Stormy and catching the men that killed Rose and wounded Flame coursed through Johnson's body like wildfire. "This is wonderful news, Duke. We must get Annie and Bill. They'll want to go with is. I'll tell James and Casey where we're going and why. They can take over until I get back. I'll throw some gear together and as soon as I find Bill, we'll be on our way to town. Call the school and tell Annie to hurry to your office. Explain to her what has happened and what we're going to do. I'll be there as fast as I can. And Duke, thanks, you don't know what this means to us!" Johnson said.

"I'll call Annie. We'll be here waiting for you and I do know what this means to you, Johnson. I was in that clearing and had to look down on Rose and watch Flame struggling for her life. I haven't forgotten. I want those men as bad as you do. Hurry and get here so we can get started," Duke said.

Johnson ran out of the barn shouting for Bill. James heard him yelling. Alarmed, he ran to see what was wrong. Johnson quickly explained. "Bill's in the lower pasture checking the early calves. I'll take a saddle horse and get him while you get your gear together," James excitedly said, then turned and raced for the barn. Johnson ran for the house to get a change of clothes and overnight gear for both himself and Ann. He was coming out of the house with two small bags when he heard hooves pounding in a hard run.

He saw Bill coming up a tractor trail in the near pasture on Thorny. James was close behind on another ranch horse. The horses were stretched out and reaching hard for more speed as their riders prodded them on. Johnson had to stop and admire the beautiful sight of capable riders on willing horses coming at high speed across the pasture. In seconds,

Bill was in the ranch yard and setting back on Thorny in a sliding stop that threw dirt far out in front of them. James, ten lengths behind, ran in and stopped beside Bill and Thorny. Bill was already out of the saddle asking Johnson questions. James came up and took Thorny's reins and said, "I'll take care of your horse. You just get going."

Johnson put both his hands out in front of him in a stopping motion and said, "Now slow down, Bill, I'll explain everything to you on the way to town. We don't even know if it's Stormy for sure, but it sounds like him and the description of the men sounds like the two we've suspected. Now let's hustle and get to town. James, we'll call you from South Dakota and let you know what's happening," Johnson said and jumped in the pickup truck.

Bill looked at James and said, "Thanks, James, I'll see you when we get back."

Bill got in the truck and heard James call out, "We'll be praying it's Stormy and that you catch the men that killed Rose!"

Johnson didn't pay much attention to the speed limit as he drove for town. Dust billowed out behind the pickup as they raced toward High Valley on the gravel road. Johnson told Bill all he knew about the call Duke received from the brand inspector in South Dakota. "For Annie's sake, I sure hope it's her colt," Bill said.

They pulled in to Duke's office and saw that he had a state vehicle parked in front with a stock trailer attached. The State of Montana emblem, with Brand Inspector lettered beneath, was emblazoned across the sides of both vehicles. "Duke's taking a trailer, he must believe it's Annie's colt," Johnson said.

They parked the truck and started for the office. The door opened and they watched Ann come running toward them. They saw tears streaming down her face. She ran to Johnson and threw her arms around him. "I knew we would find him! It's just got to be Stormy!" she cried out.

Duke came out of his office and said, "Now I want you all to listen to me. I've cleared this trip with my head office at the state capitol. They're going to give us all the support we ask for. The state would really like to capture the rustlers too. We have to get to that stock yard and identify the colt before he's sold tomorrow. Right now, unless we get there and prove otherwise, those crooks have every right to sell the horse. Their paperwork is in order, so the inspector is obligated to okay the sale. It all depends on us getting there on time. It's a long way to South Dakota, so we better start moving!"

Bill grabbed the bags out of the truck and everyone got in the state car. Duke pulled the car and trailer onto the roadway. He was in a hurry and to avoid any traffic delays going through town, he reached down and turned the siren on. "I'll turn that off when we hit the open highway. Right now, it will clear the road through town for us," he said.

Word traveled fast through school when Ann received Duke's call. She asked for and received permission to leave school to go to South Dakota in search of her colt. Everyone in school participated in one way or another in the search for Stormy and the excitement of his possible discovery spread quickly through the halls. Duke sped through town with the siren wailing. As they approached the school, he slowed down.

Everyone in the car saw a crowd of students and teachers standing in front of the school and along the street. Duke slowed even further wondering what was happening. With the siren screaming its warning, they approached the crowd. All along the street stood cheering students. They were waving their arms and giving Ann a victory signal. Teachers were holding a large hastily made banner that said, "GOOD LUCK, ANN--BRING STORMY HOME!!!" It seemed as if the whole school was cheering and waving to them in encouragement. Word also spread through town and as they sped through High Valley, people came out of stores and offices waving to them.

Tears flowed down Ann's face as Duke accelerated toward the highway. He reached down and turned off the siren. The only sound in the car as it sped toward South Dakota was the sniffling from the hopeful girl in the back seat. Johnson was overwhelmed with emotion when he saw the concern shown by their community. He withdrew into thoughts of Rose and her killers. Duke turned onto the highway and accelerated toward the far off town in South Dakota.

They were on a grave mission. Duke drove steadily through the night and only stopped to refuel. Everyone in the car kept their hopes to themselves. The only conversation was about the trip and highway directions. Ann tried to sleep during the long journey but excitement and the hum of the tires kept her awake. They traveled east across the front range of the Rocky Mountains and entered the rolling hill country of the plains. Duke drove across the barren lands of eastern Wyoming. In darkness, it was a monotonous trip. The first trace of daylight found them approaching the Black Hills near the South Dakota border. Duke was tired of driving and the dark outline of forested hills, illuminated by the coming dawn, was a welcome sight to him.

They left Wyoming and crossed into South Dakota just as the sun made its first appearance above the hills. "Another twenty miles and we'll be there," Duke said.

"Hurry, Duke, I can't wait to see if it is really Stormy. It's been so long," Ann said.

Johnson laughed and Bill said, "Hurry? What do you think we've been doing since we left High Valley?"

"Ann, if that is Stormy, remember, you haven't seen that colt in an awful long time. He'll probably look a lot different than you have him pictured in your mind. We don't know where he's been or how he has been treated for the past year and a half. Don't be shocked if he doesn't look like you recall him as a weanling," Johnson said.

"Here it is," Duke said. They came around a bend in the highway and ahead of them they could see the small town. They passed a sign that said, CASCADE, pop. 1800. Duke drove past the collection of buildings that comprised the business district. On the far side of town, he turned onto a road and followed a sign that said, CASCADE STOCK-YARDS. Up ahead they could see rambling corrals spread out over a large area. There were numerous buildings, but

Duke seemed to know exactly where he was going. He drove to a small building with a large sign on the front that said, CASCADE BRAND INSPECTOR.

Inside the building, the Cascade inspector saw the symbol of the Montana Brand Inspector's office on the side of the vehicle pulling in. He was expecting them and walked out to greet them. He saw a young woman bolt out of the car and rush toward him. "I'm Ann Olsen, can I see the horse, please," Ann excitedly said to the man.

"Yes, ma'am, you can. But first, there are a few things we better take care of before we go to the corrals," the inspector said. Everyone introduced themselves and the inspector invited them into his small office. Impatiently, Ann waited for the formalities to finish. She wanted to know if the horse, somewhere in the corrals behind her, was Stormy.

"The first thing we better do is park your official car and trailer out of sight somewhere. We don't want to make the men suspicious of seeing an official Montana car here. If it is your horse, and you can prove it, then we want to capture these men when they show up to get their paperwork. I stalled them yesterday and told them I would have their paperwork ready before today's sale. They should be back in a few hours. Duke, you could pull your rig over to that large barn on the east side of the yards and put it inside," the inspector said.

Duke left to hide the car and trailer. Johnson held on to Ann's arm trying to instill patience in the excited girl. He knew the inspector would take them to the corrals when he was ready. To Ann, it seemed like an eternity before Duke returned. He was carrying a briefcase with the reports of the crime on Gunpowder Creek inside. He also carried reports of the stolen inspection forms and travel permits taken from the State of Montana.

"We can go over the contents of this briefcase after we look at the horse," Duke said.

The inspector looked at Ann and said, "I think we better take this young lady to the corrals to see if she can identify the stallion." Johnson felt Ann jump in anticipation. They followed the inspector out of the office and down a long runway between pens holding horses and cattle. Ann walked ahead with the brand inspector. The others walked close behind. Johnson put his hand out to Duke and Bill, signaling them to let Ann go ahead. He wanted her to see the horse first, without interruption from them.

They watched as the inspector pointed to a gate on a high corral off the runway. Ann slowed her pace and approached the pen. Johnson stopped Bill and Duke a short distance from the corral. She walked to the pen and stopped. She tried looking between the planks of the corral. She stooped to peer between the boards. Ann straightened up and then climbed up the side of the corral. She looked down into the pen.

Ann could see two horses in the pen. The younger horse was a rusty color and carried a dirty, heavy, winter coat of hair. He was facing away from her, standing close beside an old horse. She could see one white sock on his left rear leg. She was uncertain. She had the picture of a young, frisky colt in her mind. The mature stallion facing away from her was big and dirty. His ribs showed and his mane was tangled with twigs and matted dirt. She couldn't see his head. She called to him. "Stormy, please let it be you," she sobbed.

The stallion heard the human voice and spun around to face the danger he had come to expect. Exhilaration exploded on Ann as she looked upon the face of the colt she loved and lost, so long ago. There was that familiar white spot on his wide forehead. It was the same finely chiseled head she knew so well. His eyes were deep set and alert. Looking at this stallion facing her, she could see the image of Flame. His appearance was rough and battered, but there was no doubt. This stallion facing her was Stormy!

The men watched as Ann rocked back and held on to the top of the fence. She cried out, "Stormy! Stormy! It's you!"

Relief flooded through the men and they rushed to the corral to see for themselves. Bill looked into the pen and exclaimed, "No doubt about it. He's the spitting image of Flame. That's Stormy."

"Duke, come see for yourself," Johnson said. Ann was crying in happiness and Johnson saw Bill wipe his eyes as they looked down on the apprehensive stallion.

"My hunch was right then. I didn't think this horse belonged at a cannery sale," the inspector said.

Ann looked at the man and then climbed off the fence and walked up to him. She said, "Thank you so much for finding him. If it wasn't for you, we would never have seen him again."

"It was your monthly flyer that kept the missing horse's description fresh in my mind. They were the reason I recognized the horse," the inspector said.

"I'd like you to look at the paperwork I have concerning this horse," Duke said.

"We don't have much time, so we better go back to the office and see if you can prove ownership," the inspector said.

Johnson called Ann from her perch on the corral fence and said, "Ann, you better come with us. We may need your help." They walked quickly to the office.

Duke opened his briefcase and began showing the reports of the stolen horse to the South Dakota inspector. "Also, someone in Montana has been stealing inspection forms and travel permits. Here is a list of the numbers of the stolen forms," Duke said. The inspector took the document and glanced down the list of numbers. He carried it over to his desk and picked up the forms the men presented when they brought the horses in. There was silence in the small office while the inspector checked the numbers against the list Duke gave him.

"We've got a match!" the inspector said. He showed Duke the forms Shorty gave him. On Duke's list of stolen forms, he pointed to the same form number that was stolen from a stock yard in Montana. "However, this doesn't prove these men stole the forms or the horse. They could have bought the horse from someone else who stole the forms. Without a brand, identification is difficult," he said.

"The description of the men that brought these horses in is the same as the pair seen in High Valley the day before the horse was stolen," Duke said.

"That doesn't prove they did the shooting or stole this stallion. Duke, you know the law, I have to have positive proof, before I can arrest these men for rustling and turn that horse over to you. As much as I believe that horse belongs to Ann, I can't turn him over on just circumstantial evidence," the inspector said.

"Isn't the description of the stolen colt on the crime report enough evidence?" Ann asked with a trace of alarm in her voice. She couldn't believe they didn't have enough proof of ownership to claim the colt.

The inspector picked up the report and looked it over. Johnson watched with a growing feeling of despair. "The report describes the colt as a sorrel with a white spot on his forehead and a white sock on his left rear leg. That could be that horse in the pen, but it could be a thousand other sorrel horses with a white spot and sock," the inspector said and shook his head from side to side. "Personally, I believe the horse is yours. However, I have to go by the laws of the state of South Dakota and they state that I must have solid proof of ownership," the inspector said firmly.

"What about the stolen forms?" Duke asked with irritation in his voice.

"Duke, we'll work with you and try to find where these men got the forms. I'll even take them into custody for possession of stolen forms, but I just don't have the positive proof I need to deny these men ownership of that sorrel horse," he sadly said. Johnson lowered his head in despair. He felt responsible. If only they had branded the colt.

"Doc Brown!" Everyone in the small room looked at Ann. "Doc Brown!" Ann said again in a louder voice.

"What do you mean?" Johnson asked.

"He treated the colt when he was only a day old, he can positively identify him," Ann said firmly.

"How?" the inspector asked.

"Our colt was mysteriously wounded on both sides of his neck when Bill found him. Doc Brown treated those wounds. He said they were teeth marks. They turned into black scars on his neck. Those scars were prominent and should still be hiding under that thick winter coat," Ann said with rising hope.

"That would be positive proof. What is his phone number?" the inspector asked. Within minutes, he was on the phone with Doc Brown in High Valley. He questioned the veterinarian about the Bent Bar colt, born during a flood two springs ago and asked him if he remembered treating him shortly after he was born. He asked if he could remember anything unusual about the colt's injuries. There was a long silence as Doc talked to the inspector. They heard the inspector say, "Okay, thank you for your time, sir." He hung up the phone and looked directly at Ann.

"If the horse in that pen has scars on both sides of his neck, resembling teeth marks, I will arrest the two men who brought him in and grant you ownership of the stallion. Your vet told me the location of the scars and if your description matches his, that's good enough for the state of South Dakota," the Cascade brand inspector said, sounding delighted.

Happily, Ann described in detail the location of the scars on the colt's neck. Excitement passed through everyone and they rushed back to the pen to look for the scars on Stormy's neck.

Stormy wouldn't let anyone near him. He fought off Duke and the inspector with threatening charges every time they tried to approach him. "We're running out of time before the rustlers return, we better run him into a narrow chute to confine him," the inspector said.

"Wait, this horse has been treated bad enough, let me try. I was the first one he saw when he was born. Colts usually remember their first contact with people, it makes a big impression on them. I found him on top of a ravine and managed to gain his trust when he was just hours old. He followed me off the mountain to where we found his mother. He just might remember and let me near him," Bill said.

Stormy backed into a corner of the corral. He was prepared to rush forward again and defend himself against the two men who tried to approach him. He watched as they talked to one of the men on the fence. Then he saw them turn and walk away. The man on the fence slowly climbed into the corral. He carefully walked along the side of the corral toward the old horse and ignored Stormy. The stallion listened as the man talked to the aged horse in a low soothing voice.

Stormy directed his full attention on the man who was now placing a hand on the old horse. The stallion welcomed the companionship of the horse, but now he watched in alarm as his new friend allowed the man to touch him. The horses were only yards apart and Stormy could plainly see the man on the far side of the old horse. He could hear the man's voice and watched as he began rubbing the other horse above his tailbone.

Stormy began to feel a comfort that he couldn't understand as he listened to the sounds coming from the man. Vaguely, he remembered noises that were familiar and meant kindness. Far off, and long ago in another place, he heard the same kind of sounds, and they did not signal danger. A new feeling of attraction to the man began to invade Stormy's fearful stance. Slowly, his fear was being replaced by curiosity. The man moved around the back of the other horse and was now between the two horses. The stallion held his ground.

Bill was within a few feet of the stallion. He slowly extended his arm to the sorrel horse's nose. Stormy stretched out toward the extended hand to see if he could recognize the scent. It was familiar, but from a time he could barely remember. Other horses and people. Running with friends and bucking high on green meadows. Being pleasantly rubbed in places that needed rubbing. Someone kind, who brought good tasting feed in dry barns. This smell and voice stirred long forgotten memories of good times and a family of horses.

Stormy's fear of this man began to crumble and he yearned to feel his touch. Carefully, Bill moved his hand to the horse's forehead and touched him. On the corral fence, Ann was almost afraid to breathe in anticipation. The touch of the man electrified Stormy and a flood of memories returned in a rush. Heavy brush above a ravine, a friendly horse and a man standing nearby. Following them to the comfort of another horse who fed and protected him from danger. Friends. This man was safe, he was a connection that could lead him out of his terrible loneliness. Stormy allowed him to move his hand from his forehead to his neck. He felt the pleasant sensation of the hand rubbing under his mane.

Bill lifted Stormy's mane away from his neck and with his other hand, brushed aside the heavy winter coat, revealing a series of short black scars that resembled teeth marks. He heard someone exhale in relief. Bill moved around the horse and gently pushed his head to the side. He used his hand to move aside the heavy hair. A series of small concise black scars stood out as if they had been branded there.

"No law in this country can argue with that evidence. That is positive proof. This is the horse stolen from you. You can take possession of him," the brand inspector said firmly.

Overjoyed, Ann slipped into the corral and gave Bill a questioning look. "I think he remembers. Ease up here and see if he recognizes his owner," Bill said. Stormy allowed Ann to move up beside him. Her touch was gentle and he stood quietly as she placed her hands on him. He wanted to give in to these familiar feelings and sounds. The stallion seemed to feel as if a heavy burden was lifted. He allowed her to put her arms around his neck. He would trust these people. A flood of tears streamed down Ann's face as she embraced the colt.

"We've got some unfinished business to take care of," Johnson said.

"Yep, you've proved your ownership. Now, let's move away from these horses so we don't arouse suspicion from the men that brought them here," the inspector ordered.

They left the corrals and went back to the office. The brand inspector placed a call to the county sheriff. He explained the circumstances and asked him to come to the stock yards. People were starting to arrive for the sale. The inspector's office became busy with people checking in horses for the sale. The inspector became involved with paperwork and inspections. Duke and the Bent Bar crew crowded into the small office and waited for Shorty and Chester to show up for their paperwork.

Bill saw an old blue truck pulling into the parking lot and asked, "Are these the ones, pulling in now?"

The inspector looked out the window and said, "You can't mistake that pair. That's them!"

Duke watched as they parked and got out. "That's the two I suspected when they brought in a few good horses to sell at High Valley. They're sure a rank looking pair and they look like the type that would shoot horses," he said. Johnson stared at the two walking toward the office and remained silent.

They were sloppy looking and their clothes were crumpled and soiled. They appeared as if they had just awakened. Johnson watched intently as they approached the office. Shorty stopped in front of the door and said something to Chester. Chester stopped and looked down at Shorty. The people inside heard Chester shout, "I should get all the money! Look at what happened to my shoulder, an' he's the cause of it!"

The people waiting in the office watched and listened as the two argued. Shorty spit out a long dark stream of tobacco juice. "You should be glad I was there. If it wasn't for me, she'd a' killed you for sure. That's why I want most of the money," Shorty said. He gave Chester a toothless grin and opened the office door.

Shorty walked in, while Chester stood in the doorway. "I come for the paperwork on them two horses we brought in yesterday. You must have it ready by now," Shorty said to the inspector behind the counter. The inspector didn't answer, he just stared hard at Shorty. Shorty looked back at him and wondered why he wasn't answering. Chester remained in the doorway. Shorty started to repeat himself and then stopped. Suddenly a feeling of foreboding flashed through him. He looked back at Chester and saw him still standing in the doorway. Shorty looked at the other people staring at him from the back of the office. Everyone in the small office had a grim look and were coldly glaring at him.

Shorty knew something was wrong. Had they been caught? The silence and grim glares he was receiving relayed a danger signal. He looked around the room, and when his gaze fell on Johnson's ice cold glare, fear shot through him. He recognized the weather worn face from somewhere and associated it with an unpleasant experience. Then he remembered the tall man and the cafe in High Valley. High Valley was close to where they stole the colt and where he shot the two mares. Panic replaced Shorty's fear. He turned and bumped into Chester in the doorway. "Let's go, Chester!" he said and rushed around him out of the office. Chester saw the look on Shorty's face and knew the worst had happened. He bolted after his partner.

The Cascade inspector started from around the counter to chase after the men. Johnson and Bill started after them too. Duke jumped in front of the inspector and stopped him. He looked in his eyes and said, "I know this is your jurisdiction and we'll respect your authority. But, a deep hurt can be put to rest, if you let these men capture that dirty pair." The inspector hesitated, he could see Duke's request came from the heart. He recalled the horrifying details of the two mares being ruthlessly gunned down in the botched rustling attempt. They had a score to settle. He nodded at Duke in understanding and left the chase up to the two men from the Bent Bar Ranch.

Shorty ran for the truck, and Chester was close behind. Halfway there, Shorty turned and looked toward the office. Cold fear enveloped him when he saw the two men running after him. He would never have time to reach the truck and escape. "This way, Chester!" he yelled and scrambled up and over a corral fence into the pens of the stockyard. Fear was driving Shorty now and he was surprisingly fast. He thought he could lose the men in the maze of corrals and pens of the stock yard.

Long legged Chester was moving as fast as he could, trying to keep up with Shorty. He clambered up the side of the corral that Shorty disappeared over. Chester caught his foot in the top rail and fell down into the pen. That pen had not been cleaned since it held cattle the day before. It was covered in a deep layer of fresh manure. Chester landed face first in the smelly mess. Before he could get up, Bill landed on his back, shoving him further into the departed cattle's excrement. Johnson raced past, after Shorty who was just going over the next fence.

Bill jerked Chester up and slammed him against the fence. He reared back his arm ready to smash his fist into the rustler's face. He hesitated. Chester's face was covered in greenish brown manure. Chester's mouth was full of the wet stuff and he coughed some out onto Bill. "You miserable scum bag," Bill said and then launched his powerful fist into Chester's face. Bill felt the satisfying crunch of teeth breaking and others rearranging themselves in Chester's mouth. Chester grunted and coughed with the force of Bill's powerful blow. He coughed out a mixture of blood and teeth, combined with a paste of fresh, green manure.

Shorty raced through the pens trying to elude the man that was relentlessly chasing him. They ran through pens holding horses and cattle. There were a few people in the stock yard preparing for the sale and they watched in wonder, as the short, dirty man ran through the runways and corrals, pursued by the tall, lean man.

Johnson knew exactly what he was doing. He let Shorty stay just far enough ahead of him to believe that he really did have a chance to get away. Johnson wanted Shorty to run far enough to be out of sight of anyone when he caught him. Johnson could see Shorty was getting close to the back side of the stock yards. He poured on the speed and closed the gap. Shorty went over the last fence and headed for the woods across a brushy field. Johnson went over the fence right on the rustler's heels and launched a flying tackle that smashed Shorty to the ground.

Quickly, Johnson grabbed Shorty and dragged him back to the corral fence. He lifted him up and slammed him into the boards of the corral. Johnson was holding Shorty in the air, with the outlaw's feet dangling a foot off the ground. Johnson looked around but could see no one. They were alone. He held Shorty pinned against the fence with one arm and with the other hand proceeded to slap Shorty hard across the face. Johnson dealt a dozen stinging blows to the rustler. He stopped hitting him and said, "You tell me why you shot those horses, or I guarantee you that you'll never walk out of here on your own two feet!"

"It wadn't me, it wadn't me that did it! It was Chester, it was all his idea. I swear!" Shorty screamed. Johnson lifted him away from the fence and slammed him back with a force that brought a loud grunt from the desperate man.

"Tell the truth, or I'll break every bone in your miserable body!" Johnson hissed into the man's face and then slammed him into the fence again.

"Okay! Okay! Just don't hurt me no more!" the terrified crook said.

"Talk!" Johnson said and tightened his grip in a threatening move.

"I had to shoot em'. They was about to kill Chester and he screamed at me to help him. That red mare was pounding him into the dirt and I shot her to save Chester. Then that old bay mare come charging at me so fast, I hardly had time to do anything but shoot her. They was both terrors and meant to kill us. They was trying to get that small colt back that we had in the trailer. That same colt that's in them corrals. It's all Chester's fault!" Shorty said in a rush and then whimpered, "Please, don't hurt me no more!"

Shorty looked into the tall man's eyes and saw the rage buried deep inside. He knew it was about to explode and he started shaking in fear.

Johnson's fury increased as he listened to Shorty's confession. He pictured the scene and visualized Rose, charging to the rescue of Flame and Stormy, under the withering gunfire that killed her. This was the man that pulled the trigger on the gun that savagely ended her life.

Johnson doubled his fist and hit Shorty in the face with all of his power. He felt the crunch of bone breaking. The next blow broke Shorty's nose and blood sprayed out from the shattered skin. Johnson cocked his arm again and punched Shorty hard in the mouth. He broke his jaw and knocked out the teeth remaining on one side of Shorty's mouth. His rage built as he vented his anger at the man who caused him so much pain. Johnson threw his arm back and swung with all his might. The force of the blow knocked the wind out of the rustler and broke two ribs in his chest. Shorty struggled to breathe, Johnson released his grip and let the vile man fall to the ground.

When Shorty regained his breath, Johnson stood him up and helped him walk back to the brand inspector's office. It took Shorty a long time to get there. His ribs hurt, his nose was swelling fast and he had trouble talking through his broken jaw. He kept spitting out pieces of broken teeth mixed with blood. "This is just a taste of what will happen to you if I ever see you around High Valley again. If you ever get out of jail," Johnson told him.

People stared as they made their way through the stockyard. Shorty looked terrible. Besides his normal filthy appearance, he now had bloodstains on his dirty clothes. He limped and held his side with one arm, while Johnson held his other arm and helped him along. They neared the office and Johnson saw a sheriff's car parked in front. There was a small crowd gathered around the car.

When they got there, they could see Chester sitting in the back seat. Blood was trickling down one corner of his mouth and he appeared to have been plastered with fresh manure. Chester looked miserable.

"Here's the other one," Johnson said and shoved Shorty toward the sheriff. Shorty looked like he had been run over by a herd of stampeding cattle.

The sheriff took one look at him and asked, "What happened to him? I suppose he got banged up like that falling off the top of the corral too!"

"He had a little accident when he was trying to escape," Johnson answered.

Bill caught Johnson's eye and a look of satisfaction passed between the two as they nodded to each other. Duke saw the exchange of a silent "well done". He felt great pleasure that his old friend finally settled the score with the men who shot his horse.

Ann walked to Johnson's side and tugged on his arm. She saw bloody knuckles on his hand. He looked down and saw tears of joy in her eyes. "I called the ranch and told Casey we would be home late tonight with Stormy," she said.

CHAPTER 19

Buster watched Ann lead the strange sorrel horse into the arena. He was curious about what she was doing. Ann had turned Buster loose in the big arena, now she was leading a stranger in and heading toward him. He was curious, but not curious enough to rush over and see who the new horse was. He could hear the girl talking to the horse as they came closer. It was a pleasant sound to Buster and by her tone, he knew the horse was probably friendly.

When they were within twenty feet of Buster, Ann stopped Stormy. The stallion was eager to see who the loose horse was. Stormy pointed his ears toward the horse and nickered. Buster heard the nicker but couldn't place it. It had sounds similar to a lot of the Bent Bar horses, but he didn't recognize the horse. The younger horse seemed friendly so Buster walked up and touched noses with him. His scent was familiar too. It carried odors similar to one of the sorrel mares. The sorrel stallion became excited and nickered, then nipped Buster on his withers. Buster snorted in annoyance and jumped back. Something far back in the recesses of his mind told him that he had been around this horse before.

Ann laughed, Stormy seemed to remember his old friend, Buster. She turned Stormy loose and watched him prance up to the older horse. Buster snorted in disapproval. Stormy jumped away and broke into a full run for the far end of the arena. With blinding speed he raced to the end of the arena, spun around and came flying back toward Buster. The gelding became nervous and pranced around in irritation. Stormy ran directly for him and at the last second veered away and slid to a stop. Buster remembered a young colt causing the same problems long ago. This looked like the same colt, only he had grown up. Buster whinnied a friendly warning to the youngster. He was glad to see him.

"Now if only Flame would be a little more friendly to you, Stormy," Ann said. Flame tolerated Stormy, but chased him off when he tried to get too friendly with her new filly. Her motherly instincts prevailed and she became protective of her new foal. She seemed to recognize him. Flame nickered and smelled him, but ran him off when he approached her young foal. Stormy recognized his mother, but couldn't understand why she kept chasing him away. "It's Mother Nature, Stormy, Flame has to take care of her new filly first. You're not number one in her mind anymore. She protected you with that same ferocity when you were the age of your little sister there," Ann said to the stallion.

Stormy's return to the Bent Bar had been a wonderful experience for everyone. The colt seemed to fall right in to the pattern of the ranch. His return boosted the morale of everyone involved in the search for him. Work on the ranch went ahead with a new enthusiasm, especially for those involved with the horse operation.

Duke called with the news that Shorty and Chester were sentenced to jail in South Dakota for stealing horses. They still faced charges for their crimes in Montana. The crime lab positively matched the paint chip found imbedded in Flame's shoe with a sample taken from the rustler's trailer. The finger prints on the whiskey bottle found at the scene matched both Shorty's and Chester's prints. Duke said, "It will be a long time before they see daylight again without steel bars blocking their view!"

Ann began working Stormy every day. The colt balked at the training at first, but slowly started to respond to her persistence. Stormy was exhilarated to be back on the ranch in the company of old friends. He looked forward to each new day and the company it brought. He put on spectacular shows in his exuberance of again being part of a group of horses. He raced around the arena showing speed that was phenomenal. He could go from a standing start to a blinding fast run in seconds.

Johnson said he had the makings of a race horse. His speed was natural and with training, he would be hard to beat. Bill said he could make a roping horse that would catch a calf in record time. Casey said that he hoped Ann didn't ask him to ride the stallion when she got ready to saddle him. "If he wanted to, I'll bet he could put on a bucking show that would stretch the britches on the best bronc rider in the country," he said.

Ann listened with pleasure to all the compliments Stormy received from everyone who saw him. "I always thought he could be a champion. Thankfully, I have him back and have the chance to see if I can make a barrel racing champ out of him. We've got a lot of work to do, but hopefully by next year at this time, I'll be riding this stallion in competition," she said.

Stormy raced around the perimeter of the arena and then slowed to a fast gallop. He loped over to the spot where Ann and Buster were watching him. His muscles rippled as he slowed to a trot. Ann looked on him with pleasure as he approached. He came right up and pushed her arm up with his muzzle. "It didn't take you long to make yourself right at home again, Stormy," she said as she rubbed his neck. The colt liked the attention she gave him and pushed again on her arm to encourage her to keep rubbing his neck. "But now, I've got to put you back in your stall. Buster and I have some serious practicing to do today and you'll just get in the way," she said.

Ann was on a barrel racing campaign. She and Buster were competing in as many rodeos as they possibly could. They were consistent and the points were piling up. She wanted to qualify for the state finals this coming fall. Buster's speed had fallen off as his age increased, but his precise execution of the pattern kept them ranked high among the finalists through the season.

Ann graduated from high school in June and began to devote more and more time to training Stormy. His ground work was going well. A week after graduation she brought Stormy into the arena and said, "Stormy! It's time that you graduated, too. We'll see if you can tolerate a saddle on your back. You're working good on the ground, so it's time to saddle you up."

She brought a saddle pad out of the tack room and slowly presented it to the colt for his inspection. Stormy sniffed it and looked away. It didn't interest him and he knew it wouldn't hurt him. Ann slid the pad along his neck and gradually worked it onto his back. He didn't pay any attention to it. She left the pad in place and went to the tack room for her saddle. When she returned, the pad was still in place. She set the saddle down in front of him and stepped back.

The colt looked at the saddle with interest. He had seen lots of them on the backs of other horses and knew what it was. He put his head down and inspected the saddle. It smelled good and he began pushing it with his muzzle. Then he picked up one of the latigo strings and began chewing. Ann stepped in and picked up the saddle. Stormy stood still and showed no fear. "Don't eat it, Stormy, they're expensive," she chided.

She pulled the off side stirrup and fender onto the seat and raised the saddle above the colt's back. Slowly and gently she lowered it onto his back. Stormy flicked his ears toward her and then turned his head to look at the saddle. He wasn't impressed with it, but he wasn't bothered either. Ann reached under Stormy and very carefully pulled the cinch to her side of the colt. She felt Stormy tense up when the cinch touched his belly. Ann talked to him in reassuring tones and he soon relaxed.

Ann held the cinch snug with her hand for a few minutes. She wiggled it around a few times to get Stormy accustomed to it. When he was completely relaxed with the cinch touching his sensitive belly, she ran the latigo through the cinch a few times and tightened it up. Stormy accepted the tightness of the cinch and stood calmly. After a few minutes, Ann tightened it all the way. She stepped back and let Stormy explore his new sensation. Ann urged the colt to walk around the arena. Soon Stormy was loping around with the saddle on his back and the stirrups flopping against his sides. He got used to it and Ann began saddling him every time she turned him loose in the arena.

Ann started standing in the stirrup to get the colt accustomed to her weight, and within a week, she was sitting in the saddle. Stormy offered no resistance and moved about with Ann on his back as if he were afraid she would fall off. He enjoyed pleasing her and was eager to learn. She started his reining lessons using a snaffle bit and the colt learned fast. Soon they were loping around the arena and Stormy was responding to Ann's cues with reins and leg pressure. Stormy carried his rider with ease and Ann never felt the colt tire or even breathe hard. He was rock hard and seemed to have a lasting endurance.

In late June, Ann decided to ride Stormy outside the arena. He was learning fast and for a green broke colt, Ann felt he was doing extremely well. She gave Buster a rest one day and rode Stormy into the hills to check the livestock. It was a big event around the ranch and everyone gave her lots of advice on being careful with a green horse. Casey was worried about her and offered to ride along. "Thanks, Case, but we'll be okay. I'll just take him up Dry Boulder and check the cows in that area. I'll make it a short day for his first time out. He's doing good and I don't have any fear of taking him into the hills," she said.

They left the ranch shortly after daylight. Ann walked him down the lane to the county road. Stormy was excited about being out in the open. He had been cooped up in the barn for months, ever since his recovery from the rustlers. He exercised regularly in the big indoor arena but that was nothing like the thrill of being out in the mountains. He was anxious to stretch his legs and kept giving Ann subtle hints by pulling on the reins.

They turned onto the county road and Ann gave in to Stormy's desire for more speed. She let him break into a trot. They trotted down the road for a quarter mile and then Stormy started nudging on the reins again. Ann liked his spirit and let him ease into a lope. She could feel his excitement about being out in the country. Stormy's desire to run was contagious and his enthusiasm rubbed off on Ann. She began to wonder just what this horse could do if she gave him his head.

It was a beautiful morning with the sun just breaking over the mountains to the east. The warm rays penetrated and warmed the horse and rider as they loped down the road. They both felt happy to be together again on this beautiful summer morning. Stormy lifted his head and tugged on the reins. "Why not!" Ann shouted and gave him his head.

Stormy accelerated so fast, Ann almost lost her seat. In just a few lengths the strong horse had rocketed into a stretching run down the county road. Ann bent at the waist and leaned forward, slacking the reins more and giving Stormy an invitation to go for all he could. He needed no further encouragement. He stretched out and reached hard for more speed as they pounded down the side of the road. The joy of the morning, combined with the invigorating feeling of being out of the barn in the open air, gave him tremendous vigor and he raced down the road in unrestrained delight.

Ann leaned into the wind and balanced herself perfectly. Stormy's speed was so great that the force of the wind caused tears to stream back from the corner of her eyes. Trees and objects flashed past so fast as to be almost unrecognizable. Ann had never known such great speed on any horse she had ever ridden. Buster had been fast in his younger years but never possessed the tremendous acceleration and unbelievable top speed Stormy was showing her this morning.

His speed was exhilarating, she made clucking sounds to encourage him even faster. She felt the stallion respond and the staccato sound of his hooves striking the road increased rapidly. Down the road they raced. For over a mile, Ann let Stormy run as fast as he wanted. She was excited and tremendously happy to be riding the colt she thought had been lost.

The joy of the moment and the thrill of the ride caused tears of happiness to mix with the wind whipped tears streaking back along her face. "Stormy, you're tremendous!"

she shouted. Stormy responded with even more effort and the beat of his hooves hitting the ground sounded like a rapid firing machine gun.

They ran past the turn off to Dry Boulder Coulee and reluctantly, Ann decided to slow the racing stallion. This was a critical time. She wondered if the running horse would obey her command to slow down or, in the heat of the moment, would he forget his training and continue running, out of her control. Ann straightened up in the saddle and gently pulled on the reins. Stormy felt the change in her posture and then felt the pressure on the bit. He wanted to keep running but his desire to please the girl was greater and he slowed his great speed.

With gentle pressure on the reins, Ann gradually slowed Stormy to a fast walk. He responded immediately to her commands. She was pleased and exhilarated with his fantastic speed. "Stormy, you are absolutely the fastest horse I have ever ridden!" she shouted when they turned and started back to the cutoff to Dry Boulder. After the long run, Ann noticed with pleasure that he wasn't even breathing hard. She reached down and patted him on his neck and said, "I think you and I are going to go places in a hurry, Stormy!"

They returned to the ranch in the late afternoon. She loped Stormy up the lane and saw Johnson and Casey watching her from in front of the barn. She rode Stormy over to them and stopped. "Stormy is absolutely the fastest horse I have ever seen," she said.

Casey looked at Johnson and said, "Now he's a race horse."

"He is fast, Casey, he'll outrun anything on the ranch. His speed is incredible," Ann said.

Johnson smiled and said, "He looks fast. He probably could be a race horse, but I'd rather see him perform for you as a barrel horse. By the way, Ann, there's a letter for you from the University. I put it on your desk in the new office," Johnson said.

Ann took care of Stormy. When he was comfortably put away in his stall, she walked over to the office. She found the letter on the desk. Apprehension gripped her as she opened the envelope. With a sinking heart, she read the letter from the University, rejecting her application for a rodeo scholarship.

Dear Miss Olsen,

Thank you for applying to the University for a rodeo scholarship. Your application was received and processed. Unfortunately our rodeo team has been filled with applicants with higher performance statistics than you have acquired to date. I note that you have performed well in barrel racing and certainly your grades meet our requirements. However, at this time, I cannot approve a rodeo scholarship for you.

As you know, the University has always produced one of the top teams in the nation. Our team must consist of the top applicants who apply, based on their previous performance in the rodeo arena and their scholastic achievements. I strongly feel with more experience at a higher level of competition, it may be possible for a re-evaluation of your application.

I am aware that you have been accepted to attend the University. I hope you will feel free to visit our training facilities when you arrive on campus. I will keep track of your performance, both scholastically and in the arena.

Glen Linsay,
Head Coach
University Rodeo Team

Scholastically, she had been accepted to the university. Now, she would have to pay her tuition without the aid of the scholarship. Dejected, Ann slumped down in the chair behind the desk. She knew there was keen competition for a slot on that rodeo team when she applied. Her performance was good. She simply had not competed enough to qualify for the higher level of competition. That higher level was found at the state finals.

She was pushing hard this year and competing in more events. She really felt she could ride Buster to the state finals. Now, it was more important than ever. She had enough funds for the first semester of college, but that was all. For her to continue after the first semester would require more money than she had.

So, it all boils down to one thing. If I want to go to college for more than just one semester, Buster and I have to win more events. That means taking more first places and not settling for second or third behind Marsha Miller, Ann thought.

CHAPTER 20

"Here she comes! I better get out of here," Casey said. Ann looked up and saw a new pickup, towing a long horse trailer, pulling into the High Valley fair grounds. Brightly painted letters, emblazoned on the side of the trailer, MARSHA MILLER --STATE BARREL RACING CHAMPION, garishly identified the owner.

"Oh, Case, why don't you just tell her you're not interested in her? Maybe then she'll stop chasing after you," Ann said and laughed.

"I have, she just doesn't take no for an answer," Casey said and walked away.

Casey got away just in time. Marsha pulled up near Ann's trailer and asked, "Hey! Have you seen Casey?" Ann looked at Marsha. She wondered why the girl was always so rude. She considered not even answering her. "Can't you hear me? Have you seen Casey?" Marsha called again from the open window.

Marsha's superior attitude irked Ann. Enough is enough, Ann thought. She was tired of trying to be nice. "He saw you coming and headed for the hills," Ann said and smiled.

Marsha frowned and said, "Sounds to me like you're a little jealous of that bronc rider." Ann didn't answer, instead she began to unload Buster from the trailer. Irritated because Ann refused to answer, Marsha pulled away to look for a parking spot.

"I think maybe she wasn't too happy with me," Ann said lightly to Buster as he backed out of the trailer.

"I don't think so either, but thanks for getting rid of her," Casey said as he walked out from behind the trailer.

Ann laughed and asked, "I thought you skeedadled out of here when she pulled in?"

"I did, but then I decided to hide behind the trailer till she left. You might need some help with Buster," Casey said.

Ann stared at Casey. He was awful handsome. She could certainly understand why Marsha was always chasing him. Why was Casey offering to help her with Buster? He knew she didn't need any help. Buster was already unloaded and she simply had to groom him before saddling him. Casey's offer was a bit strange. "Case, you know I don't need any help. How come you're asking anyway?"

"Just trying to be helpful. If I can't help you, then I guess I'll go on over to the bucking chutes. Good luck today, Ann," Casey said and walked away.

Ann watched him walk off. His behavior was strange. Usually, during a rodeo weekend, Casey was hanging out with the other bronc riders. They seemed to draw a throng of girls that chase after them over the weekend. Why was Casey showing an interest in me? Was he actually beginning to notice that I'm not a little girl any more? Ann wondered.

She groomed Buster and then went over every inch of her saddle and rigging. She wanted to be sure that there would be no equipment failure during their high speed ride through the barrels today. They were at the annual Fourth of July rodeo at the High Valley fairgrounds. She was pushing hard to gain enough points to qualify for the state finals and a win today would put them closer to that goal. Marsha was the top rider and Ann knew she would be hard to beat.

Ann remained close to Buster as the time drew near for the barrel event. She began warming the gelding in preparation for their run. It was a two day rodeo and they needed a win on both days to earn as many points as possible. Ann jogged Buster around the outside of the fairgrounds. She was slowly bringing him to a state of physical readiness. She thought the same of Buster's warmup exercises as a race car driver does when he revs his engine before the start of a race. Cold muscles will not function well at high speed. Better to have all the juices flowing before asking the horse for his top speed.

She heard the announcer calling her event and jogged over to the arena. Marsha was already in the alleyway awaiting her turn. Marsha gave her a cold stare as she rode in. She could hear the band playing and the noise of the crowd, but Marsha and the noise from the grandstands seemed remote, all of her thoughts were concentrated on the coming event. Ann learned to avoid distractions. From this point on, there existed only Buster and the three barrels awaiting them in the arena.

With the precision of a fine clock, Buster ran through the cloverleaf pattern of the barrels. Ann flowed with him and rode in a style that let the horse use her weight to his advantage. Buster's execution of the turns around each barrel was flawless. What Buster lacked in speed on the runs between barrels, he made up for in the turns. Ann guided him around the barrels in tight turns that allowed Buster to maintain a high rate of speed throughout the full circle. Once he entered the turn, Buster maintained his stride and drove hard around the barrel, accelerating quickly away toward the next barrel.

They easily won the event for the first day of the High Valley rodeo. Ann and Buster finished in first place for the day, with Marsha finishing second, a full tenth of a second behind them. The win added five points to their total for the state standings. Ann was excited about their performance and immediately began planning her strategy for the final run on Sunday.

Buster was performing like a dream. He had become a seasoned barrel horse and Ann felt more than ever that they could win at the state level. They had to earn enough points to qualify and today's win was a big help. Ann stayed at the rodeo long enough to find out the results of her event. When the announcement was made that she won, she loaded Buster and started for the ranch.

Ann would have liked to remain at the rodeo and watch the rest of the events as a spectator. Especially bronc riding. She knew it was more important to take Buster back to the ranch. The gelding had made a good run for her today. He would rest better and be more comfortable in his own stall than standing tied to the trailer for the rest of the hot afternoon. Ann wanted him to be in peak condition for tomorrow's run. She was more than willing to give up the social life at the rodeo grounds to improve her chances of an overall win on Sunday and the added points it would bring.

Ann drove out to the Bent Bar and unloaded Buster. She groomed and cared for the gelding, then put him in a cool comfortable stall. She was leaning against the gate to Buster's stall thinking about the day's event when she heard Stormy's familiar nicker.

She looked down the barn. Stormy had his head out over the gate looking toward her. Ann walked down to his stall and rubbed him on his forehead. She was still keyed up from the day's events and the stallion's friendly presence was soothing to her. "Stormy, I've got a good idea. How about you and I riding around the barrels in the new arena today. Your training is coming along good, maybe we can start you out a little early on the barrels," Ann said with enthusiasm. She remembered when Stormy had been a young colt and had run around the arena in mock fright from the three barrels she had been training Buster on. "Let's see if those barrels still interest you," she said.

Ann saddled Stormy and rode him in the arena. She jogged him around for a few minutes and then rode him to the starting line. For the next half hour, Ann walked Stormy through the pattern. Curious, she started him into the pattern again. This time she laid the reins loosely on his neck. Stormy had no guidance from her. He walked to the first barrel flicking his ears back at her in anticipation of her commands. Ann left the reins loose. When Stormy reached the first barrel he walked around it and headed for the second. The stallion walked through the complete course and returned to the starting line with no guidance at all from his rider.

Ann dismounted and fondly scratched Stormy's chest. "You're a smart horse, Stormy. I think you're going to be a natural barrel racer. You already know the pattern and what is expected. With a year of training behind you, you'll be hard to beat," she said. She mounted Stormy again and jogged him around the pattern a few more times and then put him away. Sunday morning came quickly. By ten o'clock, Ann was loading Buster and heading for High Valley. She cared for Buster at the rodeo grounds and then went to find Casey. He was never hard to find. She looked near the bucking chutes and found him talking to some of his friends. Casey saw her coming and broke away from his conversation.

"Where did you run off to yesterday?" he asked.

"Back to the ranch to put Buster away. I wanted him to be in top shape for today," she said.

"You sure beat Marsha easy enough yesterday. Congratulations," Casey said.

"How about you? How was your ride?" Ann asked.

"Fair. I had a fair horse and I made a fair ride. I've got to do better today to put me in the lead," he said.

"What kind of horse did you draw for today?" Ann asked.

"A wild eyed, crazy jughead, just the kind I can win on," Casey said and smiled.

Ann laughed and asked, "How about buying me a cup of coffee before things get too busy around here?"

"Why, Ma'am, it would be my pleasure!" Casey said.

They saw Bill at the coffee stand and Casey managed to talk Bill into paying for their coffee. "You know, Casey you're so cheap, I'll bet you still have the first dollar you ever won riding broncs," Bill said.

Casey smiled and reached in his wallet. He pulled out a crumpled one dollar bill and held it up for Bill to see. "Here it is," Casey said and grinned.

Ann laughed and said, "I've got to check on Buster. I'll see you two after my ride." Ann was first up. She was ready and waiting to enter the arena when her name was called. Buster flashed around the barrels in a perfect pattern. His performance was a repeat of Saturday's fine run. Marsha pushed the buckskin hard but fell short of overtaking Buster and Ann for the overall win. When the results were read, Ann was ecstatic. She had finally beat Marsha, fair and square, for first place. The points were quickly adding up to qualify her for the state finals.

Excited and happy, Ann rode Buster back to their trailer. She unsaddled and groomed him. When she was satisfied that Buster was comfortable, Ann headed back to the arena. She found Johnson in the spectator stands with Sam and Duke. "Move over, men, make room for the champion," Duke said, loud enough for everyone within a half mile to hear. Ann flushed with embarrassment, but happily joined the men in the stands.

The bareback bronc event got under way and it seemed like the stock contractor had saved his best horses for the last day. The horses all came out bucking hard, giving the riders good scores. "Casey is going to need a good ride to win this one today," Sam said.

"He'll be coming from behind after his low score yesterday," Johnson added.

"Casey can do it if anybody can, just watch!" Ann said with a ring of confidence in her voice.

Casey didn't let them down. When the gate swung open and his horse jumped out, Casey went to work with a vengeance. He was behind and knew he had to milk a good ride out of this horse to win. His legs were a blur. On the first jump out of the chute, Casey started raking the horse with his spurs. He reached high up the horse's neck and in time with the bucking horse's jumps, quickly dragged his spurred boot heels back down.

Casey's coordination and his ability to perfectly time the horse's next move with his body position was what made him a great bronc rider. He was able to keep his center of gravity over the horse's back during the violent maneuvers. On most all jumps, Casey came down in contact with the center of the horse's back. He wasn't thrown sideways away from the horse's next move. He had an uncanny ability to maintain control over his body position in relation to the animal under him. Casey had a natural tendency to bend and flex with the animal and he always seemed to end up centered over the horse's back, whether the horse was bucking straight up and down or sideways to the ground.

Casey's problem during this ride wasn't his ability to ride the animal. He had to not only ride him, but at the same time, infuriate the horse into bucking as hard as he could. Eight seconds is a short time and Casey pumped his legs along the horse's neck with his spurs in an attempt to make the horse surpass the others in the event.

Halfway through the ride, Casey felt the animal violently increase his bucking. He concentrated on irritating him more, so that his desire to throw him off his back would increase. The horse was angry at the rider and rose to Casey's expectations. The eight second horn sounded and Casey was satisfied with the ride as he dismounted the bucking horse onto the pick up rider's horse.

"I believe he pulled it off," Johnson said. The crowd came to their feet and applauded Casey's good ride. In the arena, Casey slid off the pick up horse and graciously pulled his hat off and waved it to the cheering crowd.

"He's sure not bashful," Duke said and laughed.

"I told you he could do it!" Ann yelled above the noise of the cheering crowd.

Casey scored an eighty-four. It was enough to boost his low score on Saturday to first place today. Casey won another buckle and the High Valley championship. "Well, Johnson, you ought to be proud of your riders. That's two champions from the Bent Bar ranch winning at the home town rodeo!" Sam said. Johnson was too pleased to even answer. He returned Sam's compliment with a wide smile.

"Now if we can only win at Twin Forks! We'll both be going to the state finals!" Ann said excitedly.

The win at High Valley put Ann in contention to qualify for the state finals in the fall. She still needed more points. It would all depend on the outcome of the Twin Forks rodeo. If she could place high in that competition, she would earn enough points. She was hoping that an appearance at the state level would be enough for her scholarship application to be reviewed by the University and be reconsidered before the end of her first semester of college.

Her future was uncertain. Her education depended on that scholarship. If she didn't receive it, she would have to drop out after the first semester. The importance of the Twin Forks rodeo became more apparent as the summer wore on.

Ann spent the rest of the summer working on the ranch and helping Bill train the young colts. She kept Buster active and competed in a few county fairs. The competition was not as stiff as the bigger rodeos, but they added a few more points to their overall standing. Ann continued to train on Buster several times a week. His condition was excellent and Ann was careful that she didn't over train him as the summer drew to a close.

She used Stormy to check the stock on the summer range. Occasionally she would run Stormy through the barrels and he seemed to enjoy chasing around them. He was young and sometimes would cut too close to the barrel, knocking it over in his haste to race to the next one. Ann held him back from his top speed and tried to develop a sense of correctness in his approach to the barrel. Ann didn't push the young horse very hard. She knew he would develop well with time.

In early September, Ann started her first semester of college. She returned home on weekends. She practiced with Buster on the barrels and spent the rest of the time studying. She had no extra time to ride Stormy and he enjoyed a leisurely life on the ranch. Ann made her final preparations for the Twin Forks rodeo. She still needed the points that a win at Twin Forks could provide. That would ensure her a spot at the state finals. Her future depended on success at Twin Forks.

Ann arrived home from school late on the night before the big rodeo. She got her equipment ready and checked on Buster. "You get some rest, big fellow, we have to leave before daylight to get to Twin Forks in time to register," she said. She loaded the trailer with her tack and put enough feed for Buster in the front compartment, and hitched the trailer to the pickup. It was late when she felt completely prepared for the trip. She fell into bed, dead tired, and slept until the clanging alarm awakened her, hours before the first light of dawn.

Johnson was ready when Ann left the house. They loaded Buster and headed for town. Bill and Casey were waiting for them in town. They tooted their horn when they passed Casey's beat up old truck. Casey's horn didn't work, but Johnson saw the old truck pull out and start following them toward the highway. "I sure hope that old wreck of a truck makes it all the way to the rodeo," Ann said.

Johnson laughed and said, "I don't know how he does it, but Casey always manages to keep that junker running!"

They arrived at the rodeo grounds in late morning. Ann and Casey went right to the office to register, while Bill and Johnson took care of Buster. Buster backed out of the trailer and looked around. "He looks weary from the trip," Bill said.

"It was a long drive. By the time Ann makes her run, Buster will already have put in a long day. I just hope he won't be too tired to make a good showing today," Johnson said.

"She sure needs the points, I know she's just a few short to qualify for the state," Bill said.

Ann came back and started brushing Buster. Everyone could see the strain she was under. She had been pushing herself too hard. She just entered college, and the heavy demands of her studies, combined with her quest for a state barrel racing championship were beginning to show. She looked tired. "Ann, why don't you rest before your event. I'll take care of Buster for you," Bill said.

"I'm okay. I'll perk up before the rodeo starts. You better look after Casey. If anybody needs help, it's him," Ann said. Everyone laughed and the tension seemed to ease on Ann's face.

Ann saw Beth and Jill while she was warming up Buster. They talked for a while and then the girls rode to the arena together. They participated in the Grand Entry and when they rode out of the arena, Beth said, "Annie, I see you're really riding hard this year. Are you trying to push Marsha out of that state title?"

"Yes, I am. I'm trying to get to the state finals. I really need to win a scholarship to continue college after this first semester. If I could place high at state, they might reconsider my application. I need a few more points to qualify. This rodeo could do it for me," Ann said.

Ann was anxious. She arrived at the arena entrance early. This rodeo was so important to her, that she didn't want to take a chance of being late when her name was called. The thirty second limit could disqualify her if she wasn't ready. She didn't intend to take any chances.

Buster seemed ready. He wasn't his usual self, but he still seemed to have lots of energy. Buster knew they were going to compete and he was anticipating a hard run. He was weary from the trip, but Ann felt he was ready to go. They called her name and she moved Buster into the arena. She jogged over to the spot where she would start. The arena judge nodded, giving her the okay to start her run.

She turned him loose and he accelerated away toward the first barrel. He was running well and Ann could feel him driving hard with his mighty hind quarters. He felt good under her and Ann rode with confidence toward the first barrel. Buster rounded the barrel fast and stretched out hard as they raced for the second.

When Buster came out of the second turn, Ann asked him for more speed on the way to the last barrel. Buster concentrated in the short distance to increase his stride. Disastrously, he took his mind off the barrel. He seemed to forget that he had to turn around the last barrel. Ann realized that he had lost his sense of purpose when Buster charged up almost to the barrel and had not even started to break his stride to maneuver around it.

She corrected him severely as they came upon the barrel. Buster realized his mistake. He tried to slow his speed and cut around the barrel at the same time. The correction was too late and as Buster clumsily attempted the turn, Ann's knee slammed into the steel barrel. Ann was a true contender. She realized their run had disintegrated to chaos for the horse. She brought him out of the turn and kicked him hard with her boot heels in an attempt to bring back some orderliness to his reasoning. Buster understood the simple command. It meant run as hard as you can.

Buster dug in and accelerated toward the finish line. His lapse of concentration cost them the race. Ann didn't look back at the barrel she hit as they ran for the finish line. She pulled Buster up from his breakneck run and slid to a stop in the alleyway. She knew the worst had happened when she saw Beth looking at her and slowly shaking her head from side to side. A feeling of dread descended on her when she saw Beth's obvious display of pity.

Ann spun around and looked back into the arena. Far away, at the end of the arena, she saw the third barrel lying on its side. They had knocked it over. An agony of defeat overwhelmed her. A five second penalty would be added to her run. At this level of competition, five seconds would put them out of contention. Ann needed to win, but now, they would not even place. The fallen barrel meant they would not add any points to their total. She felt as if the scholarship was becoming more and more elusive.

The hint of a tear began to form at the corner of her eye. She smiled at Beth and turned Buster to ride out of the arena. Marsha Miller rode up to her and brusquely said, "Tough luck, Ann, maybe now you'll retire that old nag and turn him out to pasture!" Ann was so saddened by the loss of the race that Marsha's crude comment seemed unimportant to her.

She looked at Marsha. Marsha was exquisitely dressed in an impressive western outfit. Ann wondered how she could ride so well wearing those tight pants. She was heavily made up and large earrings dangled from her ears. I suppose she dresses like that to impress the men. After all, she is the state champ. She must be uncomfortable though, Ann thought and then said, "Buster is not ready to be put out to pasture yet!" Ann nudged Buster's side and rode him out of the alleyway to her trailer, not waiting for any other comments from Marsha.

She saw the three Bent Bar men swiftly walking toward her as she dismounted. She braced herself. The loss was a tragedy. She didn't want to break down and cry in front of them. She saw concern on their faces when they walked up. "You look like you've all just lost your best friend," she said.

"Not yet, anyway. But after we're done talking to you, you may not want to be friends with us anymore!" Johnson said sternly. Shocked by his words, Ann stared at the three men looking at her with clear concern showing on their faces.

Casey took Buster's reins out of her hands and Bill immediately started unsaddling him. "We're taking over. You've been burning the candle at both ends for so long that you don't recognize how hard you've been pushing yourself. Both you and Buster need a good rest. Between your school work and trying to qualify for the state finals, you've just about worn yourself to a frazzle. You're gonna' listen to us today. You can still win tomorrow and earn five more points. You won't win this rodeo, but those five points will earn you a spot at the state championships," Johnson said.

Ann felt her eyes beginning to puff up and a tear started to form. She knew they were trying to help her. She struggled to control her emotions. Casey dropped Buster's reins and grabbed ahold of Ann's arm. "You listen now! You still have a chance, but you both have to get a good rest before tomorrow," he said. Bill led Buster to the back of the trailer and started loading him.

"Ann, I'm gonna' take you out to the ranch where we're staying. We'll put Buster in a comfortable stall so he can get a needed rest. You're gonna' spend the remainder of the day resting too! You both need it. The mistake you made in the arena today was unnecessary and was caused by fatigue. You asked a tired horse for too much. He tried to please you and you ended up knocking the barrel over. We think you can win tomorrow if you both rest," Johnson said with authority.

She knew they were right. It had been a long trip for Buster this morning. He arrived weary from the long journey. Her lack of sleep last night had impaired her judgment too. "Okay," she said weakly.

"Now, Bill and Casey are gonna' stay here. Casey still has a bronc to ride today. You and I are headed for the ranch. So why don't you climb in the truck and we'll get started," Johnson said.

Casey was still holding her by the arm. He looked down into her eyes and nodded softly to her. "Go on, Ann, get ready for tomorrow."

"Okay, I will. Good luck today, Casey," she said. She walked to the truck and got in.

Johnson drove away from the rodeo grounds. Light rain began to fall as they neared the ranch. By the time they arrived, it had increased to a steady shower. They unloaded Buster and put him into a comfortable stall. Ann wondered if the rain had affected Casey's ride. She hoped not.

Johnson said, "Buster's in a nice stall with lots of straw for bedding. He'll be able to relax until tomorrow. Why don't you go to your room and read a book or do something restful for the remainder of the day," Johnson said. Ann agreed and trudged off to the ranch house.

She was tired from her hectic schedule. She lay on the bed listening to the sounds of the rain drops pattering on the roof and thought of the barrel racing circuit. She came very close to earning enough points today for the state finals. She made a mistake by asking a tired horse for more speed, when he was already running well. The extra effort he tried to give her caused him to lose his concentration and they knocked the barrel over. Our last chance to qualify is tomorrow. I better perform with more professionalism than I showed today, Ann thought. Within minutes, she fell into a deep, restful sleep.

Ann awoke for dinner and saw the rain was still falling. She checked Buster and made sure he had feed and water. Buster seemed comfortable and hardly noticed her as she cleaned his stall. He was enjoying the quiet of the barn and seemed content. After dinner, Ann returned to her room. She lay on the bed listening to the rain and was soon asleep again.

Ann awoke to the sound of chirping birds. She looked out the window and saw the day had dawned clear. The sun was coming up and the rain had stopped. She dressed and went out to care for Buster. When Ann entered the barn, Buster gave her a friendly nicker. He seemed alert and happy to see her. "You look good and rested, Buster, I'm glad to see that," she said. Then she realized that she felt like a new person. The morning was invigorating and she felt wonderful. "Johnson was right, we both needed a good rest. If you feel as good as I do, then we'll be hard to beat today, Buster," she said.

Johnson helped her take care of Buster. "How did Casey do yesterday?" she asked. "Why don't you ask him. Here he comes," Johnson said.

Ann looked back to the house and saw Casey walking toward them with a smile on his handsome face. "By the looks of that grin, he must have won!" she said.

"I squeaked by with a win. If I can hang on again today, I just might be going to the state finals with you in a few months," Casey said when he walked up.

"That's great, Casey, but unless I win today, I won't be going," Ann said.

"Just ride smart and things might go your way," Johnson said.

They arrived at the rodeo grounds and Johnson commented on the wet conditions. "The arena might be slick today, so watch your turns. Make sure Buster is in control of his footing around those barrels. You'll be able to tell how much traction he's getting when you take the first barrel. If he feels like he has good control and the conditions aren't too slick then let him run harder around the last two. Judge how hard to push him on that first turn. If it's slippery, slow down. Everyone will have the same problem, so use caution. Since you didn't even place yesterday, your turn to run will be near the end of the event. The arena will be pretty well churned up by then, so be careful," Johnson said. He was giving her good advice and Ann listened intently to his words.

Ann could see numerous mud puddles still standing from yesterday's rainfall. A running horse could easily slip in these conditions. I'll have to be very careful today, she thought. "We're both well rested and feel fine, I think I'll saddle Buster early and ride him around so he can get used to the slick conditions. Then he'll know what to expect when we begin our run," Ann said.

"Good idea," Johnson said.

Ann began riding Buster around the arena long before her event started. There was mud everywhere and Buster avoided the worst of the puddles. The traffic coming and going from the fairgrounds made the conditions worse. By the time she rode toward the arena for the start of her event, the grounds were very sloppy. "You have a good idea what we're up against today, Buster, let's run the course only as fast as you think you can handle it," she said.

Ann saw Jill talking to Beth outside the arena entrance. The event would be starting soon, so she rode over to chat. The alleyway was slick and there was a large mud puddle in the middle. The girls were sitting on their horses off to the side of the mud, trying to stay out of everyone's way. Men were working on a stubborn tractor they used to level and condition the ground in the arena during the rodeo. Ann heard the starter of the tractor turning over in agony as the men tried to coax some life back into the old machine.

The tractor had stalled in the middle of the runway leading to the arena. "I hope they get that old thing running and smooth out the dirt in the arena before I have to make my run," Jill said.

"Look who's coming," Beth said. The girls looked and saw Marsha carefully guiding her horse around the mud puddles as she made her way toward them. She was dressed to kill. Marsha was wearing a bright red blouse, lavishly decorated with sequins. She wore tight fitting white pants with long fringe on the sides. Her western hat was white and she wore a white scarf around her neck. She was stunning. The girls heard several men whistle in admiration as Marsha rode by the bucking chutes.

"How in the world does she breathe in those tight pants?" Ann innocently asked.

"She'll have to start breathing pretty soon. She had the top time yesterday, so she's up first today," Jill said. They laughed and watched Marsha ride up.

Get ready to overlook some rude comments from her, Ann thought, as Marsha worked her way to them. A judge called out for them to be ready, they would start the event as soon as they got the tractor moved out of the way. Marsha rode around the mud puddle in the middle of the alleyway and stopped between the girls and the puddle of mud to wait for her run. She looked irritated that she couldn't just ride right into the arena but had to wait for the men to get the tractor started. She looked over at the three girls. They stared back at her. They're jealous of me, Marsha thought. There were other riders waiting along the alleyway. Marsha felt as if everyone was staring at her. She felt uncomfortable.

"Can you imagine wearing white pants on a muddy day like this," Ann said softly to Jill. She didn't think Marsha could hear her comment.

Marsha did hear her and a flash of resentment went through her. She looked at Ann and said rather loudly, "Dressing as well as I do wouldn't do you any good anyway. It would take a lot for a plain Jane like you to look good, no matter what you wore!" she said vehemently to Ann. Embarrassed by the crude attack on her looks, Ann looked at Marsha in shock. Jill started to come to Ann's defense but the sound of the tractor, trying to cough its way back to life, drowned out her words. Suddenly, the old tractor backfired and spooked the horses by its loud explosion. Surprised, Buster jumped away from the loud noise. Ann managed to keep her seat as the big gelding leaped toward the center of the alleyway. Buster collided into Marsha's buckskin horse who had also spooked from the unexpected noise. Their paths met on the edge of the big mud puddle. Buster was a working ranch horse and his superior condition was no match for the buckskin horse. The force of Buster's shoulder slamming into him, knocked the buckskin sideways into the puddle. Marsha went flying off and landed in the middle of the muddy water.

Alarmed at what had happened, Ann jumped off Buster and waded into the water to help Marsha up. She could hear people laughing behind her at Marsha's predicament. Marsha tried to scramble up out of the mud but slipped and fell back down. Ann extended her hand to help Marsha up. "You did that on purpose!" Marsha screamed at her.

"No, I didn't. The tractor backfired and spooked the horses!" Ann told her.

"I don't believe you!" Marsha screamed. Then realizing she needed help to get out, she gripped Ann's extended hand.

Ann pulled to try and lift her up. Marsha was covered in slippery mud. She got halfway to her feet when the slick mud on her hand caused her to lose her grip. Ann felt Marsha's grasp slip away and the girl fell back into the muddy water with a splash. Realizing that people were openly laughing at her, Marsha rolled over on her side in the mud and managed to scramble to her feet. Ann turned and walked back to Buster. She mounted and looked at Marsha standing in the middle of the puddle trying to clean the black goo from her soiled clothes.

Marsha was a mess. Her white pants were now black and gobs of mud smeared her sequined blouse. Her white hat was covered in mud and her face was splattered with the goop. She heard the delighted laughter of the other contestants. Never before had Marsha ever known such humiliation. Her clothes were ruined and she still had to ride in front of everyone at the rodeo.

The tractor roared to life again and was quickly driven out of the way. The judge called Marsha's name to enter the arena as the first rider of the barrel race. Marsha considered forfeiting her run. Her clothes were covered in mud and she was deeply humiliated. Tears streaked her muddy face.

Ann quickly stepped off Buster and picked up the reins to the buckskin. She led the horse over to Marsha. "Come on, Marsha, it was an accident. It's your turn to ride. You only have thirty seconds to enter the arena or be disqualified. Casey says that clothes don't make a good rider. Forget your muddy clothes and get in there and ride as hard as you can. You hold the state title. Show everyone what it takes to make a champion!" Ann shouted. Marsha stared hard at Ann. Ann wasn't sure if Marsha would take her advice or swing at her. She stared back at Marsha.

Marsha nodded quickly at Ann and took the reins from her. A determined look replaced her utter humiliation and she mounted the buckskin and rode into the arena. Ann heard the noise of the crowd increase in wonder as the muddy girl rode in. That takes some guts, Ann thought, as Marsha started her run.

The other girls watched Ann come to the aid of a person who had continually attacked and degraded her and Buster. They all shared the same feelings of admiration for Ann.

She had shown courage and integrity by helping Marsha overcome her humiliation even though Marsha had unjustly scorned her in public.

The girls watched as Marsha buckled down and attempted to forget her muddy appearance. She started her run and everyone could see they were off their usual strong pace. The episode in the alleyway was still affecting both Marsha and the buckskin. Marsha pushed the horse hard all the way through the pattern. They put in a good run, but their performance wasn't near their championship caliber.

Marsha raced across the finish line and slid the buckskin to a stop in the alleyway near the big mud puddle. She walked the horse to where Ann and Buster were waiting their turn. "It's muddy out here but the arena is good and dry. I hope you have a good run, Ann," she said. Then Marsha extended her hand to Ann in an offering of friendship.

A pleasant feeling of accomplishment surged through Ann. She had the satisfying pleasure a person feels when they have just overcome a seemingly impossible obstacle. Suddenly, a smile appeared on Ann's face and she stretched out to grasp Marsha's hand in hers. They gripped hands firmly and then Ann said, "Thanks for the information. Now, you should go and get out of those wet clothes."

Marsha smiled back at Ann. "Good idea. Thanks for lifting me up. And I don't mean just out of the mud puddle," she said. Gently Marsha pulled on the reins and walked the buckskin away toward her trailer.

There was silence for a few seconds as everyone watched Marsha ride away. "She didn't even wait to hear her time," Beth said.

"I think something more important just happened to her. Annie just taught Marsha how to be a human being and I think Marsha liked the feeling of being nice to someone for a change," Jill said.

Ann's spirits soared after the friendly encounter with Marsha. Buster was rested and eager to run. They were called to enter the arena. They were both in a great frame of mind as Ann lined Buster up. She forced herself to settle down and concentrate on the pattern. She remembered Johnson's advice to feel the course out on the first barrel. Marsha said the arena was dry. It was time to find out.

Buster pushed off swiftly for the first barrel. Ann checked his speed with an almost imperceptible touch on the reins. Buster ran fast but cautiously toward the first turn. He understood Ann's cues to be wary of the footing around the barrels. He slowed and tested the conditions as he began to wheel around the first barrel. Both Ann and Buster felt the excellent traction as his hind legs drove into the ground.

Marsha was right, the arena had good traction. There were only two barrels left between Ann and a chance to qualify for the state finals. A college scholarship could depend on their time around the remainder of the course. The conditions were good. They must win, Ann thought. It was now or never. She quickly decided to ask Buster for his top speed.

"Go Buster!" she whooped. Far up in the stands, Johnson heard her yell. He knew she was asking Buster for more than she had ever asked before. Johnson had never heard Ann shout to a horse for more speed. He jumped to his feet. She was riding as he had never seen her ride before. Ann crouched low on Buster's back. The gelding responded with a burst of speed he hadn't shown in years. He raced right up to the second barrel before checking his great speed and in a spray of dirt that almost obscured the horse and rider from the crowd, charged around the barrel. They rocketed out of the veil of flying dirt and raced for the third barrel.

The crowd saw the tremendous speed the horse and rider were attempting as they approached the last barrel. They came to their feet and cheered as Buster neared the barrel. Johnson hollered and whooped as he watched Ann ask Buster for even more speed. Buster dropped low into the turn and blazed around the barrel so fast that Ann yelled out in excitement as he accelerated to top speed for the run to the finish line. Buster kept charging right past the finish line and the crowd roared their delight as Ann brought him to a stop in the alleyway.

It was a tremendous run and the crowd kept cheering. Ann turned Buster and rode back to the arena. The applause continued and she waved to the spectators still on their feet, showing their appreciation for a tremendous performance. Ann and Buster had just made the fastest run of their career. They easily won the event for the day and earned five more points. They qualified to compete for the state championship. Ann reached down and gave Buster several loving pats on his neck. "Buster, you are one great horse!" she shouted.

CHAPTER 21

Ann left school after classes on Wednesday and started home for the ranch. She intended to be well prepared for the state barrel racing championships. Skipping two days of classes would enable her to be ready and rested for the finals. She would have no trouble making up the lost classes and Buster would not have to endure a long trip on the same day as the rodeo. Ann didn't want to make the same mistake at the state finals that she made at Twin Forks.

The state championship was held in Billings. Ann planned on arriving there early enough to give herself and Buster a full day of rest before the competition started. Since the rodeo at Twin Forks, Ann had been planning a strategy to compete in the state finals. She learned to not rush into competition without proper rest for her horse and also herself. She was always delighted to return to the Bent Bar. The familiar sights and sounds of the ranch were a soothing tonic after living on campus at the university. She arrived in the late evening and parked near the barn. Ann turned the motor off and just sat in the cab letting the pleasure of being back on the ranch soak into her soul. The pleasant aroma of hay, old leather and other barn smells entered the car and enveloped her. Content, she sat and let herself unwind from the long drive.

Her tranquility was interrupted by the unmistakable sound of Casey's voice arguing with someone on the far side of the barn. Slightly alarmed, Ann stepped out of the truck and went to see what was wrong. She walked around the barn and saw Casey's old truck parked there, but there was no sign of the bronc rider. She heard a clanking noise from under the truck and then heard Casey yell, "Come on, Nellie, give me a little help, will ya'!"

Ann walked around to the other side of the truck and saw a pair of legs sticking out from under the old wreck. The legs were wearing Casey's boots and silver spurs. "I didn't know your truck could talk, Casey!" she said.

"She doesn't, but she understands when I talk to her," Casey said. He started wiggling his way out from under the truck. Ann backed away to give him some room.

Casey stood up and grinned. He was covered in dirt and grease. "You sure look nice in your college clothes. I haven't seen you in weeks. How about giving ole' Case a welcome home hug," he said and started toward Ann.

"You're covered in grease! You stay away from me, Casey! You'll ruin my good clothes!" she shrieked.

Casey laughed and said, "I want a hug!" Ann screamed in amusement and took off running for the barn. Casey chased her into the alleyway of the barn and Ann raced to the other end screaming all the way.

Johnson heard the ruckus and came out of his office just as Casey went running by yelling, "Come on, Annie, just one little hug!" He smiled when he saw the two carrying on and obviously having fun. They were happy to see each other, he thought.

They both stopped running and began laughing when they saw Johnson watching their antics. "That grease ball wants to hug me and ruin my clothes!" Ann said to Johnson.

"As pretty as you are, I can't really blame him. Did you just get home?" Johnson asked.

"Just a minute ago. I heard Casey arguing with his truck and went to investigate. Then he started chasing me," Ann said and smiled at Casey.

"She wouldn't let me give her a welcome home hug, just cause' I have a little dirt and grease on me," Casey said.

"Are you really going to take that old truck to Billings for the rodeo?" Ann asked.

"Sure am. I'm just about finished putting a new muffler on the old girl. She'll be as good as new in a few hours," Casey said.

"Casey, I told you that you were welcome to take one of the ranch trucks. You're riding for the state championship,

I wouldn't want you to break down and miss your ride," Johnson said.

"Nellie will make it. Besides, I wouldn't want to spoil Bill by having him ride all the way to the rodeo in a good truck. Thanks for the offer, though," Casey said.

Casey made a quick feint toward Ann, as if he was going to chase her again. She screamed and ran out of the barn. They heard her yell back at them, "I'm going to the house. I've got a big day tomorrow!"

"When are you planning on leaving, Casey?" Johnson asked.

"Bill and I thought that if we got out of here in the early afternoon on Friday, that would put us in Billings soon enough," Casey said.

"That's fine with me. You can even leave earlier, if you want," Johnson said.

"No, early afternoon is good enough. How about you?" Casey asked.

"We'll leave right after lunch. That will get us there early enough to take care of Buster and get everything situated. Then Ann and Buster can take it easy on Friday. I plan on using the day to look up some old friends that I haven't seen in years," Johnson said.

"Well, I want to finish working on my truck and head home. I'll see you in the morning," Casey said.

"Okay, Casey," Johnson said. Johnson walked toward the house. He worried about leaving the ranch for so long while he was in Billings. He felt confident James could take care of anything that arose, but he still worried. He planned on calling James every night to see how things were going and to let him know how Ann and Casey were doing. Bill and Casey would be here until Friday, so there would only be a few days that James would be alone. He's a good man, he can handle it, Johnson thought.

It was late fall and daylight came later and later each day. Ann was in the barn well before the first light peeked over the eastern mountains. Buster nickered at her and Stormy poked his head out of his stall expectantly when she turned on the lights. She walked down to Stormy's stall and looked him over. "You sure have had a life of leisure since I went away to school," she said and rubbed him along his neck. He playfully nibbled at her arm with his soft lips.

"When Buster and I get back from the rodeo, you and I are going to start training every weekend in the arena, Stormy. I want to start using you for competition next year," she said. Ann fed both horses. She looked Buster over carefully. He was in good shape. His muscles were still firm. She had kept him in peak condition since the Twin Forks rodeo. "This is our last rodeo of the year and it's the biggest one we have ever ridden in. After this one, you'll get a well deserved rest," she said.

Ann packed all of her gear into the truck and trailer and went over some last minute details. She was nervous and tried to keep busy until the time came to leave. She saw Casey for a short time and asked about his truck. "Nellie's running like a top. She'll take us there and back with no trouble," he said.

"I hope so, Casey! It would be terrible if you broke down and missed your ride. This is your big chance. Just think, if you win the state championship, you could go on to ride in the national rodeos and compete with the best in the nation," Ann said.

Casey looked at her and then softly said, "So could you."

Johnson and Ann left right after lunch. They thought they would never get away. Everyone was wishing Ann luck and giving her last minute instructions. Finally, Johnson pulled away from the barn and headed down the lane for the road to town. He laughed and said, "I didn't think they'd ever let us leave!"

"I didn't either. I'm not going to relax until I see Casey and Bill drive into the fairgrounds. I don't have all the faith in that old truck that Casey does," Ann said.

"Don't worry about those two, they'll make it just fine," Johnson said.

The roads and weather were excellent. They made the trip to Billings in good time and arrived in the early evening. Johnson drove right to the fairgrounds. They made arrangements to put Buster in one of the barns right on the grounds.

Ann and Johnson had reservations to stay in a motel across the road. Ann liked the arrangements, because she would be near Buster and able to keep a close eye on him.

After unloading Buster, Ann opened a bale of straw and spread it in his stall for bedding. She filled his water bucket and grained him. Johnson hung a hay net and filled it with a flake of good Bent Bar hay. "Well, Buster, what do you think?" Ann asked.

"He's got that look on his face that translates to, 'Where are we now?'" Johnson said and laughed.

Ann patted Buster's neck and said, "Buster, we are where we have been working so hard to get for the last few years. The state championships," Ann said.

Buster whinnied and Johnson laughed. "He seemed to know exactly what you said," he said.

"He probably did," Ann said, in a serious tone.

"If you're satisfied with his accommodations, let's go check into our rooms and then get something to eat," Johnson said.

"Okay, let's go," Ann said.

Ann was up early the next morning. She walked across the road to the fairgrounds and entered the barn. Buster was glad to see her and the sound of his friendly nicker told Ann that he was lonely. She cleaned his stall and gave him a few pounds of grain. "This afternoon, I'll give you some exercise and work the kinks out, Buster," Ann said.

Contestants from all over the state boarded their horses here. The barn became busy as people arrived to take care of their animals. A twinge of nervousness trickled through Ann when she saw the people beginning to fill the barn. I'm probably going to be competing against some of these people tomorrow, Ann thought.

"Annie! There you are! I've been looking all over for you!" Ann heard the familiar voice and looked up to see Marsha coming toward her.

"Hi, Marsha, we got in last night," Ann said.

"My trailer is parked out in the parking area. I wanted to find you to see if you needed any help. I know this is your first time here and things can get pretty hectic if you don't know your way around. When you finish with Buster, why don't you stop by the trailer and we'll go to the office and check in together," Marsha said.

Pleased, Ann said, "That would be wonderful!"

"Great, I'll see you later then," Marsha said and walked away.

Happy that Marsha offered to show her around, Ann went back to work in high spirits. She finished her chores just as Johnson entered the barn. "How did Buster enjoy his new quarters last night?" he asked.

"Just fine. He was glad to see me this morning though," Ann said.

Over breakfast, Ann told Johnson about Marsha's friendly offer to show her around. "That's a pleasant turn of events. I'm glad to hear that. She just might be a big help to you, even though you'll be competing against each other," Johnson said.

"I was really pleased with her offer," Ann said.

"Good! You'll have some company while I'm visiting my friend's ranch, out past the rimrock. I'll probably be back early, hopefully Casey and Bill will be here by then and we can all have dinner together," Johnson said.

"How far do your friends live from here?" Ann asked.

"About twenty miles. I haven't been out there in years, but I won't have any trouble finding it again," Johnson said.

"Well, don't worry about me while you're gone. I'll be fine. I'm nervous about finally being here, but that will pass," Ann said.

Marsha was waiting for Ann when she knocked on the door to her trailer. They went over to the main office of the fairgrounds. Marsha introduced Ann to the people in charge of the rodeo. They all seemed to know Marsha by her first name. They congratulated Ann on qualifying. Ann was impressed by the importance they put on the fact that she did qualify. She saw a huge picture of Marsha on the wall of the office. It was a magnificent photograph of Marsha and her buckskin coming around a barrel at last year's state competition. Underneath was a caption that read "Marsha Miller-State Barrel Racing Champion".

It was an impressive photo. Ann stared at it longingly. I wonder what it would be like to actually win the event and have pictures like that of Buster and me hanging in rodeo offices all over the state, Ann thought. "That was last year," Marsha said.

Ann came out of her reverie and said, "It must be quite a feeling to be the state champion."

"It is. Unfortunately, it only lasts for one year. You have to earn it every year, and every year there are great riders like you trying to take the title away!" Marsha said and smiled.

Ann was impressed and in awe of all the photos of rodeo champions adorning the walls. Everywhere she looked, she could see photographs and mementos of past champions. There were trophies and silver buckles in glass cases. She could see spurs and ribbons encased with old photos. This is like being in the Hall of Fame of rodeo performers, she thought. "I'll bet that someday Casey's picture will be hanging here as the champion bronc rider," she said to no one in particular.

That afternoon, Ann saddled Buster and rode around the fairgrounds. Buster needed some light exercise and Ann wanted to explore the grounds. No better way to do it than horseback, Ann thought. She rode to the arena and stopped. She had never seen an arena that was so big. "Buster, this place is huge. I'll bet those stands hold a hundred times more people than the one at High Valley," she said. She rode past the bucking chutes and thought about Casey. I hope Nellie makes it here okay, she thought.

Ann was overwhelmed with what she saw. The office, with all the memorabilia of champion riders, had deeply impressed her. She thought back to all she had gone through to get here. She realized that the riders who had come before her had probably endured similar hardships to reach this level. "Buster, do you realize that we have actually made it here! After trying so hard for so many years, we are really here!" Ann said.

A happy smile broke out on Ann's face when she saw Casey's truck pulling into the fairgrounds with the two Bent Bar men inside. She trotted Buster over to meet them. They saw her coming and Casey pulled over and stopped. "Boy, I'm sure glad to see you made it!" Ann said.

Casey said, "I told you Nellie would make it. You have to have a little faith in the old girl."

"You have to have faith in her, that's the only thing that keeps this old bucket of loose and missing parts running!" Bill said.

Ann laughed. "Buster's stall is in that barn," she pointed to the barn and said, "I'll meet you there and tell you all about this place!"

After Bill and Casey checked into their room, they came back to the barn and found Ann grooming Buster. "You're gonna' rub all the hair off that poor horse if you don't stop brushing him," Bill said.

"I just want him to look good tomorrow," Ann said.

"Come on. Show us where the office is so I can check in," Casey said.

Ann happily took them to the office. They entered the building and Casey was immediately drawn to the pictures and trophies of the bronc riding champions. He stood in awe and looked at the photos of the great riders of the past. "I feel deeply honored to be here," he said. "Here are pictures of the great riders that I've only read about. To think these men actually rode here is humbling to me," he said.

"Your picture will hang here someday, Casey, I know it!" Bill said.

"I hope I ride well enough this weekend to justify the honor of being here," Casey said.

They met Johnson when he returned and after dinner Ann went to her room to be alone and rest. She went over her plans for the first day's events. It would be a busy day tomorrow. The crowds would be huge and she wanted Buster to become accustomed to all of the commotion, before their event started. She would stay with him all morning. I'll feed him a few hours before we ride and give him a chance to digest his food. I don't want him running on a full belly, but I want him to have the benefit of the energy grain gives him, she thought. She fell asleep thinking how honored she was to have the chance to compete in the state finals.

Ann had never seen so many people in one place. Billings was a big city and the crowd was tremendous. There were people and contestants from all over the state. Vendors were selling souvenirs, food and beverages in the fairway. The band was playing and there was a carnival atmosphere in the air. Ann was caught up in the excitement of the big event. As the starting time drew closer, she became nervous. I wonder where Johnson is, she thought as she brushed Buster again.

Finally, she saw him enter the barn. Bill and Casey were with him, Casey was in a one way conversation with Bill as they made their way to her. "Well, you have to come up with something, Bill, the horse just doesn't have a good reputation!" she heard Casey say as they walked up.

"What's wrong now?" she asked.

"Casey's all worked up again. He claims he drew a bad horse and wants me to think of something to help him out. He's worrying about nothin'," Bill said.

"I'm not worrying about nothing. I heard that horse just doesn't have any brains!" Casey said.

"Then you two ought to get along just fine. Neither one of you will have any, so maybe the combination of a brainless horse and a brainless rider will work in your favor," Bill said. Johnson laughed and Ann smiled at Casey's irritation with Bill's comment.

"What's the horse's name?" Ann innocently asked.

"It's a gray mare named Marbles. They told me at the chutes that they named her Marbles because she's a little short on brains and acts like she lost all her marbles. Sometimes she just doesn't think real good and does strange things," Casey forlornly said.

Bill laughed and said, "Just make her pay attention when they open the gate. Let her know that she's there to buck and that you're not gonna' put up with any monkey business."

"I hope it will be that easy. Some horses are so hardheaded that you just can't get anything out of them. Kinda' like you, Bill!" Casey said. They laughed at Casey's jab.

"Are you ready, Annie?" Johnson asked.

"I'm nervous, but I'm ready," Ann said.

"We'll be cheering for you all the way. Do you want help saddling Buster?" Johnson asked.

"No, I'll do it myself. Maybe it will help settle me down," Ann said.

"Just relax, Ann, do like you taught yourself. Put everything out of your mind except them three barrels," Casey said.

"Okay, and remember, Casey, I'll be watching you when you ride too, and good luck with Marbles," Ann said.

Ann lined up with the other contestants entered in all of the different events. They rode into the arena for the Grand Entry. Ann couldn't believe the number of people in the stands. There were thousands. It was a big rodeo and when the fans stood to sing the Star Spangled Banner, the volume was deafening. They have all come to watch us ride, Ann thought in wonder.

After the Grand Entry Parade, Ann rode into the parking area to warm up Buster and collect her jangling nerves. This is what we have been training for, calm down and use good judgment, she told herself.

The time slowly passed, but finally, Ann found herself in line near the entrance to the arena waiting for her event to start. She saw Marsha ahead of her. They waved to each other. Ann heard Marsha call back, wishing her luck. Ann tried to answer, but nothing came out. Her mouth was dry and she had butterflies in her stomach.

Marsha was introduced as the reigning state champion. She waved to the crowd. She was the first to ride and she put tremendous effort into her run. The buckskin performed faultless and Marsha came racing back across the line. Ann could see that Marsha was happy with her run. Marsha rode up beside Ann to await the announcement of her time. Neither girl spoke while they waited. Finally it was read. Fifteen point two five seconds. Marsha smiled, it was a good time. It would be hard to beat.

Marsha reached over and playfully slapped Ann on the leg. "There, Annie, you've got something to ride for now. Relax and do your best!" she said.

Ann looked at Marsha and said, "I'm sure nervous, but we're ready!" Marsha rode away and Ann moved up in line.

All the riders were turning in good times. They're all good, that's why they're here, Ann thought. She began to gain control of her nerves, the closer she came to her turn. She reached down and patted Buster on the neck. Buster had never been to anything this big. He had never seen so many people or horses before. The gelding knew this was something special and felt the importance of the occasion. Then, it was Ann's turn. She heard her name resounding over the loudspeakers! There are just three barrels out there and they're no different than the ones at home in my own arena, she told herself. She nudged Buster and they trotted into the arena.

High in the stands, Johnson stood up to watch her run. He had his fingers crossed and said a silent prayer as he waited for her to start. Casey and Bill were standing on the top of the bucking chutes, so they could watch her make the run. "Come on, Annie!" Casey yelled into the noise of the crowd.

Ann studied the course, going through each turn in her mind. Buster was anxious and began prancing sideways in anticipation of what he knew was ahead of him. Now that the moment had finally arrived, Ann settled into fierce determination and concentrated on the task at hand. The barrels were all that were important. Run around them and get back here as fast as we can, without making any mistakes. It's as simple as that, she told herself.

She turned Buster around in a three hundred and sixty degree turn and pointed him to the first barrel. Buster's ears flicked forward in the direction of the barrel and Ann turned him loose. He charged away and entered the pocket around the first barrel in perfect position. Ann urged him on. He reached his top speed and then immediately slowed and dropped down into the turn around the second barrel. Ann concentrated on the run to the third barrel. A mistake now could cost them precious time. Buster seemed to know the importance of this race. His speed was great and he broke at the right millisecond, to control himself, as he whirled around the last barrel. They were having a great run and Ann's spirits soared as Buster poured on the coal, reaching top speed as he raced for the finish line.

At full speed, Buster flashed across the finish line. Ann held the high speed for an extra stride to be sure they went past the line at top speed. So often, she had watched contestants start to slow their horses before they had crossed the finish line, adding extra time to their run.

Once past the time clocks at the finish, Ann pulled on the reins to check Buster's speed and stop before they reached the congested alleyway. There wasn't much room left for stopping. Buster went back on his haunches and with his front legs straight out began sliding to a stop. Suddenly, a horse and rider appeared in front of them blocking their path. The rider hadn't seen Ann racing into the alleyway, and walked her horse in front of them.

Buster saw them enter his line of travel. Ann was shocked when she saw the unsuspecting horse and rider in their way. She knew a collision was inevitable. People shouted warnings to the rider. She looked up and too late tried to get out of the way. Buster's reflexes took over and he tried to avoid the collision.

Buster came off his haunches and attempted to cut to the right around the other horse. He was still traveling fairly fast. Using his front legs to change directions, he managed to veer around the other horse and avoid a direct impact. His left front shoulder struck the rear quarter of the other horse in a glancing blow. Buster's quick footwork managed to keep them from slamming straight into the other horse.

Buster came to a stop and Ann quickly looked back at the horse and rider. "Are you okay?" she shouted.

"I'm okay! I'm sorry! I didn't see you coming," the other rider said. There seemed to be no harm done. Ann turned and started Buster back to wait for their time. Buster took one step and then favored his left front leg for another step, and then walked normally back toward the arena.

Ann felt Buster favor the leg and became alarmed. When he began walking normally, she felt relieved. "You scared me there for a second, Buster. You sure saved us from a bad accident. That was pretty fancy cutting!" she said.

Ann was flushed with the excitement of the run. She knew they had ridden well. The seconds ticked by while Ann waited anxiously for her time. She heard the announcer telling the crowd about her, while he waited for the judges to send her time up to him. The announcer told the crowd her home town. She heard High Valley mentioned, then Buster's name, and then he said, "Ann Olsen's time was a good run at fifteen point thirty-three seconds." The crowd applauded and Ann rode out of the alleyway.

Fifteen point three three. A good run. She was only eight-hundredths of a second behind Marsha. She felt comfortable with that time. There was still tomorrow. The times for both days would be added together. The contestant with the lowest total time would be the winner. If we run fast tomorrow and perform without errors, than we just might place high in the final standings, Ann thought.

She waited until all the riders were finished. All their times were good. When the final results of the day were in, Ann was in fifth place. She was happy. Only one half of a second separated the first place rider from the last place rider. Marsha was barely in the lead. The times were all close. It would be a very interesting race tomorrow, Ann thought.

Buster snorted and stomped a front hoof on the ground. He was still excited about the run. Ann patted him on the neck. "Great job, Buster, that was a perfect run!" she said. She walked him toward the barn and let him settle down. When Buster's breathing returned to normal she walked him into the barn. Ann put Buster away and hurried back to the arena to watch Casey's ride.

The stock contractor had supplied a lot of good horses for the bronc riders. Unfortunately, Casey didn't draw one of the good ones. Marbles was a nice mare, probably too nice. She didn't like to cause trouble. Sometimes she bucked at championship caliber, other times she forgot what was going on. Marbles was sometimes described as being scatter-brained. Casey was upset about his draw and Bill was trying to build his confidence.

Marbles was run into the chute and Casey got his first look at her. He stared at her for a moment and then said, "She doesn't look too bright, I hope she remembers what she's here for."

"Casey, in a few minutes, you're gonna' be on her back and the gate to this chute is gonna' fly open! Show her you're the boss! Sit tight on her back and spur hard, yell and scream and make her think there's a crazy man tied to her. She'll buck, because she won't want any part of you. She'll want to get rid of you in a hurry. This is the biggest rodeo you've ever competed in. You only have eight seconds to find out if you're as good as the riders that have their pictures hanging on the wall in the office. I think you are! Spend those eight seconds convincing Marbles that she's a champ and I'll bet she won't let you down!" Bill said.

They rigged Marbles and Casey settled on her back. She was fidgety, but she let Casey put his weight on her without making too much of a commotion. When Casey felt comfortable with everything, he pulled his hat down and tightened his grip in the rigging. He nodded toward the official in the arena, telling him he was ready.

The gate flew open and Marbles knew what to do. She made a fast getaway out of the chute. she made two jumps out to clear the chute and then started spinning and bucking so hard that Casey forgot about showing her who the boss was. He had his hands full. Casey concentrated on riding and trying to figure out her next move. She was spinning violently. At the same time she was kicking and twisting her body in a tremendous effort to dislodge him. All thoughts of a poor horse left Casey's mind. He was riding for all he was worth. Marbles was giving Casey more than he ever expected.

Suddenly, Marbles stopped. She just plain stopped! The unexpected move was so sudden that Casey lost his balance and went sideways to the mare's back. His grip held in the rigging and he pulled himself back to the center line of her back. Marbles just stood there with her leg's splayed out wide as if she was bracing herself on a rocking boat. A full second ticked away and then another. Casey was dumbfounded. The crowd howled in amusement at the horse. She just quit and didn't want to buck anymore.

Casey let out a blood curdling scream of frustration and spurred back into her flanks. Marbles thought that was an unfair move on the rider's part. She quit, and clearly, her determined, spread eagle stance, should have told the rider that she didn't want to go anywhere. Her rear parts were vulnerable and Casey had cowardly hit her where he shouldn't have, she thought. She wasn't going to let him get away with it.

She blew up like a cork exploding out of a champagne bottle. She jumped straight in the air and swapped ends. She warped her body around in wild contortions trying to make the rider pay for his foul play. Casey stuck with her while she tried to get even with him. The horn sounded and Casey let loose. He wanted off before she dumped him on his head. He timed her moves and released his grip. She sent him flying, upright, off her back, and Casey gracefully landed on his feet.

The crowd cheered. Casey pulled his hat off and waved it toward the spectators. Secretly, he thought the mare had come awful close to throwing him before the horn sounded. She was different than any horse he had ever ridden. The unexpected stop almost dislodged him and then the magnificent bucking, when she started again, had almost been unrideable. Marbles turned out to be an exceptional horse and Casey decided that he had been lucky to stay on her when she started bucking again.

The judges treated Casey favorable with a score of eighty-two. The bronc rider knew that score was not enough to win, but he felt lucky to have gotten any score at all. His drastic move had started her again. She could have stood still for the rest of the time and I wouldn't have gotten any score at all, he thought.

He climbed up the fence to the top of the chutes where Bill was waiting. "Casey, I think you are one lucky rider," Bill said.

"She sure had me worried when she stopped. I'm lucky to have any score at all from that mare. She sure is a tricky one," Casey said.

"I don't think you'll win today with that score, but if you can make a good draw and get an exceptional bucking horse to ride in the finals tomorrow, you might have a chance," Bill said.

"You're right. It's all going to depend on the horse I draw tomorrow. If I draw bad, I won't have a chance of even placing in this rodeo!" Casey said with a note of concern in his voice.

"Yeah, Casey, you're right. But if you draw a good horse, you could end up in first place for the overall standings and be the champ!" BIll said enthusiastically.

They picked up Casey's rigging from the pens and walked over to the motel. Bill put the rigging away while Casey washed away the dirt from his ride. They went back to the fairground and found Johnson and Ann. "What happened to your horse, Casey? Did she go on strike?" Johnson asked.

Casey smiled and said, "She just decided to quit, so I had to convince her that it wasn't a good idea."

"It was a good ride though, Case. She really bucked when she got started again," Ann said.

"Unless I draw an exceptional horse tomorrow, today's ride may not be enough to even place," Casey said woefully.

When the events were over, they all walked over to the motel. "I've been invited out to my friend's ranch for dinner tonight. We had such a good time yesterday, hashing over old times, that they wanted me to return this evening. I sure enjoyed seeing them again," Johnson said.

"You go and have fun, Johnson. We've got Casey's wreck to drive, if we want to go anywhere," Bill said.

"Nellie's not a wreck, Bill. If you don't start treating her with a little more respect, you just might find yourself walking!" Casey said indignantly.

Johnson laughed and said, "Okay! I'll see you late this evening."

When Johnson left for his friend's ranch, Bill said, "Well, let's go have some dinner. Casey wants to go to the dance tonight. We don't want him to be late and let his fan club down," Bill said and laughed. Ann felt a twinge of heartache when Bill mentioned Casey's fan club. She knew Bill was referring to the girls that always chased Casey at the dances.

After dinner they walked back to the motel. "Casey, remember, you're riding for the state championship tomorrow. Don't overdo it tonight. You need good rest to be at your best," Ann said in a stern voice when they reached the motel.

"That's good advice! You should listen to her, Casey," Bill said.

"I have to at least make an appearance, I don't want to dash any of my admirer's hopes," Casey said and grinned.

"What are you going to do?" Bill asked Ann.

"I'm going over to the barn and check Buster. I want to make sure he has enough hay and water and I'll clean his stall while I'm there. Then, I'm coming back here and read for the rest of the evening," she said.

"I'll go with you if you don't mind. I need some exercise," Casey said.

"I don't mind. I've got just the exercise for you. In fact, you're good at it," Ann said.

Bill laughed and said, "I can guess the kind of exercise you mean! Shoveling manure out of Buster's stall!"

Ann giggled and said, "Let's go!"

They walked across the road and headed for the barn. "I sure hope I get a good draw on my bronc tomorrow," Casey said.

"I hope so too! You're as good a rider as anyone here. Just think! Tomorrow at this time, you could be the new State Champion!" Ann said exuberantly.

"That goes both ways. You could be the barrel racing champ too," Casey said.

They entered the barn and walked to Buster's stall. Buster was peacefully pulling hay out of his feeder. "Hi, Buster!"

Ann said. Buster nickered and stepped toward them. Incredulous, Ann watched as Buster favored his left front leg and bobbed his head as he walked to her. Ann jerked the gate open and ran into the stall. Casey followed her and watched in dread as Ann bent to check Buster's leg.

"His leg is swollen on the back side below his knee!" Ann cried out in despair. Casey's heart sank. He knew the symptoms meant that Buster had bowed a tendon.

"How could he have done that!" Casey exclaimed.

Ann stood up and looked at Casey. He could see the anguish on her face as she tearfully cried, "He tried to avoid a horse that stepped in front of us as we raced across the finish line today. He must have strained a tendon trying to maneuver around that horse!"

She threw her arms around Buster's neck and sobbed, "Oh, Buster, I thought you were okay, but I was wrong!" Casey bent down and examined the gelding's leg. He felt swelling behind Buster's cannon bone. The area was abnormally warm to the touch and Buster flinched when he ran his fingers along the swollen tendons.

Casey stood and grabbed Ann by the arm. "This is a serious injury. Let's get a vet to look at him right away. He's in pain and maybe the vet can make him more comfortable," Casey said, and then as an afterthought added, "Ann, this is serious, you'll never be able to ride him tomorrow!" Ann stared into Casey's eyes and the magnitude of Buster's injury swept over her like a tidal wave. After coming so far, they would have to forfeit their entry. Ann began sobbing. Casey pulled her to him and held her in his arms to comfort her while she wept in disappointment.

After a few minutes, Casey said, "Come on, Ann, we can't change things, but we can get Buster some help. Let's call the rodeo vet."

She stopped sobbing and looked up at Casey. "You're right! Buster needs help right away!" They left the stall and ran back to the motel to call the veterinarian.

Ann's hopes were gone. There would be no barrel racing tomorrow. Buster would never be able to compete with that injury. She had lost her chance. All their hard work and training was lost. Dreams of scholarships and state championships were reduced to a dim memory. The simple incident in the alleyway had cost them everything.

They burst into the room Bill and Casey were sharing. Bill jumped up in surprise. He had been lying on the bed reading a magazine. "What happened?" he asked in alarm.

"Big trouble, Bill! Buster's bowed a tendon. We need the vet to look at him right away!" Casey cried.

"What! How did he do that?" Bill shouted.

"It must have been when we were finishing our run today. He tried to avoid a horse and rider that walked in front of us while he was trying to stop in the alleyway," Ann said.

Casey picked up the telephone and dialed the motel office. "Could you get in touch with the rodeo veterinarian and have him call our room as quick as you can. We have an injured barrel horse that needs attention right away," Casey said. There was a pause while Casey listened to the operator. "Thank you very much," he said and hung up. "She's gonna' get ahold of him and have him call our room as soon as possible," Casey said.

"Are you sure Buster has a bowed tendon?" Bill asked.

"Positive, Bill. His leg is swollen from his ankle to his knee on the back side. When you touch him there, you can feel heat and he flinches. It's a severely strained tendon alright," Casey said.

"Then you'll never be able to ride him tomorrow!" Bill said and looked at Ann. He could see her heartache and realized the terrible loss Buster's injury meant to her.

"Your only chance is to find another horse to ride tomorrow. That would be better than forfeiting," Bill said, trying to be helpful to Ann.

"We don't have any other horse trained to run the barrels," Ann mournfully said. There was silence while the three Bent Bar riders tried to think of a solution to the terrible problem suddenly facing Ann.

"How about trying to borrow a horse somewhere?" Casey asked.

"I think that either Jill or Beth would let me use their horse in these circumstances, but Twin Forks is another two hundred miles past High Valley. I don't see how we could travel that distance and be back here in time for the event," Ann said.

"That leaves only Stormy or Thorny," Bill said with finality.

"Bill, I have never run either one of those horses at top speed around the barrels. That would be an awful gamble," Ann said.

"Gambling is a lot better than forfeiting!" Casey said. They fell silent again while Ann thought about the only two horses she could possibly ride tomorrow. Maybe there was still a thread of hope, Ann thought.

"It will take all night to get back to the ranch and trailer one of those horses back here before the rodeo starts tomorrow. We have to think of something. You've come too far to forfeit now," Bill said.

"I remember back before Stormy was stolen, how he used to run around the barrels following you and Buster while you practiced. He was just a little colt then but he ran at full speed," Casey said and smiled at Ann. Ann recalled Stormy chasing them around the barrels as a colt. The fond memories roused her to smile.

"I don't know if Stormy could handle these crowds. He's not accustomed to all this noise and commotion. It might terrify him. I know he has blazing speed, but whether I could control his speed around the barrels is another question. It would be a huge gamble," Ann said.

"I don't think you have any choice," Bill said.

"The only other choice you have is to quit. You're too tough to quit, so let's go and get Stormy!" Casey said.

"We'll have to find Johnson and get the pickup. Do you have the phone number of his friend's ranch?" Bill asked.

"No! I neglected to get it from him. I don't even know where their ranch is. Out past the rimrock somewhere, he said," Ann answered.

"We'll have to find him somehow, we don't have much time to play with. We just barely have time to make a round trip to the ranch to get Stormy," Bill said.

"Nellie! We'll take her! She's our only hope. We don't have time to run around out past the rimrock trying to find Johnson. That's a lot of country out there. It would be like trying to find a needle in a haystack. It's gonna' be close as it is, to drive clear to the Bent Bar and get back here in time," Casey said.

"You're right, Casey, but do you think your old truck can handle that long of a haul," Bill asked.

"I don't see where we have any other choice. If we want to see Annie racing for the championship tomorrow, then we have to trust Nellie. Don't worry, she'll make it!" Casey said.

"Oh, Casey! What if something happens, you might miss your ride and your chance at the championship. That would be terrible!" Ann said.

"Don't worry. Leave it to me to keep Nellie running. It means more to me to see you ride tomorrow than worrying about missing my own ride. And don't argue with me!" Casey said.

The phone rang and Bill answered it. It was the veterinarian. Bill explained Buster's condition and gave the vet Buster's stall number. He listened for a few seconds and then said, "Thank you, sir, I'll be there waiting for you." He placed the receiver back in its cradle and said, "That was the vet. He said he'd be right over. I'll meet him there, so don't worry about Buster, he'll be in good hands. You two better get started for the Bent Bar. I'll call James and tell him what happened and ask him to have Stormy ready when you get there. Drive careful and we'll look for you early tomorrow."

Casey looked at Ann. He could see the indecision in her eyes. She's not sure what to do. Everything's happened so fast, Casey thought. "Right now, Ann, you don't have a sliver of a chance of riding tomorrow unless we get you a horse. You can sit there and think about it, or we can get started for the Bent Bar and Stormy. It's your only chance. Now, go get what ever you want to take with you and I'll drive Nellie over to the barn and hook up the trailer. Buster will be all right. Don't worry about him," Casey said with authority.

Ann looked at him for a few seconds and then said, "I'll get my things and meet you at the barn."

They were on their way to the Bent Bar within thirty minutes after the decision was made to bring Stormy to Billings for Ann's final ride. Casey coaxed his old truck down the highway toward the Bent Bar Ranch. Nellie groaned her way up and down the mountainous country heading west toward High Valley.

Ann told Casey of her fears about using Stormy in the rodeo. "He has absolutely no experience with crowds and noise. Remember, he grew up alone in the mountains for over a year, until we found him. I've never pushed him hard around the barrels and I just don't know what to expect from him. I won't even have time to make a practice run with him before the race! For all I know, he might run right on past the barrel and not obey my commands. Besides that, he's a stallion. How will he act around other strange horses?" Ann said.

"We'll keep our fingers crossed. Has he ever disobeyed you when you were riding him?" Casey asked.

"No. Not since I started his training from the saddle. He's still a youngster though, he's not even three yet," Ann said.

"When we get back to Billings with him, we'll put him in the stall with Buster. He'll be glad to see his old friend and that will reassure him. He'll know he's with friends. If you have time, maybe you can walk him around the grounds and get him accustomed to everything before you ask him to race," Casey said.

"I hope I'll have time. Stormy reaches such an incredible speed so quickly that if I could get good turns out of him around the barrels, then there might still be a chance of placing in the overall standings. That would be a lot better than just dropping out," Ann said.

"Stormy is an intelligent horse, he might surprise you and really do good. He sure has the ability to turn in a great time," Casey said.

"How about you, Casey? What about your ride?" Ann asked.

"I'm behind. My score today wasn't high enough to make me comfortable. I'll have to draw an exceptional horse and then ride him well enough for the judges to give me a score a few points above any one else. That's the only way I know I can come from behind and take the lead. It really doesn't look too good and I'm concerned about it. The chance of drawing a horse that will go out of his way to throw me and buck harder and wilder than any other horse there is pretty slim. I don't even know if there is a horse there capable of giving me a winning ride. It all depends on the draw. If I draw a really rank bronc, I might have a chance. If I don't, then I'm out of luck. It's discouraging, but don't worry about me," Casey said.

The hours passed and they neared High Valley. When they finally turned onto the lane leading to the ranch they were both weary from the long day and night. They could see lights on in the barn. Casey drove up and parked next to the barn. He shut off the motor and gave the old truck a pat on the dashboard. "Good job, Nellie, I told everybody you'd make it," Casey said tiredly to his truck. Ann laughed and then stifled a yawn as she climbed out of the truck. It was almost two o'clock in the morning.

James walked out of the barn. He heard them drive up. "Well, you made it in good time," he said. They all walked into the barn toward Stormy's stall.

"When you have a good truck, you make good time," Casey said.

"No comment," James said.

"How's Stormy?" Ann asked.

"Curious about why I'm bothering him so early in the morning," James answered. They walked to Stormy's stall and Ann saw the colt had been brushed, watered and fed.

"Thank you, James, I see you've been working on him," Ann said.

"When Bill called and explained what happened, I was heartbroke for you. But then I thought, what the heck', Ann and Stormy just might be able to win. So I went to work. I checked his shoes too! He's ready to go," James said.

"Great! We have to load him and hurry right back to make it in time for Ann to ride," Casey said.

"It's a long way," Ann wearily said.

James looked at them. He saw how tired they were and felt compassion. "Well, don't worry about it. You're both going to get some sleep on the way back to Billings. I'm driving!" James said with authority. Surprised, Ann and Casey looked at James.

"It's about time I went to one of those fancy rodeos and got a chance to watch you two ride. You're both worn out and too tired to drive. I'll drive you back. It'll give you a chance to rest before you have to compete. You're Bent Bar riders and so am I. I'm gonna' make sure you get back there ready to ride in top shape. How about that old wreck of yours, Casey? Can she make it back?" James asked.

Casey looked at James and a smile spread across his face. "James, you're a real friend. We can sure use some sleep," he said.

"Don't worry about it. I seem to recall that you always volunteer to help me out when I need it, pal," James said.

"How about the ranch? Who will watch it while we're gone?" Ann asked.

"Duke. I called him right after Bill called and I explained everything. He said to call him as soon as you arrived and he would come right out. He'll stay here and look after things till' we get back," James said brightly.

James called Duke while Ann and Casey loaded Stormy. The colt was happy to see Ann and he stepped into the trailer with no trouble. That's a good start, Ann thought. Stormy had not been in a trailer since they brought him back from South Dakota.

Duke arrived. He wished them luck and told them not to worry about a thing at the ranch. With James driving and Stormy safely in the trailer, they pulled out and headed back to Billings. They had been at the ranch less than one hour.

James chattered away as they drove down the valley. He was excited about going to the rodeo in Billings. They drove through town and pulled onto the highway. James kept up a steady stream of jabber as Nellie rolled along the highway. Within fifty miles it became a one way conversation. Casey and Ann stopped answering. James looked over and saw both riders had fallen sound asleep. Ann was comfortably snuggled against Casey's shoulder. Casey was leaning against the door. James smiled to himself and thought, I better quit running at the mouth and let them get some rest.

Ann awoke just outside of Billings. "Ten miles to go, and Nellie's purring like a kitten!" James said when he saw Ann awaken.

"Did you every have any doubts?" Casey asked with his eyes still closed.

"What time is it?" Ann asked.

"Ten o'clock. We've got about three hours before your event begins," Casey said.

"How do you two feel?" James asked.

"Thanks to you, I feel rested," Ann said.

"I feel pretty good too. You didn't push Nellie too hard while I was asleep, did you?" Casey asked.

James laughed and said, "No! She's been ticking like a clock the whole way."

Casey directed James through Billings to the fairgrounds. They pulled into the grounds and James parked by the barn. Johnson and Bill saw them coming and were at the truck before the riders even got out. "James, what a surprise to see you here! I'm glad you came," Johnson said.

"I took one look at these two when they pulled into the ranch. I saw how tired they were and decided I better drive them back so they could get some sleep," James said.

"That's not true. He just wanted a chance to drive Nellie," Casey said grinning.

"Duke's watching the ranch," Ann added.

They unloaded Stormy and Ann ran into the barn to see how Buster was. He greeted her with a nicker. Ann entered his stall and saw his leg wrapped in a bandage. Bill came in behind her and said, "He did strain a tendon, the vet said he would be okay, but that you'll have to stay off of him for several months. You would never have been able to ride him today."

"Buster, you'll get a well deserved rest. It's up to Stormy now!" Ann said. Casey led Stormy into the stall. Buster and Stormy nickered to each other and everyone saw Stormy's obvious pleasure of finding his old friend here.

"Maybe we should leave these two alone and let Stormy get used to the place," Bill said.

"I'm headed for the office to have them change the horse I'm riding from Buster to Stormy, then I'm going to my room to freshen up and come back to ride Stormy around. I want to try to get him accustomed to all the people and horses," Ann said.

"I'm going to stay here and watch these horses," Johnson said. He didn't want to take a chance of anything else going wrong.

Ann left and Johnson asked James how things were at the ranch. "Just fine, it's just lonely there with everyone gone," James said.

"Casey, how about you? How do you feel today? You've got a big ride ahead of you this afternoon," Johnson asked.

"I'm in good shape. I'm just worried to death about getting a good horse to ride. I'm behind, and it will be hard to catch up unless I get something really wild to ride," Casey said, sounding disheartened.

Ann spent over an hour in her room. She took a cold shower in hopes that the icy water would wash away her fatigue. She stood under the cold, stinging, jets of water for fifteen minutes. It was frigid. Ann stepped out of the shower and dried herself. She felt invigorated and refreshed. The cold water had done the job. She dressed in the clothes she brought especially for this ride. She wouldn't have time to come back and freshen up before her event, so she put on some light make-up and looked at herself in the mirror. Not bad for someone who has only slept a few hours in the front of a pickup in the last two days, she thought.

With less then two hours before the start of the event, Ann walked back to the barn. As she entered, she heard someone whistle. She turned and saw two cowboys sitting on a fence watching her as she walked by. "You sure look nice today," one of them said. The other man smiled and whistled again, obviously, admiring her good looks.

Ann smiled at them and said, "Thank you."

Casey was at Buster's stall and saw the men flirt with Ann. He rushed up and grabbed Ann by the arm, and gave the men a mean look. "Come on, Annie, don't pay any attention to them, but you really do look nice today!" Casey said and hurried her along the barn to the stall.

Ann smiled to herself, could Casey be jealous of those two guys sitting on the fence, she wondered. He sure acted like he was coming to my rescue, she thought. She saw Stormy hanging his head out over the stall gate and her thoughts quickly changed to the stallion. "I've got less then two hours before I ride. I better get busy with Stormy," she said.

"Now, you be careful with him. Remember, he's still a green colt!" Casey said.

Ann slipped a halter on Stormy. She snapped a lead rope on the halter and led him out of the stall. For fifteen minutes, she walked him up and down the alleyway. Stormy was nervous, but followed Ann obediently. He craned his neck around and looked at all the strange people and horses. There was lots of noise and occasionally he would prance sideways when something startled him. Gradually, by degrees, he started to accept the commotion around him. Ann felt the tenseness easing in the stallion. Stormy was more uneasy than Ann realized. The only thing that kept him from breaking and running was his complete trust in Ann and knowing that his great old friend, Buster, his link to warm memories, was standing nearby. People were rattling buckets and slamming stall gates, there were vehicles driving by outside, and everywhere he looked, there were people and horses.

Stormy was wary. He had spent most of his life in the solitude of the mountains, all of this congestion and commotion was alien to him. He was not comfortable in this atmosphere. He remained alert and vigilant to any danger that might threaten him. Shorty had deceived him and Mouse and his rider pretended friendship and then betrayed him when he gave them his trust. Stormy could not fully accept all of these strange people and horses without staying on guard against a sudden attack.

Time was running out and Ann knew she had to forge ahead quickly in order to bring Stormy to accept the crowds.

He remained alert, but slowly began to accept the smaller distractions that surrounded him. She walked him back to the stall and noticed that the things that caught his attention when she first led him through the barn did not bother him now. James was waiting for her when she returned to Buster's stall. "How is he?" James asked.

"It's time to ride him into the middle of everything he fears!" Ann said.

As Ann saddled Stormy, she could feel his tension. His muscles were rock hard. He was ready for any danger that might show itself. Ann murmured softly to him while she worked. She slipped a snaffle bit in his mouth and wondered if she should use something harsher to control him if he broke and ran. No! I'll have to control him with his absolute trust in me. I wouldn't be able to control this strong stallion if he decided to run away, she thought.

She walked the saddled horse out of the stall. Almost immediately, people in the congested barn stopped and stared at the magnificent stallion. Stormy was something to see. His muscular build was beautiful. His sorrel coat was shining and the saddle and bright blanket on his back made his appearance sensational. Ann was proud of the stallion. She heard comments about what an exceptional horse he was from the crowd of onlookers that stopped to admire him.

Johnson, Bill and Casey appeared when she brought Stormy out of the stall. She looked at them and smiled. She could see concern on their faces. "You men look like you're worried to death," she said and smiled.

"How's he doing?" Johnson asked.

"Nervous, but in control," Ann said. She stepped into the saddle and looked down at them. They could see the determined look in her eye. Stormy uttered a low, expectant nicker. Bill started to give her some advice, but then decided against it. It was too late, she was on her own now, he thought.

Ann began walking Stormy out of the barn. She looked behind her, the Bent Bar men were following her. "For heaven sakes, you'd think this was the first time I've ever ridden a horse!" she said.

They stopped in their tracks. "Remember, Ann! You're a Bent Bar rider, show em' what we can do!" Casey called out. Ann waved and rode Stormy out of the barn.

She walked the wary horse through the crowds, and across the rodeo grounds. They worked their way to the far end of the fairgrounds where there was less congestion. Ann talked to Stormy. He flicked his ears back at her while she talked in soothing tones. Stormy realized something special was happening and the sound of Ann's voice had a calming effect on him.

Ann began trotting him along a fence line. She decided not to ride in the Grand Entry. That would be asking too much of the stallion. She would save the shock of the noisy crowded arena for that one big race around the barrels. Exposing him to the crowds unnecessarily might cause him to resist going back into the arena when their turn came to race.

Hope flickered through Ann. She saw a trash barrel overflowing with rodeo litter. She trotted Stormy to the barrel and then turned him around it. He darted around the barrel and trotted away. Ann turned and loped him back to the barrel. Stormy's ears went up and he spun around the barrel with just the slightest rein pressure on his neck. Well, at least you remember what to do, Ann thought.

She kept the stallion busy loping around the outside of the fairgrounds. Stormy was glad for the exercise. He eagerly increased his speed to a gallop when Ann asked him for more speed. She asked for a quick stop and he dropped back on his haunches in a smooth slide to a full stop. So far, so good, Ann thought.

The rodeo was well underway, but still, Ann kept the stallion away from the commotion. She kept Stormy busy, loping and galloping as the time for the final barrel race neared. Ann stopped and dismounted. Stormy had been exercising fairly hard for over an hour. She felt his chest and neck. There was not even the slightest hint of sweat. His breathing was perfectly normal. "You are certainly in good physical condition, Stormy. You're not even sweating or blowing after that workout," Ann said.

She was waiting until the last possible moment before riding to the arena. Finally, she heard the announcer's voice over the loud speakers talking about the barrel race as the next event. "This is it, Stormy. We've got to go!" she said. She mounted and rode straight for the entrance of the arena where she knew the rest of the barrel racers would be lining up in readiness for their runs for the title.

Ann rode toward the crowded alleyway. Stormy cautiously entered the noisy congestion of the holding area, where riders were lined up and awaiting their turns. She felt the stallion tense under her as they made their way through the crowd. Stormy's ears were flickering back and forth as he tried to keep track of all the potential threats around him. Ann continually reassured him with the soothing tones of her voice. Stormy was tense, and he alertly looked at every possible thing that could be a threat to him. Ann's voice was the only assurance that it was safe to be here.

"Ann! Where did you get that magnificent animal?" Marsha cried out. Ann saw Marsha riding toward her and waved. "You never told me you had a secret weapon!" Marsha said when she rode up beside them.

Stormy warily sidestepped away from the buckskin and Ann quickly stopped his movement with light heel pressure. "Buster sprained a front leg yesterday. We drove all night back to the ranch to get Stormy. He's young and I've been training him. He's the only other horse I had to ride," Ann said.

"He's absolutely gorgeous!" Marsha said.

They heard Marsha's name called out as the first rider. "Time to go! I'm first up!" Marsha said and rode into the arena. Ann moved Stormy over to the other riders and lined up in the fifth place position. Stormy was cautiously enduring the noise and commotion in the alleyway. He continually turned his head, watching every move made by those near him.

345

People were sitting all along the fences leading to the arena. There were pens full of cattle next to the alleyway. They were being sorted for the roping event that followed the barrel race. The pens were noisy with bawling cattle and men yelling as they moved them into chutes in preparation for the roping. Stormy watched nervously but remained firmly under Ann's control.

Ann leaned down and patted Stormy on the neck. "You have to trust me, Stormy, everything is going to be okay," she said. A concerned, low nicker escaped the stallion. He had never before been surrounded by so many potential threats.

The cheering crowd told Ann that Marsha was starting her run. The noise was almost unbearable to Stormy. He had never heard anything so loud before, and stomped his feet in annoyance. Ann leaned to the side, trying to see around the other riders and watch Marsha as she raced around the barrels. They were fast. The buckskin seemed to know this was the big race and he put tremendous effort into their run. They came flying back across the finish line, running full speed into the alleyway. Stormy backed quickly against the fence in surprise as the buckskin ran by. Ann gently moved him back in line with the other horses. Stormy didn't like being confined in this small area with other horses running by him.

Marsha stopped and rode back to wait for her time. She knew she had a good run and anxiously waited on the far side of the runway. Marsha threw her hands in the air when she heard her time read. Fifteen point one three seconds! That would be hard to beat, Marsha knew. It would probably win her another championship, she happily thought. Marsha stayed in the area to watch the other riders attempt to beat her time.

Swiftly, the racers made their runs. Ann and Stormy moved up. Ann felt Stormy's uneasiness growing, the longer she held him in check, awaiting their turn. "Whatever happens, we are really here! It's not a dream, Stormy!" Ann said. The last rider in front of them rode into the arena. "We're next, Stormy!" Ann said, as the rider started her run.

The holding pens next to the alleyway were being cleared of the last of the cattle. Most of them had been pushed into smaller pens that led into the roping chutes. A few stubborn steers ran to the far end to escape being driven into the narrow chutes. One hardheaded steer refused to budge from the corner of the pen he lodged himself in.

Ann watched as the rider spun around the first barrel and raced for the second. Only a few seconds left before our turn, and not too soon. Stormy is really getting fidgety, she thought.

One of the men driving the cattle ran up and tried to spook the stubborn steer back down to the chutes. The animal refused to move. He had been pushed from one pen to another all morning and was tired of it. He was going to stay where he was. The man yelled at the animal to no avail. The steer stayed put. On the far side of the pen another man yelled out, "Here, Slim, slap him a lick with this rope! That'll get em' going!" With a flip of his wrist, he threw a coiled rope down into the pen.

The rider came around the last barrel and Ann heard her urging the horse to top speed as they raced for the finish line.

Slim picked up the coiled rope and shook out a loop. He climbed onto the fence to get above and behind the obstinate steer. He yelled down at the animal and then swung the rope above his head to let it fly down onto the steer.

Stormy caught sight of the rope flying in the air behind them. Images of Shorty and Gunpowder Creek, gunfire and high corrals, flashed through his mind. Visions of Mouse double crossing him and ropes entrapping him blazed across his consciousness. It was too much! He broke and ran! He bolted away so fast that Ann lost her seat and frantically grabbed for the saddle horn as Stormy raced out of the alleyway. Marsha wheeled her buckskin out of the way to avoid the stallion's flight from the threatening rope. By the time the last barrel racer ran into the alleyway, Stormy was running full speed across the fairgrounds with Ann back in the saddle, crouched low over his back.

Ann let him run. She knew any attempt to stop him now would fail. She had seen the rope flying and knew why

Stormy bolted. She understood the terror the colt associated with ropes. Stormy flashed across the fairgrounds dodging surprised people and horses. He cut around vehicles and jumped over obstacles in his path. They reached the end of the fairgrounds and Stormy lifted off the ground and easily jumped the fence.

Ann lightly touched his neck with the reins to see if he would respond. Stormy hesitated and then turned in the direction she asked. Ann straightened slightly in the saddle and then gently put pressure on the snaffle bit in the stallion's mouth. Gratefully, she felt him slow and knew he would obey her commands. Thoughts of the barrel race flashed through her mind. Stormy spooked at the worst possible time.

The last rider before them had been racing for the finish line when Stormy bolted. They were just seconds away from riding into the arena. It was their turn. They only had thirty seconds to enter the arena or be eliminated. Far off, Ann could hear her name resounding from the booming loudspeakers. She was being called to enter the arena!

Stormy was still galloping away from the fairgrounds. Ann called out to him, "Stormy! You have to trust me. We have to run back to the arena! Time is running out! We'll be eliminated from the race. Trust me, Stormy!"

Stormy heard her voice. It soothed his jittery nerves. Ann pulled on the reins and kicked him hard with one of her boots. She had never been so forceful giving him a command. Her intensity overpowered his desire to escape. The stallion spun around in the direction Ann directed him. Ann kicked him again and urged him to high speed. He accelerated back toward the fence and the fairgrounds beyond.

Maybe we'll be too late, but I'm going to try. I've been through too much to give up now, Ann thought, as Stormy raced for the fence. They neared the fence and Ann touched her heels to the stallion's sides. Stormy launched himself in the air and effortlessly rose above the high fence again. They landed at a dead run and Stormy raced for the arena.

Ann guided the racing stallion back to the alleyway. People dodged out of their way as Stormy twisted and turned around trucks and trailers as he raced back the way he came. The effort was exhilarating and he forgot about the rope in the excitement of the run. Ann had him fully under control when they neared the alleyway. Stormy's adrenalin was flowing hard and he was eager now to follow Ann's cues.

Apprehension gripped Johnson when he heard Ann's name being repeatedly called. She had not entered the arena and was nowhere in sight. "Something's happened!" James said. They were not able to see Stormy bolt out of the alleyway and had no idea he ran away. They stood up and tried to see across the arena into the alleyway. Despair spread through them when they heard the announcer call out again, "Last call for Ann Olsen, your time is running out!"

"Look!" James shouted and pointed into the fairgrounds. Johnson looked in the direction James was pointing. He was shocked! Clearly, he could see people running to get out of the path of a bright sorrel stallion racing swiftly through the parking area toward the arena. "It's Stormy and Ann!" James shouted.

Marsha heard the announcer call down to the judge, "Call the next rider into the arena!"

Anxious for her new friend, Marsha yelled to the judge, "Give her a few more seconds!" Then, Marsha heard people yelling out in the parking area and she turned to see what was happening. Stunned, she caught glimpses of the sorrel stallion with Ann crouched on his back racing toward the alleyway.

People were moving out of his way and calling warnings to others of the stallion's approach. Marsha could hear Ann calling for more speed and heard the pounding hooves as they neared the alleyway. "Wait! Here she comes!" Marsha yelled to the judge.

Ann guided the racing stallion at full speed right into the alleyway. She slowed him as they approached the other riders. Marsha yelled at Ann, "Run right into the arena! Hurry!" Ann urged Stormy on and he ran past the next barrel racer who was starting to enter the arena.

"Ann Olsen on Stormy!" she called to the amazed judge, while she pulled Stormy into a sliding stop. Stormy came out of his slide and reared high in the air. He pawed the air and every spectator of the rodeo heard his wild, shrill scream of excitement. The crowd came to their feet to better see the stallion, still on his hind legs screaming his wild call while the rider clung to him.

The judge called out to Ann while Stormy walked on his hind legs and pawed the air, "Start your run now or I'll have to disqualify you!"

Crouched high over Stormy's withers, Ann reached up and slapped the stallion's neck hard. Stormy reacted and came down prancing sideways. "The barrels, Stormy! We have to run them now!" The crowd heard her command the excited horse.

She spun Stormy around in a circle and pointed him at the barrels. Stormy saw them and knew what they meant. His ears flashed forward toward them and Ann knew he was ready. "Go, Stormy!" she yelled and kicked her heels into his sides.

The great stallion needed no further urging. He wanted to run. Stormy exploded from the starting line and accelerated directly to the first barrel. Ann lightly touched a rein against his neck and he turned slightly as he charged forward. As he reached the first barrel, he dropped down and rolled around it faster than Ann could believe. Stormy wanted to run as hard as he could. He knew he had to turn around the barrel first and then could open up going to the next one. The faster he got around the barrel the faster he could return to a flat out run.

He went around the second barrel so fast that the crowd knew something exceptional was taking place. They had remained on their feet since Stormy raced into the arena and now they started cheering in appreciation of the incredible speed the sorrel horse was showing. Stormy's speed was electrifying. He was away from the second barrel running faster than anyone could believe. It seemed that at such great speed he would never be able to slow enough to make the turn around the last barrel.

Stormy had grown up in the mountains, racing full speed through dense forests. He could dodge trees and jump fallen timber at a full run. He had developed an uncanny ability to turn at top speed around obstacles in his path. His muscles were developed running straight uphill, jumping and dodging boulders. It never entered his mind that he couldn't maneuver around the last barrel at this phenomenal speed.

Ann was totally engrossed in the ride. Her concentration was absolute. She knew she must keep Stormy from knocking the last barrel over as he approached at high speed. Stormy never slowed until just before reaching the barrel. At the last instant, he changed his stride and spun around the barrel. The stallion went around the barrel so low that Ann felt the toe of her boot drag the ground.

She also felt the hard steel of the barrel scrape against her thigh as they came out of the turn. The barrel teetered back and forth as Stormy raced away. He quickly reached incredible speed and raced for the finish line. Ann crouched above him and shouted, "Run, Stormy, Run!"

They flashed across the finish line in a blur of speed. Stormy slowed and then Ann touched the reins and brought him into a jarring stop in the alleyway. Fearfully, Ann spun around and looked back into the arena to see if the last barrel had fallen over. At the far end of the arena she could clearly see the barrel. Amidst the thunder of the cheering crowd, Ann saw that the barrel had remained upright.

The crowd cheered and roared their delight. Never had they seen a horse show so much speed and maneuverability in this arena. Ann started to walk Stormy out of the alleyway but then turned him and walked back toward the arena. She knew they had made a remarkable run. She wanted to hear the time before she rode away. Stormy pranced and sidestepped into the arena. The noise of the crowd was deafening.

Marsha suddenly appeared beside her and shouted above the noise, "That was the most fantastic ride I have ever seen! You deserve the victory!"

Ann heard the announcer calling for quiet. Finally the noise diminished and she could hear him saying, "I have just received confirmation, it's official. Ladies and Gentlemen, it is a new state record! Ann Olsen and her young stallion, Stormy, have broken the record with a fantastic time of fourteen point eight two seconds!"

The crowd roared again and people surged around her, congratulating her and Stormy. Stormy was still excited and Ann kept him moving through the crowd of well wishers toward the sanctuary of the barn. She was ecstatic. Stormy had performed beyond her wildest dreams.

They made it to the barn and Ann rode Stormy right up to Buster's stall. There was a crowd of people already there and she was glad to see James, Bill and Johnson waiting for her. Buster greeted them with a loud whinny. Stormy answered Buster's call with a piercing scream. Ann was forced to pose for pictures and Stormy jumped when the flash bulbs went off. Bill helped her calm the excited horse and James took the reins from her. Ann insisted that Buster be included in the photos, "Buster got us here and he should be in the pictures too!" Ann said to the photographers.

Everyone was congratulating her and asking questions at the same time. They wanted to know all about the sorrel stallion and why they had never seen him before. Ann looked at Johnson, who was beaming with pleasure. Her eyes pleaded with him to help her with the people. His smile widened and he came to her side and began answering the crowd's questions.

Ann looked at Bill and asked, "Where is Casey?"

"He's coming! Casey saw your ride and he's so proud, he's about to bust! He went to pick up his draw for the bronc riding so he'd know what horse he has to ride. Casey waited until after your race. He should be back by now," Bill said.

Johnson was doing his best to help Ann with the crowd. A well dressed man in a western suit and tie made his way through the throng to Ann. Johnson watched curiously as he stopped in front of her and stared at Stormy. "Miss Olsen, did you train that horse?" the man asked.

"Yes, I did," Ann answered.

"You've done a wonderful job, young lady. That horse is incredible," he said.

"Thank you, sir," Ann answered.

The man stared at Ann and said, "I should introduce myself. My name is Glen Linsay. I'm the head coach of the University rodeo team."

Surprised, Ann could only say, "Oh!"

Coach Linsay smiled and said, "We are going to review your application for a scholarship. With your talent, it would be a great loss to us if you were not on our team. I'm sure we'll be able to make a favorable decision for you."

Ann cried in joy and said, "Thank you, sir, thank you!"

Casey came running into the barn and saw the crowd around Ann. He was excited. "Ann!" he shouted. Ann looked and saw his smiling face as he made his way toward them.

"It does my heart good to see Casey so happy. I hope he drew a good horse to ride. He's been down in the dumps since his ride yesterday," Bill said.

Casey pushed through the crowd and picked Ann up in a bear hug. He planted a kiss on her cheek to the amusement of the onlookers. "No one beat your overall time! You not only broke the state record but you won the state championship, too!" Casey shouted. Casey set Ann down and then looked wickedly at Bill.

"Look at this, Bill!" he said and handed Bill the card with the name of the horse he drew to ride. Bill took the card from Casey and looked at it. Everyone watched curiously as a smile began to spread across Bill's face.

"MOON SHOT! You drew MOON SHOT to ride for the finals!" Bill shouted.

"I sure did! We better get over there and make sure he remembers me!" Casey excitedly said.

Bill grabbed Casey's hand and began shaking it in happiness. "Come on, let's get over to the chutes so you won't be late for your ride!" Bill said.

They started working their way through the crowd and Ann yelled after them, "Good luck, Casey! And remember, you're a Bent Bar rider! Show them what we can do!"

Casey stopped and looked back at Ann. He stared at her for a few seconds and then said, "Hey, Ann! When the rodeo is over, how about riding back to the Bent Bar ranch with me in my old truck, Nellie!"

To order additional copies of **STORMY THE BARREL HORSE**, complete the information below.

Ship to: (please print)

Name _____

Address _____

City, State, Zip _____

Day phone _____

_____ copies of *STORMY THE BARREL HORSE* @ $16.95 each $_____

Postage and handling @ $3.00 per book $ _____

Total amount enclosed $ _____

Send check or money order to : **Horseman's Press**
P.O. Box 687
Silver Star, Montana 59751

To order additional copies of **STORMY THE BARREL HORSE**, complete the information below.

Ship to: (please print)

Name _____

Address _____

City, State, Zip _____

Day phone _____

_____ copies of *STORMY THE BARREL HORSE* @ $16.95 each $_____

Postage and handling @ $3.00 per book $ _____

Total amount enclosed $ _____

Send check or money order to : **Horseman's Press**
P.O. Box 687
Silver Star, Montana 59751

For a free catalogue of the art work of Don Greytak, please write or call:
Don Greytak • Old Library Gallery, 439 4th Ave., Havre, Montana 59501
406-265-8165